Praise for the novels of
#1 *New York Times* bestselling author
Debbie Macomber

"Macomber never disappoints."

—*Library Journal*

"Macomber's patented recipe of idyllic small-town life with a touch of romance is sure to result in a summer best-seller."

—*Booklist* on *Cottage by the Sea*

"Exudes Macomber's classic warmth and gentle humor."
—*Library Journal* on *Three Brides, No Groom*

"Macomber is a skilled storyteller."

—*Publishers Weekly*

"Whether [Debbie Macomber] is writing lighthearted romps or more serious relationship books, her novels are always engaging stories that accurately capture the foibles of real-life men and women with warmth and humor."

—*Milwaukee Journal Sentinel*

"With first-class author Debbie Macomber, it's quite simple—she gives readers an exceptional, unforgettable story every time, and her books are always, always keepers!"

—*ReaderToReader.com*

"Debbie Macomber tells women's stories in a way no one else does."

—*BookPage*

DEBBIE MACOMBER

Autumn Nights

The Playboy and the Widow and *Almost an Angel*

mira

mira™

ISBN-13: 978-0-7783-1208-6

Autumn Nights

Copyright © 2021 by Harlequin Books S.A.

The Playboy and the Widow
First published in 1988. This edition published in 2021.
Copyright © 1988 by Debbie Macomber

Almost an Angel
First published in 1989. This edition published in 2021.
Copyright © 1989 by Debbie Macomber

For questions and comments about the quality of this book, please contact us
at CustomerService@Harlequin.com.

Mira
22 Adelaide St. West, 41st Floor
Toronto, Ontario M5H 4E3, Canada
www.Harlequin.com

Printed in Lithuania

Recycling programs
for this product may
not exist in your area.

MIX
Paper from
responsible sources
FSC® C021394

Also available from Debbie Macomber and MIRA

Blossom Street

The Shop on Blossom Street
A Good Yarn
Susannah's Garden
Back on Blossom Street
Twenty Wishes
Summer on Blossom Street
Hannah's List
"The Twenty-First Wish"
  (in *The Knitting Diaries*)
A Turn in the Road

Cedar Cove

16 Lighthouse Road
204 Rosewood Lane
311 Pelican Court
44 Cranberry Point
50 Harbor Street
6 Rainier Drive
74 Seaside Avenue
8 Sandpiper Way
92 Pacific Boulevard
1022 Evergreen Place
Christmas in Cedar Cove
  (*5-B Poppy Lane* and
  A Cedar Cove Christmas)
1105 Yakima Street
1225 Christmas Tree Lane

The Dakota Series

Dakota Born
Dakota Home
Always Dakota
Buffalo Valley

The Manning Family

The Manning Sisters
  (*The Cowboy's Lady* and
  The Sheriff Takes a Wife)

The Manning Brides
  (*Marriage of Inconvenience* and
  Stand-In Wife)
The Manning Grooms
  (*Bride on the Loose* and
  Same Time, Next Year)

Christmas Books

Home for the Holidays
Glad Tidings
  (*There's Something About Christmas*
  and *Here Comes Trouble*)
Christmas in Alaska
  (*Mail-Order Bride* and
  The Snow Bride)
Trading Christmas
Christmas Letters
The Perfect Christmas
  (includes *Can This Be Christmas*)
Choir of Angels
  (*Shirley, Goodness and Mercy,*
  Those Christmas Angels and
  Where Angels Go)
Call Me Mrs. Miracle
The Gift of Christmas
A Country Christmas
  (*Kisses in the Snow* and
  The Christmas Basket)

Heart of Texas

Texas Skies
  (*Lonesome Cowboy* and
  Texas Two-Step)
Texas Nights
  (*Caroline's Child* and
  Dr. Texas)
Texas Home
  (*Nell's Cowboy* and
  Lone Star Baby)
Promise, Texas
Return to Promise

CONTENTS

THE PLAYBOY
AND THE WIDOW

One

"Mom, I don't have any lunch money."

Diana Collins stuck her head out from the cupboard beneath the kitchen sink and wiped the perspiration from her brow. "Bring me my purse."

"Mother," eight-year-old Katie whined dramatically, "I'm going to miss my bus."

"All right, all right." Hurriedly Diana scooted out from her precarious position and reached for a rag to dry her hands.

"We're out of hair spray," Joan, Katie's elder sister, cried. "You can't honestly expect me to go to school without hair spray."

"Honey, you're in fifth grade, not high school. Your hair looks terrific."

Joan glared at her mother as though the thirty-year-old were completely dense. "I need hair spray if it's going to stay this way."

Diana shook her head. "Did you look in my bathroom?"

"Yes. There wasn't any."

"Check the towel drawer."

"The towel drawer?"

Diana shrugged. "I was hiding it."

Joan frowned and gave her mother a disapproving look. "Honestly!"

"Mom, my lunch money," Katie cried, waving her mother's purse under Diana's nose.

With quick fingers, Diana located five quarters and promptly handed them to her younger daughter.

Five minutes later the front screen door slammed, and Diana sighed her relief. No sound was ever more pleasant than that of her daughters darting off to meet the school bus. The silence was too inviting to resist, and Diana poured herself a cup of coffee and sat at the kitchen table, savoring the quiet. She grabbed her laptop and, automatically went in search of part-time positions. It was tempting, although Diana wanted to wait until the girls were a bit older. Before Stan had died, there'd been few problems with money. Now, however, they cropped up daily, and Diana was torn with the desire to remain at home with her children, or seek the means to provide extra income. For three years Diana had robbed Peter to pay Paul, juggling funds from one account to another. Between the social security check, the insurance check and the widow's fund from Stan's job, she and the girls were barely able to eke by. She cut back on expenses where she could, but recently her options had become more limited. There were plenty of macaroni-and-cheese dinners now, especially toward the end of the month. Diana could always ask for help from her family, but she was hesitant. Her parents lived in Wichita and were concerned enough about her living alone with the girls in far-off Seattle. She simply didn't want to add to their worries.

"Pride cometh before a fall," she muttered into the steam rising from her coffee cup.

A loud knock against the screen was followed by a

friendly call. "Yoo-hoo, Diana. It's Shirley," her neighbor called, letting herself in. "I don't suppose you've got another cup of that."

"Sure," Diana said, pleased to see her friend. "Help yourself."

Shirley took a cup down from the cupboard and poured her own coffee before joining Diana. "What's all that?" She cocked her head toward the sink.

"It's leaking again."

Shirley rolled her eyes. "Diana, you're going to have to get someone to look at it."

"I can do it," she said without a whole lot of confidence. "I watched a YouTube video online that tells you how to build a shopping center in your spare time. If I can repair the outlet in Joan's room, then I can figure out why the sink keeps leaking."

Shirley looked doubtful. "Honey, listen, you'd be better off to contact a plumber…"

"No way! Do you have any idea how much those guys charge? An appointment with a brain surgeon would be cheaper."

Shirley chuckled and took a sip of her coffee. "George could check it for you tonight after dinner."

"Shirley, no. I appreciate the offer, but…"

"George was Stan's friend."

"But that doesn't commit him to a lifetime of repairing leaking pipes."

"Would you stop being so darn proud for once?"

Funny how that word "pride" kept cropping up, Diana mused. "I'll call him," she conceded, "but only in case of an emergency."

"Okay. Okay."

Diana closed her laptop. "Let me save you the trouble of small talk. I know why you're here."

"You do?"

"You're dying to hear all the details of my hot date with the doctor I met through Parents Without Partners."

"Not many women have the opportunity to have dinner with Dr. Benjamin Spock."

A smile touched the edges of Diana's soft mouth. "He's a regular pediatrician, not Dr. Spock."

"Whoever!" Shirley said excitedly, and leaned closer. "All right, if you know what I want, then give me details!"

Diana swallowed uncomfortably. "I didn't go out with him."

"What?"

"My motives were all wrong."

Shirley slumped forward and buried her forehead against the heel of her hand. "I can't believe I'm hearing this. The most ideal husband material you've met dances into your life and you break the date!"

"I know," Diana groaned. "For days beforehand I kept thinking about how much money I could save on doctor bills if I were to get involved with this guy. It bothered me that I could be so mercenary."

"Don't you think any other woman would be thinking the same thing?"

Diana's fingers tightened around the mug handle. "Not unless they have two preteens."

"Don't be cute," Shirley said frowning. "I have trouble being angry with you when you're so witty."

Standing, Diana walked across the kitchen to refill her cup. "I don't know, Shirl."

"Know what?"

"If I'm ready to get involved in a relationship. My life

is different now. When Stan and I decided to get married, it wasn't any surprise. We'd been going together since my junior year in high school and it seemed the thing to do. We hardly paused to give the matter more than a second thought."

"Who said anything about getting married?"

"But it's wrong to lead a man into believing I'm interested in a long-term relationship, when I don't know if I'll ever be serious about anyone again."

"You loved Stan that much?" Shirley inquired softly.

"I loved him, yes, and if he hadn't been killed, we probably would have lived together contentedly until a ripe old age. But things are different now. I have the girls to consider."

"What about you?"

"What about me?"

"Don't you need someone?"

"I—I don't know," Diana answered thoughtfully. The idea of spending her life alone produced a sharp pang of apprehension. She wanted to be a wife again, but was afraid remarriage would drastically affect her children's lives.

Shirley left soon afterward, and Diana rinsed the breakfast dishes and placed them inside the dishwasher. Her thoughts drifted to David Fisher, the man whose dinner invitation she'd rejected at the last minute. He obviously liked children or he would have chosen a different specialty. That was in his favor. She'd met him a couple of weeks before and listened over coffee to the gory details of his divorce. It was obvious to Diana that he was still in love with his ex-wife. Although Shirley viewed him as a fine catch, Diana wasn't interested.

Not until she closed the dishwasher did Diana notice

the puddle of water on her kitchen floor. The sink again! It would be a simple matter of tightening the pipes if the garbage disposal didn't complicate the job.

Unfortunately the malfunctioning sink didn't heal itself, and after Diana picked up Joan from baseball practice, disaster struck.

"Mom," Katie cried, nearly hysterical. "The water won't stop!"

When Diana arrived, she found that the pipe beneath the sink had broken and water was gushing out faster than it would from a fire hydrant.

"Turn off the water," Diana screamed.

Katie was dancing around, stomping her feet and screaming. By the time Diana reached the faucet, the water had reached flood level.

"Get some towels, stupid," Joan called.

"I'm not stupid, you are."

"Girls, please." Diana lifted the hair off her forehead and sighed unevenly. Either she had to call George or wipe out any semblance of a budget by hiring a plumbing contractor. Given that option, she reached for the phone and dialed her neighbor's number.

The male voice that answered sounded groggy. "George, I hope I didn't wake you from a nap."

"No…"

"Did Shirley mention my sink?"

"Who is this?"

"Diana—from next door. Listen, I'm in a bit of a jam here. The pipe burst under the sink, and, well, Shirley said something about your being able to help. But if it's inconvenient…"

"Mom," Katie screamed. "Joan used the *S* word."

"Just a minute." Diana placed her hand over the telephone mouthpiece. "Joan, what's the matter with you?" she asked angrily.

"I'm sorry, Mom, it just slipped out."

"Are you going to wash out her mouth with soap?" Katie demanded, hands on her hips.

"I haven't got time to deal with that now. Both of you clean up this mess." She inhaled a calming breath and went back to the phone, hoping she sounded serene and demure. "George?"

"I'll be right over."

Ten seconds later, a polite knock sounded on the front door. Diana was under the sink. "Joan, let Mr. Holiday in, would you?"

"Okay."

"Mom," Katie said, sticking her head under the sink so Diana could see her. "How are you going to punish Joan?"

"Katie, can't you see I've got an emergency here!" She raised her head and slammed her forehead against the underside of the sink. Pain shot through her head and bright stars popped like flashbulbs all around her. She blinked twice and abruptly shook her head.

"Mom," Joan announced. "It wasn't Mr. Holiday."

Pushing her hair away from her forehead, Diana opened one eye to find a pair of crisp, clean jeans directly in front of her. Slowly she raised her gaze to a silver belt buckle. Above that was a liberal quantity of dark hairs scattered over a wide expanse of muscular abdomen. A cutoff sweatshirt followed. Diana's heart began to thunder, but she doubted it had anything to do with the bump on her head. She never did make it to his face. He crouched in front of her first. His blue eyes were what she noticed immediately. They were a brilliant shade that reminded her of a Seattle sky in August.

"Who—who are you?" she managed faintly.

"Are you all right?"

Diana was ready to question that herself. Whoever this man was who had decided to miraculously appear at her front door, he was much too good to be true. He looked as though he'd stepped off the hunk poster hanging in Joan's bedroom.

Diana knocked the side of her head with her palm to clear her vision. "You're not George!" It wasn't her most brilliant declaration.

"No," he admitted with a lopsided grin. "I'm Cliff Howard, a friend of George's."

"You answered the phone?" This was another of her less-than-intelligent deductions.

Cliff nodded. "Shirley's at some meeting, and George had to run to the store for a minute. I'm watching Mikey. I hope you don't mind that I brought him along."

She shook her head.

Cliff was down on all fours by this time. "Now what seems to be the problem?"

For a full moment all Diana could do was stare. It wasn't that a man hadn't physically attracted her since Stan's death, but this one hit her like a sledgehammer, stunning her senses. Cliff Howard was strikingly handsome. His eyes were mesmerizing, as blue and warm as a Caribbean sea. She couldn't look away. He smiled then, and character lines crinkled about his eyes and mouth, creasing his bronze cheeks. She'd never stared at a man quite this unabashedly, and she felt the heat of a blush rise in her face.

"There's a problem?" he repeated.

"The sink," she murmured, and pointed over her shoulder. "It's leaking."

"Bad," Katie added dramatically.

"If you'd care to move, I'd be happy to look at it for you."

"Oh, right." Hurriedly Diana scooted aside, sliding her rear end into a puddle. As the cold water seeped through her underwear, she bounded to her feet, wiping off what moisture she could.

Something was drastically wrong with her, Diana concluded. The way her heart was pounding and the blood was rushing through her veins, she had to be afflicted with some serious physical ailment. Scarlet fever, maybe. Only she didn't seem to be running a temperature. Something else must be wrong—something more than encountering Cliff Howard. He was only a man, and she'd dated plenty of men since Stan, but none of them—not one—had affected her like this one.

"Does your husband have a pipe wrench?" he called out from under the sink. "These pliers won't work."

"Oh dear." Diana sighed. "Can you tell me what a pipe wrench looks like?"

Cliff reappeared. "Does he have a toolbox?"

"Yes…somewhere."

Women! Cliff doubted he would ever completely understand them. This one was curious, though; her round, puppy dog eyes had a quizzical look, as though life had tossed her an unexpected curveball. The bang on her head had to be smarting. She shouldn't be working under a sink, and he wondered what kind of husband would leave it to her to handle these types of repairs. This was a woman who was meant for lace and grand pianos, not greasy pipes.

"When do you expect him home?" he asked patiently. The flicker of pain that flashed into her eyes was so fleeting that Cliff wondered at her circumstances.

"I'm a widow."

Cliff was instantly chagrined. "I'm sorry."

She nodded, then forced a smile. In an effort to bridge the uncomfortable silence, she asked, "Does a pipe wrench look like a pair of pliers, only bigger, with a mouth that moves up and down when the knob is twisted?"

Cliff had to think that over. "Yes, I'd say that about describes it."

"Then I've got one," Diana said cheerfully. "Hold on a second." She hurried into the garage and returned a minute later with the requested tool.

"Exactly right."

He smiled at her as though she'd just completed the shopping center project. "Should I be doing something?" she asked, crouching.

"Pray," Cliff teased. "This could be expensive."

"Damn," Diana muttered under her breath, and looked up to find Katie giving her a disapproving glare. In her daughter's mind, *damn* was as bad as the *S* word. "Don't you have any homework?" she asked her younger daughter.

"Just spelling."

"Then hop to it, kiddo."

"Ah, Mom!"

"Do it," Diana said in her most stern voice.

A few minutes later, Cliff climbed out from under the sink. "I'm afraid I'm going to need some parts to get this fixed."

"If you'll write down what's necessary, I can pick them up tomorrow and—"

"You don't want to go without a sink that long. I'll run and get what you need now." He wiped his hands dry on a dish towel and headed toward the front door.

"Just a minute," Diana cried, running after him. "I'll give you some cash."

"No need," he said with a lazy grin. "I'll pay for it and you can reimburse me."

"Okay," she returned weakly. The last time she'd looked, her checkbook balance had hovered around ten dollars, give or take a dime or two.

Cliff took Mikey Holiday with him, but not because he was keen on having the youth's company. His reasons were purely selfish. He wanted to grill the lad on what he knew about his neighbor with the sad eyes and the pert nose.

"You buckled up?" he asked the eight-year-old.

Mikey's baseball cap bobbed up and down.

"Say, kid, what can you tell me about the lady with the leaky sink?"

"Mrs. Collins?"

"Yeah." Cliff had to admit he was being less than subtle, but he often preferred the direct approach.

"She's real nice."

That much Cliff had guessed. "What happened to her husband?"

"He died."

Cliff decided his chances of getting any real information from the kid were nil, and he experienced a twinge of regret. He'd met far more attractive women, but this one got to him. Her appeal, he suspected, was that wide streak of independence and that stiff upper lip. He admired that.

It had been a while since he'd been this curious about any woman, and whatever it was about her that attracted him was potent. A smile came and went as he thought about her dealing with the problem sink. It was all too obvious she didn't know a thing about plumbing. Then he recalled the pair of puzzled brown eyes looking up at him and how she'd sensibly announced that he wasn't George.

He laughed softly to himself.

* * *

The knock on the front door got an immediate response from Diana. "You're back," she said, rubbing her palms together. She seemed to have a flair for stating the obvious.

Cliff grinned. "I shouldn't have any problem fixing that sink now."

"Good."

The house was quiet as she led him back into the kitchen. Diana hadn't been this agitated by a man since...she couldn't remember. The whole thing was silly. A strange man was causing her heart to pound like a locomotive. And Diana didn't like it one bit. Her life was too complicated for her to be attracted to a man. Besides, he was probably married, even though he didn't wear a wedding band. If Cliff was George's friend, and if he was single, it was a sure bet that Shirley would have mentioned him. And if Cliff was available, which she sincerely doubted, then he was the type to have plenty of women interested in him. And Diana had no intention of becoming a groupie.

"I really appreciate your doing this," she said after a long moment.

"No problem. What happened to the kids?"

"They're upstairs playing video games," she explained, and hesitated. "I thought you might work better with a little peace and quiet."

"I could have worked around the racket."

Diana nervously wiped her hands on her thighs. Then, irritated with herself, she folded them as though she were about to pray. Not a bad idea under the circumstances. This man was so virile. He was the first one since Stan to cause her to remember that she was still a woman. Five minutes in the kitchen with Cliff Howard and she was thinking about satin sheets and lacy underwear. Whoa, girl! She reined in her thoughts.

"Could you hand me the wrench?" he asked.

"Sure." Diana was glad to do anything but stand there staring at the dusting of hairs above his belly button.

"I don't think I caught your first name," he said next.

"Diana."

He paused, his hands holding the wrench against the pipe. "It fits."

"The pipe?"

"No," he said, grinning. "Your name." He pictured a Diana as soft and feminine, and this one was definitely that. Her hair was the color of winter wheat. She smelled of flowers and sunshine; summer at its best. Her face was sensual and provocative. Mature. She'd walked through the shadow-filled valley and emerged strong and confident.

Self-consciously Diana placed her hand at her throat. "I was named after my grandmother."

Cliff continued to work, then altered positions from lying under the sink on his back to kneeling. "It looks like I'm going to have to take off the disposal to get at the problem."

"Should I be doing something to help?"

"A cup of coffee wouldn't hurt."

"Oh, sorry, I should have thought to offer you some earlier." Diana hurried to her antique automatic-drip coffee-maker and put on a fresh pot, getting the water from the bathroom. She stood by the cantankerous machine while it gurgled and drained. Soon the aroma of freshly brewed coffee filled the kitchen.

When the pot was full, Diana brought down a mug and knelt on the linoleum in front of Cliff. "Here."

"Thanks." He sat upright, using the cupboard door to support his back.

"Do you have children—I mean, you claimed you could work around the noise, so I naturally assumed that you…"

"I've never been married, Diana," he said, his eyes serious.

"Oh." He had the uncanny ability to make her feel like a fool. "I just wondered, you know." Her hands slipped down the front of her Levi's in a nervous reaction.

"I was wondering, too," he admitted.

"What?"

"How long has your husband been gone?"

"Stan died in a small plane crash three years ago. Both my husband and his best friend were killed."

Three years. He was surprised. He would have thought a woman as attractive as Diana would have been snatched up long before now. She was the marrying kind and…ultimately out of his league.

"I shouldn't have pried." He saw the weary pain in her eyes and regretted his inquisitiveness.

"I'm doing okay. The girls and I have adjusted as well as can be expected. I'll admit it hasn't been easy, but we're getting along."

The phone rang, and before Diana could even think to move, Joan came roaring down the stairs. "I'll get it."

Diana rolled her eyes and smiled. "That's one nice thing about her growing up. I never need to answer the phone again."

"It's Mr. Holiday." Joan's disappointment sounded from the hallway. "He wants to speak to his friend."

"That must be you." The moment the words were out, Diana wanted to cringe. She was making such an idiot of herself!

Cliff rolled to his feet and reached for the wall phone.

Because she didn't want to seem as though she were eavesdropping, Diana moved into the living room and straightened the decorator pillows on the end of the sofa, positioning them just so. They were needlepoint designs her mother had given her last Christmas.

Five minutes later, hoping she wasn't being too conspicuous, she returned to the kitchen. Cliff was under the sink, humming as he worked. The garbage disposal came off without a hitch, and he set it aside. Next he added a new piece of pipe.

"There wasn't anything in the video about replacing pipe—at least in the one I viewed, anyway," she explained self-consciously.

"I'm happy to do it for you, Diana," he said, tightening the new pipe with the wrench. "There." He stood and faced the sink. "Are you ready for the big test?"

"More than ready."

Cliff turned on the faucet while Diana squatted, watching the floor under the sink. "It looks worlds better than the last time I peeked."

"No leaks?"

"Not a one." She straightened and discovered they were separated by only a couple of inches. She blinked and eased back a couple of steps. Neither spoke. Sensual awareness was as thick as a London fog; Diana's blood pounded through her veins. Her gaze rested on the V of his shirt and the smattering of curly, crisp hairs. Gradually she raised her gaze and noticed that his lower lip was slightly fuller than the upper. It had been so long since she'd been kissed by a man. Really kissed. The memory had the power to stir her senses, and her hands gripped the sink to keep herself from swaying toward him. She was behaving like

Joan over a new boy in class. Her hormones were barely under control. "I don't know how to thank you," she managed finally, her voice weak.

"It isn't necessary."

Feeling awkward, Diana said, "Let me write you a check for the supplies."

"They were only a few dollars."

That was a relief! He named a figure that was so ridiculously low that she could hardly believe it. She thought to question him, but recognized intuitively that it wouldn't do any good and quietly wrote out the check.

"I don't suppose I could have a refill on the coffee?" Cliff surprised himself by saying. Standing there by the sink, he'd nearly kissed her. She'd wanted it. He'd been partially amused by her obvious desire, until he'd realized that he wanted it, too.

"A refill? Of course. I don't mean to be such a poor hostess." She moved to the glass pot and brought it over to Cliff, who had claimed a chair at the table. Diana topped his cup and then her own, returned the pot and took a seat opposite him.

"Do you like Chinese food?" he asked unexpectedly, again surprising himself. It wasn't her beauty that attracted him so much as her spirit.

Diana nodded. Her stomach churned and she knew what was coming. She hoped he would ask her, and in the same heartbeat prayed he wouldn't.

"Would you have dinner with me tomorrow night?"

"I…"

"If you're looking for a way to repay me, then make it simple and share an evening with me."

"Joan's got baseball practice." Instead of looking for excuses, she should be thanking God he'd asked. "But Shirley could pick her up."

Cliff grinned, his blue eyes almost boyish. "Good, then I'll see you at six-thirty."

Diana responded to the pure potency of his smile. "I'll look forward to it."

The minute Cliff was out the door, Diana phoned her neighbor.

"Shirley, it's Diana," she said, doing her best to curtail her excitement. "Where have you been hiding him?"

"Who? I just walked in the door. What are you talking about?"

"Cliff Howard!"

"You met Cliff Howard?"

"That's just what I said. After all these months of indiscriminately tossing men at me, why didn't you introduce us earlier?"

A lengthy, strained silence followed. "I'm going to shoot George."

"Shoot George? What's that got to do with anything?"

Shirley raised her voice in anger. "I told that man to keep Cliff Howard away from you. He's trouble with a capital *T*, and if you have a brain in your head you won't have anything to do with him."

Two

"Mom, do you want to borrow my skirt?" Joan held up a skimpy piece of denim that was her all-time favorite.

"No thanks, sweetheart." Diana was standing in front of the mirror in her bathroom, wearing only her slip and bra.

"But, Mom, this skirt is the absolute!"

Diana sighed. "I appreciate the offer, sweetie, but it's about four sizes too small. Besides, I have no intention of looking like Katy Perry."

"But Cliff's so handsome."

Leave it to Joan to notice that. This year Diana had seen a major transformation take hold of her elder daughter. After one week of fifth grade, Joan had wanted her ears pierced and would have killed for fake nails. The youngster argued that Diana was being completely unreasonable to make her wait until junior high before wearing makeup. Everyone wore eye shadow and Diana must have been reared in the Middle Ages if she didn't know that. Boys were quickly becoming all-important, too. Fifth grade! How times had changed.

"Are you going to wear your pearl earrings?" Joan asked next.

The pair were Diana's best and saved for only the most festive occasions. "I—I'm not sure."

She wasn't sure about anything. Shirley seemed convinced Diana was making the mistake of her life by having anything to do with Cliff.

Her nighbor claimed he was a notorious playboy who would end up breaking her fragile heart. He was sophisticated, urbane and completely ruthless about using his polished good looks to get what he wanted from a woman, or so Shirley claimed. Next she had admitted that she was half in love with him herself, but as Diana's self-appointed guardian, Shirley couldn't bear thinking what could happen to her friend in the hands of Cliff Howard.

After Shirley's briefing, Diana was too curious to find out to consider cancelling the date.

"Mom, the earrings," Joan repeated impatiently.

Her daughter's shrill voice broke into Diana's thoughts. "I don't think so."

"Do it, Mom."

"But if I wear them now, I won't have anything to razzle-dazzle Cliff with later."

Joan chewed on the corner of her lower lip, grudgingly accepting her mother's decision. "Right, but what about your hair?"

"What about it?" Diana's hair was styled the way she always wore it, parted on the side and feathered back away from her face.

Joan looked unsure. "You look so ordinary, like this is an everyday date or something."

"I don't think now would be the time to experiment with something different."

"I suppose you're right," Joan admitted reluctantly.

Diana checked her watch; she had plenty of time, but the way Joan kept suggesting changes wasn't doing a whole lot for her self-confidence. Maybe her daughter was right, and it was time to do something different with her hair and makeup. But age thirty was upon her, and no matter how she parted her hair or applied her makeup, she wasn't going to look like Stacey Q., Joan's favorite female rock star. Well, almost favorite. Stacey Q. ran a close second to Katy Perry.

When Diana came out of the bathroom, she discovered her daughter sorting through her closet. "I have what I'm going to wear on the bed."

"But, Mom, black pants and a blouse are so boring."

"The blouse is silk," she told her coaxingly.

"Men like black silk, not white."

Diana preferred not to know where Joan had gotten that little tidbit of information. The child was amazing. While Diana slipped into the pants, Joan lay across the queen-size mattress and propped her chin up with her hands.

"You know who Cliff reminds me of?" Joan asked with a dreamy look clouding her blue eyes.

"Who?"

"Christian Bale."

"Who?" Diana stopped dressing long enough to turn around and face her daughter.

"You know, the actor."

Diana sighed. "I suppose he does faintly resemble him, but Cliff's hair is dark."

"Cliff's hot stuff, Mom. He's going to make your blood boil."

"Joan, for heaven's sake. The way things are going, I may never see him again after tonight."

Alarmed, Joan bolted upright. "Why not?"

"Well, for one thing my clothes are boring, and for another I don't look a thing like Katy Perry and my hair's all wrong."

"I didn't say that," Joan returned defensively.

The doorbell chimed and Joan tore out of the room. "It's him. I'll get it."

Diana let out an exasperated breath, squared her shoulders and did one last check in the mirror. She'd dressed sensibly, hoping to be tactful enough to remind Cliff that she was a widow and a mother. According to Shirley, Cliff had previously dated beauty queens, centerfolds and an occasional actress. Diana was "none of the above." Her reflection revealed round eyes and a falsely cheerful smile. Good enough, she decided as she reached for her sweater and placed it over her arm; nights still tended to be nippy in May.

Joan came rushing back to the bedroom. "He brought you flowers," she announced in a husky whisper. "Mom," she continued, placing her hand over her heart, "he's so-o-o handsome."

As Joan had claimed, Cliff stood inside the living room with a small bouquet of red roses and pink carnations. It had been so long since a man had given her flowers that Diana's throat constricted and she couldn't think of a single word to say.

He smiled, and the sun became brighter. Shirley was right. This man was too much for a mere widow.

"You look lovely."

Somehow Diana managed a feeble thank-you.

"Mom's got terrific legs," Joan inserted smoothly, standing between Diana and Cliff and glancing from one to the other. "I keep telling her that she ought to show them off more often." She slapped her hands against her sides. "But my mother never listens to me."

Diana glared at her daughter, but said nothing. "I'll find a vase for these." As she left the room, Joan's chatter drifted after her. Her daughter found it important that Cliff know she was much too old to have a babysitter. Katie was over at the Holidays', but at eleven, Joan was far too mature to have anyone look after her.

"I thought you had baseball practice?" Diana heard Cliff ask.

"Normally I do," Joan explained with a patient sigh, "but I skipped today because my mother needed me."

Diana reappeared and Joan escorted the couple to the front door. It was on the tip of Diana's tongue to remind Joan of the house rules when she was alone, but one desperate glance begged her not to. Diana grudgingly complied and said everything that was needed with one stern look.

"Have a good time," Joan said cheerfully, holding the front door open. "And, Cliff, you can bring Mom home late. She doesn't have a curfew."

"I'll have her back before midnight," Cliff promised.

Joan nodded approvingly. "And don't worry, Mom, I'll take care of everything here."

That was what concerned Diana most. She kissed Joan's cheek and whispered, "Remember, bedtime is nine." Shirley would be over then to sit with the girls until Diana returned.

"Mom," Joan said under her breath, "you're treating me like a child."

Diana smiled apologetically. However, it would be just like her daughter to wait up half the night to hear the details of this date, and Diana couldn't face Joan and Shirley together.

Cliff's sports car was parked in front of the house. It was a two-seater that Diana couldn't identify. Cool. Very cool. He held open the door and helped her inside. She mumbled her thanks, feeling self-conscious and out of her element. Diana drove a ten-year-old SUV and wouldn't know the difference between a BMW and an MGB.

Cliff joined her a moment later, inserted the key in the ignition and turned to her, smiling. "Is she always like that?"

"Always. I hope she didn't embarrass you."

"Not at all." He looked more amused than anything.

"I sometimes wonder if I'm going to survive motherhood," Diana commented, her hands clenching her purse.

"You seem to be doing an admirable job."

"Thanks." But Cliff hadn't seen her at her worst. Katie called her the screaming meemie when she let loose. Diana didn't lose her cool often, but enough for the girls to know that the best thing for them to do was nod politely and agree to everything she shouted, no matter how unreasonable.

Cliff started the engine, doing his best to hold back his amusement. This daughter of Diana's was something else. He'd been looking forward to seeing this widow all day. He continued to be confounded by the attraction he felt for her. True, she was pretty enough, but years older than the women he normally dated. Diana had to be close to his age.

Several times during the day, he'd discovered his thoughts drifting to her, wondering what she was doing and what catastrophe she was fearlessly facing now. After he'd finished with her sink, he'd gone to the Holidays' and drilled George, wanting to ferret out every detail about Diana he could. Shirley arrived home then, and when she learned that he planned to take Diana to dinner, her disapproval had been tangible. She'd mumbled some dire warning about the wrath of God coming down upon his head if he ever hurt Diana.

However, it was never Cliff's intent to hurt any woman. He realized George and his other golfing friends credited him with the playboy image, but he wasn't Hugh Hefner.

He wasn't even close. Oh, there'd been a few relationships over the years, but very few. It was true that most women found him attractive, and it was also fair to say he liked variety. The truth was his reputation far outdistanced reality.

When Cliff had drilled his friend about Diana, George hadn't been able to say enough good things about the young widow. To escape Shirley's threats, the two men had gone to the local pub and talked late into the night. Cliff went away satisfied that he'd learned everything George knew about his next-door neighbor.

In the car seat, Diana clasped and unclasped her purse. She was nervous. She hadn't felt this uptight since…never, she decided. A man had stepped out of the pages of *Gentleman's Quarterly* and into her life. This shouldn't be happening to her. Events like that were reserved for fairy tales and gossip magazines. Not widows whose money couldn't stretch till the end of the month.

Diana wanted to stand Shirley up against a wall and shoot her for filling her with doubts. One date! What possible damage could one dinner date do? The one and only time she was interested in finding out details about a man, and all Shirley could do was point out that Diana was headed down the road to destruction. Shirley claimed lesser women crumbled under Cliff's charm. He broke their hearts, but he hated to see them cry. Diana, according to Shirley, was too gentle natured to be hurt by this playboy.

Consequently Diana didn't know anything more about Cliff than she had when he'd left her house the night before.

"How do you know George?" she asked, breaking the silence.

"George and I golf together," Cliff explained.

George was a real sports fanatic.

"Do you play?" Cliff asked.

"I'm afraid not." No time. She was the room mother for Katie's second grade class, did volunteer work at the elementary school the girls attended, taught Sunday school and was heavily involved in Girl Scouts. "I used to play tennis, though," she added quickly. "Used to" being the operative expression. Every Thursday had been her morning on the court, but that was before Joan was born and... oh, good grief, that was eleven years ago. Where had all the years gone?

They arrived at the Chinese restaurant and were seated in a secluded booth. "This place isn't high on atmosphere, but I promise you the food's terrific," Cliff said.

Diana studied the menu, and her stomach growled just reading over the varied list of entrées. If the food tasted half as good as it sounded, she would be satisfied. "You needn't worry," she said, "I'm easy to please. Anything that I don't have to cook is fine by me."

The waiter appeared, and they placed their order. Diana cradled a small teacup in both hands. "I know you fix leaky sinks in your spare time, but what do you normally do?"

"I'm an attorney." His gaze settled on her mouth. "Are you a working mother?"

Diana bit back a defensive reply. A man who had never been married wouldn't appreciate the fact that *every* mother was a working mother. "Not outside the house," she explained simply. "I keep thinking I should find a part-time job, but I'm delaying it as long as possible."

"What have you trained for?"

"Motherhood."

Cliff grinned.

"I suppose that sounds old-fashioned. But you have to remember that Stan and I married only a few months after

I graduated from community college. The first couple of years, while Stan worked for Boeing, I attended classes at the University of Washington, but I got pregnant with Joan and didn't earn enough credits for a degree. At one time I'd hoped to enter the nursing profession, but that was years ago."

Their hot-and-sour soup arrived. "Why don't you do that now?" Cliff wanted to know.

"I could," she admitted, and shrugged, "but I feel it's too important to spend time with the girls. They still need me. I'm all they've got and I'd hate to be torn between attending Joan's baseball games and doing homework, or squeezing in an additional night class." She paused and dipped her spoon in the thick soup. "Maybe that's an excuse, but my children are the most important investment I have in this life. I want to be there for them."

"What if your husband were alive?"

"Then I'd probably be in nursing school. The responsibilities of raising the girls would be shared." She hesitated. She doubted that Cliff would understand any of this—a bachelor wouldn't. "To be honest, I'm not toying with the idea of getting a part-time job because I want one. Money is tight and it gets tighter every year. I suppose by the time Joan's in junior high, the option will be taken away from me, but by then both girls will be better able to deal with my being away from home so much."

"Joan seemed eager enough to have you leave tonight."

Diana nodded, hiding a smile. "That's because she thinks you look like Christian Bale."

"I'm flattered."

Diana noted that she didn't need to explain to him that Christian Bale was an actor. "I hope you don't find this rude, but how old are you, Cliff?" Diana knew she was older. She had to be—if not in years, then experience.

"How old do you think?"

She shrugged. "Twenty-five, maybe twenty-six."

"How old are you?"

A hundred and ten some days. Fifteen on others. "Thirty last September."

His grin was almost boyish. "I'm thirty-one."

The conversation turned then, and they discussed local politics. Although they took opposing points of view, Diana noted that he respected her opinions and didn't try to sway her to his way of thinking. Cliff was far more liberal than Diana. Her views tended to be conservative.

From their conversation, she discovered other tidbits of information about him. He skied, and had a condo at Alpental on Snoqualmie Pass. His sailboat was docked at the Des Moines Marina and he enjoyed sailing, but didn't get out often enough. He was allergic to strawberries.

Diana hated to see the evening end. It had been years since she'd had such a fun date. Cliff was easy to talk to, and she was astonished when she happened to notice the time. They'd been sitting in the booth talking for nearly three hours.

"How about a movie?" he suggested on the way to the restaurant parking lot.

Regretfully Diana shook her head. "Sorry, Cliff, but it's after ten. I should think about heading back."

It looked for a moment as though he wanted to argue with her, but he changed his mind. Diana was sure that most of his dates didn't need to rush home. More than likely they lingered over wine in front of a romantic fireplace, shared a few kisses and probably more. It was the "probably more" that got her heart pumping. It would be a foolish mistake to let this relationship advance beyond friendship. All right, she admitted it. She was attracted to the man. Good grief, what red-blooded female wouldn't be? But they lived in different worlds. Cliff was part of the swinging singles scene and she was like a modern-day Betsy Ross, doing needlepoint in her rocking chair in front of the television.

"You're looking thoughtful," he said as they left the restaurant.

"I do?" she murmured.

Once again he opened the car door for her, and she scooted inside as gracefully as she could manage. Again her fingers moved to the clasp on her purse. For some reason she was nervous again. She liked Cliff more than any man she'd dated since Stan's death, but it went without saying that she wasn't the woman for him.

Cliff pulled out of the parking lot and was soon on the freeway heading south. They chatted easily, and Diana could see where Cliff would make a good attorney. He could be persuasive when he wanted to be. Darn persuasive.

"That was my exit," she told him when he drove past it. She jerked her head over her shoulder as though it were possible for them to reverse their direction.

"I know."

"Where are you taking me?" She was more amused than irritated.

"If you must know, I want to kiss you and I wasn't exactly thrilled to do it in front of an audience."

As Joan had predicted it would, Diana's blood reached the simmering point. A kiss would quickly accelerate it to the boiling stage.

"Joan and Katie will be in bed by now." He needn't worry about them peeking through the living room drapes.

"I was thinking more of George and Shirley," Cliff told her.

Diana laughed; he was probably right. She could picture Shirley waiting by her front window, drapes parted, staring at the street.

Cliff took the next exit to the small community in the south end of Seattle called Des Moines. "I want you to see something," he explained.

"Your sailboat?"

"No," he said softly. "The stars."

Romantic, too! She could resist anything but romance. It wasn't fair that in a few hours he could narrow in on her weaknesses and break down all her well-constructed defenses.

There were several dozen cars in the huge parking lot. A wonderful seafood restaurant was an attraction that brought many out on a lovely spring evening.

Cliff parked as far away from the restaurant as he could. He turned off the ignition and climbed out of the car. By the time he was around to her side, Diana's heart was pounding so hard it threatened to break her ribs.

With his arm draped around her shoulders, Cliff led her down onto the wharf. The night was lovely. A soft breeze drifted off the water and the scent of seaweed and salt mingled with the crisp air. The sky was blanketed in black velvet, and the sparkling stars dotted the heavens like diamonds.

"It's lovely, isn't it?" she said, experiencing the wonder of standing beneath a canopy of such splendor.

Cliff's answer was to turn her in his arms. She looked up at him, and her hair fell away from her face. He raised his hands to touch her cheeks and stared down at her. His fingertips slowly glided over each feature. Such smooth skin, warm and silky, and eyes that could rip apart a man's heart. Slowly he lowered his mouth to hers, denying himself the pleasure for as long as he could endure it.

Their mouths gently brushed against each other's like rose petals caught in a breeze. Velvety smooth. Soft and warm. Infinitely gentle, but electric. Again he kissed her, only this time his mouth lingered, longer this time, much longer.

Diana felt her knees go weak and she swayed toward him, slipping her arms around his neck. A debilitating sensation overcame her. She couldn't think, couldn't breathe, couldn't move.

Cliff groaned and his grip tightened and moved to the back of her head. He slanted his mouth across hers, sampling once more the pure pleasure of her kiss. He'd been right; she tasted incredibly of sweet butterscotch. Hungrily, his lips devoured hers, again and again, unable to get enough of her. Diana felt the tears well in her eyes, and was at a loss to know where they came from or why. One slipped from the corner of her eye and rolled down the side of her face, leaving a shiny trail.

At first her tears were lost to him, he was so involved with the taste of her. When he realized she was crying, he stopped and drew away from her.

"Diana?" he asked tenderly, concerned.

Embarrassed, she tucked her chin against her shoulder, not knowing what to say.

"Then why…"

"I don't know. I am such an idiot." She jerked her hand across her face and smudged her carefully applied mascara. "I don't know, Cliff. I honestly don't know."

He tried to hold her, but she wouldn't let him.

"Because it was good," she offered as an explanation.

"The kiss?"

"Everything. You. The dinner. The stars." She sobbed once and held her hands over her face. "Everything."

"I didn't have anything to do with making the stars shine," he teased softly. Although she didn't want him to hold her, Cliff kept his hands on her shoulders, seeking a way to comfort her.

Diana knew he was attempting to lighten the mood, but it didn't help.

"Come on, let me take you home." This wasn't what he wanted, but he didn't know what else to do.

Miserable, she nodded.

"I have to admit this is the first time my kisses have caused a woman to weep."

She attempted to laugh, but the sound that came out of her throat was like the creak of a rusty hinge. No doubt this was a switch for him. Women probably swooned at his feet. Tall, handsome, rich men were a rare species.

He draped his arm around her shoulders again as he led her back to his car. When he opened the door for her, he paused and pressed a finger under her chin, lifting her face so that she was forced to meet his gaze.

"It was just as good for me," he told her softly.

Diana longed to shout at him to stop. All this wasn't necessary. The last thing she wanted was for him to sweep her off her feet, and already she was so dangerously close to tumbling that it rocked her to the bottom of her soul. They weren't right together. Cliff was wonderful, too good to be true. His tastes leaned toward someone young and sleek, not a widow with two daughters whose lifetime goals were to grow up and succeed Katy Perry.

All the way back to the house, Diana mentally rehearsed what she planned to say at the door. He'd ask her out again, and she'd tell him in hushed, regretful tones that she had to decline. She had to! The option had been taken away from her the instant he'd pulled her into his arms. Shirley was right—this man was more dangerous than fire!

Only Cliff didn't give her the opportunity to refuse him. Like the perfect gentleman, he escorted her to the door, thanked her for a lovely evening, gently kissed her forehead and walked away.

Diana was grateful he hadn't made her say it, but her heart pounded with regret. Cliff had realized there could be no future for them, and although she would have liked to find a way, it was impossible.

A week passed, a long, tedious week when life seemed to be an uphill battle. Joan went through two packages of press-on nails, and they turned up in every conceivable corner of the house. Katie's allergies were acting up again, and Diana spent two dreary afternoons sitting in a doctor's office waiting for the nurse to give Katie her shot.

Shirley was over daily for coffee and to reassure Diana that she'd made the right decision about not seeing Cliff again. It seemed Cliff had recovered quickly and was said to be dating Dana Mattson, a local television talk show hostess. Diana thought of Cliff fondly and wished him well. In many ways she was grateful for their one evening together. She'd felt more alive than at any other time since Stan's death. She was grateful that he'd shown her the light, but now she didn't know if she could be content with living in the shadows again.

The Thursday afternoon following their dinner, Diana planted marigolds along the edges of the flower bed in the backyard. The huge old apple tree was in bloom and filled the air with the sweet scent of spring, but Diana was too caught up in her own thoughts to notice. All day she'd been in a blue funk, depressed and irritable. Every time she saw the wilted bouquet of roses and carnations in the center of the kitchen table, she felt faint stirrings of regret. Friday there wouldn't be any choice but to toss the flowers. It was silly to allow a lovely bouquet to mean so much.

After depositing her garden tools in the garage, she stepped into the bathroom to wash her hands. Joan was standing on top of the toilet, leaning across the sink and staring in the mirror. Her young mouth was twisted in a grimace.

"What are you doing?" Diana demanded.

"I'm practicing so I look cool. See," She turned to face her mother, her mouth twisted in a sarcastic sneer that would have wilted daffodils.

"You look terrible."

"Great. That's exactly the look I'm going for."

"Joan, sweetheart," she said with growing impatience, "I just put five hundred dollars down at the orthodontist's so that you could have lovely, straight teeth."

Joan stared at her blankly.

"Do you mean to tell me I'm spending thousands of dollars to straighten the teeth of a child who plans never to smile?"

"Boy, are you a grouch," Joan announced as she jumped down off the toilet. "What's the matter, Mom, is Aunt Flo visiting?"

It took Diana a moment to make the connection with her monthly cycle. When she did, her knees started to shake. In an even, controlled voice, she turned toward her daughter. "When did you learn about Aunt Flo?"

"A year ago."

"But…" So much for the neat packet she'd mailed away

for that so carefully explained everything in the simple terms that a fifth grader would understand.

"I figured you'd get around to telling me one of these days," Joan said, undisturbed.

"Oh, dear." Diana sat on the edge of the tub.

"It's no big deal, Mom."

"Who told you…when?" Diana's voice shook as she realized that her little girl wasn't so little anymore. "Why didn't you come to me?"

"Honestly, Mom, I would have, but you think a fifth grader is too young for panty hose."

"You are!"

"See what I mean?" Joan declared, shaking her head.

"Who told you?"

"The library…"

"The Kent library?" Good grief, it wasn't safe to take her daughter into the local library anymore.

"You see," Joan explained, "we had this discussion in fourth grade that sort of left me hanging, so I checked out a few books."

"And the books told you everything?"

Joan nodded and started to speak, but was interrupted by her younger sister, who stuck her head in the bathroom door.

"I'm starved—what's for dinner?"

"I haven't decided yet."

Katie placed her hands on her hips. "Is it going to be another one of *those* dinners?"

"Can't you see we're having a serious mother-daughter discussion here?" Joan shouted. "Get lost, dog breath."

"Joan!" Diana cried, and quickly diverted an argument. "Don't call your sister that. Katie, I'm hungry, too. Why don't you check what's in the refrigerator? I'm open for suggestions."

"Okay," Katie cried eagerly, and hurried back into the kitchen.

"Are you mad?" Joan asked in a subdued voice. "I didn't tell you before, well, because...you know."

"Because I won't let you wear panty hose."

Joan nodded. "You've got to remember, I'm growing up!"

Diana swiped the hair off her face. At this moment she didn't need to be reminded of the fact her elder daughter was turning into a woman right before her eyes.

Katie had emptied half the contents of the refrigerator on top of the counter by the time Diana entered the kitchen. "Find anything interesting?"

"Nothing I'd seriously consider eating," Katie said. "Can we have Kentucky Fried Chicken tonight?"

"Not tonight, honey."

"How about going to McDonald's?"

"If we can't afford KFC, we can't afford McDonald's."

"TV dinners?" Katie asked hopefully.

"Let me see what we've got." She opened the freezer door and glared inside, hoping against hope she'd somehow find three glorious flat boxes.

The doorbell chimed in the distance. "I'll get it," Joan screamed, and nearly knocked over the kitchen chair in her rush to get to the front door first.

"Oh, hi." Joan's voice drifted into the kitchen. "Mom, it's for you."

The list of possibilities ran through Diana's mind. The paperboy, Shirley Holiday, the pastor. She rejected each one. Somehow she knew even before she came into the room who was at the door. She'd longed for and dreaded this moment.

"Hi," Cliff said, smiling broadly. "I was wondering if the three of you would like to go on a picnic with me."

"Sure," Joan answered first, excited.

"Great," Katie chimed in.

Cliff's gaze didn't leave Diana's. "It's up to your mother."

Three

"I thought we'd go to Salt Water Park," Cliff said, his gaze holding Diana's. He resisted the urge to lift his hand, touch her cheek and tell her she'd been on his mind from the minute he'd left her. After their dinner date he'd instinctively realized that if he were to ask her out again, she'd refuse. The only way he could get her to agree to see him again would be to involve her daughters.

"Can we have Kentucky Fried Chicken?" Katie asked, jumping up and down excitedly.

"Katie!" Diana cried. That girl worried far too much about her stomach.

"As a matter of fact," Cliff answered, "I've got a bucket in the car now."

"Mother," Katie pleaded, her eyes growing more round by the second. "KFC!"

"I'll get a blanket," Joan said, rushing through the living room and down the hall to the linen closet.

"I've got to change shoes," Katie added, and zoomed after her sister, leaving Diana and Cliff standing alone.

"I take it this means you're going?"

Diana decided his smile was far too sexy for his own

good, or for hers. "I don't appear to have much of a choice. If I refuse now, I'm likely to have a mutiny on my hands."

Cliff grinned; his plan had worked well. A streak of dried dirt was smeared across her chin, and her blond hair was gathered at the base of her neck with a tie. Her washed-out jeans had holes in the knees. Funny, but he couldn't remember the last time a woman looked more appealing to him. She was everything he'd built up in his mind this past week, and more.

What he'd told her that night was true—he'd never had a woman respond to his kisses with tears. Unfortunately, what Diana didn't know was that he'd been equally shaken by those moments in the moonlight. He'd been attracted to her from the minute she'd stared up at him from beneath her kitchen sink and described a plumber's wrench. She'd amused him, challenged his intelligence, charmed him, but what had attracted him most was her complete lack of pretense. This wasn't a woman whose life centered around three-inch long fingernails. She was gutsy and authentic.

Over dinner, he'd discovered her wit and humor. On social issues she was opinionated but not dogmatic, concerned but not fanatical. She was unafraid of emotion and possessed a deep inner strength. All along he'd known how much he wanted to kiss her. What he hadn't anticipated was the effect it would have on them both. A single kiss had never touched his heart more. Diana had been trembling so badly, she hadn't noticed that he was shaking like a leaf himself. He experienced such a gentleness for her, a craving to protect and comfort her. He felt like a callow youth, unpracticed and green. Thrown off balance, he hadn't enjoyed the feeling.

On the way home from the marina, they'd barely talked. By then Cliff was confident he wouldn't be seeing her again. That decided, a calmness had come over him. A widow with children was no woman to get involved with, and Diana was the take-home-to-mother type he generally avoided.

Picturing himself as a husband was difficult enough, but as a father...well, that was stretching things. He'd always enjoyed children and looked forward to having his own someday; he just hadn't planned on starting with a houseful. He did like Joan and Katie—they were cute kids. But they were kids. He hardly knew how to act around them.

Then why had he gone back to Diana's? Cliff had asked himself that same question twenty times in as many minutes. He'd been out a couple of times that week, but neither woman had stimulated him the way those few hours with Diana had. He heard her laugh at the most ridiculous times. A newscast had left him wondering what her opinion was on an important local issue. He'd waited a couple of days for her to contact him. Women usually did. But not Diana.

Interrupting his thoughts, Joan returned to the living room, dragging a blanket with her. The eleven-year-old was quickly followed by a grinning, happy Katie.

"You ready?" Cliff asked.

"We won't all fit in your sports car," Diana said, fighting the natural desire to be with Cliff and angry with herself for wanting it so much. She'd changed clothes and washed her face, but she still felt like Cinderella two nights after the ball.

"We can take two cars," Joan suggested, obviously not wanting anything to ruin this outing.

Palm up, Cliff gestured toward her elder daughter. "Excellent idea."

Joan positively glowed. "Can I ride with Cliff?"

Diana's brows involuntarily furrowed in concern.

"I…ah."

"It's fine with me," Cliff told her, and noticed that Katie looked disappointed. "Then Katie can ride with me on the way home."

"Okay," Diana agreed reluctantly.

Diana followed Cliff to Salt Water Park, which was less than ten minutes from the house. She'd taken Joan and Katie there often and enjoyed the lush Puget Sound beachfront. On their last visit, the girls had watched several sea lions laze in the sun not more than twenty feet off the shore on a platform buoy.

When Cliff turned off the road and into the park entrance, Diana saw him throw back his head and laugh at something Joan had said. A chill went up Diana's back at the thought of what her daughter could be telling him. That girl had few scruples when it came to attractive men. But Diana was concerned for another reason. Both her girls liked Cliff, which was unusual, and although she'd dated a number of men during the past few years, rarely had she included the children in an outing. As much as possible, she tried to keep her social life separate from her family.

Cliff pulled into a space in the parking lot, and Diana eased the SUV into the spot beside him. Even though it was a school night, there seemed to be several families out enjoying the warm spring evening. Both Joan and Katie climbed out of the respective cars and rushed across the thick grass. Within seconds they returned to inform Cliff that there was an unused picnic table close to the beach.

Diana waited while Cliff took the bag of food from the trunk of his car. She felt awkward in her sweatshirt and wished she'd taken the time to change into a new pair of shorts. Had she known she was going on a picnic with Cliff, she would have washed her hair that afternoon and tried to do something different with it. That would have pleased Joan. Suddenly her thoughts came to an abrupt halt. She was traipsing on dangerously thin ice with this playboy.

"I've been meaning to ask you what kind of car this is?" she asked as he closed the trunk.

"A Lamborghini."

"Oh." She didn't know a lot about sports cars, but this one had a name that sounded expensive.

The girls were waiting at the table for them when Diana and Cliff arrived. Joan had unfolded the blanket and spread it out beneath a tall fir tree.

"Can we go looking for seashells?" Joan asked.

"I want to eat first," Katie complained. "I'm hungry."

"I bought plenty of food." Cliff said, opening the sack and setting out four individual boxes. Each one contained a complete meal.

"What's for dessert?" Already Katie had ripped open the top of her box, and a chicken leg was poised in front of her mouth.

"Ice cream cones, but only if you're good," Cliff answered.

"What he means by 'good,'" Joan explained in a hushed voice, "is giving him plenty of time alone with Mom. They need to talk."

Diana's eyes flared with indignation. "Did you tell her that?" she demanded in a low whisper.

Cliff looked astonished enough for her to believe in his innocence. "Not me."

From the corner of her eye, Diana saw him give Joan a conspiratorial wink, and was all the more upset. Rather than argue with him in front of the children, Diana decided to wait. However, maintaining her anger with Cliff was impossible. He shared the picnic table bench with Katie and sat across from Diana. He was so charming that he had all three females under his spell within minutes. Diana found it only a little short of amazing the way he talked to the girls. He didn't talk down to Joan and Katie, but treated them as miniature adults, and they adored him for it. From Diana's point of view, this man could do with fewer worshiping females.

The girls finished their meal in record time and were off to explore. While Diana tossed their garbage into the proper receptacle, she shouted out instructions.

"Don't you dare come back here wet!" she cried, and doubted that they'd heard her.

"Wet?" Cliff asked.

"Leave it to them to decide to go swimming."

"Once they find out how cold the water is, they'll change their minds," he said confidently.

Cliff had moved from the picnic table to the blanket and sat with his back propped against the tree, watching Diana as she made busywork at the picnic table.

"I'm sure the birds will appreciate your dumping those crumbs on the ground," he said, and patted the area beside him. "Come and sit down."

Unwillingly Diana did as he asked, but sat on the edge of the blanket. It was too dangerous to get close to Cliff; such raw masculinity unnerved her. She'd been three years without a man, and this one made her feel things she would have preferred to forget.

"I wish you hadn't done this," she said in a small, quiet voice.

"What?"

"Don't play dumb with me, Cliff Howard. You know exactly what I'm talking about."

"Why are you sitting so far away from me?"

"Because it's safe here."

"I don't bite." His mouth curved up in a sensual smile that did uncanny things to Diana's equilibrium.

"Maybe not, but you kiss," she told him irritably.

His eyes held hers. "It was good, wasn't it?"

She nodded. "Too good."

His smile was lazy. "Nothing can be *too* good."

Diana couldn't find it within herself to disagree, although she knew she should. "What's this about your suggesting to Joan that they give us time together alone?"

His mouth broadened into a deeper grin. "Actually, that was her idea."

Diana rolled her eyes heavenward. That sounded exactly like something Joan would suggest.

"I like your girls, Diana," he said gently. "You've done a good job raising them."

"They're not raised yet—besides, you're seeing their good side. Just wait until they start fighting. There are days when I think they're going to seriously injure each other."

"My brother and I were like that. We're close now, although he's living in California." Cliff paused and told her a couple of stories from his youth that produced a smile and caused her to relax. "Rich and I talk at least once a week now. Joan and Katie will probably do the same once they leave home."

Bringing her legs up, Diana rested her chin on top of her knees. One hand lazily picked up a long blade of grass. It felt right to be with Cliff. Right and wrong.

"Why haven't you married?" The question was abrupt and tactless, slipping out before she could temper the words.

Cliff shrugged, and then his answer was as direct as her question. "I haven't found the right woman. Besides, I'm having too much fun to settle down."

"Usually, when a man's over thirty there's a reason... I mean...some men can't make a commitment, you know." Oh, heavens, she was making this worse every minute.

"To be honest, I've never considered marriage." There hadn't been any reason to. That wasn't to say he hadn't been in love any number of times, but generally the emotion was fleeting and within a few weeks another woman would capture his attention. Once he'd had a girl move in with him, but those had been the most miserable months of his life, and the experience had taught him valuable lessons. Expensive ones. He would never again accept that kind of arrangement.

"Shirley mentioned a Becky somebody."

Bless Shirley's black heart, Cliff mused. "She lived with me for three months."

"You didn't want to marry her?"

"Good grief, no. I was never so glad to get rid of anyone in my life."

Diana frowned. The knowledge that Cliff had lived with a woman proved that he was a swinging single, as she'd suspected. That he'd want to spend time with her was only a little short of amazing. Perplexed, she wrapped her arms around her legs and briefly pressed her forehead to her knees.

"You don't approve of a man and woman living together?" The troubled look that clouded her eyes made her opinion all the more evident.

Diana lifted her head and her eyes held his. "It isn't for me to approve or disapprove. What other people do is their own business as long as it doesn't affect me or my children."

"But it's something you'd never do?"

Her hesitation was only slight. "I couldn't. I have Joan

and Katie to consider. But as I said, it's not up to me to judge what someone else does."

Her answer pleased him. Diana was too intelligent to get caught in a dead-end relationship that would only end up ripping apart her heart.

Unfortunately Cliff had been forced to learn his lessons the hard way.

"You were on my mind every day, all day, all week," he said softly, enticingly. "I thought about you getting up and taking the girls to school. Later, I remembered you telling me you wanted to plant marigolds. That's what you did today, isn't it?"

Diana nodded and closed her eyes. "I had a crummy week." She didn't want Cliff to court her. Her attraction to him was powerful enough without his telling her he hadn't been able to get her off his mind.

"The fact is, I couldn't stop thinking about you," he added.

"I filled out an application for a job with the school district this morning," she told him brightly. She was desperate for him to stop leading her on. She didn't need for him to say the things a woman wants to hear. They weren't necessary; she had been fascinated from the moment he'd walked into her house. "There's a good chance they'll be able to hire for September."

"When I wasn't thinking about you," he continued, undaunted, "I was remembering our kisses and wondering how long it would be before I could kiss you again."

Her fingers coiled into hard fists. "I'll probably be working as a teacher's aide," she said, doing her utmost to ignore him.

"Don't make me wait too long to kiss you again, Diana."

Her hands were so tightly bunched that her fingers

ached. She forced herself to ignore him, to pretend she hadn't heard what he was saying. Closing her eyes helped to blot out his image, but when she opened them again, he had moved and was sitting beside her.

"How long are you going to make me wait?" he asked again, in a voice that would melt concrete.

His eyes rested on her mouth. Diana tried to look away, but he wouldn't let her. Even when he raised his hand and turned her face back to him, his gaze didn't stray from her lips. He pressed his index finger over her mouth and slid it from one corner of her lips to the other. Diana couldn't have moved to save her life.

"You don't need to tell me anything. I know what you're thinking and that you weren't able to get me off your mind, either. I know you want this."

One of his hands cupped the side of her face, and her eyes fluttered closed. His other hand slipped around her waist as he brought her into his arms. In that moment Diana couldn't have resisted him to save the world. He knew her, knew that he'd been on her mind all week, knew how much she regretted that things couldn't be different for them.

Cliff lowered his head and pressed his lips over hers. The kiss was gentle and so good, that Diana felt her heart would burst. Emotionally rocked, she trembled as though trapped in the aftermath of an earthquake.

Slowly his mouth worked its way over hers, and she opened her lips to him in silent invitation, the way a flower does to the noonday sun, seeking its warmth, blossoming. Diana groaned, and her arms curled around his torso until her hands met at his spine. Before she was aware of how it had happened, Cliff placed his hands on her shoulders and pressed her backward, anchoring her to the blanket. He raised his head, and his eyes delved into hers.

Diana sank her fingers into the dark hair at his temples and smiled tentatively. It was the sweetest, most tender expression Cliff had ever seen, filled with such gentle goodness that he felt his heart throb with naked desire. He longed to press her body under his.

"Do you feel it, too?" he asked, needing to hear her say the words.

Diana nodded. "I wish I didn't."

"No, you don't," he returned with supreme confidence. A surge of undiluted power gripped him.

"I think he kissed her."

A girlish giggle followed the announcement.

"Katie?" Cliff asked Diana.

She nodded.

Cliff levered himself off Diana and helped her into a sitting position. Self-conscious in front of her children, Diana ran her fingers through her hair, lifting it away from her face.

"We found a starfish," Joan said, delivering it to her mother and sitting on the blanket.

Diana didn't notice the proud find as much as the fact that her daughter's shoes were missing and the bottoms of her jeans were sopping wet. Chastising Joan in front of Cliff would embarrass the eleven-year-old, and Diana resisted the urge.

"Isn't he gorgeous?" Katie demanded.

"Who?" Diana blinked, thinking her daughter could be talking about Cliff.

"The starfish!" Both girls gave her a funny look.

"Yes, he's perfectly wonderful. Now take him back to the water or he'll die."

"Ah, Mom..."

"You heard me." She brooked no argument.

Joan picked up the echinoderm and rushed back to the beach. Katie lingered behind, her head cocked at an angle as she studied Cliff.

"Do you like to kiss my mother?" she asked curiously.

Cliff nodded. "Yes. Does that bother you?"

Katie paused to give some consideration to the question. "No, not really, as long as she likes it, too."

"She likes it, and so do I."

Katie's pert nose wrinkled. "Does she taste good?"

"Real good."

"Gary Hidenlighter offered me a baseball card if I'd let him kiss me. I told him no." She wrapped her hands around her neck, then, graphically pretending to strangle herself. "Yuck."

"It matters who you're kissing, sweetheart," Diana explained. A fetching pink highlighted her cheekbones at her daughter and Cliff talking about something so personal.

Having satisfied her curiosity, Katie ran toward the pathway that led to the beach and to her elder sister.

"I have the feeling that if Gary Hidenlighter had offered her Kentucky Fried Chicken, she would have gone for it."

Cliff chuckled, his eyes warm. "What do I need to trade to gain your heart, Diana Collins?"

Ignoring the question, Diana picked up the blanket and took care to fold it with crisp corners. She held the quilt to her stomach as a protective barrier when she finished.

"I asked you something."

"I have no intention of answering such a leading question." In nervous agitation she flipped a stray strand of hair around her ear.

"Can I see you again tomorrow?" he asked. "Dinner, a show, anything you want."

Diana's heart constricted with dread. Now that she was

faced with the decision of whether to see him again, the answer was all too clear.

"Listen," she murmured, wrapping her arms around the blanket to ward off a chill, "we need to talk about this first."

"I asked you to go to a movie with me."

"That's what I want to talk about."

"Is it that difficult to decide?"

"Yes," she whispered.

Cliff stood and leaned against the tree, bracing one foot against the trunk. "All right, when?"

Diana was uncertain. "Anytime the girls aren't around."

"Later tonight?"

She'd never felt more unsure about a man in her life. The sooner they talked, the better. "Tonight will be fine."

"Don't look so bleak. It can't be that bad."

It was worse than bad. Shirley's warnings echoed in her ears, reminding her that she'd be a fool to date a prominent womanizer who was said to have little conscience and few scruples. Diana's insides were shaking and her nerves were shot. She was a mature woman! She should be capable of handling this situation with far more finesse than she was exhibiting.

"I—I wish you hadn't come back." Her emotions were so close to the surface that she tossed the blanket on the picnic table and stalked away, upset with both Cliff and herself.

For half a minute, Cliff was too stunned to react. This woman never ceased to astonish him. She'd wept in his arms when he'd kissed her, and when he'd told her how attracted he was to her and asked her out again, she'd stormed away as though he'd insulted her.

Driven by instinct, Cliff raced after her, his quick stride catching up with her a few feet later.

"Maybe we should talk now," he suggested softly, gesturing toward a park bench. "We can see the girls from here. If there's a problem, I don't want it hanging over our heads. Now tell me what's got you so upset."

She gaped at him. He honestly didn't know what was wrong. He was driving her crazy, and he seemed completely oblivious to the fact. Gathering her composure, Diana nodded in silent agreement and sat down.

Cliff joined her. "Okay, what's on your mind?"

You! she wanted to scream, but he wouldn't understand her anger any more than she did. "First of all, let me tell you that I am very flattered at the attention you've given me. Considering the women you usually date, it's done worlds of good for my ego."

A frown marred his brow. "I don't know what you're talking about."

"Oh, come on, Cliff," she said in an effort to be flippant. "Surely you realize that you're 'hot stuff.'"

"So they tell me."

She expelled her breath slowly, impatiently. "A date with you would quicken any female's heart."

"I'm flattered you think so."

"Cliff, don't be cute, please—this is difficult enough."

He paused, leaned forward and clasped his hands. "I don't understand what any of this has to do with a picnic supper. I like you. So what? I think your daughters are wonderful. Where does that create a problem?"

"It just does." She felt like shouting at him.

"How?" he pressed. Women generally went out of their way to attract his attention. He found it an ironic twist that the one woman who had dominated his thoughts for an entire week would be so eager to be rid of him. Her defiance pricked his ego. "All right, let's hear it," he said, his voice low and serious.

Still, he wouldn't look at her, which was just as well for Diana, since this was difficult enough.

"I don't want to see you again," she said forcefully, although her voice shook. There—it was out. Considering the way she responded to his kisses, she must be out of her mind. Although she had to admit she didn't feel especially pleased to decline his invitation, it was for the best.

Cliff was silent. The thing was he knew she was right, but he felt he was on the brink of some major discovery about himself. Ego aside, he realized he could have just about any woman he wanted, except Diana Collins.

"I suppose Shirley told you I have the reputation of being some heartless playboy. Diana, it's not true."

Diana paused to take in several deep breaths. She'd hoped that he'd spare her this. "I think you're wonderful...."

"If you honestly felt that way, you wouldn't be so eager to be rid of me."

"Don't, Cliff," she pleaded. She wasn't going to be able to explain a thing with his interrupting every five seconds.

"What I can't understand," he said, shaking his head, "is why you're making it out to be some great tragedy that I find you attractive."

"But I'm not your...type," she declared for lack of a better description. "And if we continue to see each other, it will only lead to problems for us both."

"It seems to me that you're jumping to conclusions."

"I'm not," she stated calmly.

Cliff was losing his temper now. "And as for your not being my type, don't you think I should be the one to decide that?"

"No," she argued. Diana could hardly believe she was

telling the most devastating man she'd ever known that it would be better for them not to see each other again.

"Why not?" he shot back.

"Because."

"That doesn't make a lot of sense."

Diana clamped her mouth closed. It wasn't going to do any good to try to reason with him. He probably was so accustomed to women falling into his arms that he wasn't sure how to react when one resisted. A few years earlier she would have been like all the others, she noted mentally.

"Diana," he said after a calming minute. "I don't know what's going on in that twisted mind of yours, but I do think you're being completely unreasonable. I like you, you like me..."

"The girls..."

"Are terrific."

"But, Cliff, you drive a Lamborghini."

The car bothered her! "What's that got to do with anything?"

Diana wasn't sure she could explain. "It makes a statement."

"So does your Ford SUV."

"Exactly! What I can't understand is why a man who drives an expensive sports car is interested in seeing a thirty-year-old widow who plows through traffic in a ten-year-old bomber."

"Bomber?"

Diana's grin was fleeting. "That's what the girls call the Ford."

Cliff's gaze drifted to the two youngsters running along the rolling surf. Their bare feet popped foam bubbles with such mindless glee that he found himself smiling at their antics.

Diana's gaze followed his and her thoughts sobered.

"This doesn't really have anything to do with what cars we drive, does it?"

"No," Diana admitted softly. "Shirley warned me about you."

"I'm not going to lie," Cliff murmured. "Everything she said is probably true. But of all the women I've met, I would have thought you were one to form your own opinions."

"If it were just me, I'd be accepting your offer so fast it would make your head spin," she answered honestly. "But the girls think you're the neatest thing since microwave popcorn and they're at a vulnerable age."

"Somehow I got the feeling that what's bothering you isn't any of these things. Not the car, not the girls, not the other women I date."

He read her thoughts so well it frightened her. She clenched her hands together and nodded. "I can't be the woman you want."

He frowned. "What do you mean?"

"I haven't got the body of a centerfold or the looks of a beauty queen. I've had children."

"Hey, I'm not complaining. I like what I see."

"You might not be so sure if you saw more of me."

"Is that an offer?"

Color bloomed full force in her cheeks. "It most certainly was not."

"More's the pity."

"That's another thing. I'm...not easy."

"You're telling me. I've spent the past fifteen minutes trying to talk you into a movie. After all this I certainly hope you don't intend to turn me down."

She laughed then, because refusing him was impossible. He was right; she was the type of person to make up her own mind. Shirley would have her hide, but, then, her neighbor hadn't been the sole subject of his considerable charm.

"You will go with me, won't you?"

"Where?" Katie cried, running up from behind them.

"Cliff wants to take me to a movie."

Katie clapped her hands. "Oh, good. Can Joan and I go, too?"

Four

"I hope you know what you're getting yourself into," Diana's neighbor muttered, her brow puckered. She paused and stared at the bottom of her empty coffee cup. "George told me he's seen Cliff Howard bring lesser women to their knees."

"Listen, Shirley, I'm a big girl. I can take care of myself."

Shirley snickered softly. "The last time you told me that was when you decided to figure your own income tax, and we both know what happened."

Diana cringed at the memory. In an effort to save a few dollars a couple of years back, she'd gone over her financial records and filled out her own tax forms. It hadn't appeared so difficult, and to be truthful, she'd been rather proud of herself. That was until she'd been summoned for an audit by an IRS agent who had all the compassion and understanding of a grizzly bear. It had turned out that she owed the government several hundred dollars and they weren't willing to take Mastercard. They were, however, amicable to confiscating her home and children if she didn't come up with the five-hundred-dollar discrepancy. Scraping the money together on her fixed income had made the weeks following the audit some of the most unpleasant since her husband's death.

"I just don't want to see you get hurt," Shirley added in thoughtful tones. "And I'm afraid Cliff Howard's just the man to do it."

"What I want to know is why I've never seen Cliff before now?" Diana asked in an effort to change the subject. "You know so much about him, like he was a longtime family friend. I didn't even know he existed."

"George plays golf with him a couple of times a month. They meet at the country club. Until the other night, Cliff had only been to our house once." Her mouth tightened. "I should have known something like this would happen."

"Like what?"

"You falling head over heels for him."

Diana laughed outright at that. "Rest assured, I am not in love with Cliff Howard."

"But you will be," Shirley said confidently. "Every woman falls for him eventually. Some of the stories going around the clubhouse about him would shock you."

"Well, you needn't worry. I'm not going to fall for him."

"That's what they all say," Shirley told her knowingly.

Diana avoided her friend's gaze. Her neighbor wasn't saying anything she hadn't already suspected. She liked Cliff, was strongly attracted to him, but she wasn't going to fall for him. She was too intelligent to allow herself to be taken in by a notorious playboy. But, no matter what her feelings, Diana couldn't completely discredit Shirley's advice. Her neighbor could very well be right, and Diana could be headed down the slick path to heartache and moral decay.

She paused and cupped her hands around her coffee

mug. "He's been wonderful with the girls," she said, hoping that alone was excuse enough to date Cliff.

"I know," Shirley answered softly, shaking her head. "That confuses me, too. I never thought Cliff Howard would like children."

"Mikey thinks he's great."

"Yeah, but Cliff won him over early by bringing him an autographed baseball."

Shirley had a point there. Besides, Mikey was the friendly sort and not easily offended. "Joan and Katie are crazy about him."

Shirley's eyes narrowed. "Just don't make the mistake of thinking you're different from all the other women who have wandered in and out of his life."

Diana pondered her friend's words. Shirley had gone to great lengths to describe Cliff's "women." To hear her neighbor tell it, Cliff Howard hadn't so much as looked at a woman over thirty, much less shown an interest in dating one. It went without saying that he usually avoided women with children. Cliff had told her himself that she was the first widow he'd taken out. Diana didn't know what was different about her, wasn't sure she wanted to know. He seemed to honestly enjoy being with her and the girls, and for now that was enough.

"What makes you think you'll be different?" Shirley pressed.

"But I am different. You said so yourself," Diana answered after a lengthy pause, holding her neighbor's concerned gaze.

"I don't mean it like that." An exasperated sigh followed. "Just keep reminding yourself that Cliff could well be another Casanova."

Diana laughed outright. "Unfortunately he's got his good looks."

"You're about as likely to have a lasting relationship with Cliff as you are with Casanova, so keep that in mind."

"Yes, Mother," Diana teased softly. She found Shirley's concern more touching than irritating.

"Just don't make me say 'I told you so,'" her neighbor returned, and the doubt rang clear in her voice.

Diana mused over their conversation for most of the day. Shirley wasn't telling her anything she hadn't already considered herself. She'd been playing with fire from the minute she'd agreed to that first dinner date with Cliff, and she knew it, but the flickering flames had never been more attractive. She was thirty, and it was time to let her hair down and kick up her heels a little.

For his part, Cliff wasn't stupid, Diana realized. He knew what kind of physical response he drew from her, knew she had been teetering with indecision when he had suggested they see each other again. So when Katie had piped in and asked to go to the movies with them, Cliff had jumped on the idea. By including the girls, he'd known she wouldn't refuse. How could she, with Joan and Katie doing flips over the idea? The man was a successful attorney and he'd read her ambivalence with the ease of a first grade primer. Although she'd been determined to put an end to this silliness, her well-constructed defenses had tumbled with astonishing unconcern and she was as eager for the drive-in as the girls. It was one of the last left in the country and in South King Country, in the countryside.

"Mom," Katie cried as she rushed into the kitchen the minute the school bus dropped her off. "Can Mikey go to the drive-in movie with us?"

Diana hedged. "I don't know, honey. Cliff has to agree."

"He won't care. I know he won't, and besides, he knows Mikey and Mikey's parents know Cliff." She slapped her hands against her side as though that fact alone were enough for anyone to come to the same decision, then grinned beguilingly.

Arguing with such logic seemed fruitless. "Let's wait and talk to Cliff once he arrives."

"Okay."

Diana watched in amazement as Katie grabbed an apple from the fruit basket and dashed out the front door to join her friends. Usually Diana was subjected to a long series of arguments whenever the girls were after something, and Katie's easy acceptance pulled her up short.

"Well, all right," she muttered after her daughter, still bemused.

By the time Cliff arrived, Diana was convinced that half the neighborhood was waiting. He parked his sports car in the driveway, and was instantly besieged by a breathless, excited Joan and two or three of Joan's friends. Katie and Mikey followed a second later. Both Diana's girls grabbed for Cliff's hand, one trying to outdo the other. With a patience that pleased and surprised Diana, Cliff stopped their excited chatter. He directed his first question to Joan.

Watching the humorous scene from the front porch, Diana saw her elder daughter issue an urgent plea for Cliff to allow her to invite their very best friends in all the world to the drive-in with them.

Katie started in next. Cliff's gaze went from the girls to a series of neighborhood kids who stood in the background, awaiting his reply.

From her position, Diana could clearly see Cliff's confusion. He'd asked for this, she mused, having trouble holding in her laughter.

"Hi," she greeted him, coming down the steps.

"Hi." His bewildered gaze sought hers as he motioned toward Joan and Katie and the accumulated friends. "What do you think?"

"It's up to you."

"Please, Cliff," Katie cried, her hands folded as if praying.

Cliff glanced down on Diana's daughter and released a long, frustrated sigh.He'd thought about this evening all day, and planned—or at least hoped—the drive-in movie would quickly put the girls to sleep so he could kiss Diana. Once again he'd discovered she'd dominated his thoughts most of the afternoon. His plans certainly hadn't included dragging half the neighborhood to the drive-in with him.

"I thought of a way it could work," Diana told him. "Come inside, and we'll talk about it."

Her compromise wasn't half bad, Cliff mused an hour later as he parked his sports car beside the SUV full of kids at the drive-in. They'd agreed earlier to take Diana's vehicle simply because his car wouldn't hold everyone. Diana had suggested they drive both cars and park next to each other. That way the adults could maintain their privacy and still manage to keep an eye on the kids, who were feeling very mature to have their own car. Now that he thought about it, Diana's idea had been just short of brilliant.

"How does everyone feel about popcorn?" Cliff asked once they'd situated the cars halfway between the screen and the snack bar.

"I already popped some," Diana informed him, climbing out of the driver's seat. Joan eagerly replaced her, draping her wrist over the steering wheel and looking as though she were Jeff Gordon ready for the Indy 500.

Diana sorted through something in the rear of the SUV and returned with her arms full. She handed each child his own bag of popcorn and a can of soda. "Don't eat any until the movie starts," she instructed, and was greeted by a series of harmonizing moans. "That goes for you, too," she told Cliff, her eyes twinkling.

He grumbled for show and shared a conspiratorial wink with Joan, who, he could see, had already managed to sample her goodies. He held his car door open for Diana before walking around the front and joining her in the close confines of his Lamborghini.

Diana scooted down low enough in the seat to rest her head against the back of the thick leather cushion. The contrast between them had never been more striking. She wore Levi's and a pink sweatshirt, while Cliff was fashionably dressed in slacks and a thick crewneck sweater. Diana sincerely doubted that any of his other dates had ever dressed so casually. Nor did she believe other women had six kids tagging along. Knowing Cliff's game, Diana considered the neighborhood tribe poetic justice.

"This is turning into a great idea," he said, wondering how much longer it would take before it got dark.

Before Diana could answer, a Road Runner cartoon appeared on the huge white screen. The kids in the car next to them cheered with excitement, and even from her position in Cliff's sports car, she could hear them rip into their bags of popcorn.

"You're a good sport," Diana said, feeling self-conscious all of a sudden. "I mean about the kids and everything."

"Hey, no problem."

"How'd work go?" She felt obligated to make small talk, certain he wouldn't possibly be interested in the cartoon.

"Good. How about your day?"

"Fine." She clenched her hands together so hard her fingers ached. "Joan went to the orthodontist." Now that made for brilliant conversation! She'd bore him to death before the end of the previews.

"So she's going into braces?"

Diana nodded and reached for her bag of popcorn so she'd have something to do with her hands. "I told her she's enough of a live wire as it is."

Cliff chuckled. "I'm glad to hear she's going straight."

Now it was Diana's turn to laugh. What had seemed the perfect solution an hour before now had the feel of a disaster in the making. Alone with Cliff, she'd seldom been more uncertain about anything. Joan and Katie had been her shield, protecting her from the wealth of emotion Cliff was capable of raising within her. She sat beside him, quivering inside, never having felt more vulnerable. He could make cornmeal mush of her life if he chose to, and like a fool, she'd all but issued the invitation for him to do so. Shirley's warnings sounded in her ears like sonic booms, and for an instant, Diana had the sinking feeling that one of Custer's men must have experienced the same sensation as he rode into battle, wondering what he was doing there. Diana wondered, too. Oh, man, did she wonder.

The credits for the Lucas film rolled onto the huge screen, but Diana's thoughts weren't on the highly rated movie. The open bag of popcorn rested on her lap, but she dared not eat any, sure the popcorn would stick halfway down her desert-dry throat.

"Diana?"

She jumped halfway out of her seat. "Yes?"

Cliff's smile was lazy and gentle and understanding. "Relax, will you? I'm not going to leap on you."

If there'd been a hole to crawl into, Diana would have gladly jumped inside. "I know that."

"Then what's the problem?"

There didn't seem to be enough words to explain. She was a mature, capable woman, but when she was around him, all her hard-earned independence evaporated into thin air like an ice chip on an Arizona sidewalk. He brought back feelings she preferred to keep buried, churning emotions that reminded her she was still a young, healthy woman. When she was with Cliff, she was a red-blooded woman, and her body felt obliged to remind her of the needs she didn't want to remember. With Cliff so close beside her, the last thing on her mind was motherhood and apple pie. His proximity caused her to quiver from the inside out. She wanted him to kiss her, longed for his touch. And it scared her to death.

"Diana?"

Slowly she turned to look at him. Her face felt hot against the crisp evening air, and Cliff's look brushed lightly over her features. He was kissing her with his eyes, and she was burning up with fever. Suddenly the interior of the car made her feel claustrophobic. She set the popcorn aside and reached for the door handle.

His hand stopped her. "You're beautiful."

He whispered the words with such intensity that Diana felt them melt in the air like cotton candy against her tongue. She wanted to shout at him not to say such things to her, that it wasn't necessary. She didn't need to hear them, didn't want him to say them. But the protest died a speedy death as he reached for her shoulders. His gaze held her prisoner for what seemed an eternity as he slowly slid his hand from the curve of her shoulder upward, until he found her warm nape. He didn't move, hardly breathed, anticipating her reaction. When he could wait no longer for an invitation, he wove his fingers into her hair and directed her mouth toward his.

Cliff's lips claimed hers in a fury of desire. His mouth slanted against hers in a full, lush kiss that spoke of fervor and timeless longing. The shaking inside Diana increased and she raised her hands to grip his shoulders just to maintain her equilibrium. Her skin was hot and cold at the same time.

Suddenly it all seemed too much. Using her arms as leverage, Diana abruptly broke away. Head bowed, she drew in ragged breaths. "Cliff, I…"

He wouldn't allow her to speak and gently directed her mouth back to his. All the resolve she could muster, which wasn't much, had gone into breaking off the kiss. When he reached for her again, unwilling to listen to any argument, there was nothing left with which to refuse him. His mouth opened wider, deepening the kiss, and Diana let him. Folding her arms around his neck, she leaned into his strength. He brought her against him possessively until her ribs ached and the heat of his torso burned its way down the length of her own. Cliff felt her body's natural response to him and he groaned. At this moment he'd give anything to be anyplace besides a drive-in. He wanted to lift the sweatshirt over her head and toss it aside. The pain of denial was strong and sharp as he buried his face in the sloped curve of her neck. With even, steady breaths, he tried to force his pulse to a slow, rhythmical beat as he struggled within himself. It had been a long time since he'd experienced such an intensity of need.

The battle that waged inside Diana was fierce. She

wanted to push herself away from him and scream that she wasn't like his other women. There'd been only one lover in her life, and she wasn't going to become his next conquest simply because her hormones behaved like jumping beans whenever he touched her. But the words that crossed her mind didn't make it to her lips.

"Diana…" Cliff spoke first, his voice filled with gruff emotion. "Listen, I know what you're thinking."

"Don't, Cliff, please don't." She twisted her face away from him, unable to form words to explain all that she was thinking and feeling. She felt both tormented and compelled by what was happening to them.

Cliff tensed, and his fingers dug into her shoulders.

"What's wrong?" She lifted her head and bravely raised her gaze to meet his own.

"Don't look now, but we've got an audience."

"Joan?"

"And…others."

"How many others?"

"Five."

"All six of the kids are staring at us?" The hot flush that had stained her neck raced toward her cheeks and into the roots of her hair. She'd assured all the neighborhood parents that the drive-in movie was rated PG, and here she was giving them an R-rated sideshow.

"Six noses are pressed against the window, and six pairs of eyes are glued on us," Cliff interjected with little humor.

"Oh, no," Diana groaned, hanging her head in abject misery.

"Joan's giving me the thumbs-up sign, Katie looks shocked and Mikey's obviously thoroughly disgusted. He's decided to cover his eyes."

"What should we do?" Diana asked next, horribly embarrassed.

"Good grief, why ask me? I don't know a thing about kids."

His hold was tight enough to cause her shoulders to ache, but Diana didn't complain. She was as much at a loss about what to do as Cliff was. "I think we should smile and wave, and then casually go back to watching the movie."

"This isn't the time to be cute."

"I wasn't trying to be funny. That was my idea."

"If that's the best you can come up with, then I suggest you turn in your Mother of the Year Award."

"What?" Diana cried.

"We could be warping young minds here, and all you're doing is coming up with jokes."

"Oh, for heaven's sake, I think it's safe to assume they've seen people kiss before now," Diana said, growing more amused by the moment.

"Hey, Mom."

Joan's shout interrupted their discussion. Forcing herself to appear calm and collected, Diana twisted around, painted a silly smile on her face and rolled down the window. "Yes, sweetheart?" she answered in a perfectly controlled voice. She was actually proud of herself for maintaining her cool. She prayed her expression gave away none of the naked desire she'd been feeling only moments before.

"Why are you arguing with Cliff?"

"What makes you ask that?"

"You weren't fighting a minute ago."

"You were kissing him real hard," Katie popped in. She was leaning from the back seat into the front and sticking her head out the side window next to her sister. "Judy Gilmore's boyfriend kissed her like that the time she baby-sat for us. Remember?"

"Say, aren't you kids supposed to be watching the movie?" Cliff asked, having trouble disguising his chagrin.

"It's more fun looking at you," Joan answered for the group.

"Mom, I've got to go to the bathroom."

"Me, too." Three other voices chimed in from behind Katie.

"I'll take you." Diana couldn't get out of the car fast enough. Rarely had she been more grateful for the call of nature.

By the time Diana returned, Cliff's mood had improved considerably. He was munching on popcorn and staring at the screen. When she eased into the seat beside him, he glanced in her direction and grinned. "The movie's actually pretty good."

Diana suspected it wasn't half as amusing as they'd been. She had to give Cliff credit—he really was a good sport.

By the time the second feature had started, Joan, Katie and their friends were sound asleep.

"I should have waited until now to kiss you," Cliff joked, staring across at the car filled with snoozing youngsters. "Problem was, I was too eager."

That had been Diana's trouble, as well. From the minute she'd sat beside him and they'd been alone, she'd known what was bound to happen. She'd wanted it too much.

Cliff looped his arm around her shoulder and brought her head down to his hard chest. "Now that we haven't got a crowd cheering us on, do you want to try it again?" He gave her a self-effacing, enticing half smile.

Diana laughed, and although the console prevented her from cuddling up close to his side, she adjusted herself as best she could. "When I was a teenager, we used to call the drive-in the 'passion pit.'"

"Hey, I'm game. I don't know if you recognize it or not, but there's chemistry between us." He brushed the hair from her brow and pressed his lips there.

"I noticed it all right." His kiss just then was like adding water to hot grease. "It's more potent than I care to dwell on."

"I'll say."

He did kiss her again during the second movie, but more for experimentation than anything. His fingers, tucked under her chin, turned her mouth to his as his warm lips touched, stroked and brushed hers. Temporarily satisfied, Cliff settled back and watched the movie for a few minutes more. He reached for her again later and nibbled along her neck. He refused to hold her tight, as aware of the danger as she of this explosive fireworks between them. A drive-in movie with a carload of kids parked in the next space was not the place to get overly romantic.

The second movie over, Cliff met her back at the house after Diana had dropped off Joan and Katie's friends. Both girls were more interested in sleeping than climbing out of the car. Finally Cliff lifted the sleeping Katie into his arms and carried her inside and up the stairs. A dreamy-eyed Joan followed behind, yawning as she went.

Diana tucked the blankets around her elder daughter. Joan planted her hands beneath her pillow and rolled onto her side. "Mom?"

"Yes, honey."

"Thank Cliff for me, okay?"

"Will do."

Joan forced one eye open. "Are you going to see him again?"

"I...don't know, honey. He hasn't asked me out."

"You should invite him to dinner. You make great spaghetti."

"Honey, I don't think that's a good idea."

"I happen to love good spaghetti," Cliff answered.

Diana turned and found him standing in the doorway of Joan's bedroom. "Why don't you make up a batch and bring it sailing?"

"Sailing?"

"You and the girls." Having heard Diana's hesitation, he resigned himself to including her daughters in every outing until she learned to trust him. "We'll make a day of it."

"When?"

Cliff thought about waiting another week to see Diana again, and knew that was much too long. His schedule for the next week was hectic and he'd be lucky to find the time to spend more than an hour or two with her. He had two cases going to trial and a backlog of work awaiting his attention. "Tomorrow," he suggested.

Joan bolted upright. "Hey, that sounds great. Count me in."

Irritated, Diana glared down at her daughter. "Cliff, I don't know. I'd think you'd have had your fill of me and the girls for one weekend."

"Let me be the judge of that."

"I've never been sailing before," Joan reminded Diana, her two round eyes gazing up at her pleadingly. "And you know how Katie loves anything that has to do with the water."

"We'll talk about it later," Diana told her firmly, and walked out of the bedroom. Cliff followed her down the stairs.

"Well, what do you say about tomorrow?" he asked, standing in front of the door.

"I'm...not sure." She remained on the bottom step, so that when he walked over to her, their eyes were level.

He smiled at her then and slipped one arm around her waist to pull her against him. In an effort to escape, Diana pried his arm loose and climbed one stair up so she rose a head above him.

If she thought he was going to let her go so easily, Cliff mused, then Diana Collins had a great deal to learn about him.

He brought her into his arms and kissed her until everything went still as hot, tingling shivers raced through Diana. She closed her eyes and stopped breathing.

"Tomorrow," she said in a tight, strained whisper. "What time?"

"Noon," Cliff mumbled, and dropped his hands.

Diana gripped the banister until her nails threatened to bend. "Thank you for tonight."

It was all Cliff could do to nod. He backed away from her as though she held a torch that was blazing out of control. Already he was singed, and all he could think about was coming back for more.

Five

"How long will it take before I catch a fish?" Katie asked impatiently. Her fishing pole was poised over the side of the sailboat as the forty-foot sloop lazily sliced through the dark green waters of Puget Sound.

"Longer than five minutes," Diana informed her younger daughter. She tossed an apologetic glance in Cliff's direction. He'd been the one so keen on this outing. She wasn't nearly convinced all this time together with the girls would work. Cooping the four of them up in the close confines of a sailboat for an afternoon wouldn't serve anyone's best interests as far as she could see. But Cliff had assured her otherwise, and the girls continued to swoon under the force of his charm. With such resounding enthusiasm from both parties, Diana certainly wasn't going to argue.

"The secret is to convince the fish he's hungry," Joan said haughtily with the superior knowledge of a girl three years Katie's senior.

"How do you do that?"

Diana was curious herself.

"Move your line a little so the bait wiggles," Joan answered primly, and gyrated her hips a couple of times as an example. "That makes the fish want to check out what's happening. In case you weren't aware of it, fish are by nature shy. All they need is a little encouragement."

"All fish are shy?" Diana muttered under her breath for Cliff's benefit.

"Especially sharks," he returned out of the corner of his mouth.

"I've met a few of those in my time." Chuckling, Diana watched as he finished baiting Joan's hook and handed her the pole. Cliff could well be a shark, but if so, he was a clever one.

When he'd completed the task, he paused and grinned at her.

"What about you?" Diana asked as he settled down by the helm. "Aren't you going to fish?"

"Naw." He slouched down and draped his elbow over the side of the sloop. Squinting, he smiled into the sun and expertly steered the sailboat into the wind.

For a full minute, Diana couldn't look away. Shirley had painted Cliff in such grim tones—a man without conscience who freely used women. When he was finished, Shirley had said, he hurled them aside for fresh conquests. Looking at him now, Diana refused to believe it. Cliff was patient with the girls, and exquisitely gentle with her. Just being with him was more fun than she could remember having had in months. He appeared completely at ease with her and Joan and Katie. But, then, she reminded herself, women were said to be his forte. If Cliff were indeed the scoundrel her neighbor so ardently claimed him to be, then he'd done an excellent job bamboozling her.

"Mom, come and look," Katie called, and Diana moved closer to her daughter.

Cliff smiled. He was enjoying this outing with Diana and her family. Getting the girls occupied fishing had helped.

He had them using his outdated equipment, so nothing expensive could be ruined. Actually, he was rather proud of himself for being so organized. He'd set the fishing gear the girls could use on one side of the boat and his own on the other. That way, there would be no confusion.

Now, with the girls interested in catching "shy" fish, he could soak up the sun and take time to study Diana. She was nothing like the women he was accustomed to dating. The attraction he felt for her was as much a shock to him as it apparently had been to her.

She'd finished with Katie and sat next to him. They were so close that Cliff could feel the warmth radiating from her. He longed to put his arm around her and bring her closer to his side. Okay, he'd admit it! He wanted to kiss her. Her butterscotch kisses were quickly becoming habit forming. All he'd need to do was lean forward. Their torsos would touch first, and his mouth would quickly find hers. No matter where he looked—the sky, the green water, the billowing sails, anyplace—he couldn't dispel every delicate, womanly nuance of Diana. Frustrated, he deliberately turned his thoughts to other matters.

"How's it going, girls?" he called, seeking a diversion.

"Great," Joan shouted back.

Cliff was impressed with her enthusiasm.

"All right, I guess," Katie said, peering over the side. "Here, fishy, fishy, fishy."

"That isn't going to help," Joan snapped, and as if to prove her point, she swung her fishing pole back and forth a couple of times, looking superior and confident.

Contented, Cliff grinned, and his gaze drifted back to Diana. She was a widow, no less. He'd always pictured widows as old ladies with lots of grandchildren, which was illogical, he realized. Diana was his own age. It wasn't that he'd avoided dating women thirty and over, he simply hadn't been attracted to any. But he was attracted to Diana.Oh yes, was he attracted! He wasn't so naive not to realize his playboy reputation had put her off. He'd give his eyeteeth to know what she'd heard—it would do wonders for his ego. Smiling, he relaxed and loosened his grip on the helm. He didn't know what George Holiday had told his wife, but apparently Shirley had repeated it in graphic detail. Luckily Diana had a decent head on her shoulders and was smart enough to recognize a bunch of exaggerations when she heard them.

Diana had never been on a sailboat before and she loved it, loved the feeling of relaxed simplicity, loved the wind as it whipped against her face and hair, loved the power of the sloop as it plowed through the water, slicing it as effectively as a hot butcher's knife through butter. Earlier, Cliff had let her man the helm while he'd moved forward to raise the sails, and she had been on a natural high ever since.

"You're looking thoughtful," Cliff said to Diana a moment later.

Her returning smile was slow and lazy. She closed her eyes and let the wind whip through her hair, not caring what havoc the breeze wreaked. "I could get used to this," she murmured, savoring the feel of the noonday sun on her upturned face.

"Yes," Cliff admitted. He could get used to having her with him just as easily. When he stopped to analyze his feelings, he realized that she was the down-home type of woman he didn't feel the need to impress. He could be himself, relax. He was getting too old and lazy for the mating rituals he'd been participating in the past few years.

"Cliff!" Joan screamed into the wind, her shrill voice

filled with panic. "I've...got something." The fishing pole was nearly bent in two. "It's big."

"Joan caught a whale," Katie called out excitedly.

"Hold on." Cliff jumped up and gave the helm to Diana.

"Here, you take it," Joan cried. "It's too big for me."

"You're doing fine."

"I'm not, either!"

"Joan, just do what Cliff says," Diana barked, as nervous as her daughter.

"But he hasn't said anything yet."

"How come Joan can catch a fish and I can't?" Katie whined. "I wiggled my hips and everything."

"Honey, now isn't the time to discuss it."

"It's never the time when I want to ask you something."

"Reel it in," Cliff shouted. The urge to jerk the pole out of the eleven-year-old's hands and do it himself was strong. The once confident Joan looked as if she would have willingly forgotten the whole thing.

Cliff watched as the fifth grader's hand yanked against the line. "Don't do that—you'll lose him!"

"I don't care. You do it—I didn't really want to kill a fish, anyway."

"Don't be a quitter," Cliff said, more gruffly than he'd intended. "You're doing fine."

"I am not!"

Exasperated, Cliff moved behind Joan and helped her grip the pole. With his hand over hers, he reeled for all he was worth, tugging the line closer and closer to the boat.

"I can see him," Katie shouted, jumping up and down.

"It's a salmon," Cliff called out as they got the large fish close to the boat. "A nice size sockeye from the look of him." He left Joan long enough to retrieve the net, then leaned over the side of the boat to pull the struggling salmon out of the water.

"Gross," Joan muttered, and closed her eyes. "No one told me there was going to be blood."

"Only a little," Diana assured her.

"I want to catch a fish," Katie cried a second time. "It's not fair that Joan caught one and I didn't."

"Don't worry about it," Joan said with a jubilant sigh. "I'll help you."

"I don't want your help. I want Cliff to show me."

"Cliff has to steer the sailboat," Diana explained to her younger daughter. She knew this peaceful afternoon was too good to be true. The girls would erupt into one of their famous fights and shock poor Cliff. He wasn't used to being around children—he wouldn't understand that they bickered almost constantly.

"I'm hungry," Katie decided next.

In order to appease her younger daughter, Diana climbed below deck to the galley, where Cliff had stored the picnic basket, and got Katie a sandwich and a can of her favorite soda.

Within a half hour, both girls were back to fishing, and serenity reigned once again.

"How much longer will it take?" Katie demanded within a few minutes. The irritating question was repeated at regular intervals.

Cliff's smile was getting stiffer by the minute. He wished he hadn't invited the girls along. He wanted Diana to himself, but he realized she would have refused the invitation if Joan and Katie hadn't been included. For the past thirty minutes, he'd been sitting watching Diana and wanting to kiss her. He couldn't do half the things he longed to do with Joan and Katie scrutinizing his every move. They were good kids, but it wasn't the same as being alone with Diana. And with Katie whining every few minutes, Cliff sorely felt the need for a little peace and quiet. His musings were interrupted by Katie's excited shout.

"Mommy, I got a fish, I got a fish!"

"I'll show you how to bring him in!" Joan yelled, and quickly moved to her sister's side, dragging her fishing pole with her.

"Hey! Watch your lines." Cliff's warning came too late, and before anyone could do anything to prevent it, the two fishing lines were hopelessly entangled.

"What do we do now?" Joan asked, tossing Cliff a look over her shoulder.

Once Cliff had assessed the situation, he shrugged and sadly shook his head. "There's nothing to do. I'll have to cut both lines."

"But my fish…"

"Honey, you can't reel him in now," Diana hastened to explain, praying Katie wouldn't be too terribly disappointed.

Cliff hated to cut the fishing lines, too, and was angry for not having warned the girls about what would happen if they didn't mind their poles. In addition to losing the fish, he was throwing away good lures and weights. Thankfully, there was nothing of real value like his— It was then that he saw his open tackle box on the other side of the boat. Cliff went stark still. He'd given both girls specific instructions to stay out of his gear. His swift anger could not be contained.

"Who got into my stuff?" he demanded, and knelt down to examine his box. His worst fears were quickly realized. "My lucky lure is missing. Who took my lucky lure?"

"Joan, Katie, did either of you get into Cliff's box?" Already Diana feared the answer. Cliff looked as though he'd like to strangle both girls for so much as touching his equipment.

"Where is my lucky lure?" Cliff repeated, his face hard and cold.

"You…you just cut it off." Katie's head dropped so low Diana could see her crown.

For a minute it looked as though Cliff would jump overboard in an effort to retrieve his silver lure from the murky green waters.

"That was my lucky lure," Cliff repeated, as if in a daze. "I caught a forty-pound rock cod with that silver baby."

"Katie," Diana coaxed, "why did you get into Cliff's equipment when he asked you not to?"

Cliff slammed the lid to his tackle box closed, and the sound reverberated around the inside of the sailboat like a cannon shot. He stood and turned his back to the three women. Diana and her girls couldn't appreciate something like a special lure. To them it was just a five-dollar piece of silver. To him it was his "sure bet." The success of an entire fishing expedition depended on whether he had that silver lure. He might as well hang up his fishing pole for good without it. A woman couldn't be expected to appreciate how much it meant. Burying his hands inside his pants pockets, Cliff muttered something vile under his breath and decided there wasn't anything he could do about it now. The lure was gone.

"Mom, I just heard Cliff swear," Joan whispered.

"Cliff, I'm sorry." Diana felt obliged to say something, although she realized it wasn't nearly enough. She felt terrible. With one look at the way the hot color had circled his ears, she knew how truly angry he was.

"It's my fault," Katie blubbered, hiding her face against her mother's stomach. "Joan caught a fish and I wanted one, too, and I thought Cliff's pretty lure would help."

"You'll replace the lure out of your allowance money," Diana said sternly.

Tears welled up in the small, dark eyes as she nodded, eager to do anything to appease Cliff.

With slow, deliberate action, Cliff returned to the helm and sat down heavily. His brooding gaze avoided Diana and the girls. "Don't worry about it," he said as calmly as possible.

"I'm sorry, Cliff," Katie whispered in a small, broken voice.

He forced his gaze to the youngster. "Don't give it a second thought," he said almost flippantly.

"I'll buy you a new silver lure just as pretty."

"I said, don't worry about it."

If possible, Katie's brown eyes grew more round. Tears rolled down her pale cheeks.

"How about something to eat?" Diana interjected, rubbing her palms together, hoping to generate interest in the packed lunch.

"We're not hungry," Joan answered for both her and her sister.

"Cliff?"

"No, thanks."

"I guess I'm the only one." She got out a sandwich and even managed to choke down a couple of bites.

Cliff's gaze drifted to Diana, who was valiantly pretending nothing was wrong. If she didn't watch it, she was likely to gag on that sandwich. Joan and Katie were huddled together, staring at him like orphans through a rich family's living room window on Christmas Eve. Joan had her arm draped over her sister's shoulders, while Katie looked thoroughly miserable. Finally Cliff couldn't stand it anymore.

"How come she loses my lure and I'm the one feeling guilty?" If there'd been a place to stalk off to, he would have done it. As it was, he was stuck on the boat with all three of them, and he wasn't in the mood for company or conversation.

"I think it's time to head back to the marina," Diana murmured, and sat beside her daughters.

Cliff couldn't have agreed with her more. He mumbled some reply and quickly tacked across the wind, heading in the direction of Des Moines Marina. Every now and then, his gaze reverted to Diana and her daughters. The three sat in the same dejected pose, shoulders hunched forward, eyes lowered to the deck, hands planted primly on their knees. The sight of them only made Cliff feel worse. All right, he'd lost his temper, but only a little. His conscience ate at him.So he shouldn't have yelled, and Joan was right, he had sworn. He'd overreacted. Talk about the wrath of Khan! But for crying out loud, Katie had gotten into his equipment, when he'd given specific instructions for her to stay out.

Diana longed to say or do something to alleviate this terrible tension. Cliff had every reason to be upset. She was angry with Katie, too, but the eight-year-old was truly sorry, and other than replacing the lure, which Katie had already promised, there was nothing more the little girl could do.

"Cliff..."

"Diana..."

They spoke simultaneously.

"You first," Cliff said, and gestured toward her, unable to tolerate the silence any longer.

"I want you to know how sorry I am." When Cliff opened his mouth, she knew before he spoke what he planned to say, and it irritated her more than an angry argument. Squaring her shoulders, she gritted her teeth and waved her index finger at him. "Please don't tell me not to worry about it."

"Let's forget it, okay?" His smile was only a little stiff. He didn't want this unfortunate incident to ruin a promising relationship. When it came to dealing with women, he did fine—more than fine. It was Joan and Katie who had placed him out of his element.

"It's obvious you're not going to forget it."

"It's just that it was a special lure," Cliff said, although that certainly didn't excuse his anger.

Katie placed her hands over her face and burst into sobs.

If Cliff had been feeling guilty before, it was nothing compared to the regret that shot through him at Katie's teary tirade. He'd lost his favorite lure; *he* felt guilty, and she was crying. He didn't understand any of this, but the one thing he did know was that he couldn't bear to see the youngster so miserable. Without forethought, he left the helm and went over to Katie. He picked her up and hugged her against his chest before turning to steer the sloop with Katie cradled in his lap. "It's all right, sweetheart," he whispered, wrapping his arms around her.

"But... I...lost...your...lucky lure," she bellowed.

"It was just an ordinary lure. You can buy me another one just like it, and then that one will be my luckiest lure ever."

"I'm...so-o-o sorry." She kept her face hidden in his shoulder.

"I know."

"I'll never ever get into your fishing box again. I promise."

She raised her head, and Cliff wiped a tear from the corner of her eye. The surge of tenderness that overtook him came as a surprise. He'd been angry, but he was over that. There were more important things in life than a silly lure, and he'd just learned that an eight-year-old's smile was one of them.

"We've both learned a valuable lesson, haven't we?"

Katie responded with a quick nod. "Can I still be your friend?"

"You bet."

Her returning grin was wide.

"You want to learn how to steer the sailboat?"

She couldn't agree fast enough. "Can I?"

"Sure."

Diana felt the burden of guilt lift from her shoulders. She enjoyed Cliff's company and liked the way he'd included the girls in their dates. He'd gone out of his way to be good to her, and she would have hated to see everything ruined over a lost lure. He had a right to be upset—she was mad herself—but anger and regret weren't going to replace his "silver baby."

Diana watched as Cliff patiently showed Katie the importance of heading the sailboat into the wind. The eight-year-old listened patiently while Cliff explained the various maneuvers. He looked up once, and their eyes happened to meet. Cliff smiled, and Diana thought she'd never seen anything more dazzling. From now on she wasn't listening to anything Shirley Holiday had to say. She knew everything she needed to know about Cliff Howard.

Remembering how good Cliff had been with Katie after she'd lost his lure made the days that followed the sailing trip pass quickly as she anticipated seeing him again. They'd left the marina, had dined on Kentucky Fried Chicken, Katie's favorite, and had headed back to Diana's house. Cliff had discreetly kissed her goodbye, invited her to dinner and promised to phone.

Joan sauntered into the kitchen, paused and glanced at

the two chicken TV dinners sitting on top of the kitchen counter. "Is Cliff taking you to dinner?"

"Good guess."

Joan wrinkled up her nose. "I hate to tell you this, but Katie's not going to eat chicken unless it's from the Colonel."

Diana opened the microwave and placed the frozen meals inside. "She'll live."

"A starving woman wouldn't eat that, either."

Diana sighed. "You'll enjoy the chicken, so quit worrying about it."

"Okay."

The phone rang, and Joan leaped to answer it as if there were some concern that Diana would fight her for it.

"Hello."

Diana rolled her eyes as her daughter's voice dipped to a low, seductive note, as though she expected Justin Bieber to phone and ask for her.

"Oh, hi, Cliff. Yeah, Mom's right here." She placed the receiver to her stomach. "Mom, it's Cliff."

Diana wiped her hands dry on a kitchen towel and reached for the phone. "Hello."

"Hi."

The sound of his voice did wondrous things to her pulse. She wouldn't need an aerobics class if she talked to Cliff Howard regularly. "The kids' dinner is in the microwave, and the girls are going over to Shirley's afterward, so I should be ready within the hour."

"That makes what I have to tell you all the more difficult." He'd been looking forward to this dinner date all week and was frustrated.

"You can't make it?" Diana guessed. She should have known something like this would happen. Everything had gone too smoothly. The girls were going to Shirley's, she'd found a lovely pink silk dress on sale and her hair looked great, for once. Naturally Cliff would have to cancel!

"I'm sorry," he stated simply, and explained without a lot of detail what had happened. A court date had been changed and he had to prepare an important brief by morning. He wouldn't be able to get away for hours. He hated it, would have done anything to get out of it, but couldn't. Then he waited for the backlash that normally followed when he was forced into breaking a dinner engagement.

"I know you wouldn't cancel if it wasn't something important," Diana said, hiding her disappointment.

"You're not angry?"

His question took Diana aback. "Should I be?"

"I…no."

"I'm not saying I won't miss seeing you." She marveled that she was so willing to admit that. When it came to Cliff, she continued to feel as though she were standing on shifting sand. She was afraid of letting her emotions get out of control, and she didn't want to rely on him for more than an occasional date. And yet every time he asked to see her again, she was as giddy as Joan over the rock group U2.

"I'll make it up to you," Cliff promised.

"There's no reason to do that."

"How about dinner Thursday?"

Diana checked the calendar beside the phone. "The PTA is electing its officers for next year, and since I'm a candidate for secretary, I should at least make a showing."

"How about—"

"Honestly, Cliff, you don't need to make anything up to me. If you're so—"

"Diana," he cut in, "I haven't seen you or the girls in three days. I'm starting to get withdrawal symptoms. I actually found myself looking forward to watching the Disney Channel this week."

Diana laughed.

"If you can't go out with me Thursday, then how about Friday?" Now that he'd gained her trust, he felt more comfortable about having her accept an invitation without having to include her daughters.

"Cliff, listen, I'm already going to be gone three nights this week."

"Three?"

"Yes, I went to a Girl Scout planning meeting on Monday. I had a quick Sunday school staff meeting Tuesday and now the PTA thing on Thursday. I don't mind leaving the girls every now and then, but four nights in one week is too much. If you want the truth, it's probably a good thing you have to cancel tonight. I don't like being gone this much."

Cliff leaned back in his desk chair and chewed on the end of his pencil. After the fishing fiasco, he'd hoped to avoid including the girls in any more of their dates for a while. "Okay," he said reluctantly, "let's do something with the girls on Friday."

"Cliff, no."

"No?"

"Really. Both Joan and Katie have been up late every night this week. Katie's got a cold, and I really don't want to take her out again. Friday night, I planned on ordering pizza and getting them both down early." She wasn't making excuses not to see him, and prayed he understood that. Everything she'd said was the complete truth.

"Saturday night, then?" He wasn't giving up on her, not this easily.

Her breath was released on a nervous sigh. "All right."

Six

The house was still, and Diana paused for a moment to cherish the quiet. After loud protests and an argument with Joan, who seemed to think a fifth grader should be allowed to stay up and watch MTV, both girls were in bed. Whether they were asleep or not was an entirely different question. Peace reigned, and that was all that mattered to Diana.

She brewed herself a cup of tea and sat with her feet up, reading. In another two weeks school would be out, and then Joan and Katie would find even more excuses to put off going to bed. If it were up to those two ruffians, Diana knew they'd loiter around until midnight. Only Diana wouldn't let them. In some ways she was eager to spend the summer with the girls, and in other ways she dreaded three long months of total togetherness. Her parents had insisted on having them fly to Wichita and had even paid for their airline tickets. Diana was looking forward to those two weeks as a welcome reprieve. She missed seeing her family and in the past had briefly toyed with the idea of moving back to her hometown. That had been her original intention after Stan had died. Her parents had planned to come and help her with the move, but Diana had hedged, uncertain. Now she was convinced she'd made the right decision to stay in the Seattle area. With the loss of their father, the girls had already experienced enough upheaval in their young lives. A move so soon afterward wouldn't have been good for any of them. Although Diana dearly loved her family, she did better when they weren't hovering close by.

Her wandering thoughts were interrupted by the doorbell. She paused and checked the time. It was only a few minutes past nine, but she rarely received company this late.

Setting aside her book and her tea, she answered the door. "Cliff."

"Hi." His ready smile was filled with charm. "Did you win the election?"

Diana was more than a little surprised to see him. After their telephone conversation a couple of days before, she hadn't known what to think. She stepped aside so he could come in. "Win the election?" she repeated, not following his line of thought.

"Yes, you told me you were up for PTA secretary."

"Oh, yes. I was running unopposed, so there wasn't much chance I'd lose."

"Is that Cliff?" Katie, dressed in her pink flannel nightgown, appeared at the top of the stairs.

"Hi, Katie." Cliff raised his hand to greet the youngster, his smile only a little forced. He preferred to spend time with Diana alone tonight.

"Katie, you're supposed to be asleep."

"Can I give Cliff his lure?"

"Okay." Diana knew it would do little good to argue. While shopping in a local store the day before, Katie had found a similar fishing lure, and they'd bought it as a replacement for Cliff's. At the time, Diana had wondered if there would be an opportunity to see Cliff again. He had asked to see her on Saturday, but she half expected him to cancel. She wasn't sure where their relationship was headed. He seemed determined to see her again, but she hadn't heard a word from him since their abrupt telephone conversation a few days earlier.

Katie flew down the stairs and raced into the kitchen. "Mom, where'd you put it?"

"In the junk drawer."

As if by magic an exasperated Katie reappeared, hands on her hips. "Mom," she said with a meaningful sigh, "all the drawers are filled with junk."

Rather than answer, Diana stepped into the kitchen and retrieved the fishing lure for her daughter.

Katie eagerly ripped it from Diana's fingers and hurried back to Cliff, who was sitting in the living room. "Here's another lucky lure," she said, her eyes as round as grape-fruits. "I'm real sorry I lost yours."

Cliff's gaze sought Diana's as he accepted the lure. "I told you not to fret over it."

"But you got real angry, and I felt bad because I wasn't supposed to get into your fishing gear and I did. Mom's making me pay for it out of my allowance."

"I'd rather you didn't." Cliff directed the comment to Diana.

Before Diana could respond, Katie broke in. "But I have to!" she declared earnestly. "Otherwise I won't learn a les-son—at least that's what Mom said."

"Moms know what's best," Cliff managed to murmur, looking uncomfortable.

Katie brightened. "Besides, I thought that if I bought you another lucky lure, then you'd take Joan and me out in your sailboat again. Next time I promise I won't get into your fishing box." As though to emphasize her point, she spit on the tips of her fingers and dutifully crossed her heart.

Before Cliff realized Katie's intention, the little girl hurled her arms around his neck and gave him a wet kiss on the cheek.

Diana smiled at his shocked look. "Tell Cliff good-night, honey."

Without argument, Katie paused long enough to give her mother another hug and kiss, then dutifully traipsed back upstairs.

"It seems women have a way of throwing themselves into your arms," Diana teased once Katie had left the room. She hoped to lighten the mood. She didn't know why Cliff had come, especially when he looked as though he'd rather be anyplace else in the world than with her.

"I sincerely hope the trait runs in this family," Cliff teased back. He held out his arms to her, then complained with a low groan when Diana chose to ignore his offer.

Cliff wasn't exactly sure what was going on with him. After their last adventure on the sailboat, he'd decided that although he enjoyed Joan and Katie, he preferred to keep the kids out of the dating picture. It was Diana who interested him. In fact, he couldn't stop thinking about her.

She wasn't as beautiful as other women he'd seen. Her hips were a tad too wide, but where physical attributes had seemed important in the past, they didn't seem to matter with her.

When it came to women, Cliff wasn't being conceited when he admitted he could pick and choose. Yet the one woman who filled his thoughts was a young widow with two preteens. He'd been so astonished at the desire he felt for Diana that he'd phoned his brother in California and told him about her.

Rich had listened, chuckled knowingly and laughed outright when Cliff mentioned that Diana was a widow with two daughters. Then he'd made some derogatory comment about it being time for Cliff to find a real woman. Cliff had been vaguely disappointed in the conversation. Subconsciously he'd wanted his brother to tell him to wise up and stay away from a woman with children. Cliff had almost *wanted* Rich to tell him to avoid Diana and insist that a relationship with her would be nothing but trouble. Maybe that was what Cliff wanted to hear, but it wasn't what he felt.

Even if Rich had advised him to break things off with her, he doubted that he would have been able to. She was in his blood now, increasing the potency of his attraction each time they were together. That evening as he'd sat in his office, he hadn't been able to get his mind off Diana. Twice he'd picked up the phone to call her. Twice he'd decided against it. He didn't like what was happening to him. No one else seemed to notice that he was sinking fast. And there wasn't a life preserver in sight.

Sitting in the overstuffed chair beside Cliff, Diana took a sip of her tea and attempted to put some order to her thoughts. She was happy to see Cliff. More than happy. But a little apprehensive, too.

"How was your day?" she asked finally when he didn't seem inclined to wade into easy conversation.

"Busy. How about yours?"

"I went in for a job interview with the school district this morning." Cliff couldn't possibly understand what courage that had taken. She hadn't worked outside the home since Joan had been born, and had no real credentials. "I'm hoping they'll hire me as a teacher's aide. That way I'll have the same hours as the girls."

"Do you think you'll get the job?"

Diana answered with a soft shrug. "I don't know. The principal from Joan and Katie's school gave me a recommendation, since I've done a substantial amount of volunteer work there. The last school levy passed and the district's been given the go-ahead to hire ten teacher's aides. I have no idea how many applications they took or how many they interviewed."

"If that doesn't pan out, I'm sure I could find a part-time position for you in my law firm." The minute Cliff made the offer, he regretted it. Having Diana in his office two or three times a week could end up being a source of personal conflict.

"Thank you, Cliff, but, no."

"No?" This woman continued to astonish him. He'd expected her to jump at the offer. "Why not?"

"It's downtown, and I'd prefer to be as close to the girls as I can in case they get sick and need to come home...." That was the first plausible excuse to surface. Although it was the truth, Diana didn't have a great deal of choice when it came to finding employment. She'd turned down his offer because she preferred not to work in the same place as Cliff.

"I can understand that," he said, relieved and irritated at the same time. Diana had him so twisted up in knots he couldn't judge his own emotions anymore. He shouldn't have come tonight, he knew that, but staying away had been impossible.

"I'm pleased you stopped by," Diana said next.

He was happy she was pleased, because he was more confused than ever. He had thought that if he stopped off and they talked, then maybe he'd know what was happening to him. Wrong. One look at Diana and all he wanted to do was make love to her.

"I want you to know I feel bad about our conversation the other day." Diana felt as though she were sailing into uncharted waters, her destination unknown. Their telephone conversation had gone poorly, and she wasn't sure whose fault it was. Cliff had kept insisting on seeing her again, and she had kept refusing, finally giving in. More than that, it seemed that Cliff had been expecting her to be angry because he'd had to cancel their dinner date. She hadn't been. Then Cliff had sounded as though he'd wanted to start an argument and was confused when she wouldn't be drawn into a verbal battle.

"You feel bad because I canceled dinner?" Cliff asked.

"No, because I had to turn down your offer for another date."

Cliff felt more than a little chagrined. He'd admit it— her refusal had irked him. For all his suave sophistication, he wasn't accustomed to having a woman turn him down. It had taken a fair amount of soul-searching to decide he wanted to see Diana again—without Joan and Katie. Her rejection, no matter how good her reasons, had been a blow to his considerable pride.

"You turned me down for dinner *and* Friday night," he reminded her.

"I thought I explained…"

"I know."

Diana lowered her gaze to her mug of tea, which she was gripping tightly with both hands. "You don't know how hard that was."

"Then why did you?"

"For the very reasons I told you."

His brow puckered into a deep frown.

"I like you, Cliff. Probably more than I should." She didn't know what weapon she was handing him by admitting her feelings, but she was too old for silly games, too wise to get tangled up in a web of emotion and too intelligent not to look at him with her eyes wide open. They weren't right for each other, but that hadn't seemed to matter. They'd weathered their relationship much better than she had ever imagined they would. If they were going to continue to see each other, then she preferred that they be honest about their feelings. Honest and up-front.

"I like you, too, Diana," he admitted softly, his eyes holding her all too effectively. "I'm not sure I'm ready for what's developing between us, but I want it. I want you."

The muscles in her stomach constricted with his words. She'd asked for his honesty, and now she was forced to deal with her own reactions to it. Cliff frightened her because he made her feel again; he'd reawakened the deep womanly part of her that craved touch. Intuitively she'd known the first time he'd kissed her how potent his caress would be. In the years since Stan had died, she'd effectively cast the hunger for love and desire from her life.

Until Cliff.

Knowing this made each minute they spent together all the more exciting. It made each date all the more dangerous.

Diana tore her gaze from his. "What are we going to do about it?"

"I don't know."

"I...don't, either."

Cliff drew in a hard breath and held out his arms to her. "Come here, Diana."

Of its own volition, her hand set the tea mug aside. She stood and walked over to Cliff and offered no resistance when he pulled her down and cradled her in his lap. Her hands rested against his shoulders as his eyes gently caressed her face. It was almost as if he were asking her to object.

She couldn't. She wouldn't. A long, uninterrupted moment passed before Cliff lifted her hair from her shoulder and tenderly kissed the side of her neck. His lips felt cool against her skin, and she turned her head to grant him the freedom to kiss her where he willed.

At the sound of her soft gasp, his tongue made moist forays below her ear. Cliff loved the scent of her. Other women relied on expensive perfumes, and yet they couldn't compare to the fresh sunshine smell that was Diana's alone.

An all-too-warm, tingling sensation raced through Diana. Against her will, she closed her eyes. Her fingers gripped his shirt collar as his lips slowly grazed a trail across the underside of her chin.

"Cliff..." she moaned. "Please..."

"Please what?"

Her throat constricted, and she felt as if she were going to cry again. When she spoke, the words came out sounding like someone trying to speak while trapped underwater. "I want you to kiss...me."

His hands covered each side of her face and directed her mouth to his. Their lips slid across each other's with sweet familiarity. Diana was eager, so eager, but the urgency was gone, leaving in its wake a pure electric, soul-stirring sensation.

She clung to him even as the tears burned their way down her face. When he paused, as though unsure, she kissed him back, her mouth parted and pliant over his. She'd come this far and she refused to let him back away from her now.

Diana's kiss was all the encouragement Cliff needed. His arms tightened around her, and he gently rocked her, unable to get close enough. He felt the moisture on her face and tasted the salt of her tears. The reason for their being there humbled him. She was opening up to him as she never had before, trusting him, granting him custody of her wounded heart.

Diana moaned as his hands roamed over her back, bringing her as close as it was humanly possible.

At her soft cry tenderness engulfed him like a tidal wave. He wanted Diana in that moment more than he'd ever craved anything in his life. The passion she aroused in him was almost more than he could bear. He tried to tell her what she did to him by kissing her again and again, but it wasn't enough. Nothing seemed to satisfy the building fire within him. "Diana," he moaned, "I'm afraid if we continue like this we're going to end up making love in this chair."

The words made no sense to Diana. Cliff had transported her from limbo into heaven in a matter of moments. She had no desire to leave her newly discovered paradise. Her only response was a strangled, nonsensical plea for him not to stop.

"Upstairs," he said a minute later. "I want to make love to you in a bed."

Somehow the words made it through the thick haze of desire that had clouded her brain. He wanted to make love to her in a bed! Upstairs. Joan and Katie—her daughters— were upstairs.

"No," she managed.

"No?" Cliff echoed, shocked.

"The...girls."

"So? Aren't they asleep?"

"I...don't know. It doesn't matter."

"It matters to me," he argued. "I need you, Diana."

She didn't need to guess how much he wanted her—she

was feeling the same urgency. It had been slowly building in her for three long years.

"I want you," he reiterated forcefully. Pressing his hands over her ears, he kissed her long and hard so she'd know he wasn't just muttering the words.

Diana drove her fingers into his hair and slanted her mouth over his in eager response. "I need you, too," she whispered against his lips. "Right now, I could almost die I want you so much."

"Good."

"But, Cliff, I can't. I…"

"Come on, honey, don't argue with me. We're mature adults—we both know what we want—so what's stopping you?"

"Cliff, you don't understand."

He closed his eyes and groaned. "Somehow I knew that you were going to say that."

"Joan and Katie are up there."

"They're asleep, for heaven's sake." He could argue with her if she were being reasonable, but he was defenseless against such logic. "They won't even know."

"I'll know."

His hold on her torso tightened as he buried his face in the smooth silk of her skin. He drew in a ragged breath as the battle between his conscience and his raw need raged within him. Without too much trouble, he knew he could change her mind. She wanted him nearly as much as he craved her, and all it would take to convince her of that was a few more uninterrupted minutes. He released an anguished sigh when his conscience won. There would be another chance, another place, and the next time it would be right.

"Are you angry?" Diana asked.

He thought about it a moment, then shook his head. "No."

"I feel like I've been a terrible tease."

"Then tease me anytime you want," he managed on the tail-end of a sigh. "Now," he said, easing her off his lap, "walk me to the door and kiss me good-night while I still have the power to leave you."

She rose unsteadily. The carpet under her feet seemed to buckle and sway beneath her.

Cliff held out his hand to steady her. "Are you okay?"

"I don't know," she admitted with a half smile. She didn't know if she'd ever be the same again. Every part of her was throbbing with need, and yet all she could taste was frustration and regret.

He wrapped his arm around her and let her walk him to the front door. Their kiss was ardent, but brief. His arms continued to hold her. "Saturday night," he reminded her. "I'll pick you up at six-thirty."

It was all Diana could do to nod.

She remained leaning against the door frame long after Cliff had left. A strange chill rattled her as she realized how close she had come to walking up the stairs and making love with Cliff. It was then that she realized there was no real commitment between them, not even whispered words of love, only the pure physical response of a lonely widow to an exceptionally handsome man. Diana gripped her stomach as a wave of nausea passed over her. She felt ill and frightened.

Somehow she made it up the stairs and into bed, but that didn't guarantee sleep. Over and over again she thought about what had nearly happened with Cliff. No doubt women regularly fell into bed with him. Diana couldn't blame them; he would be a wonderful lover. Gentle and considerate. Even now, hours after he'd left, her body tingled from the memory of his touch.

She wanted him, but the situation was impossible. Her life was filled with responsibilities now. She wasn't carefree and single—she was a mother.

After twenty more minutes of tossing and turning, Diana glanced at the clock. Life wasn't simple for her anymore. Not with two daughters who watched her every move. When she'd been dating Stan, there'd been no real thought to the future. It had all been so easy. They were in love, so they got married. Diana was burdened with obligations now on all sides. Ones she willingly accepted.

For two days, she agonized over what she was going to say to Cliff. She wanted to set the record straight, explain that what had nearly happened wasn't right for her. She couldn't deny that she desired him; he'd see through that fast enough.

When Cliff arrived promptly at six-thirty to pick her up on Saturday night, she kissed the girls goodbye and stiffly followed Cliff to his car. Although he'd told her they were going to dinner, he hadn't said where.

"You look as jumpy as a pogo stick," he said once they were seated inside his Lamborghini. He was dying to kiss her. Already he ached with the need to hold her in his arms and taste her kisses.

"I…we need to talk."

Cliff placed the key in the ignition, then leaned over to gently brush his mouth over hers. "Can't it wait until dinner?"

Diana shook her head. "I don't think so. It's about what nearly happened the other night."

"Somehow I thought you'd bring that up." His hands

tightened around the steering wheel. He'd gone too fast for her, but she'd amazed him with how ready and eager she was. It hadn't been right for them Thursday, but it would be tonight—he'd make certain of that.

"I'm not ready for...it." Her face flushed with embarrassment. She'd never talked to a man this way, not even with Stan.

"Lovemaking." If she wouldn't say the word, he would. He didn't know what her problem was. The fact that she would deny what was happening between them surprised him, especially after all her talk about honesty. Their making love was inevitable. He'd known it almost from the first.

He wanted her desperately. Every time he closed his eyes, he pictured her in his bed, satin sheets wrapped around her, with her arms stretched toward him, inviting him to join her. She wouldn't need to ask him twice. These past two days without her had been hell. He wanted her so much that he felt naked and vulnerable without her, and now he was determined to have her. It hadn't felt right to walk away from her the other night. The memory of her kisses had returned to haunt him.

"All right, lovemaking," Diana echoed, her voice firm but low. "After the other night, I'm afraid I've given you the wrong impression."

Cliff reached over and squeezed her fingers. "Don't worry, honey, we're not going to do anything you don't want."

Diana should have felt better with his reassurance, but she didn't. She'd dreaded this evening from the moment he'd left her, and yet the hours hadn't gone by fast enough until she'd seen him again. She thought she knew what she wanted, but one look at Cliff and she was unsure of everything.

"You didn't say where we were going for dinner," she said, making conversation.

He smiled, and his face lit up with boyish charm. "It's a surprise."

He drove toward Des Moines and Diana was certain he was taking her to the fancy seafood restaurant the marina was famous for, but he drove past it and instead headed up the back roads to the cliff above the water.

"I didn't know there was a restaurant up this way," she confessed.

"There isn't," he told her with a wide grin. "We're going to my condo. I've been cooking all day."

"Your place," Diana echoed, and the words seemed to bounce around the car like a ricocheting bullet. Her heart slammed against her breast with dread.

"I'm a fabulous chef…wait and see."

Her responding smile was weak and filled with doubt.

Cliff parked his car in the garage and came around to help her out. He tucked his arm protectively around her waist as she climbed out of his car, then paused to gently kiss the side of her neck. His tender touch went a long way toward chasing away Diana's fears, and she smiled up at him.

Cliff was eager to show her his home and proudly led her into his condominium. The first thing Diana noticed was the flickering flames of the fireplace. The table was set for two, with candles ready to be lighted. The room was dark, and music played softly from the expensive speakers.

As she surveyed the room, a chill shimmied up her spine. "You haven't heard a word I've said, have you?"

Seven

"Of course I've been listening," Cliff insisted. He didn't know what was bothering Diana, but she'd been acting jumpy from the minute he'd picked her up.

"I told you, I'm not ready."

"For dinner?" He couldn't understand why she was so riled up all of a sudden. He'd been looking forward to this evening for days. The crab was cracked for their appetizers, hollandaise sauce simmered on top of the stove, ready to be poured over fresh broccoli. The thick T-bone steaks were in the refrigerator, just waiting to be charcoal grilled. He wanted everything perfect for tonight, for Diana. The wine was chilled—he'd seen to it all.

"In case you weren't aware of it," Diana cried, pointing a finger at her chest, "I live in this body!"

"What in the world are you talking about?"

"This." She gestured wildly with her arm toward the open space of his living room. "Tell me, Cliff, exactly what have you planned for tonight?" She flopped down on his white leather couch, crossed her legs and glared at him with wide, accusing eyes.

"A leisurely candlelight dinner. Is that a crime, or did I miss something in law school?"

Diana ignored his sarcasm. "And that's all? What about after dinner?"

He scooted the ottoman in front of the couch, sat down and leaned forward so his eyes were level with hers. "I thought we'd share a couple of glasses of wine in front of the fireplace."

"And sample a few stolen kisses, as well?" she coaxed.

Cliff grinned, relaxing. "Yes."

The lilting strains of the music from a hundred violins drifted through the room. She noticed the way the lights in the hallway that led to the master bedroom had been dimmed invitingly. The door to his room was cracked open, a ribbon of muted light beckoning to her. The romance in the condominium was so thick, Diana could hardly see the romancer.

"But you're planning on something else happening, aren't you?" she asked, her eyes effectively holding his.

Cliff opened his mouth to deny it, then quickly decided against trying to bluff his way out of the obvious. He didn't have any choice but to be honest with Diana. Before he could say anything, she cut him off.

"Don't lie to me, Cliff Howard," she declared, folding her arms defiantly around her torso. "Do you think I'm stupid? Do you honestly believe I'm so naive to not know that you've planned the big seduction scene?"

"All right. All right." He eased her arms loose and reached for her stiff fingers, holding them between his hands. "Maybe I'm going off the deep end here, but after the other night, I thought maybe…"

"Exactly what did you think?"

"That you and I had something special going for us. Something very special."

"You want to make love to me?"

"You're right I do," he murmured, and raised her fingertips to his lips. His gaze didn't leave hers, as though seeking confirmation. "And you want me, too, so don't try to deny it."

"I have no intention of doing so. You're right on target... things could easily have gotten out of hand the other night."

Cliff was beginning to feel more confident now. He realized that some women required more assurances. "Then you can understand—in light of Thursday night—why I'm thinking what I'm thinking." He raised his eyebrows suggestively, seeking a way to alter the sober tone of this conversation. Diana was becoming far too defensive over something that was inevitable. Wanting her in his bed shouldn't be considered a felony. Surely she realized that.

Diana felt incredibly guilty. She couldn't be angry with Cliff when she'd given him every reason to believe she was willing to sleep with him. Not until he'd left and her head had cleared did she realized how wrong a physical relationship with Cliff was for her. Unfortunately Cliff had no way of knowing about her sudden change of heart. The anger rushed out of her as quickly as it had come. She freed one hand from his grip and gently traced the underside of his well-defined jaw. She wasn't sure what she'd gotten herself into, but she wanted to make it right for them both.

Cliff captured her hand and held it against his cheek, needing her more and more by the minute. If she didn't stop looking at him with those incredibly lovely brown eyes, he couldn't offer any guarantee he'd be able to serve the meal he'd spent so much time preparing.

"Cliff, I feel bad about all this, but I'm simply not ready."

He stared at her for a full moment, weighing his options. She was frightened, he could see that, and he didn't blame her for acting like a nervous virgin. It had been a long time since a man had properly loved her. Thursday night she'd been as hot as a firecracker. It had hurt Cliff to leave her, both physically and mentally. She had to know him well enough to realize that he wasn't going to rush her into something she didn't want. First he had to make sure everything was right for her.

"Honey," he whispered, and leaned forward to sample her sweet lips. Their mouths clung, and when he sat back down, he closed his eyes at the bolt of passion that surged through him. "Trust me, you're ready."

Diana blinked back the dismay. Nothing she'd said had sunk into Cliff's thick skull. She tugged her hands free and clenched them together. "Answer me this, Cliff. Do you love me?"

Groaning inwardly, Cliff forced a smile. Over the years he'd come to almost hate that word. Women hurled it at him continually, as if it were a required license for something they wanted as much as he did. "I believe there's magic between us."

Diana's returning grin was infinitely sad. "Oh, Cliff, it sounds as if you've used that phrase a hundred times. I expected you to be more original than that."

She shamed him, because he *had* used that line before—not as often as she said, but enough to warrant a guilty conscience. Her look told him how much she disapproved of glib, well-worn words. To hear her tell it, he was another Hugh Hefner. Well, he had news for her—she wasn't exactly Mother Teresa. He didn't know how she could deny the very real and strong sexual tension between them. Diana was warm and loving, and confused. All he wanted to do was show her how good things could be between them, and Diana was making it sound as though he should be arrested for even thinking about taking her to bed.

She dropped her gaze and sighed. "It would be best if I went home."

Her words were as unexpected as they were unwelcome. "No!"

"No?"

"Diana, we've got something magical here. Let's not ruin it." Cliff was grasping at straws and knew it, but he didn't want her to leave.

"What we've got is a bunch of hormones calling out to one another. There's no commitment, no love!"

"You don't believe that."

"Am I wrong?" she asked with eyes that ripped into his soul. "Are you ready to offer your life to me and the girls?" She knew the answer, even if he didn't. Love preceded marriage, and although he cared for her, he didn't love her.

Commitment was another word Cliff had come to abhor. He jerked his fingers through his hair, almost afraid to speak for fear of what he'd say. "I can't believe we're having this conversation."

Already she was on her feet, her purse clenched under her arm. "Goodbye, Cliff."

He stood and crossed the room. "Why are we arguing like this, when all I want to do is make love to you?"

Dejected, Diana paused, her hand on the doorknob. "In case you haven't figured it out, that's exactly our problem."

Cliff was growing more impatient by the minute. Impatient and overwhelmingly frustrated. Okay, so she'd read his intentions; he hadn't exactly tried to cover up what he'd planned for the evening. She could be a good sport and play along, at least until after dinner. He wasn't going to force her into anything if she honestly objected. "Is wanting you such a sin?" he asked.

"No," she answered smoothly, "but I need something

more than magic." She couldn't explain it any better. If Cliff didn't understand love and commitment, then it was unlikely he'd be able to follow her reasoning. And she had no intention of trying to justify it anyway.

"Come on, Diana, wake up and smell the coffee. Times have changed. Men and women make love every night."

"I know." She had no more arguments. There was nothing more to say. She twisted the knob and pulled.

Cliff's fist hit the door, closing it with a sharp thud. "I don't know what happened between Thursday night and now, but I think you're being entirely unreasonable."

"I don't expect you to understand."

His anger and disappointment were almost more than he could bear. "Please don't leave."

"I can't see any other option."

He gritted his teeth, trying to come up with some way to make her understand. "Diana, listen to me. I'm a sexual person. I haven't been with a woman in a long time. I've got to have you for the pure physical release, I…"

Her stunned look caused him to swallow the rest of what he was saying.

"Goodbye, Cliff," she said, and then jerked open the door and walked out.

Cliff stared at the closed front door for a full minute. He couldn't believe he'd said that to her, as though she and she alone were responsible for easing his sexual appetite. He couldn't have made a bigger mess of this evening had he tried.

Diana didn't know she could walk so fast. Instead of going along the sidewalk, she cut between parked cars and crossed the street. Within a few minutes she was close to the marina. A Metro bus pulled to a stop at the curb, and its heavy doors parted with a whoosh. Without knowing its destination, Diana climbed on board. She had already taken her seat, when she saw Cliff's sports car race past the bus and chase after a taxi. Her eyes followed Cliff and the taxi until they were out of sight.

Diana was able to get a transfer from one bus to another, and an hour later she walked inside her house, exhausted and furious.

"Mom, where were you? What happened?" Joan cried, running to the door to greet her. "Cliff's been calling every ten minutes."

She ignored the question and headed for the refrigerator. For the past half hour, she'd been walking. She was dying of thirst, and her feet hurt like crazy—a lethal combination. Both Joan and Katie seemed to recognize her mood and went out of their way to avoid her.

Diana had been home fifteen minutes, when the phone rang again. Joan sprinted into the kitchen to answer it.

"If it's Cliff, I don't want to talk to him," Diana yelled after her daughter.

Joan reappeared a couple of minutes later. "He just wanted to know that you got home okay."

"What did you tell him?"

"That you were mad as hops."

Diana groaned, sagged against the back of the overstuffed chair and hugged a pillow to her stomach. That wasn't the half of it. The next time she went racing out of a man's condominium, she'd make sure she carried enough cash to take a cab home. She'd ridden on the bus with two winos and a guy who looked like a candidate for the Hell's Angels.

"Are you mad at Cliff, Mom?" Katie wanted to know, plopping down at her mother's feet.

"Yes."

"But I like Cliff."

"Don't worry, kid, I got all the bases covered." Joan sank onto the carpet beside her sister. "Cliff just phoned. I advised him to wait a couple of days, then send roses. By that time, everything will be forgotten and forgiven."

The pressure Diana applied to the pillow bunched it in half. "Wanna bet?" she challenged.

Shirley poured herself a cup of coffee and sat at the kitchen table beside Diana. "It's been a week."

"I told you I didn't want to hear from him." Diana continued copying the recipe for yet another hamburger casserole that disguised vegetables. She had only a few minutes before the girls would be home from school, then the house would become an open battlefield. Both Joan and Katie had been impossible all week. Without understanding any of what had happened between Cliff and her, her daughters had taken it upon themselves to champion his case. Diana refused to talk about him and, as a last resort, had forbidden either girl to mention his name again.

For the first few days after their argument, Diana had held out hope that things could be settled between her and Cliff, It didn't take long for her to accept that it was better to leave matters as they were. They were in a no-win situation. The bottom line was that they'd only end up hurting each other. Despite everything, Diana was pleased to have known Cliff Howard. She'd been living her life in a cooler; she'd grieved for Stan long enough. It was time to join the land of the living and soak up the sunshine of a healthy relationship again. Dating Cliff had shown her the way out of the chill, and she would always be grateful to him for that. In the past three years, she'd dated only occasionally.

Cliff had helped her to see that she was ready to meet someone, pick up the pieces of her shattered life and move on.

"But I feel bad," Shirley continued, holding the coffee
mug with both hands. "George told me I had the wrong
impression of Cliff—he isn't exactly the playboy I led you
to believe."

"Honestly, Shirley, I'd think you'd be happy. I've finally agreed to a dinner date with Owen Freeman." For
two years her neighbor had been after Diana to at least
meet this distant relation of hers. Diana had used every
excuse in the book to get out of it. She simply hadn't been
interested in being introduced to Shirley's third cousin, no
matter how successful he was. Cliff had changed that, and
Diana would have thought her neighbor would appreciate
this shift in attitude.

"I know I should be thrilled you're willing to meet
Owen, but I'm not." Shirley ran the tip of her index finger
around the rim of her mug. She hesitated, as though she'd
noticed the flower vase in the center of the table for the
first time. It came from a florist. "Who sent the flowers?"

"Cliff."

"Cliff Howard?"

Diana nodded, intent on copying the recipe. He'd taken
Joan's advice and sent the bouquet of red roses with a quick
note of apology scribbled across the card. In other words,
the next move was up to her. It had taken Diana several
days of soul-searching to decide not to contact him. The
decision hadn't been an easy one, but it was the right one.

"But if he sent you flowers, then he must be willing to
patch things up."

"Maybe." Diana dropped the subject there.

Her neighbor paused. "The least you could do is tell me

what he did that was so terrible. If you can't talk to me, then who can you talk to?"

Diana's fingers tightened around the pencil. Shirley wasn't asking her anything Joan and Katie hadn't drilled her about a dozen times. Both girls had been out of joint from the minute Diana informed them she wouldn't be seeing Cliff again. Katie had argued the loudest, claiming she wanted to go on his sailboat one more time. Joan had ardently insisted she liked Cliff better than anyone, and had gone into a three-day pout when Diana wouldn't change her mind. As patiently as she could, Diana explained to both girls that there would be other men they would like just as well as Cliff.

"What I want to know," Diana said, reaching for her own coffee as she studied her friend, "is why you've changed your tune all of a sudden. When I first started going out with Cliff, you were full of dire warnings. And now that I've decided not to see him again, you're keen for me to patch things up with him."

"You're miserable."

"I'm not," Diana shot back, then realized what Shirley said was true. She missed Cliff, missed the expectancy that he'd brought back into her life, the eagerness to greet each day as a new experience. She missed the little things—the way his hand reached for hers, lacing her fingers with his. She missed the way his eyes sought her out when the girls were jumping up and down at his feet, wanting something from him. She hadn't realized how lonely she was until Cliff had come into her life, and now the emptiness felt like a huge, empty vacuum that needed to be filled.

"It's best this way," Diana said after a thoughtful moment.

Shirley's hand patted hers. "Okay," she said reluctantly, "if you say so."

"I do."

Neither spoke for a long time. Finally Shirley ventured into conversation. "When are you having dinner with Owen?"

"Tomorrow," Diana answered. Now all she had to do was pump some enthusiasm into meeting Shirley's third cousin, who taught English literature at the local community college.

The following evening, Diana tried to convince herself what a good time she was going to have. She showered and dressed, while Joan followed her around the bedroom, choosing her outfit for her.

"How come you're wearing your pearl earrings?" Joan demanded. "You didn't wear them for..." She started to say Cliff's name, then hurriedly corrected herself since he was a forbidden subject. "You know who—and now you're putting them on for some guy you haven't even met."

Diana's answering smile was weak at best. She needed the boost in confidence, but explaining that to her daughter would be difficult.

When her mother didn't answer, Joan positioned herself in front of Diana's bedroom window that looked down onto the street below. "A car just pulled into the driveway."

"That will be Mr. Freeman. Joan, please, be on your best behavior."

"Oh, no."

"What's wrong?"

"He just got out of the car—he's wearing plaid pants."

Diana reached for her perfume, giving her neck and wrists a liberal spray, and rolled her eyes toward the ceiling. "It's not right to judge someone by the clothes he wears."

"Mom, he's a nerd to the tenth power." Joan sagged onto

the end of the mattress and buried her face in her hands. "If you end up marrying this guy, I'll never forgive you."

"Joan, honestly!"

"Mom, Mr. Freeman is here," Katie screamed from the foot of the stairs after peeking out the living room window. She raced up to meet her mother, who was coming out of the bedroom. "Mom," she whispered breathlessly. "He's a geek. A major geek!"

Feigning a smile, Diana placed her hand on the banister and slowly walked down the stairs to answer the doorbell.

As far as looks went, the blonde won over Diana, hands down, Cliff decided. He smiled at the sleek beauty who clung to his arm, and tried to look as though he were enjoying himself. He wasn't. In fact, he'd been miserable from the minute Diana had walked out of his condominium. At first he'd been furious with her. For a solid hour he'd driven around, searching for her, desperate to locate her. Only heaven knew where she'd run off to—it was as though aliens had absconded with her.

Twice he'd broken down and phoned her house, nearly frantic with worry. Joan had assured him, on the third call, that her mother was home and safe. It was then that Cliff had decided that whatever was between Diana and him was over. She was a crazy woman. One minute she was melting in his arms, and the next she was as stiff as cement, hissing accusations at him.

Two days later, after he'd had a chance to cool down, Cliff changed his mind. He'd behaved like a Neanderthal. The remark he'd made about being a sexual person returned to haunt him. It was no wonder she was angry, but she'd played a part in their little misunderstanding, leading him on, letting him think there was a green light in her eyes where it was actually a flashing red one. He didn't possess ESP—how was he supposed to read her mind? Okay, he'd make the first move toward a reconciliation, he decided, and then leave the rest up to her. On his instructions, his secretary ordered the roses with an appropriate message. Cliff had sat back and waited.

When he hadn't heard from Diana by the end of the week, he was stunned. Then shocked. Then angry. All right, he'd play her game—he was a patient man. In time she'd come around, and when she did, he'd play it cool. If anyone was sitting home nights, alone and frustrated, it wouldn't be him. He'd make sure of that.

Hence Marianne—the blonde.

"Who are you going out with tonight?" Joan asked her mother as she sat at the kitchen table and glued on a false thumbnail.

"Not Mr. Freeman again," Katie groaned, and reached for an apple.

"He's a nice man."

"Mom, if you wanted nice, I could set you up with Mr. Rogers or Captain Kangaroo."

Diana hated to admit how right Joan was. Owen Freeman excited her as much as dirty laundry. He'd brought her candy, escorted her to a classical music concert and treated her with kindness and respect. He'd even supplied her with letters from his colleagues attesting to his character, just in case she was worried about being alone with him. Maybe Cliff wasn't so out of line to have mentioned magic. She felt it with him, but she certainly didn't with Owen Freeman. There were so many frogs out there and so few princes.

"Have you read through his references yet?" Joan asked.

"Honey, that was a very nice gesture on Mr. Freeman's part."

"He's a geek."

"Katie, I want you to stop calling him that."

Her younger daughter shrugged.

Joan spread contact cement across the top of the nail on her little finger. A pile of fake fingernails rested in front of her. "It's your life, Mom. You know how Katie and I feel about Mrs. Holiday's cousin, but you do what you want."

"Well, don't worry about it—you're not having dinner with him. I am."

Joan rolled her eyes toward the ceiling. "Lucky you."

Owen arrived a half hour later. He brought Joan and Katie a small stuffed animal each and a small bouquet of flowers for Diana. He really was an exceptionally nice man, but, as Joan had said, so were Mr. Rogers and Captain Kangaroo.

When Owen headed toward Des Moines and the restaurant at the marina, Diana tensed. Of all the places in the south end to eat, he had to choose this one.

"I understand the food here is excellent," Owen said once they were seated.

"I've heard that, as well," Diana said, looking over the top of her menu. Her heart was pumping double its normal rate. She was being silly. There was absolutely no reason to believe she would run into Cliff Howard simply because this restaurant was close to his condominium. No sane reason at all.

Owen ordered a bottle of wine, and Diana nearly did a swan dive into the first glass. Alcohol would help soothe her jittery nerves, she reasoned. After tonight, Diana decided, she would tell Owen that it simply wasn't going to work. He was such a nice person, and she didn't want to lead him on when there was no reason to believe anything would ever develop between them. Her mind worked up a variety of ways to tell him, then she decided to take the coward's way out and leave a voice mail message after he dropped her off following dinner.

"You're quiet this evening," Owen said softly.

"I'm sorry."

"Are you tired?"

She nodded. "It's been a long week." Diana turned her head and looked out over the rows and rows of watercraft moored in the marina. Without much trouble, she located Cliff's forty-foot sloop.

"Do you sail?" she asked Owen, without taking her eyes from Cliff's boat.

"No, I can't say that I do."

"Fish?"

"No, it never appealed to me."

Diana pulled her gaze away. Owen was forty, balding and incredibly boring. Nice, but boring.

"I did go swimming once in Puget Sound," he said, his voice rising with enthusiasm.

Diana's smile was genuine. No doubt, Owen saw himself as a real daredevil. "I did, too—once, by accident."

"Really?"

She nodded, and the silence returned. Finally she said, "I enjoy picnics."

Owen's forehead puckered into a brooding frown. "I don't get much time for outdoor pursuits."

"I can imagine...with school and everything."

"Bridge is my game."

"Bridge," Diana repeated, amused. Owen Freeman was really quite predictable. "I imagine you're good enough to play in tournaments."

The literature professor positively gleamed. "As a matter of fact, I am. Have you ever played?"

"No," she admitted reluctantly.

The hostess escorted another couple to the table across from their own. Diana didn't pay much attention, but the blonde was stunning.

"I would thoroughly enjoy teaching you," Owen continued. "Why, we could play couples."

"I'm afraid I don't have much of a head for cards." Except when it came to her VISA or Mastercard. Then she knew all the tricks.

"Don't be so hard on yourself. You've just lacked a good teacher, that's all. I promise to be patient."

Diana felt someone's stare. She paused and looked around and didn't recognize anyone she knew. Taking another sip of her wine, she relaxed. "Is it warm in here? Or is it just me?" she asked Owen.

"It doesn't seem to be overly warm," Owen responded, and turned around as though to ask the opinion of those sitting at the table closest to their own.

Feeling feverish, Diana frantically fanned her face. It was then that she saw Cliff. The voluptuous blonde she'd noticed a few minutes before sat beside him, her torso practically draped over his arm. Diana's hand froze in midair as her breath caught in her lungs. Her worst nightmare had just come true. Cliff was dating Miss World, and she was with Captain Kangaroo.

Eight

"Katie, will you kindly come down from that tree!" Diana yelled as she jerked open the sliding glass door that led to the backyard. It seemed she was going to have to cut down the apple tree in order to keep her younger daughter from climbing between its gnarled limbs. The girl seemed to think she was half monkey. Two days into summer vacation, and already Diana was beginning to sound like a banshee.

"Mom…"

"Katie, just do it. I'm in no mood for an argument." She slammed the door, furious with herself for being so short-tempered and angry with Katie for disobeying her. A rush of air escaped her lungs as she slouched against the kitchen wall and hung her head in an effort to get a firm grip on her emotions.

"Mom?"

Diana lifted her eyes to find Joan standing on the other side of the room, studying her with an odd look. She frowned. "What?"

In answer to her mother's question, Joan pulled out a chair and patted the seat. "I think it's time for us to have another of our daughter-mother talks."

If her preteen hadn't looked so serious, Diana would have laughed. Not again! Diana had only just recovered from the first such conversation. Joan had spoken to her about the importance of not doing anything foolish—such as marrying Owen on the rebound from Cliff.

"Again, Joan?" she asked, her eyes silently pleading for solitude.

"You heard me."

Diana rolled her eyes toward the ceiling and seated herself. While Diana waited, Joan walked around the counter and brewed a cup of coffee. Once she'd delivered it to her mother, she took the chair across from Diana and plopped her elbows onto the tabletop, her hands cupping her face as she stared at her mother.

"Well?"

"Don't rush me. I'm trying to think of a diplomatic way of saying this."

"I've been a grouch. I know, and I apologize." Diana could do nothing less. She'd been snapping at the girls all week. School was out, and it took time to adjust. At least, that was what she told herself.

"That's not it."

"Is it Owen? You needn't worry. I won't be seeing him again."

In a spontaneous outburst of glee, Joan tossed her hands above her head. "There is a God!"

"Joan, honestly!"

"So you're not going to date Owen anymore. What about…" She paused abruptly. "You know…the one whose name I've been forbidden to mention."

"Cliff."

Joan pointed at her mother's chest. "He's the one."

"What about him?" Diana asked, ignoring her daughter's attempt at humor.

The amusement drained from the eleven-year-old's dark eyes. "You still miss him, don't you?"

Diana lowered her gaze and shrugged. She preferred not to think about Cliff. Ever since the night she'd seen him with that bimbo clinging to him like a bloodsucker, Diana had done her best to avoid anything vaguely connected with Cliff Howard. It was little wonder they hadn't been able to get along. Obviously, Cliff's preference in women swayed toward the exotic. Their breakup had been inevitable. He might have been satisfied with apple pandowdy for a time, but his interest couldn't have lasted. Not when he could sample cheesecake anytime he wished. Diana had been intelligent enough to recognize that from the first, but she'd been so flattered—all right, attracted to Cliff—that she'd chosen to ignore good old-fashioned common sense. Joan was right, though. She did miss him. But more important, she'd gotten out of the relationship with her heart intact. No one had been hurt; she'd been lucky.

"Anyway, Katie and I have been thinking," Joan continued.

"Now that's dangerous." Diana took a sip of her coffee and nearly choked as the hot brew slid down the back of her throat. Joan had made it strong enough to cause a nuclear meltdown.

"Mom, Katie and I want you to know something."

"Yes?"

"Whatever Cliff did, *we* forgive him. We think that you should be big enough to do the same."

Marianne batted her thick, mascara-coated lashes in Cliff's direction, issuing an invitation that was all too obvious. He pulled her into his arms and kissed her hard. Harder than necessary, grinding his mouth over hers, angry with her for being so transparent and even angrier with himself for not wanting her.

The woman in his arms moaned, and Cliff obliged by kissing her again. He didn't need to be an Einstein to realize he was seeking something. Every time he kissed Marianne, it was a futile effort to taste Diana.

The blond wound her arms around his neck and seductively rubbed her breasts over his torso. Cliff couldn't force any desire for her, and the realization only served to infuriate him.

His hands gripped Marianne's shoulders as he extracted himself from her grasp.

She looked up at him, dazed and confused. "Cliff?"

"I've got a busy day tomorrow." He offered the lame excuse, stood and reached for his jacket. "I'll give you a call later." He hurried out the door, hardly able to escape fast enough. Once inside his car, he gripped the steering wheel with both hands and clenched his jaw. What was happening to him? Whatever it was, he didn't like it. Not one bit.

Diana stood at the sliding glass door and checked the sleeping foursome on the patio. In an effort to make up for her cranky mood, and in a moment of weakness, she'd agreed to let the girls each invite a friend over for a slumber party. Now all four were sacked out in lawn chairs, with enough pillows, blankets, radios and stuffed animals to supply a small army. They'd talked, laughed, carted out half the contents of the kitchen and had finally worn themselves out. Peace and goodwill toward men reigned for the moment.

Diana had just poured herself a cup of decaffeinated coffee, when the doorbell chimed. Surprised, she checked her watch and noticed it was after ten. She certainly wasn't expecting anyone this late.

Setting aside her coffee, she moved into the entryway and pressed her eye to the peephole in the front door. Her gaze met the solid wall of a man's chest—one she'd recognize anywhere. Cliff Howard's.

There wasn't time to react, or time to think. Her heart hammered wildly as she unbolted the lock and gradually opened the door.

"Hi," he said awkwardly. "I was in the neighborhood and thought I'd stop in. I hope you don't mind."

He was dressed in a dinner jacket, his tie was loosened and the top two buttons of his shirt were unfastened. Cliff didn't need anyone to tell him he looked bad. That was what he felt like, too. So the dragon lady wasn't going to come to him. Fine, he'd go to her, and they'd get this matter settled once and for all. Hard as it was to admit, he missed her. He even missed Joan and Katie. It hadn't been easy swallowing his pride this way, and he sincerely hoped Diana recognized that and responded appropriately.

"No, I don't mind." Actually, she was pleased to see him now that she'd gotten over the initial shock. They hadn't exactly parted on the best of terms, and she wanted to clear the air and say goodbye without a lot of emotion dictating her words. "I'd just poured myself a cup of coffee. Would you care for some?"

"Please." He followed her into the kitchen, sat down, noticed the open drape and pointed toward the patio. "What's going on out there?"

"School's out, and the girls are celebrating with a slumber party."

He grinned and nodded toward the large pile of blankets.

Only one hand and the top of a head were visible. "I take it the one with the six-inch bright red fingernails is Joan."

Grinning, Diana delivered his cup to the table and nodded. "And the one clenching sixteen Pooh bears is Katie." As she moved past Cliff, she caught a whiff of expensive perfume and the faint odor of whiskey.

"It's good to see you, Diana." The fact was, he couldn't stop looking at her.

"There wasn't any need to tear yourself away from a hot date to visit, Cliff. I'm here most anytime." Her words were more teasing than angry, and she smiled at him.

He smiled back. "The least you could do is pretend you're happy to see me."

"But I am."

She really did have the most beautiful eyes. Dark and deep, wide and round. They were capable of tearing apart a man's heart and gentle enough to comfort an injured animal. He remembered how their color had clouded with passion when he'd kissed her, and wondered how long it would be before he could do it again. He longed for Diana's kisses as much as he missed her quick wit.

Diana settled herself in the chair across from him, not wanting to get too close. Cliff had that look in his eyes, and she was beginning to recognize what it meant. If she gave him the least amount of encouragement, he would reach for her and cover her mouth with his own. Then everything she'd discovered about herself these past days without him would be lost in the passion of the moment.

"Why did you come? Did your dinner companion turn you down?"

She didn't know the half of it, he thought to himself.

Diana grinned into her coffee cup. "Was she the same girl as the other night?"

"Yes," Cliff admitted sheepishly. "Unfortunately all her brains are situated below her neck."

"Now, Cliff, that was unkind." So her own estimation of Miss World had been right on; the blonde was a bimbo. It was tacky to feel so good being right about the other woman. Tacky, but human.

"Well, your date certainly resembled William F. Buckley."

Diana was unable to hold back her laugh. "He brought me references."

"What?"

"He's Shirley's third cousin, and apparently he thought I needed to know something more about him. Honestly, Cliff, I thought I'd die. He'd had someone from Highline Community College write up a letter telling me what a forthright man he is, and there was another letter from his dentist and a third from his apartment manager."

They laughed together, and it felt incredibly good. Diana wiped a tear from the corner of her eye and sighed audibly. "Joan and Kate were scared to death I'd marry him."

"How have the girls been?"

"They're great." Actually, Diana was grateful both her daughters were asleep; otherwise they might have launched themselves into Cliff's arms and told him how miserable their mother had been without him.

"And you?"

"Good. How about yourself?"

"Fair." Cliff didn't know the words to describe all that had been happening to him. Nothing had changed, and yet everything was different. He'd dated one of the most sought-after women in Seattle, and she'd left him feeling cold. His little black book was filled with names and phone numbers, and he hadn't the inclination to make one phone call.

"Actually, I'm glad you stopped by," Diana said, wading into the topic they'd both managed to avoid thus far. "I owe you an apology for running off on you that way."

"Diana, honestly, I still don't know what I did that was so terrible."

"I realize that."

"I thought we had something really good going. I didn't mean to rush you—I assumed—falsely, it seems—that you were as ready for the physical part of our relationship as I was."

Diana lowered her gaze, and her hands tightened around the mug. "I wish I could be different for you, but I can't."

"You wanted me. I knew that almost from the first."

She still did, but that didn't alter her feelings. "Unfortunately I need something more than magic."

"What?" If he could give it to her, he would.

Her eyes were infinitely sad, dark and soulful. "You know the answer to that without my having to spell it out for you."

At least she had the common sense not to say it: love and commitment. He wasn't pleased at the thought of either one.

"Listen," she said, slowly lifting her eyes to capture his. "I'm glad you're here, because we do need to talk. A lot of things have been going through my mind the past couple of weeks."

"Mine, too."

"I like you, Cliff. I really do. It would be so easy to fall in love with you. But I'm afraid that if I did, we'd only end up hurting each other."

Feeling confused, he frowned darkly at her. "How do you mean?"

"When we first started going out, you automatically included the girls—mainly because I had them gathered around me like a fortress, and you recognized that you had to deal with them in order to get to me."

He grinned because she was right on target; that had been his plan exactly.

"Later, after the fishing fiasco, you realized that having the girls around wasn't the best thing for a promising relationship. I can't say that I blame you. There's no reason for you to be interested in children—a ready-made family isn't for you, and children do have a tendency to mess things up."

Cliff opened his mouth to contradict her, then realized that basically she was right. After the sailing trip, he had more or less decided the time had come to wean Diana away from her girls. To be honest, he'd wanted her all to himself. Oh, he'd planned to include Joan and Katie occasionally, but he was mainly interested in Diana. Her daughters were cute kids, but he could easily have done without them, and as much as possible, he'd hoped to keep them in the background of anything that developed between him and Diana.

"You make me sound pretty mercenary." Actually, when he thought about what he'd been doing, he realized that his actions could be construed as selfish. All right, so he'd been selfish!

"I don't mean to place you in a bad light."

"But it's true." It hadn't been easy for him to admit that, and he felt ashamed.

"Herein we have the basic problem. I can't be separated from the girls. You may be able to ignore them, but I can't. We're one, and placing me in the middle and asking me to choose between you and my daughters would only make everyone miserable."

Cliff's smile was wry. "You know, you would have made a great attorney."

"Thanks."

"The way I deal with Joan and Katie could change, Diana." His gaze continued to hold hers. She was right; he'd been thinking only of himself, and he'd been wrong. But now that the air had been cleared, he was more than willing to strike up a compromise.

"Perhaps it could change." She granted him an A for effort, and was pleased that he cared enough to want to try. "But there's more."

"There is?"

"Cliff, for some reason you have a difficult time making a commitment to one woman. I suspect it has a lot to do with the girl who lived with you. Shirley told me about her."

"Becky." He didn't even like to think about her or the whole unfortunate experience. It had happened a long time ago, and as far as he was concerned, the whole affair was best forgotten.

"You might not be thrilled with this, but I think you cared a great deal for Becky. I honestly believe you loved her."

Unable to remain seated, Cliff stood and refilled his coffee cup, even though he'd taken only a few sips. "She was a selfish bitch," he said bitterly, his jaw tight.

"That makes admitting you loved her all the more difficult, doesn't it?"

"Who do you think you are? Sigmund Freud?"

"No," she admitted softly. "Believe me, I know what you went through when she moved out. Although the circumstances were different, I was unbelievably angry with Stan after he died. I'd take out the garbage and curse him for not being there to do it for me. I'd never been madder at anyone in my life. As crazy as it sounds, it took me months to forgive him for dying."

"Stan's death has absolutely nothing in common with

what happened between me and some airhead. Becky wandered in and out of my life several years ago and has nothing to do with the here and now."

"Perhaps you're right."

"I know I am," he reiterated forcefully.

"But ever since then, you've flitted in and out of relationships, gained yourself a playboy reputation and you positively freeze at the mention of the word love. I'd hate to think what would happen if marriage turned up in casual conversation."

"That's not true." He felt like shouting now. Diana hadn't even known Becky. He was lucky to have gotten away from the two-timing schemer. Diana had it all wrong—he was planning on falling in love and getting married someday. It wasn't as if he'd been soured on the entire experience.

"I understand how you feel, believe me. Loving someone makes us vulnerable. If we care about anyone or anything, we leave ourselves wide open to pain. Over the years, the two of us have both shielded our hearts, learned to keep them intact. I'm as guilty as you are. I've wrapped my heart around hobbies. You use luxuries. The only difference between the two of us is that I have Joan and Katie. If it hadn't been for the girls, they might as well have buried me in the casket with Stan. It would have been safe there—airless and dark. Certainly there wouldn't have been any danger of my heart getting broken a second time. You see, after a while the heart becomes impenetrable and all our fears are gone."

Standing across from her, Cliff braced his hands on the back of the chair. He said nothing.

"I guess what I'm trying to say is that I finally understand the reason I couldn't sleep with you. Yes, you were right on target when you said I was physically ready, but emotionally and spiritually I'm miles away. You were right, too, when you claimed there was magic between us. After dating Owen, I recognized that isn't anything to sneeze at, either." She paused, and they shared a gentle smile. "But more than that, I realized that without love, without risking our hearts, the magic would fade. A close physical relationship would leave me vulnerable again and open to pain." She dropped her gaze to the tabletop. "It hurts too much, Cliff. I don't want to risk battering my heart just because something feels good."

When she'd finished, the silence wrapped itself around them.

Diana was the first one to speak. "But more than anything, I want you to know how grateful I am to you."

"Me? Why?"

"You woke me up. You made me feel again."

"Glad to oblige, Sleeping Beauty." Cliff hadn't liked what she'd said—maybe because it hit too close to the truth. She was right; he had changed after Becky, more than he'd ever realized. He wasn't particularly impressed with the picture Diana had painted of him, but the colors showed through all too clearly. She was right, too, about surrounding himself with luxuries. The sailboat, the fancy sports car, even the ski condo—they were extravagances. They made him feel good, made him look good.

After a long moment, Cliff moved away and emptied his coffee cup into the sink. "You've given me a lot to think about," he said with his back to her.

She'd given them both a lot to think about. Diana walked him to the front door and opened it for him. "Goodbye, Cliff."

He paused for a moment, then reached for her, folding her in his arms, pressing his jaw against the side of her head. He didn't kiss her, didn't dare, because he wasn't sure he would still be able to walk away from her if he did.

Diana slowly closed her eyes to the secure warmth she experienced in his arms. She wanted to savor these last moments together. After a while, she gently eased herself free.

"Goodbye, Diana," he whispered, and turned and walked away without looking back.

"Hey, Cliff, how about a cold beer?"

"Great." He stretched out his hand without disturbing his fishing pole and grabbed for the Bud Light. Holding the chilled aluminum can between his thighs, he dexterously opened it with one hand and guzzled down a long, cold drink.

"This is the life," Charlie, Cliff's longtime fishing buddy, called out. His cap was lowered over his eyes to block out the sun as he leaned back and stretched out his legs in front of him. The boat rocked lazily upon the still, green waters of Puget Sound.

"It doesn't get much better than this," Cliff said, reaching for a sandwich. The sun was out, the beer was cold and the fish were sure to start biting any minute.

The weather forecast had been for a hot afternoon sun. It was only noon, and already it was beginning to heat up. Charlie and Cliff had left the marina before dawn, determined to do some serious fishing. Thus far neither man had had so much as a nibble.

"I'm going to change my bait," Charlie said after a while. "I don't know what's the matter with these fish today. Too lazy, I guess. It looks like I'm going to have to give them reason to come my way."

"I think I'll change tactics, too." Already Cliff was reeling in his line. It was on days like this, when the fish weren't eager and the sun was hot, that he understood what it meant to be a fisherman. Once he had his pole inside the boat, he reached for his tackle box and sorted through the large assortment of hand-tied flies and fancy lures. A flash of silver stopped his search. His replacement lucky lure. His fingers closed around the cold piece of silver as his thoughts drifted to Katie. She was rambunctious and clever, and whenever she walked, the eight-year-old's pigtails would bounce. Grinning, he remembered how she'd leaned over the side of his sailboat and called out to the fish, trying to lure them to her hook before her sister's. His grin eased into a full smile as he recalled the girls' antics that Saturday afternoon.

"You know what I've been thinking?" Charlie mumbled as he tossed his line over the side of the boat.

Cliff was too caught up in his thoughts to care. He'd done a lot of thinking about what Diana had said the other night. In fact, he hadn't stopped thinking about their conversation. He hadn't liked it, but more and more he was beginning to recognize the truth in what she'd had to say.

"Cliff?"

Sure, he'd missed Diana, regretted his assumptions about their casually drifting into a physical relationship. But he missed Joan and Katie, too, more than he'd ever thought he would. The instant flare of regret that constricted his heart at the sight of the lure shocked him. He was beginning to care for those two little girls as much as he did for their mother.

"Cliff, good buddy? Are you going to fish, or are you going to kneel and stare into that tackle box all day?"

There was a reason Diana hated Monday mornings, she decided as she lifted the corner of Joan's double bed and tucked the clean sheet between the mattress and the box spring. She hated changing sheets, and once a week she was reminded of the summer job in her junior year of high school. She'd been a hotel maid and had come to hate anything vaguely connected with housekeeping.

When she finished with the girls' sheets, she was going to wash her hair, pack a picnic lunch and treat Joan and Katie to an afternoon at Seahurst beach in Burien, another South Seattle community. She might even put on a swimsuit and sunbathe. Of course, there was always the risk that someone from Greenpeace might mistake her for a beached whale and try to get her into the water, but she was willing to chance it.

Chuckling at her own wit, Diana straightened and reached for a fresh pillowcase. It was then that she heard a faint but sharp cry coming from outside, and recognized it immediately as something serious. It sounded like Katie. She tossed the pillow aside and started out of Joan's bedroom. The last time she'd looked, both girls were in the backyard playing. Mikey Holiday had been over, as well as a couple of other neighborhood kids.

"Mom!" Joan shrieked, panic in the lone word. "Mom! Mom!"

It was the type of desperate cry that chills a mother's blood. Diana raced down the stairs and nearly collided with her elder daughter. Joan groped for her mother's arms, her young face as pale as the sheet Diana had just changed.

"It's Katie...she fell out of the apple tree. Mom, she's hurt...real bad."

Nine

Diana walked briskly down the wide hospital corridor. Katie was at her side, being pushed in a wheelchair by the nurse who'd met her at the emergency entrance. The eight-year-old sobbed pitifully, and every cry ripped straight through Diana's soul. She hadn't needed a medical degree to recognize that Katie had broken her arm. What did astonish Diana was how calmly and confidently she'd responded to the emergency. Quickly she had protected Katie's oddly twisted arm in a pillow. Then she'd sent Joan and Mikey over to his house with instructions for Shirley to contact Valley General Hospital and tell them she was on her way with Katie.

"You'll need to fill out some paperwork," the nurse explained when they reached the front desk.

Diana hesitated as the receptionist rose to hand her the necessary forms.

Katie sobbed again and twisted around in her chair. "Mom...don't leave me."

"Honey, I'll be there as fast as I can." It wasn't until Katie had been wheeled out of sight and into the cubical that Diana began to shake. She gripped the pen between her fingers and started to complete the top sheet, quickly writing in Katie's name, her own and their address.

"Could… I sit down?" Now that her hands had stopped trembling, her knees were giving her problems. The entire room started to sway, and she grabbed the edge of the counter. She was starting to fall apart, but couldn't. At least not yet, Katie needed her.

"Oh, sure, take a seat," the woman in the crisp white uniform answered. "There are several chairs over there." She pointed to a small waiting area. A middle-aged couple was sitting there watching the *Noon News*. Somehow Diana made it to a molded plastic chair. She drew in several deep breaths and forced her attention to the questionnaire in front of her. The last time she'd been in Valley General was when Stan had been brought in.

Her stomach heaved as unexpected tears filled her eyes, blurring her vision as she relived the horror of that day. Three years had done little to erase the effects of that nightmare. Her throat constricted under the threat of overwhelming sobs, and again Diana forced her attention to the blank sheet she needed to complete.

But again the memories overwhelmed her. She'd been contacted at home and told that Stan had been in an accident. Naturally she'd been concerned, but no one had told her he was in any grave danger. She'd left the girls with Shirley and rushed to the hospital. Once she'd arrived, she'd been directed to the emergency room, given a multitude of forms to complete and told to wait. There'd been another man who'd just brought his wife in with gall bladder problems, and Diana had even joked with him in an effort to hide her nervousness. It seemed they kept her sitting there waiting for hours, and every time she inquired, the receptionist told her the doctor would be out in a few minutes. She asked if she could see Stan and was again told she'd have to wait. Finally the physician appeared, so stiff and somber. His eyes were filled with reluctance and regret as he spoke. And yet his message was only a few, simple words. He told Diana he was sorry. At first, she didn't understand what he meant. Naturally, he was sorry that Stan had been hurt. So was she. It wasn't until she asked how long it would be before her husband could come home and seen the pity in the doctor's eyes that she understood. Stan would never leave the hospital, and no one had even given her the chance to say goodbye to him. Diana had been calm then, too. So calm. So serene. It wasn't until later, much later, that the floodgates of overwhelming grief had broken, and she'd nearly drowned in her pain.

Katie's piercing cry cut sharply into Diana's thoughts. Her reaction was instinctive, and she leaped to her feet. The hospital staff hadn't let her go to Stan, either.

She stepped to the receptionist's desk. "I want to be with my daughter."

The woman took the clipboard from Diana's numb fingers and glanced over the incomplete form. "I'm sorry, but you'll need to finish these before the doctor can treat your daughter."

"Please." Her voice cracked. "I need to be with Katie."

"I'm sorry, Mrs. Collins, but I really must—"

"Then give her something for the pain!" The sound of someone running came from behind her, but Diana's senses were too dulled to register anything more than the noise.

"Diana." Cliff joined her at the counter, his eyes wide and concerned. "What happened?"

"Katie...they won't let me be with Katie."

Tears streamed down her face, and Cliff couldn't ever remember seeing anyone more deathly pale. It was then that he realized that he'd never imagined that Diana could be so unnerved. One look at her told him why he'd found it so urgent to rush here. Somehow he'd known that Diana would need him. Until a half hour ago, his day had been going rather smoothly. He'd been eating a sandwich at his desk, thinking about a case he was about to review, when his secretary had stuck her head in the door and announced that someone named Joan was crying on the phone and asking to speak to him. By the time Cliff had lifted the receiver, the eleven-year-old was almost hysterical. In between sobs, Joan had told him that Diana had taken Katie to the hospital. She'd also claimed that her mother couldn't afford to pay the bill. Cliff had hardly been able to understand what had happened until Shirley Holiday had gotten on the line and explained that Katie had broken her arm. Cliff had thanked her for letting him know, then had sat quietly at his desk a few minutes until he'd decided what he should do. After a moment he'd dumped the rest of his lunch in the wastepaper basket, stood and reached for his suit jacket. He'd tossed a few words of explanation to his secretary and crisply walked out the door.

A broken arm, although painful, was nothing to be worried about, he'd assured himself. Kids broke their arms every day. It wasn't that big a deal. Only this wasn't just any little kid, this was Katie. Sweet Katie, who had tossed her arms around his neck and given him a wet kiss. Katie who would sell her soul for a bucket of Kentucky Fried Chicken. Diana's Katie—his Katie.

He hadn't understood why he felt the urgent need to get to the hospital, but he did. Heaven or hell wouldn't have kept him away. It was a miracle that the state patrol wasn't after him, Cliff realized when he pulled into the hospital parking lot. He'd driven like a crazy man.

"Mrs. Collins has to complete these forms before she can be with her daughter," the receptionist patiently explained for the third time.

Diana's hand grasped Cliff's forearms, and her watery eyes implored him. "Stan...never came home."

Cliff frowned, not understanding her meaning. He reached for the clipboard and flipped the pages until he found what he wanted. "Diana, all you need to do is sign your name here." He gave her the pen.

"I'm sorry, but I will have to ask Mrs. Collins to fill out all the necessary—"

Cliff silenced the receptionist with one determined look. "I can complete anything else."

Diana scribbled her name where Cliff had indicated and gave the clipboard back to him.

"Take Mrs. Collins to her daughter," he stated next in the same crisp, dictatorial tone.

The woman nodded and stood to walk around the desk and escort Diana to where they'd wheeled Katie.

Cliff watched Diana leave, reached for the clipboard and took a seat. It wasn't until he read through the first few lines she'd completed that he understood what Diana had been trying to tell him about Stan. The last time she'd been in the hospital was when her husband had been brought in after the airplane accident. From the information George Holiday had given him, Cliff understood that Stan had been badly burned. On the advice of Stan's physician, Diana had never seen her husband's devastated body. One peaceful Saturday morning, Diana kissed her husband goodbye and went shopping with her daughters, while he took off in a private plane with a good friend. And she never saw her high-school sweetheart again.

Less than an hour later, Diana appeared and took a seat beside Cliff. She'd composed herself by this time, embarrassed to have given way to crying as she had.

"They're putting a cast on Katie's arm," she said when Cliff looked to her. "She's asking to see you."

"Me?"

"Yes, Cliff, you."

They stood together. Diana paused, feeling a bit chagrined, but needing to thank him. "I don't know who told you about the accident or why you came, but I want you to know how much I appreciate your…help. Something came over me when we arrived at the hospital, and all of a sudden I couldn't help remembering the last time I was here. I got so afraid." Her voice wobbled, and she bit into her bottom lip. "Thank you, Cliff."

"No problem." He was having a hard time not taking her in his arms and offering what comfort he could. His whole body ached with the need to hold her and tell her he understood. But after their last discussion, he didn't know how she'd feel about him touching her. He buried his hands in his pants pockets, bunching them into impotent fists. "I'm here because I want to be here—there's nothing noble about it."

Although he made light of it, Diana knew he'd left his law office in the middle of the day to rush to the hospital. His caring meant more than she could ever tell him. She wanted to try, but the words that were in her heart didn't make it to her tongue.

"Cliff!" Katie brightened the minute he stepped into the casting room.

"Hi, buttercup." Her face was streaked with tears, her pigtails mussed with leaves and grass and a bruise was forming on the side of her jaw, but Cliff couldn't remember seeing a more beautiful little girl. "How did you manage that?" He nodded toward her arm.

"I fell out of the apple tree," she told him, and wrinkled up her nose. "I wasn't supposed to climb it, either."

"I hope you won't again," Diana interjected.

Katie's young brow crinkled into a tight frown. "I don't

think I will. This hurt real bad, but I tried to be brave for Mom and Joan."

"I broke my leg once," Cliff told her. The thought of Katie having to endure the same pain he'd suffered produced a curious ache in the region of his heart. He watched as the PA worked, wrapping her arm in a protective layer of cotton. Then he dipped thick plaster strips in water and began to mold them over Katie's forearm and elbow.

"I've missed you a whole lot," the little girl said next.

"I've missed you, too." Cliff discovered that wasn't a lie. He'd tried not to think about Diana and her daughters since the night of their talk. The past couple of days, he'd been almost amused at the way everything around him had reminded him of them. He'd finally reached the conclusion that he wasn't going to be able to forget these three females. Somehow, without his knowing how, they'd made an indelible mark on his heart. What Diana had said about Becky and him had been the truth. Funny, he'd once told Diana to wake up and smell the coffee, and yet he had been the one with his head buried in the sand.

"Mom missed you, too—a whole bunch."

"Katie!"

"It's true. Don't you remember you were cranky with me and Joan, and then you told us you were sorry and said you were still missing Cliff and that was the reason you were in such a bad mood."

A hot flush seeped into Diana's face and circled her ears. With some effort, she smiled weakly in Cliff's direction, hoping he'd be kind enough to forget what Katie had told him.

"Don't you remember, Mom? Joan thought it was Aunt Flo again and you said—"

"I remember, Katie," she said pointedly.

"Who's Aunt Flo?" Cliff wanted to know.

"Never mind," Diana murmured under her breath.

"Will you sign my cast?" Katie asked Cliff next. "The only boys who can sign it are you and Mikey."

"I'd be honored."

"And maybe Gary Hidenlighter."

"Who's he?" The name sounded vaguely familiar to Cliff, and he wondered where he'd heard it.

"The boy who offered her a baseball card if she'd let him kiss her."

"Ah, yes," Cliff answered with a lopsided grin. "I seem to recall hearing about the dastardly proposition now."

"Kissing doesn't seem to be so bad," Katie added thoughtfully after a moment. "Mom and you sure do it a lot."

Cliff lightly slipped his arm around Diana's shoulders and smiled down on her. "I can't speak for your mother, but I know what I like."

"I do, too," she responded, looking up at Cliff, comforted by his feathery touch.

Getting Katie out of the hospital wasn't nearly as much a problem as getting her in had been since Cliff was there to smooth the way. While Diana filled in the spaces Cliff had left blank on the permission forms, he wheeled Katie up to the hospital pharmacy and had the prescription for the pain medication filled. By the time they returned, Diana had finished her task. As the two came toward her, the sight of them together filled her with an odd sensation of rightness.

"Can I ride in Cliff's car?" Katie asked once they were in the parking lot.

"Katie, Cliff has to get back to his office."

"No, I don't," he countered quickly, looking almost boyish in his eagerness. "While we were waiting, I phoned my secretary and told her I was taking the rest of the day off."

"Oh, goodie." Katie's happy eyes flew from her mother to Cliff and then back to Diana again. "Since Cliff isn't real busy, can I go in his car?"

Diana's gaze went to Cliff, who acquiesced with a short nod.

All the way into Kent, Katie chatted a mile a minute. The physician had claimed that the pain medication would make the little girl drowsy, but thus far it had had just the opposite effect. Katie was a wonder.

"I used my new lucky lure the other day," Cliff said when he was able to get a word in edgewise.

"Oh, good. Did it work?"

"Like a dream." His change in luck had astonished him and had amazed Charlie, who'd wanted to know where Cliff had bought that silver lure. Cliff had sailed back into the marina that afternoon with a good-size salmon and a large flounder, while Charlie hadn't gotten so much as a curious nibble.

Katie let out a long sigh of relief. "I was real afraid the new one wouldn't have the same magic."

"Then rest assured, Katie Collins, because this new lure seems to be even better than the old one. In fact, you might have done me a favor by losing the original."

"Really? Are we ever going to go fishing on your sailboat again? I promise never to get into your gear unless you tell me I can."

"I think another fishing expedition could be arranged, but let's leave that up to your mother, okay?" He wasn't sure Diana would agree to seeing him again, and didn't want to disappoint Katie.

"That sounds okay," Katie assented.

When Cliff pulled into the driveway behind Diana's gray

bomber, it seemed that half the kids in the neighborhood rushed out to greet Katie.

They followed her into the house, and she sat them down, organized their questions and patiently answered each one, explaining in graphic detail what had happened to her. As he looked on from the kitchen, it seemed to Cliff that she was holding her own press conference.

While Katie was hailed as a heroine, Diana brewed coffee and brought a cup to Cliff. "Do you mind if I take a look around your garage?" he asked her unexpectedly after taking a sip.

"Sure, go ahead." She wondered what he was up to and was mildly surprised when he reappeared a couple of minutes later with a handsaw.

"Here," he said, handing her his suit jacket, and marched outside.

Katie noticed he was gone right away. "What's Cliff doing?"

Diana was just as curious as her daughter and followed him out the sliding glass door. She paused, watching him from the patio as he methodically started trimming off the lower branches of the backyard's lone tree.

By the time he'd finished, Cliff had loosened his tie, unfastened the top buttons of his starched shirt and paused more than once to wipe the sweat from his brow.

Grateful for his thoughtfulness, Diana started issuing instructions. Soon the neighborhood kids had gathered around him and stacked the fallen limbs into a neat pile. Diana was so busy watching Cliff and telling the kids to keep out of his way that he was nearly finished before she noticed that Joan was missing.

Diana wandered through the house, looking for her daughter. When she didn't find her on the lower level, she wandered up the stairs.

"Joan?"

She heard a muffled sob and peeked inside the first bedroom, looking past all the Justin Timberlake posters to her daughter, who had flung herself across the top of her half-made bed.

"Joan?" she asked softly. "Don't you want to come and see Katie?"

"No."

"Why not? She wants you to sign her cast."

"I'm not going to. Not ever."

Diana moved to her daughter's side and sat on the edge of the mattress. Puzzled by Joan's odd behavior, she brushed the soft wisps of hair from the eleven-year-old's furrowed brow.

Huge tears filled the preteen's dark brown eyes. She muttered something about Cliff that Diana couldn't understand.

"You phoned him at his office?"

Joan nodded. "I… I don't know why. I just did."

"Do you think I'm angry with you because of that?"

Joan shrugged in open defiance. "I don't care if you are mad. I wanted to talk to Cliff and I did… Katie was hurt and I thought he had the right to know."

The realization that both girls had turned to Cliff in the emergency was only a little short of shocking to Diana. Katie had asked about him even before Diana had had a chance to tell the youngster he was in the hospital waiting room, filling out the forms. And Joan had contacted him at his office, knowing she would probably be punished for doing so. No other man Diana had ever dated had had this profound effect on her daughters. Without trying, without even wanting to, Cliff Howard had woven himself into their tender hearts. Although it hurt, Diana understood now that she'd made the right decision to break off her relationship with him. Cliff possessed the awesome power to hurt her children, and it was her duty, as their mother, to protect them.

"Mom," Joan sobbed, straightening up enough to hurl herself into her mother's arms, "I was so afraid."

"I know, sweetheart." Fresh tears filled Diana's eyes at the memory of those first minutes at the hospital. "I was, too."

"I...thought Katie would never come home again."

Diana's own fears had been similar. In all the confusion, she hadn't considered what had been going on in Joan's mind. As the eldest, Joan could remember the day her father had died. She had only been eight at the time, and although she might not have understood everything, she could vividly remember the horror, just as Diana had earlier in the day.

"You can have my allowance if you need it...."

"I don't need your allowance, honey."

Embarrassed now by the display of emotion, Joan wiped the moisture from her cheek and gave her mother a determined, angry look. "That Katie can be really stupid. You know that, don't you?"

"Cliff cut off the lower limbs so Katie won't be able to climb into the apple tree again."

Joan nodded approvingly. "It's a good thing, because that Katie can be so stupid. Knowing her, she wouldn't learn a single lesson from this. If something hadn't been done, she'd probably break her other arm next week."

Diana hid her smile, and the two hugged each other. "Come downstairs now, and you can talk to your sister."

Joan nodded. "All right, but don't get mad at me if I tell Katie she's got the brains of a rotting tomato."

* * *

"Mom, is there room in your suitcase for my iPad?"

Diana groaned, glanced toward the ceiling and prayed for patience. "Unfortunately I need some space for my clothes," she said, and attempted to shut the suitcase one last time. It wouldn't latch. "Your iPad has low priority at the moment."

"Mom!" Katie hurried into the bedroom. "Did you tell Cliff we were going to Wichita to visit Grandma and Grandpa?"

Diana hedged, trying to recall if she had or not. She had, she thought. "Yes."

"How come he hasn't come over since he brought me home from the hospital?"

The tight, uncomfortable feeling returned to Diana's chest. "I...don't know."

"But I thought he would."

So had Diana. She'd laid her cards out on the table, and the next move was his. He'd been wonderful with Katie that day she'd broken her arm, more than wonderful. While Katie had slept during the afternoon from the effects of the medication, he'd taken Joan out shopping. Together they'd purchased Katie a huge stuffed Pooh bear. At dinnertime he'd insisted on providing Kentucky Fried Chicken, much to her younger daughter's delight. But after they'd eaten, he'd said a few words of farewell, and that had been the last Diana or the girls had heard from him.

Actually, Diana was grateful for this vacation. These next two weeks with her parents would help all three of them take their minds off one Cliff Howard.

"He didn't even sign my cast."

"I think he forgot," Diana said, sitting on her suitcase in an effort to latch it.

"I think we should call him," Joan chimed in.

"No."

"But, Mom…"

One derisive look from Diana squelched that idea.

"What is it with that man, anyway?" Joan asked next. "I don't understand him at all."

Joan wasn't the only one baffled by Cliff.

"I thought he was hot for you."

"Joan, please."

"No, really, Mom. The day he brought Katie home, he could hardly take his eyes off you."

Diana had done her share of looking, too. She'd wanted to talk to him, let him know how much she appreciated what he'd done for her and the girls, but he had left before the opportunity arose, and they hadn't heard from him in four days. Now that she'd had some time to give the matter thought, she'd decided not to protect the girls from the danger of Cliff denting their tender hearts. She'd seen how wonderful he'd been with Katie and how thoughtful with Joan. He'd never intentionally hurt them.

"Cliff told me he'd take me fishing again," Katie said. Her cast was covered with a multitude of messages and names in a variety of colors, but she'd managed to save a white space for Cliff under her elbow. "But he said if we went again, it would be up to you. We can go, can't we, Mom?"

Before Diana could answer Katie, the phone rang. Joan pounced on the receiver next to Diana's bed like a cat on a cornered mouse.

"Hello," she said demurely, sat down and grinned girlishly. She crossed her legs and thoughtfully examined the ends of her fingernails. "It's good to hear from you again."

It was obviously a boy, and Joan was in seventh heaven.

"Yes, she's recovered nicely. Katie always was the brave

one. Personally, at the sight of blood, I get the vapors. It's a good thing my mother kept her wits about her."

Diana bounced hard on the suitcase and sighed when the latch snapped into place. Success at last.

"Yes, she's sitting right here. She's packing. You do remember we're leaving for Wichita tonight, don't you? You didn't? Well, that's strange... Mom claims she did tell you. Yes, of course, just a minute." Grinning ear to ear, Joan held out the phone to her mother. "It's for you, Mom. It's Cliff."

Diana's heart fell to her knees and rebounded sharply before finally settling back into place. Joan had to be joking. "Cliff Howard?"

"Honestly, Mother, just how many Cliffs are you dating?"

"At the moment, none."

As diplomatically as possible, Joan steered her younger sister out of the bedroom and started to close the door.

"But," Katie protested, "I want to talk to Cliff, too."

"Another time," Joan said, and winked coyly at her mother.

Clearing her throat, Diana lifted the telephone receiver to her ear. "Hello."

"Diana? What's this about you leaving for Wichita?"

"Yes, well, I thought I mentioned it."

A short silence followed. "How long are you going to be gone?"

"Two weeks."

Her answer was followed by his partially muffled swearing. "Listen, would it be all right if I came over right away?"

Ten

Cliff pulled his sports car into Diana's driveway and turned off the engine. For a long moment he kept his hands on the steering wheel, his thoughts heavy. Maybe Diana had told him about this trip to Wichita, but if she had, he sure didn't remember it. He'd reached a decision about himself and his relationship with Diana and her girls. The process had been painful, but now that he knew his mind, he wasn't going to let a planned two-week vacation stand in his way.

Determined, he climbed out of his car, slammed the door and headed for the house.

Diana met him on the front porch, and once again Cliff was struck by her simple beauty. Her dark eyes with their long, thick lashes searched his face. Her lips were slightly parted, and a familiar ache tightened Cliff's midsection. If everything blew up in his face today, if worse came to worse and he never saw Diana Collins again, he'd always remember her and her kisses. They'd haunt him.

"Hello, Cliff." Diana was amazed how cool and unemotional she sounded. She wasn't feeling the least bit controlled. From the minute they'd finished their telephone conversation, she'd been pacing the upstairs, wandering from room to room in a mindless search for serenity. She'd never heard Cliff sound quite so serious. Now that he'd arrived, she noted that his piercing blue eyes revealed an unfamiliar intensity.

"Hello, Diana."

She opened the screen door for him.

"Where are the girls?" he asked once he was inside the house. He kept his hands in his pockets for fear he'd do something crazy, like reach for her and kiss her senseless. He'd been thinking about exactly that for four long days. Being with her only increased his need to taste her again.

"Joan and Katie are saying goodbye to all their friends in the neighborhood. You'd think we were going to be gone two years instead of two weeks." Actually, this time alone with Cliff had been Joan's doing. Her elder daughter hadn't been the least bit subtle about suggesting to Katie that perhaps they should take this opportunity to bid their friends a fond au revoir. Katie, however, had been far more interested in seeing Cliff. Diana estimated they'd have fifteen minutes at the most, before Katie blasted into the house.

Cliff jerked a hand out of his pocket and splayed his fingers through his hair. Now that he was here, he found he was tongue-tied. He'd practiced everything he wanted to say and now he didn't know where to start.

"Would you like some coffee?"

"No, thanks, I came to talk." That sounded good.

"Okay." Diana moved into the living room. Whatever was on Cliff's mind was important. He hadn't so much as cracked a smile. She imagined his behavior was similar when he stood in the courtroom before the jury box. Each move would be calculated, every word planned for the maximum effect.

Diana lowered herself into the overstuffed chair, and Cliff took a seat directly across from her on the sofa. He sat on the edge of the cushion, his elbows resting on his thighs, and clenched his hands into tight fists.

"How's Katie?"

Diana's smile came from her heart. "She's doing great. After the first day she didn't even need the pain medication."

"And you?"

Without his having to explain, Diana understood. "Much better, I... I'm not exactly sure I know what happened that day in the hospital, but emotionally I crumbled into a thousand pieces. I was about as close to being a basket case as I can remember. I'll always be grateful you were there for Katie and me."

"Her accident taught us both several valuable lessons."

"It did?" Diana swallowed around the uncomfortable tightness in her throat. She hardly recognized the Cliff who sat across from her; he was so grim-faced and unreadable.

Cliff seemed unable to take his eyes off her. There was so much he longed to tell her, and he'd never felt more uncertain about how to express himself. Knowing she would be leaving for her parents' had thrown him an unexpected curveball. He wished he could have taken her to an expensive restaurant and explained everything on neutral ground. Now he felt pressured to clear the air between them before she left for Wichita.

"Until Katie broke her arm," he went on to say, "I'd more or less decided, after our late-night conversation, that you were right and it was best for us not to see each other again." He sat stiffly, feeling ill at ease. "It didn't take you long to see through me— I'm definitely not the marrying kind, and you knew it. You appealed to my baser instincts and I appealed to yours, but anything more than that between us was doomed. Am I right?"

Out of nervous agitation, Diana reached for the pillow

with the cross-stitch pattern and fluffed it up in her lap. "Yes... I suppose so."

"Not seeing me again was what you wanted, wasn't it?" Cliff challenged.

Regretfully Diana nodded. It was and it wasn't. A relationship with Cliff showed such marvelous promise, and at the same time contained the coarse threads of tragedy. If the only threat had been *her* heart and *her* emotions, Diana might have risked it.

At least those had been her thoughts before the accident, when she'd seen how good Cliff had been with her girls. Joan and Katie were already involved.

"I see."

Diana wasn't sure he did. If he understood all this, then there wasn't any reason for this urgent visit now. Suddenly she understood what he was getting at. Her cheeks flushed, and she stood, holding the decorator pillow to her stomach. "Cliff, I apologize."

"You do?" He was the one who wanted to ask her forgiveness.

"Yes. I had no idea Joan would contact you when Katie was hurt. I'll make sure it doesn't happen again. I don't know why she did it...but I've talked with her since and explained that she should never have made that call, and she promised she..."

Cliff stormed to his feet. "I'm not talking about that!"

"You're not?"

"No." He lowered his voice, paused and ran his hand along the back of his neck a couple of times. "Listen, I'm doing a poor job of this."

She stared at him in wide-eyed wonder, not knowing what to think.

"Sit down, would you?"

Diana lowered herself back into the chair.

Cliff paced the space in front of her as though she were a stubborn member of the jury and he were about to make the closing argument in an important trial. He couldn't believe he was making such a mess of something this basic. Talking to Diana should have been a simple matter of explaining his change of heart, but once he arrived, he felt as nervous as a first-year member of a debate team.

Diana pressed her hands between her closed knees and studied Cliff as he moved back and forth in the small area in front of her chair. It was on the tip of her tongue to tell him that if he didn't hurry, the girls would be back and then their peace would be shattered. With Katie doing cartwheels at the sight of him, there wouldn't be a chance for a decent discussion.

Perhaps, Cliff decided, it would be best to start at the beginning. "Do you remember the night I came over after work and we sat and talked?"

Diana grinned and nodded. "As I recall, we did more kissing than talking."

Cliff relaxed enough to share a smile with her, and when he spoke his eyes softened with the memory of how good the gentle lovemaking between them had been then. "It didn't feel right to walk away from you that night."

Diana's gaze dropped to the carpet. It hadn't felt right to her, either, but there was so much more at stake than her feelings or his.

"After I left you, I decided a romantic evening alone together in my condo would be just the thing to seal our fates. Do you remember?"

She wasn't likely to forget. "Listen, Cliff, I don't know what your point is, but…"

Cliff wasn't entirely sure anymore, either. "I guess what

I'm having such a difficult time telling you is that I don't bed every woman I date." Diana was special, more than special. She had never been, and never would be, a number to him—someone he'd use to boost his ego. He wanted to explain that, and it just wasn't coming out the way he'd planned.

"It's none of my business how many women you've slept with." If he was going to make some grand confession, she wasn't interested in hearing it.

"But this does involve you."

She stood again, because it was impossible to remain seated. "Listen, Cliff, if you're going to tell me you slept with that...that bimbo blonde then...don't."

"Bimbo blonde? Oh, you mean Marianne. You think I made love to her? Diana, you've got to be joking."

"No, I'm not." The unexpected pain that tightened her chest made it almost impossible to talk evenly. The power Cliff Howard wielded to injure her heart was lethal. Diana had recognized that early in their relationship and had taken steps to protect herself. Yet here he was, stirring up unwelcome trauma.

"I didn't sleep with her! Diana, I swear to you by all that I hold dear, I didn't go to bed with Marianne." His words were little more than a hoarse whisper.

She walked across the room and looked out the window. Where were the girls when she could really use them? "That's hardly my business."

"I'm trying to make a point here."

"If so, just do it," she said, and whirled around to face him, shoulders stiff. She was on the defensive now and growing more impatient by the minute.

"I want to apologize for..."

"That's exactly what I thought," she flared, resisting the

urge to place her hands over her ears to blot out his words. "And I don't want to hear it...so you can save your breath."

"For the night at my condominium," Cliff continued, undaunted. "I set up that seduction scene because we both felt the magic, and I wanted you." He lowered his voice to an enticing whisper of remembered desire. "Heaven knows I wanted you." And nothing had changed.

Now it was Diana's turn to pace, and she did so with all the energy of a raw recruit eager to please his sergeant. She stopped when she realized how ridiculous she must look and slapped her hands against the sides of her thighs. "Just what is your point?"

For a minute Cliff had forgotten. "When you walked out on me that night, I can't remember ever being angrier with anyone in my life. I figured if you were into denial, then fine, but I was noble enough to be honest about my feelings."

"I wonder if there's a Pulitzer Prize for that," she murmured sarcastically, and wrapped her arms around her waist.

Cliff ignored her derision. "Later I had a change of heart and decided I could be forgiving, considering the circumstances. I gave you ample time to come to me, and when you didn't, I was forced to swallow my pride and bridge the uneasiness between us. You may be impressed to know that I don't do that sort of thing often."

A snicker slipped from Diana's clogged throat. She tightened her grip on her waist. The longer he spoke, the more uncertain she was as to how to take Cliff. He was being sarcastic, but it seemed to be at his expense and not hers.

"That night you lowered the boom and told me a few truths," Cliff continued. "Basically, let it be known that you weren't interested in falling into bed with me because of some mystical, magical feeling between us. You also took it upon yourself to point out a couple of minor flaws in my personality. As I recall, shortly afterward I was left to lick my wounds."

A smile cracked the tight line of Diana's mouth. "Was I really so merciless?"

"Wanna see the scars?"

"I didn't mean to be so ruthless," she said tenderly, filled with regret for having injured his pride, although she'd known the nature of their talk would be painful for him.

"The truth hurts—isn't that how the saying goes?"

Diana nodded.

"I've done a lot of thinking since that night." Only a few feet separated them, and he raised his hands as though to reach for her and bring her close to him. Reluctantly he dropped his fists to his side and took a step in the opposite direction.

"And?" Diana pressed.

"And I think we may have something, Diana. Something far more valuable than magic. Something I'm not likely ever to find again. I don't want to lose you. I realize I may have ruined everything by trying to rush you into bed with me, and I apologize for that. I'd like a second chance with you, although I probably don't deserve one."

His eyes softened and caressed her with such tenderness that Diana stopped breathing until her lungs ached. When she spoke, the words rushed out on the tail end of a raspy sigh. "I think...that could be arranged."

"Whatever it is between us is potent—you'll have to agree to that."

Diana couldn't deny the obvious.

"I know you have your doubts and I honestly can't blame you. But if you agree to letting me see you again, I promise to do things differently. I'm not going to pressure you into lovemaking—you have my word on that."

"I've made my share of mistakes, too, and I think it would only be fair if I came up with a few promises of my own."

He looked at her as though he hadn't had a clue as to what she was talking about.

"I have no intention of rushing you into making a commitment. And the word *love* will be stricken from my vocabulary." Feeling almost giddy with relief, she smiled warmly.

Cliff smiled in return. "I wonder if we could seal this bargain with a kiss."

"I think that would be more than appropriate."

Cliff had reached for her even before she'd finished speaking. He needed to hold her again and savor her softness pressing against him. She was halfway into his arms, when the front door burst open.

"Cliff!" Katie leaped into the living room with all the energy of a hydroelectric dam. Her pigtails were swinging, her eyes aglow. "I didn't think you'd ever get here. You forgot to sign my cast, and I saved you a space, but it's getting dirty."

Joan followed shortly after Katie. "Hi, Cliff," she said nonchalantly. She tossed her mother an apologetic look.

Cliff pulled a pen from inside his suit pocket and knelt in front of Katie.

"What took you so long?" Katie demanded as Cliff started penning his message on her cast.

"I don't know, buttercup," he answered, looking up to Diana and smiling.

"I can't get over how much the girls have grown," Joyce Shaffer, Diana's mother, said with an expressive sigh, alternately glancing between Joan and Katie.

"It's been a year, Mom." The long flight from Seattle to

Wichita had left the girls and Diana exhausted. Joan and Katie had fallen asleep ten minutes after they arrived at Diana's family home. Diana longed to join her daughters, but her parents were understandably excited and wanted to chat. Diana and her mother gathered around the kitchen table, nibbling on chocolate chip cookies, drinking tall glasses of milk and talking.

"Poor Katie," her mother went on to say sympathetically. "Is her arm still hurting?"

"It itches more than anything."

Burt Shaffer pulled up a chair and joined the two women. "Who's this Cliff fellow the girls were telling me about?"

Diana hesitated, not exactly sure how to explain her relationship with Cliff. She didn't want to lead her family into thinking she was about to remarry, nor did she wish to explain that she and Cliff had reached a still untested understanding.

"Cliff and I have dated a few times." That was the best explanation she could come up with on such short notice. She should have been prepared for this. The minute the girls had stepped off the plane, Katie had shown her grandparents where Cliff had signed her cast and told the detailed story of how he'd let her ride in his car on the way home from the hospital. First Katie, then Joan, had spoken nonstop for a full five minutes, extolling his myriad virtues, until Diana had thought she'd scream at them both to cut it out.

"So you've only dated him a few times." Her father nodded once, giving away none of his feelings. "The girls certainly seem to have taken a liking to him. What about you, rosebud? Do you think as highly of this Cliff fellow as Joan and Katie seem to?"

"Now really, Burt," her mother cut in. "Don't go quizzing poor Diana about the men in her life the minute she walks in the door. Diana, dear, did I tell you Danny Helleberg recently moved back to town?"

Diana and Danny had gone to high school together a million years ago. Although they'd been in the same class, Diana had barely known him. "No..."

"I talked to his mother the other day in the grocery store and I told her you were flying out for a visit. She says Danny would love to see you again."

"That would be nice." Not really, but Diana didn't want to disappoint her mother.

"I'm glad you think so, honey, because he phoned and I told him to call again in the morning."

"That'd be great." Her smile was weak at best. She had hardly said more than a handful of words to Danny Helleberg the entire time they were in school together. Recounting the memory of their high-school days should take all of five minutes. It was the only thing they had in common.

"His wife left him for another man. I did tell you that, didn't I? The poor boy was beside himself."

"Yes, Mom, I think you did mention Danny's marital problems." She tried unsuccessfully to swallow a yawn, gave up the effort and planted her hand over her mouth, hoping her parents got the hint.

They didn't.

"Danny and his wife are divorced now."

Diana did her best to try to look interested. It was the same way every visit—her parents seemed to think it was their duty to supply her with another husband. Every summer a variety of men were paraded before her while Diana struggled to appear grateful.

"Tell us about Cliff," her dad prompted.

Diana's fingers tightened around her milk glass. "There really isn't much to tell. We've only gone out a few times."

"What's his family like?" her mother wanted to know, looking as though she already disapproved. If Diana was going to remarry, it was her mother's opinion that the man should be from Wichita. Then Diana wouldn't have any more excuses to remain in Seattle.

"Really, Mom, I don't have any idea—I haven't met his parents."

"I see." Her mother exchanged a look with her father that Diana recognized all too well.

"Cliff's an attorney," she added hurriedly, hoping that would impress her parents.

"That's nice, dear." But her mother didn't seem overly swayed by the information. "We just hope you aren't serious about this young man."

"Why?" Diana asked, surprised.

Her mother looked more amazed than Diana. "Why, because Danny Helleberg is back in town. You know how well his mother and I get along."

Diana felt like grinding her teeth. "Right, Mom."

Cliff leaned back on his leather couch and stretched out his legs in front of him, crossing his ankles. Diana's first email had arrived. Already adrenaline was pumping through him. Four days. She'd been gone only four days, and he missed her more than he thought it was possible to miss another human being. He thought about their last minutes together while he'd driven her and the girls to the airport. Diana had lingered as long as she could, seeking to delay their parting. So much had remained unsaid between them. She'd wrapped her arms around his neck and kissed him soundly. The memory of that single, ardent kiss still had the power to triple his pulse rate. It was the type of kiss men remember as they go into battle. A kiss meant to forge time and distance. She'd looked as dazed as he felt. Without saying anything more, she'd turned and left him, rushing into the airport with Joan and Katie at her side. Cliff had remained at the airport drop-off point far longer than necessary, wishing she were back in his arms. Two weeks, he'd thought. That shouldn't be so long, but the way the time was dragging, each minute seemed longer than the one before. Two weeks was an eternity.

He grinned as he read over the first few lines that told him about Joan and Katie and how Katie had told her parents about him before Diana had had the opportunity to mention his name. The smile faded when he read how her parents were pressuring her to move to Wichita so they could look after her properly. He sighed audibly as he scrolled down to the second page. Diana assured him this was an old argument and that she had no intention of leaving Seattle. She loved her parents, but being close to them would slowly, surely, drive her crazy. Cliff agreed with that. He loved his family, but they had the same effect upon him.

Cliff continued reading. Diana told him she regretted the impulsive kiss at the airport. Now all she could think about was getting back to Seattle and seeing him again. Nothing had ever been that good—not even their first kiss at the marina under the starlight.

Cliff agreed.

If she experienced half the emotion he had over that kiss, she'd call her family vacation short and hurry back to him. All he could think about was Diana coming home and his holding her again.

He left the computer and went into the kitchen to fix himself something for dinner. Five minutes later he returned, pausing over the last few words she'd written about the kiss.

On impulse he reached for the phone. If he didn't hear her voice, he'd be the one to slowly, surely, go crazy. Getting her parents' number wasn't a problem, and he quickly punched it out, checking his watch and figuring out the time difference.

"Hello."

Cliff would have staked his life savings that Joan would answer. He was right.

"Hi, Joan."

"Cliff! How are you?"

"Fine." Okay, so that was a minor exaggeration; he would be once he talked to Joan's mother.

"We went to Sedgwick County Zoo today. It was great. I saw a green snake and a black-necked swan."

She paused, and Cliff heard muffled arguing.

"Joan," Cliff called after a long pause, "are you there?"

"Yes, Cliff," she said a bit breathlessly. "It seems my darling younger sister wants to talk to you."

"Okay." Briefly Cliff wondered if he'd end up speaking to everyone in the entire household before he was able to talk to Diana.

"Hi, Cliff," Katie shouted. "I told Grandma and Grandpa all about you, and Grandpa says he's going to take me fishing here in Wichita."

"That sounds like fun. Where's your mother?"

"There was a bad storm the other night and there was lightning and thunder, and I woke up scared and Mom came in and told me there was music in the storm. Did you know that? And guess what? She was right. I went back to sleep, and in the morning I could still remember the funny kind of drums that played."

Cliff was impressed at Diana's genius. "I'm glad you're not afraid of thunder anymore."

Once again Cliff heard muffled words and then silence. "Katie? Is someone on the phone?"

"Hello, Cliff."

Joan again. "Listen, sweetheart, could I speak to your mother?"

"I'm afraid that poses something of a problem," Joan whispered huskily into the receiver, as though she'd cupped her hand over it.

"It does?"

"Yes. You see, she isn't here at the moment."

"What time do you expect her back?"

"Late. Real late."

"How late?"

"She didn't get in until after midnight last night."

Cliff grinned. "I suppose she's seeing a lot of her old high-school friends."

"Especially one old friend. A *boyfriend*," Joan said heavily.

"Oh?"

"Yes, his name is Danny Helleberg. He's not nearly as good-looking as you, but Grandma told me that looks aren't everything. Grandma insists that Danny will make an excellent stepdad. Katie and I aren't sure. Out of all the men Mother's been dating—including the man with references—we vote for you."

Eleven

A week! It hadn't even taken Diana a week to forget about him. The minute she was out of Cliff's sight, she'd started dating another man behind his back. Outrage poured over him like burning oil, scalding his thoughts. He should have learned from Becky that women weren't to be trusted. He'd been a fool to allow another woman, someone he'd thought he could trust, to do this to him a second time.

Pacing seemed to help, and Cliff did an abrupt about-face and marched to his living-room window with a step General Mac Arthur would have praised. All along, Diana had probably planned and plotted this assault on his pride. Look at how cleverly she'd manipulated him thus far! Why, she'd had him eating out of the palm of her hand! With his fists clenched tightly at his sides, Cliff turned away from the unseen panorama before him and stepped into his kitchen, opening the refrigerator. He stared blankly at its contents, shook his head, wondered what he was doing there and closed the door. Diana was ingenious, he'd grant her that much. She had him right where she wanted him— lonely, miserable and wanting her. From the minute he'd met her, he hadn't been himself. It was as though he were out of sync with his inner self while he mulled over what this young widow and her daughters were doing in his life. He'd listened to her while she tore him apart, searched deep within himself and recognized the truth of what she'd said. And all the while she'd waited patiently for him to return to her. And he had. Diana had been so confident that she hadn't so much as tried to contact him. Not once.

Then this sweet, innocent widow had duped him into believing this two-week jaunt to Wichita was a vacation to visit her family. She was visiting all right, but it wasn't her family she'd been so eager to get home to see. Oh, no, it was some old-time boyfriend she could hardly wait to date again. While she'd been looking at Cliff with those wide, deceiving eyes of hers, she'd been scheming to hook up with this Danny whatever-his-name-was.

And another thing—some mother she turned out to be, leaving Joan and Katie this way. Both girls had bubbled over with excitement, they'd been so happy to hear from him. The poor kids were lonely. And what children wouldn't be, left in a strange house with people they hardly knew, while their mother was gallivanting around Wichita with another man?

Cliff knew one thing. If Diana was painting the town, he wasn't going to idly sit at home, pining away for her. He was through keeping the *TV Guide* company, through missing Diana or even thinking about her. In fact, he was finished with her entirely, he decided suddenly. He didn't need her, and it was all too obvious that she didn't need him, either. Fine. She could have it her way. In fact, she could have her old high-school boyfriend. Being the noble man he was, Cliff determined that he would quietly bow out of the picture. He'd even wish the two childhood sweethearts every happiness.

Now that he'd made a decision, Cliff took out his little black book and flipped through the pages. The names and phone numbers of the women listed here would give Diana paranoia. Grinning, he ran his finger down the first section and stopped at Missy's phone number. One look at Missy, and Diana would know she was out of the running. Already he felt better. The thought of Diana comparing herself to another one of his dates and falling short was comforting to his injured ego. As he'd told himself a minute before, Cliff Howard didn't need Diana Collins.

He reached for the phone and hit the first three digits of Missy's number, then abruptly disconnected. He wasn't in the mood for Missy. Not tonight.

Determined, he turned the page and smiled again when he saw Ingrid's name. The pretty blond Swede was another one Diana would turn green over. This time, however, it wasn't the voluptuous body that would pull the widow up short, although heaven knew Ingrid was stacked in all the right places. No, Ingrid was a well-educated corporate attorney, in addition to being independently wealthy. Cliff knew how much Diana would have loved to get her college degree. Soothed by the thought, Cliff reached for the phone and punched out a long series of numbers, but he hung up before the first ring.

Diana wasn't such a terrible mother. Look at how she'd calmed Katie down in the middle of a thunderstorm. The unexpected, unwanted thought caused him to frown.

Okay, so she hadn't exactly left her daughters in the hands of strangers, but Joan and Katie hardly knew their grandparents. It seemed to Cliff that Diana would want to spend her time with her mother and father. He sagged against the back of the couch and let out his breath in a heated rush.

He didn't want to be with Missy tonight, not Ingrid, either. Diana was the only woman who interested him, and had been the only one for weeks. He had an understanding with Diana, unspoken, but not undefined. They had something wonderful going—they wanted to test these feelings, explore this multifaceted attraction. If she felt the need to date other men, then that was up to her. For his part, he'd been living in the singles world for a long time; he didn't need another woman in his arms to tell him what he already knew. His gaze fell to the black book in his hands. He riffled through the pages, stopping now and again at a name that brought back fond memories. Yet there wasn't anyone listed whom he'd like to wrap in his arms, no one he longed to kiss and love. Given a magic wand and a bucketful of wishes, Cliff would have conjured up Diana Collins and only Diana Collins. Widow. Mother. And, he added painfully, heartbreaker.

Cliff must have dozed off watching television, because the next thing he was aware of was the phone. Its piercing rings jolted him awake. He straightened, rubbed his hand over his eyes, then reached for his cell.

"Hello."

"Cliff, it's Diana."

The sound of her voice was enough to send the blood rushing through his veins. When he spoke, he attempted to hide the sarcasm behind banter. "So how was your hot date with Danny Heartthrob?"

"That's what I called about. Listen, Cliff, I don't know what the girls told you…"

"Quite a bit, if you must know." Again he made it sound as though the entire evening had been a joke to him.

"Are you mad?"

She sounded worried and uptight, but Cliff thought it was poetic justice. "Should I be?"

"No!"

"Then why all the concern?"

Diana hesitated, not liking the condescending note in his voice. "I thought, you know, that you might have gotten upset because…well, because I'd gone out to dinner with Danny."

"Two nights in a row, according to Joan."

"I swear I don't even like him. He's a dead bore, but my mother's got this thing about my remarrying before I shrivel up and become an old woman. To hear her tell it, that's likely to happen in the next six weeks. Time is running out."

"Listen, if you want to see this Danny every night of your vacation, it's fine with me."

"It is?" came Diana's stunned response. "I…thought we had an understanding."

Cliff felt shut out and hurt, but he wasn't about to let her know that. Yes, they did have an agreement, but apparently it didn't mean a whole lot to Diana. Obviously she considered herself free to date other men, when he still hadn't recovered from the shock of not finding a single name in his black book that interested him. The only woman he wanted was Diana Collins, but unfortunately she was with another man.

"If you think I'm going to fly into a jealous rage, then you've got me figured all wrong. I'm just not the type," Cliff said, wondering exactly what this bozo Danny looked like. "The way I see it, you're on vacation and you're a big girl. You can do what you want."

Diana pondered his tone more than his words. She'd been sick when Joan and Katie had told her Cliff had phoned. He wouldn't understand that she'd gone out with Dan to appease her mother. These two dates had been part of a peacekeeping mission.

"You mean you're honestly not angry?"

"Naw."

"If the circumstances were reversed, I'm not sure I'd be as generous." She made an impatient, breathy sound, then burst out, "I know this is none of my business, but maybe you're being understanding about this because you've been seeing someone…since I've been in Wichita?"

Cliff would have loved to let her think exactly that, but he wasn't willing to lie outright. Misleading her, however, was an entirely different story.

"I'm sure there's been ample opportunity," Diana added, feeling more miserable by the minute.

"Well, as a matter of fact…"

"Forget I asked that," she insisted. "If you're going out with Bunnie or Bubbles or any of the other girls listed in your bachelor directory, I'd rather not know about it."

"Do you doubt me?" he asked, trying to sound casual. She had a lot of nerve. He was the one sitting home nights staring at the boob tube while she was flirting with everything in pants on the other side of the Rocky Mountains.

"It isn't a matter of trust," Diana answered after a long moment.

"Then what is it?"

"I'm not sure." The frustration was enough to make her want to cry. "We had so little time together before I had to leave. I'd been looking forward to this trip for weeks and then I didn't even want to go. There was so much I wanted to tell you, so much I wanted to say."

A pulsating silence stretched between them.

"It's ten-thirty here," Cliff said at last, checking his

watch and figuring the time difference. It was past midnight there. "Did you just get in?"

"About twenty minutes ago."

"Did you have a good time?"

"No."

Naturally she'd tell him that, and just as naturally he believed her, because it hurt too much for him to think otherwise.

"I will admit that I was a little bit jealous when I first talked to Joan." He didn't like telling her that much; it went against his pride. But letting her know his feelings would help.

Diana relaxed and closed her eyes.

"But it wasn't anything I couldn't work out myself," he added magnanimously. "I didn't like it one bit, if you're looking for the truth, but beyond anything else, I trust you."

The line went quiet for a moment. "Oh, Cliff, I've been so worried."

"Worried," he repeated, realizing Diana was close to tears. "Whatever for?"

"After what happened with you and… Becky, I had this terrible feeling that you'd think I was… I don't know, cheating on you."

"You haven't even cheated *with* me yet."

Her soft laugh was like a refreshing sea mist on a hot, humid afternoon. Cliff savored the sweet musical cadence of her voice.

It struck him then, struck him hard.

He was in love with Diana. No wonder he'd reacted like a lunatic when Joan had told him her mother was out with an old high-school flame. He'd been a blind fool not to acknowledge his feelings before now. He'd been attracted to her physically almost from the first, and the pull had been so strong that sharing a bed with her had been the only thing on his mind. Her reaction to that idea had left him reeling for days. She wanted more, demanded more. At the time he hadn't learned that the physical response she evoked in him only skimmed the surface of his feelings for her.

"I can't tell you how boring tonight was," Diana went on. "Dan doesn't like women who wear Levi's. Can you believe that, in this day and age? I spent the entire evening listening to his likes and dislikes, and I'm telling you—"

"Diana," Cliff interrupted her.

"Yes?"

The need to say it burned on his tongue, but he held back. A man didn't tell a woman he loved her over the phone. "Nothing."

The line went completely silent for a moment. "I'm not seeing him again. I made that perfectly clear to Dan tonight." She could deal with her mother's disappointment more readily than she could handle another date with a fuddy-duddy thirty-year-old.

"Don't let me stand in your way," Cliff returned almost flippantly. He was still shaking with the realization that he loved Diana. When a man cared this deeply for a woman, he shouldn't need those kinds of reassurances.

Suddenly angry, Diana frowned at the receiver. "That's a rotten thing to say."

"What is?"

"Oh, don't play stupid with me, Cliff Howard. I hadn't planned on seeing Dan again, but since you have no objection, then fine."

He could feel the heat of her anger a thousand miles away. Her words were hurled at him with the vehemence of a hand grenade. "What's made you so mad?"

"You. Do I honestly mean so little to you?"

"What on earth are you talking about?"

"That…that last statement of yours about my dating Dan, as though you couldn't care less and…"

"I couldn't care less," he echoed, and feigned a yawn.

"Fine, then."

Cliff couldn't so much as hear her breathe. It was as though they'd been caught up in a vacuum, both struggling to find an escape, but discovering they were trapped.

She'd do it, too. Diana would go out with this clown again just to spite him. Women! He'd made a major concession on her behalf, and she didn't have the good sense to appreciate it. "Okay, you want me to say don't go out with Dan…then I'm saying it."

It was exactly what Diana had needed to hear five minutes before. Unfortunately his admission had come too late. "You've got no claim on me. I can see anyone I please, and you…"

"The hell I don't have a claim on you."

"The hell you do!"

"I love you, ," he shouted. "That must give me some rights."

"You don't need to shout it at me!"

"How else am I supposed to get you to listen?"

"I… I don't know." If she had felt like crying before, it was nothing compared to what she was experiencing now. "You honestly love me?" Her voice was little more than a whisper.

"What's wrong now?" True, he hadn't planned on telling her like this, but he expected some kind of reaction from her. What he'd honestly hoped she'd do was to burst into tears and tell him she'd been crazy about him from that first night when he'd repaired her sink.

"Why did you tell me something like this when I'm a thousand miles away?"

"Because I couldn't hold it inside any longer. Are you going to keep me in suspense here? Don't you think you should let me know what you feel toward me?"

"You already know."

"Maybe, but I'd still like to hear you say it."

"I love you, too." The words were low and seductive, rusty and warm.

"How much longer are you going to be gone?" he asked, having difficulty finding his voice.

"Too long."

Cliff couldn't have agreed with her more.

"Will Cliff be at the airport?" Joan wanted to know, returning the flight magazine to the pocket in the seat in front of her.

"Yeah, Mom, will he?" Katie asked, tugging on Diana's sleeve.

Diana nodded. "He said he would."

The Boeing 737 was circling Sea-Tac airport before making its final approach for landing.

Joan and Katie had been far less impressed with flying on the return trip from Wichita, and Diana felt mentally and physically drained after coming up with twenty different ways to keep the pair entertained.

Cliff had promised he'd be waiting in the airport when they landed. Although Diana was dying for a glimpse of him, she almost wished she had time to take a shower and properly touch up her makeup before their reunion. She felt haggard, and it wasn't entirely due to the long flight.

Diana had made the mistake of admitting to her parents that she was in love with Cliff. She'd been honest in the hope that her mother would understand why she didn't want to date anyone else while she was in Wichita. Instead the announcement had been followed by a grueling question-and-answer session. Her mother and father had demanded to know everything they could about Cliff and his intentions toward her and the girls. Diana couldn't reassure them since she didn't know herself. Instead of being pleased for Diana, her parents seemed all the more concerned. Consequently, her last week in Wichita had been strained and uneasy for everyone except the girls.

"You talked to him lots."

"Who?" Diana blinked, trying to listen to Katie.

Her younger daughter gave her a look that told Diana she was losing it. "Cliff, of course. Every time I turned around, you two were on the phone."

"We spoke a grand total of six times."

"But for hours."

"Yeah," Joan piped in. "The first week we were there, you hardly mentioned his name. In fact, you got mad at Katie for telling Grandma and Grandpa about him and then the second week you hogged the phone, talking to him every minute of the day."

"I did not hog the phone!"

"Someone could have been trying to get through to me, you know," Joan said defensively.

"Who?"

"I…don't know, but someone, maybe a boy."

"Is Cliff going to marry you?" Katie asked. "I think I'd like it if he did."

Oh, no, not the girls, too. First her parents wanted to know his intentions, and now Joan and Katie. It was too much. "I have no idea what's going to happen between Cliff and me," Diana answered forcefully. It was little wonder that Cliff hated the word *commitment*—she was beginning to have the same reaction herself.

"I, for one, think it would be fabulous to have a father who looks like Cliff," Joan said, tilting her head in a thoughtful pose.

"Speaking of rock stars," Diana said pointedly, her gaze narrowing on her elder daughter, "did you really tell the boy who carried out Grandma's groceries that we're a distant relation to Phil Collins?"

Joan's bemused gaze slid to the other side of the plane. "Well, I'm sure we must be related one way or another. Just how many Collinses could there be? It is a small world, Mother, in case you hadn't noticed."

The plane landed on the runway with hardly more than a timid bounce, then the taxi to the receiving gate took an additional ten minutes. By the time the 737 had pulled to a stop and passengers were starting to disembark, Diana's nerves were frayed. The girls were right; she had talked to Cliff nearly every night. But now that they were home, she was skittish and self-conscious. She wished she'd done something glamorous with her hair before they'd left Wichita, but at the time, she'd been so eager to get on the plane and back to Seattle that she hadn't planned ahead.

Joan and Katie tugged at her arms, urging her to hurry as they briskly walked down the narrow jetway. It seemed as if everyone was hurried toward baggage claim, and although Diana didn't readily see Cliff, she knew he was there.

"Diana."

She'd just made it past the first large group crowding around the carousel.

"Over here."

Before Diana could think, Joan and Katie had left her

side and hurled themselves at Cliff as though they'd just spent the past ten years in boarding school.

He crouched to receive their bear hugs and nearly toppled when he looked up and smiled at Diana.

"Welcome home," he said, straightening. Lightly he wrapped his arm around her shoulder and brushed his lips over hers. He paused to inhale the fragrance of spring that was hers alone and briefly closed his eyes in gratitude for her and the girls' safe return.

"Do you want to see my suntan?" Joan asked.

"Sure." Cliff was so glad to have them back that he would have agreed to anything.

"I got another Pooh bear from Grandma."

Cliff grinned down on Katie, and would have willingly given her a whole warehouse full of her favorite bear. Oh yes, it was good to have them back.

"What about you?" Cliff asked, slipping his arm around Diana's waist. "Is there anything you want to show me?"

"Maybe."

"Later?"

"Later," she agreed with a soft smile.

They weren't back in the house five minutes before Joan and Katie were out the door, eager to let their friends know everything about Wichita.

Cliff had just finished delivering the last suitcase to Katie's bedroom. He paused at the top of the stairs and waited for Diana to meet him.

"If I don't get to properly kiss you soon, I'm going to go crazy." He held his arms out to her. "Come here, woman."

Without hesitation, Diana walked into his arms as though she'd always belonged there. It didn't matter to her that the front door was wide open, or that the girls were likely to burst in at any minute. All that concerned her was Cliff.

His hands knotted at the base of her spine as his gaze drifted hungrily over hers. "Did you see any more of Danny-boy?"

"You know I didn't."

"Good, because I was insanely jealous." His mouth found hers in an expression of fiery need, and he poured everything he'd learned about himself into the kiss. Everything he'd learned about what was right for them. Nothing had gone according to schedule while Diana was away. Every second, every minute of their separation had only heightened his need to have her back. Again and again he kissed her, needing her and showing her how much. His lips branded her and cherished her, and his tongue dipped into the secret warmth of her mouth.

Fire streaked through Diana's veins, and a delicious throbbing ache spread through every part of her body. The Boeing aircraft had landed in Seattle, she had even carried her suitcases into the house, but she hadn't been home until exactly this minute. The realization of how much Cliff had come to mean to her in such a short time was both powerful and frightening. She slid her arms around him, needing the reassurance of his closeness. Her hands traced his back, slowly playing over his ribs and the taper of his spine. She savored the feel of this man who held her and loved her and needed her as much as she needed him.

Diana's breathing became raspy when Cliff's mouth moved from her lips to the side of her neck. She trembled and snuggled closer in his embrace.

"Welcome home, Diana." His own breathing was shaky.

"If I go to the grocery store, to the dentist, to the bank, anywhere, promise you'll greet me this way when I return."

"I promise." His grip on her shoulders relaxed, but he didn't release her. Not yet.

"Oh, I nearly forgot." She broke away and hurried into her bedroom. "I brought you something."

Cliff followed her inside. "You did?"

Already Diana had tossed her suitcase on top of the mattress and was sorting through a stack of neatly folded clothes for the T-shirt.

"Diana?"

"It's right here. Just hold on a minute."

"Listen, I know this is soon and everything..."

"It's blue—the same color as your eyes." When she'd first seen the T-shirt, her heart had almost broken, she'd missed him so much.

Cliff buried his hands in his pockets. This wasn't exactly how he planned to do this, but he'd done a lot of thinking while Diana had been away and seeing her again proved everything he thought to question. "Diana..."

"It's here. I know it is." She paused and twisted around. "I may have tucked it in Joan's suitcase." Determined to find it, she hurried into her daughter's bedroom, paused and whirled around. "I'm sorry, Cliff, what were you saying?"

"Nothing." He felt like a fool.

"Okay." Diana went back and started rooting through the suitcase. The shirt was perfect for Cliff, and she was eager to give it to him.

"Actually, I had some time to mull over our relationship while you were away, and I was thinking that maybe we should get married."

At last Diana found the shirt, lifted it out and turned to face him, her eyes wide with triumph. The excitement drained from her as quickly as water through a sieve.

"What was it you just said?"

Twelve

"Mom, what do you think?" Joan paraded in front of her mother as though the eleven-year-old were part of a Las Vegas floor show. She wiggled her girlish hips and demurely tucked her chin over her shoulder while placing her hands on bended knee. "Well?"

Diana successfully squelched a smile. "You look at least fifteen, if not older."

Joan positively glowed with the praise.

"How come we have to wear a dress?" Katie grumbled, following her sister into the living room. Diana's younger daughter wasn't the least bit thrilled at the prospect of a dinner date with Cliff if she had to wear her Sunday clothes. "How come Cliff can't just bring over KFC? I like that best."

"Hey, dog breath, I want to eat in the Space Needle," Joan blasted her.

In a huff, Katie crossed her arms and glared defiantly at her sister. "I think it's silly."

The dinner date with the girls to announce their engagement had been Cliff's suggestion. He'd wanted to take Joan and Katie someplace fancy and fun and had chosen the famous Seattle landmark from the 1962 World's Fair.

"Come on, girls," Diana pleaded, "this night is special, so be on your absolute best behavior."

"Okay," the two agreed simultaneously.

Cliff arrived ten minutes later, dressed in a crisp pin-striped three-piece suit and looking devilishly handsome. The minute he walked in the house, the girls burst into excited chatter, gathering around him like children before a clown. Although he was listening to Joan and Katie, his eyes sought out Diana's and were filled with warmth and gentle promise. One look confirmed that his wild imagination hadn't conjured everything up out of desperation and loneliness. She did love him, and heaven knew he loved her.

Seeing Cliff again made Diana feel nervous, impatient and exhilarated. She'd only arrived back in Seattle the day before, and her whole world had been drastically changed within a matter of a few hours. The memory of Cliff standing on the other side of Joan's bedroom from her, looking boyish and uncertain as he suggested they get married, would remain with Diana all her life. Anyone who knew this man would never have believed the confident, sophisticated Cliff Howard could be so unsure of himself. In that moment, Diana knew she would never again doubt his love. She didn't recall how she'd answered him. A simple yes or a nod—perhaps both. What she did remember was the joy of Cliff crushing her in his arms and kissing her until they'd been forced to part when Joan and Katie returned.

"Can I order KFC at the Space Needle?" Katie asked a second time, breaking into Diana's musings.

"Every restaurant serves chicken, dummy," Joan inserted. "Personally, I'm going to order shrimp."

If dishes were wishes, Cliff would order two weeks alone in a hotel room with Diana. He dreamed about making love to her, about lying in bed and experiencing the feel of her skin brushing against him. He thought about waking up with her in the morning and falling asleep with her at night. Night after night, day after day. The mere suggestion excited him, filled him with anticipation for the good life that lay before them. The physical desire he felt for her was deep, honest and powerful. On the twenty-minute drive into Seattle, both Joan and Katie were excited and anxious and kept the conversation going, bantering back and forth, then squabbling, then joking.

The elevator ride up the 605-foot Space Needle left Joan and Katie speechless with awe. Diana treasured the brief silence. She didn't know what had gotten into her girls lately, but they seemed either to be constantly chattering or else endlessly bickering.

The hostess seated them by a window overlooking Puget Sound and the Olympic mountain range. The two girls sat together, and Cliff sat beside Diana. Once they were comfortable, they were handed huge menus. Diana's eyes skimmed over her own, and when she'd made her decision, she glanced in the girls' direction.

"Katie," she whispered, both embarrassed and amused, "honey, the napkin's not a party hat. Take it off your head."

"Oh." Katie's dark eyes were filled with chagrin.

Joan smothered a laugh, which only proved to embarrass Katie more.

"How was I supposed to know these things?" Katie demanded.

Joan opened her mouth to explain it all to her younger sibling, but Diana interceded with a scalding look that instantly silenced her oldest daughter.

Cliff set his menu aside when the waitress appeared, and after everyone had made their selection, he ordered champagne cocktails for the adults and Shirley Temples for the girls. While waiting for their drinks to arrive, Cliff placed his arm around Diana, cupping her shoulder. She raised her hand and linked her fingers with his. His touch was light, almost impersonal, but Diana wasn't fooled. Cliff was as nervous about this evening as she was. So much rested on how Joan and Katie reacted to their news.

"Cliff and I have something we'd like to tell you," Diana said softly after the waitress had placed a drink in front of each one of them. She knew how much the girls liked Cliff, but she wasn't sure how they'd feel about him becoming a major part of their lives. It had been just the three of them for a long time.

Joan took a long sip of her Shirley Temple. Her eyes were raised, but her head was lowered. She looked like a crocodile peering at them from just above the waterline. For her part, Katie was busy spreading out the linen napkin across her lap.

Diana resisted the urge to shout at them both that this was important and they should pay attention.

"Cliff and I are trying to tell you something," Diana said forcefully, gritting her teeth with impatience.

"What?"

The fact that they'd decided to get married wasn't something to be blurted out without preamble. Diana had hoped to start off by explaining to her daughters how she'd come to love Cliff and how her love would affect Joan's and Katie's life.

"Cliff and I have discovered that we love each other very much." Diana's fingers tightened around his. Just being able to say the words and not having to hide them in her heart produced a special kind of joy.

"So?" Katie murmured, lifting the tiny, plastic sword from her drink and shoving both maraschino cherries into her mouth at once.

"I already knew that," Joan said knowingly.

"So," Diana said slowly, and expelled her breath, "Cliff and I were thinking about getting married."

"And we wanted to know your feelings on the matter," he inserted, studying both Joan and Katie. He was as uptight about this evening as Diana. But the girls seemed more concerned about sucking ice cubes than listening to what their mother had to say.

Joan shrugged. "Sure, if you want to get married, I don't care."

"Me, either," Katie agreed, and juice from the two cherries slid down the side of her chin.

"Oh, gross," Joan cried, and pointedly looked in the opposite direction.

Diana's patience was quickly wearing thin. "Girls, please, we're not talking about what we're going to have for breakfast tomorrow morning. If Cliff and I do get married, it's going to be a major change in all our lives." She was about to relay that the marriage would mean they'd be moving and the girls would be changing schools, but Joan interrupted her.

"Will I get a bigger allowance?"

"Can I have a new bike?" Katie asked on the tail end of her sister's question.

"Can I tell people we're going to be rich?" Joan asked without guile.

"If we're going to be rich, then I should be able to get a new bike, shouldn't I?"

"We are not going to be wealthy because I'm marrying Cliff," Diana cried, raising her voice and doing a poor job of hiding her disappointment in her daughters. She wasn't sure what she'd expected from Joan and Katie but it certainly hadn't been indifference and greed.

"Gee, Mom, why are you so mad?" Joan asked, studying her mother with a quizzical frown. "Katie and I already knew you were in love with Cliff. We couldn't help but know from the way you've been acting all summer."

Both girls seemed to want an answer.

"I see," Diana answered softly, briefly regaining a grip on her emotions.

"Then neither of you has any objection to our getting married?" Cliff asked.

Diana was as tense as a newly strung guitar. What upset her most was the way the girls were behaving; the entire dinner was about to be ruined.

Joan and Katie shared a look and answered his question with a short shake of their heads.

"I think it'd be great if you married Mom," Joan answered. "But if it's possible, I'd like to be able to get my ears pierced before the wedding." Briefly she fondled her thin earlobe. "What do you think, Cliff?"

As an attorney, Cliff was far too wise to get drawn into those mother-daughter power games. "I think that's up to your mother."

"And you already know my feelings on the matter, Joan!"

"Okay. Okay. Sorry I asked."

Any further argument was delayed by the waitress, who delivered their order, and for a brief time, all dissension was forgotten. Katie dug into her crispy fried chicken, while Joan daintily dipped her jumbo shrimp in the small container of cocktail sauce.

"Mom, will Cliff be my father?' Joan asked a minute later, cocking her head in a thoughtful pose.

"Your stepfather."

Joan nodded and dropped her gaze, looking disappointed. "But would a stepfather be considered a real enough father for the banquet?"

It took Diana only a moment to understand Joan's question. The Girl Scout troop Joan had been involved with throughout the school year was sponsoring a father-daughter dinner at the end of the month. Diana had read the notice and not given the matter much thought. Unless someone from church volunteered to escort them, the girls generally didn't attend functions that involved fathers and daughters.

"I'm sure a stepfather will be acceptable," Cliff answered. "Would you like me to take you to the banquet?"

"Would you really?"

"I'd be more than happy to."

It seemed such a minor gesture, but a feeling of such intense gratitude filled Diana's heart that moisture pooled in her eyes. She turned to Cliff and offered him a watery smile. "Thank you," she whispered. She wanted to say more, but speaking was quickly becoming impossible.

His eyes held hers in the most tender of exchanges, and it took all the strength and good manners Cliff could muster not to kiss Diana right there in the Space Needle restaurant. His insides felt like overcooked mush. He was ready for a wife, more than ready, and he was willing to learn what it meant to be a father.

It wasn't his intention to take the memory of Stan away from Joan and Katie, nor would he be the same kind of father they'd known. He was sure to make mistakes; he wasn't perfect and this father business was new to him, but he loved Joan and Katie and he planned to care for them as long as he lived. Somewhere along the way to discovering his feelings for Diana, her daughters had neatly woven strings around his heart.

"It's because of me, isn't it?" Katie asked, waving a chicken leg in front of Diana's and Cliff's nose as though it were a weapon.

"What is?" Diana asked.

"That you and Cliff are going to get married."

"How come?" Joan asked sharply, reaching for her napkin. "I think it's because of me."

"No way!" Katie cried. "I was the one who broke my arm and Cliff came back to Mom because of that!"

"Yeah, but I was the one who called and told him you were in the hospital—so it's all my doing. If it hadn't been for me, we could have ended up with Owen, or worse yet, Dan from Wichita, as our new dad."

"Will you girls kindly stop arguing?" Diana hissed. Embarrassment coated her cheeks a shade of hot pink. People were turning around to stare at them. Diana was certain she could feel disapproving looks coming their way from the restaurant staff.

"Who did it, then?" Katie demanded.

"Yeah, who's responsible?"

Both girls stopped glaring at each other long enough to turn to look at their mother.

"In a way you're both responsible," Diana conceded, praying the two would accept the compromise.

"Ask Cliff." Once again the chicken leg was waved under their noses.

"Yeah, Cliff, what do you think?"

"I think…"

"Drop it, girls," Diana insisted in a raised voice the girls readily recognized as serious. "Immediately!"

The remainder of the dinner was a nightmare for Diana. Whereas Joan and Katie had chattered all the way into Seattle, they sat sullen and uncommunicative on the drive home to Kent. A couple of times Cliff attempted to start up a conversation, but no one seemed interested. Diana knew she wasn't.

Back at the house, Joan and Katie went upstairs to their rooms without a word.

Diana stood at the bottom of the stairs until they were out of sight and then moved into the kitchen to make coffee. Cliff followed her and placed his hands on her shoulders as she stood before the sink.

Miserable and ashamed of her children's behavior, Diana hung her head. "I am so sorry," she whispered when she could speak.

"Diana, what are you talking about?"

"The girls—"

"Were exhausted from a two-week vacation with their grandparents. You haven't been back twenty-four hours, and here we are hitting them with this." Gently his hands stroked her bare arms. He felt bad only because Diana did. "I love you, and I love the girls. Tonight was the exception, not the norm. They're good kids."

She nodded because tears were so close to the surface and arguing would have been impossible. Cliff must really love her to have put up with the way Joan and Katie had behaved. Diana couldn't remember a time when her daughters had been worse. After all these years as a single mother, Diana had prided herself on being a good parent and in one evening she'd learned the truth about her parenting skills.

"Diana," Cliff whispered, "put that mug down. I don't want any coffee. I want to hold you."

The mug felt as if it weighed a thousand pounds when Diana set it on the counter. Slowly she turned, keeping her eyes on the kitchen floor, unable to meet his gaze.

His arms folded around her, bringing her against him. He didn't make any demands on her, content for the moment to offer comfort. His chin slowly brushed against the top of her head, while his hands roved in circles across her back. The action had meant to be consoling, but Cliff had learned long before that he couldn't hold Diana without wanting her. Diana looped her arms around his neck and directed his mouth to hers. The kiss was possessive, filled with frustration and undisguised need. Diana shuddered at the wild, consuming kiss.

Cliff was pacing outside the gates of heaven. He loved this woman, needed her physically, mentally, emotionally— every way there was to need another human being. But she was driving him crazy The drugged kiss went on unbroken, and so did the way she moved against him. "Diana," He pulled his mouth from hers and buried his face in her shoulder while he came to grips with himself.

They remained clenched in each other's arms until their strained, uneven breathing calmed. Gathering her courage, Diana tilted back her head until she found his eyes.

Cliff smiled at her, bathing her in his love. His thumb brushed the corners of her mouth, needing to touch her.

Little could have gone worse tonight, and Diana felt terrible. "You don't have to go through with it, you know."

He frowned, not understanding.

"With the wedding… After tonight, I wouldn't blame you if you backed out. I think if the situation were reversed, I'd consider it."

Cliff's frown deepened. She had to be nuts! He'd just found her and he had no intention of doing as she suggested. He saw the doubt in her eyes that told him of her uncertainty. He met her gaze steadily, his own serious. "No way, Diana," he whispered, and cupped her face, tilting her head upward to meet his descending mouth. The kiss was deep and long, warm and moist. When he broke away, his shoulders were heaving and his breathing was fast and harsh. He didn't move a muscle for the longest moment. Then, slowly, regretfully, he dropped his arms.

"I'd better go," he said with heavy reluctance. It was either go now or break his promise to her.

Diana wanted him to stay, needed him with her, but she couldn't ask it of him. Not tonight, when everything else had gone so wrong. Wordlessly she followed him to the front door.

He paused and lifted his hand to caress her sweet face. Diana placed her own over his and closed her eyes.

"I'll call you tomorrow."

She nodded.

"Mom, when will Cliff be here?"

Diana finished removing Joan's hair from the hot curler before glancing at her wristwatch. "He's due in another hour."

"Do you think he'll like my dress?"

"I'm sure he'll love it. You always did look so pretty in pink."

"Really?"

Diana couldn't remember Joan ever being more anxious for anything. The Girl Scout banquet was a special night for her daughter and for Cliff. The wedding was set for the second week of August; they'd found a house near Des Moines that everyone was thrilled with, and they planned to make the big move before the first day of school. Diana had already started some of the packing.

Her parents were flying out for the ceremony, as were Cliff's. His brother, Rich, and his wife and family were driving up from California. But for Joan, the wedding and all the planned activities that went along with it ran a close second to the father-daughter banquet. Cliff had told her he was ordering an orchid for Joan, and out of her allowance money Joan had proudly purchased a white rose boutonniere for Cliff.

The phone pealed in the distance, and a minute later Katie stuck her head in the bathroom door. "It's for you, Mom. It's Cliff." Katie paused and glanced at her elder sister. "Wow, you look almost grown up."

"You really think so, Katie?"

Smiling, Diana hurried into the upstairs hallway and picked up the telephone receiver. "Hi, there. Oh, Cliff, you wouldn't believe how pretty Joan looks. I've never seen her—"

"Diana, listen…"

"She's more excited than on Christmas morning—"

"Diana." This time his voice was sharp, sharper than he'd intended. He was in one heck of a position, torn between his job and his desire to be with Joan for her special night. He didn't mean to blurt it out, but there didn't seem to be any other way to say it. "I can't make it tonight."

Diana was so stunned she sagged against the wall and closed her eyes. "What do you mean you can't make it?" she asked after a tortuous moment when the terrible truth had begun to sink in. Surely she'd misunderstood him. She hoped there was some kind of mix-up and she hadn't heard him right.

"The senior vice president has asked me to take over a case that's going to the state supreme court. I just found out about it. The first briefing is tonight."

"But surely you can get out of one meeting."

"It's the most important one. I tried, Diana."

"But what about Joan?" This couldn't be happening—it just couldn't. The new dress, Joan's first pair of panty hose, her hair freshly permed and set in hot rollers. "What about the father-daughter banquet?"

Cliff couldn't feel any worse than he already did. "I phoned George Holiday, and he's agreed to take her. There will be other banquets."

"But Joan wants to go with you."

"Believe me, if I could, I'd take her. But I can't." He was growing impatient now, more angry at the circumstances than with Diana, who couldn't seem to believe or accept what he was telling her.

"But surely they'd have let you know about something this important before now."

"Diana, I'll explain it to Joan later. I've got to get back to the meeting. I'm late now. Honey, believe me, I'm as upset about this as you are."

"Cliff," she cried, "please, you can't do this to her." But it was too late, the line had already been disconnected. When she turned around, Diana discovered Joan watching her with wide brown eyes filled with horror and distress.

"Cliff's not going, is he?" she asked in a pained whisper.

"No...he's got an important meeting."

Without a word, Joan turned and walked into her bedroom and closed the door.

The minute it was feasibly possible, Cliff prepared to leave the meeting. He shoved the papers into his briefcase and left with no more than the minimal pleasantries. He felt like a heel. His conscience had been punishing him all night. Okay, okay, it wasn't his fault, but he hadn't wanted to disappoint Joan. His only comfort was that he'd be able to take her to the father-daughter banquet the following year and the year after that. Surely she'd understand this once and be willing to look past her disappointment.

The porch light was on at Diana's, and he hurriedly parked the car. To his surprise, Diana met him at the front door. She looked calm, but she didn't fool him; he knew her too well. Anger simmered just below the surface. He'd hoped she would be more understanding, but he'd deal with her later. First he had to talk to her daughter.

"Where's Joan?"

"In her room. She cried herself to sleep."

"Oh, no." Cliff groaned. He moved past Diana and up the stairs into the eleven-year-old's bedroom. The room was dark, and he left the light off and sat on the corner of her mattress. His heart felt heavy and constricted with regret as he brushed the curls off her forehead.

"We need to talk," Diana whispered from outside the doorway. Her arms were crossed over her chest and her feet were braced apart, as though to fend off an attack.

"How did the banquet go?" he asked as he followed her down the stairs.

Diana shrugged. "Fine, I guess. Joan hardly said a word when she got home."

"Honey, I'm sorry, I really am. This kind of thing doesn't come up that often, but when it does, there's nothing I can do."

"You broke her heart."

Cliff didn't need Diana piling on any more guilt than what he already had. It wasn't as though he'd deliberately gone out of his way to disappoint Joan. He certainly would rather have spent the night with Diana's daughter than cooped up in a stuffy, smoke-filled office.

"I know a banquet with an eleven-year-old girl isn't high on your priority list…"

"Diana, that's not true—"

"No…you listen to me. You want to break a date with me, then fine. I'm mature enough to accept it. But I can't allow you to hurt one of my children. I absolutely refuse to allow it."

Cliff ran his fingers through his hair and angrily expelled his breath. "You're making it sound like I deliberately planned this meeting just so I could get out of the banquet."

"All I know," Diana said, holding in the anger as best she could, "is that if it had been Stan, he would have been here!"

Stan's name hit Cliff with all the force of a brick hurled against the back of his head. He reeled with the impact and the shock of the pain. "Are you going to throw his name at me every time something goes wrong?"

"I don't know," she murmured. "All I know is that I don't want you to hurt Joan and Katie."

"You're making it sound like I'm looking for the opportunity."

"I've had all night to think about what I want to say," Diana confessed, dropping her gaze, unable to meet the cutting, narrowed look he was giving her. "All of a sudden I'm not so sure marriage would be the best thing for me and the girls."

Cliff knotted his hands into tight, impotent fists. "Okay, you want to call off the wedding, then fine."

His willingness shocked her. "I don't know what I want."

"Well, you'd better hurry up and decide."

A horrible silence stretched between them like a rolling, twisting fog, blinding them from the truth and obliterating the love that had once seemed so strong and invincible.

"I'll give you a week," Cliff announced. "You can let me know then what you want to do." With that, he turned and walked out the front door.

Thirteen

"Are you making poached eggs again?" Joan whined when she came down the stairs for breakfast.

"Yes," Diana said. "How'd you know?"

"Oh, Mom, honestly." The preteen plopped down at the kitchen table and shook her head knowingly. "You always make poached eggs when you're upset. It's a form of self-punishment—at least, that's what I think. Katie says it's because you still haven't made up with Cliff." She paused to study her mother. "Katie's right, too. You know that, don't you?"

Mumbling something unintelligible under her breath, Diana cracked two raw eggs over the boiling water. A frown gently creased her forehead. "Just how many times this week have I served poached eggs?"

"Three," Joan came back quickly. "Which is exactly as many days since you and Cliff had your big fight."

"We didn't have a big fight," Diana answered in a calm, reasonable voice.

Joan shrugged and took a long drink of her orange juice before answering. "I heard you. You and Cliff were shouting at each other—well, maybe not shouting, but your voices were raised, and I could hear you all the way up-stairs." She paused as though considering whether to add a commentary. "Mom, I think you were wrong to talk to Cliff that way."

Diana groaned and scraped the butter across the top of the hot toast. "This isn't a subject I want to discuss with you, Joan."

"But I saw Cliff when he came into my bedroom, and he felt terrible about missing the banquet."

"I thought you were asleep!"

"I wasn't really... I had my eyes closed and everything, but I was peeking up at him through my lashes. He felt really bad. Even I could see that."

Diana wielded the butter knife like a sword, waving it at her daughter. "You should have said something then."

Looking guilty, Joan reached for her orange juice a second time. "I was going to, but you started talking and saying all those mean things to Cliff, and I was glad because I was still angry with him." She paused and sighed. "Now I wish I'd let him know I was awake. Then maybe I wouldn't be eating poached eggs every morning."

Diana served her daughters breakfast, but she didn't bother to eat any herself. She didn't need a week to decide if she wanted to marry Cliff. Within twenty-four hours after their argument, she recognized that she'd behaved badly. Joan and Katie were far more than willing to confirm her suspicions about the way she'd acted. Diana was forced into admitting she'd been unreasonable. More than anything, she deeply regretted throwing Stan's name at Cliff. Beyond whatever else she'd said, that had been completely unfair. She owed Cliff an apology, but making one had never come easy to her—the words seemed to stick in her throat. But if she didn't do it soon, she'd have a mutiny on her hands. Already Katie had hinted that she was going to move in with Mrs. Holiday if she had to eat poached eggs one more morning.

The girls went swimming that afternoon, and while they were at the pool, Diana paced the kitchen floor, gathering up the courage to contact Cliff. With a stiff finger, she punched out the number to his office as she rehearsed again and again what she planned to say.

"Hello," she said in a light, cheerful voice. "This is Diana Collins for Cliff Howard."

"I'll connect you with one of his staff," the tinny receptionist's voice returned.

Diana was forced to ask for him a second time.

"Mr. Howard's in a meeting," his secretary explained in a crisp professional tone. "Would you like to leave a message?"

"Please have him return my call," Diana murmured, defeated. She was convinced Cliff had given his secretary specific instructions to inform her that he was out of the office. The suspicion was confirmed when, hours later, she still hadn't heard from him. He'd said a week, and he seemed determined to make her wait that long, Diana mused darkly after Joan and Katie were in bed asleep. He wanted her to sweat it out. Either that, or he'd decided to cut his losses and completely wash his hands of her.

Depressed and discouraged, Diana sat in front of the television, flipping channels, until she stumbled upon an old World War II movie. For an hour she immersed her woes in the classic battle scenes and felt tears course down her cheeks when the hero died a valiant death. The tears were a welcome release. Once she started, she couldn't seem to stop. Soon there was a growing pile of damp tissue on the end table beside her chair.

The doorbell caught her by surprise. There was only one person it could be. Cliff. Loudly she blew her nose, then quickly rubbed her open hands down her cheeks to wipe away the extra moisture. With her head tilted at a regal angle, she moved into the entryway, her heart pounding at a staccato beat.

"Hello."

Cliff took one look at her and blinked. "Are you okay?"

She nodded and pointed to the television behind her. "John Wayne just bit the dust, but he took the entire German army with him."

Cliff stepped inside the house. "I see."

He looked good, Diana thought unkindly. The very least he could do was show a little regret—a few worry lines around the mouth. Even a couple of newly formed crow's-feet at his eyes would have satisfied her. At the very least, he could say something to let her know he'd been just as miserable as she. Instead he was the picture of a man who had recently returned from a two-week vacation in the Caribbean. He was tan, relaxed, lean and so handsome he stole her breath.

"I understand you called the office," he said stiffly.

Diana nodded, but couldn't manage to get the practiced apology past the clog in her throat.

"You wanted something?"

Again she nodded. His expression was tightening—she was losing him fast. Either she had to blurt out how sorry she was, or she was going to let the most fantastic man she'd ever met silently slip out of her life.

"Is it so difficult to tell me?"

Confused, she nodded, then abruptly shook her head.

Cliff released a giant sigh of frustration and impatience, then reached for her, gripping her shoulders. His fingers dug deep into the soft flesh of her upper arms. "I'm not letting you go this easily."

"What?" She blinked at the shock of his harsh treatment.

"I know what you're going to say and I refuse to accept it."

She slapped her hand over her heart, her eyes as round and as wide as full moons. "You know what I'm going to say?"

In response, he nodded, released her shoulders and instead captured her face. If she'd wished to witness his pain and regret, she saw it now. It filled his face, twisting his mouth and hardening his jaw. "I love you, Diana." With that, he lowered his mouth to hers in a punishing kiss that robbed her of her breath and her wits.

Cliff groaned, and Diana slipped her arms around his neck, melting her body intimately against his. "Cliff." Reluctantly she broke away, lifting her soft brown eyes to capture his. Her hands bracketed his face as a slow, sweet smile turned up the corners of her mouth. "I love you so much. I'm so sorry for what happened— I was unreasonable. Forgive me. Please."

Shock and disbelief flickered briefly across his taut features.

"You can't honestly believe I'm going to cancel the wedding," she whispered, humbled by this man and his love for her. "The reason I called you today was to tell you how much I love you." The moisture that brightened her eyes now had nothing to do with the emotion brought on by the sentimental movie. These tears came all the way from her heart.

Cliff looked for a moment as though he didn't believe her. He kissed her again because he couldn't remain with his arms wrapped around her and not sample her familiar sweet taste. He felt weak with relief and, at the same moment, filled with an incredible, invincible strength.

Cliff's kiss filled Diana with desire, left every muscle in her body quivering. Her passion matched his. Cliff pressed his lips over hers in mounting fervor, and Diana rose onto her toes to align herself more intimately with his body.

"Diana." He groaned and tore his mouth from hers. "We...we have things to settle here."

"Shh." She kissed him hungrily, slanting her mouth over his as she wove her fingers through his thick hair, savoring the feel and taste of him.

Cliff could refuse her nothing. The golden glow of a crescent moon outlined her beautiful face. Cliff released a deep sigh of awe at the priceless gift she was granting him—herself, without restraint, without restriction.

"Let's go upstairs," she whispered.

Cliff blinked and raised his hands to capture her face, holding her steady so he could look into her passion-drugged eyes. When he spoke, his voice was husky and deep. "Aren't the girls up there?"

"Yes, but...?"

Their breaths warmed each other's mouths. "I can't believe I'm doing this," he groaned, and closed his eyes to a silent agony.

"Doing what?"

"Refusing you."

"Cliff, no." Diana couldn't believe it, either. After all the times he'd tried to seduce her, now he was turning her down. "Why?" she choked. "I want you."

"Believe me, honey, I want you, too—so much it hurts." He spoke through clenched teeth, his hands gripping her upper arms. Diana went still in his arms, and he relaxed as though a great tension had eased from him.

"Not the first time we make love," he murmured into her hair, his voice low and raw. "Not like this. We'll be married in ten days. I can wait."

"I don't know that I can," she complained.

"Yes, you can. The loving is going to be very good between us."

If it was going to be like it had been tonight, Diana didn't know if she'd survive the honeymoon.

It took Cliff almost an hour to find the headstone. He'd wandered around the graveyard in the early morning sunlight, intent on his task. Today was to be his wedding day. Friends and relatives crowded around him at every turn. His sane, sensible mother had become a clucking hen. His father kept slapping him across the back, smiling and looking proud. Even his brother seemed to follow him around like a pesky shadow, just the way he'd done in their youth. There were a thousand things left to be done on this day, but none so important as this.

Now that he'd located the place, Cliff wasn't sure what had driven him here. He squatted and read the words engraved with such perfection into the white marble: STANLEY DAVID COLLINS, HUSBAND, FATHER. The date of his birth and death were listed. No epitaph, no scripture verse, just the blunt facts of one man's life.

Slowly Cliff stood and placed his hands in his pockets as he gazed down at the headstone. His heart swelled with strong emotion, and in that space of time, he knew what had driven him to this cemetery on this day. He hadn't come to seek solitude from all the hustle and bustle, nor had he sought escape from the people who had suddenly filled his home. He didn't need a graveyard to be alone. He'd come to talk to Stan Collins. He'd come because he had to.

"I wish I'd known you," he said, feeling awkward, the words low and gruff. "I think we would have been friends." From what he'd learned from George Holiday and the information he'd gleaned from Diana and the girls, Stan had been a good man, the type Cliff would gladly have counted as a friend.

Only silence greeted him. Cliff wasn't sure what he'd expected, certainly no voice booming from heaven, no sounds from the grave. But something—he just didn't know what.

"You must have hated leaving her," he said next. He didn't know much about Stan's death, only bits and pieces he'd picked up from Diana the day he'd gone to the hospital when Katie had broken her arm. Between Diana's non-sensical statements and her panic, he'd learned that she hadn't been able to see Stan when they'd brought him into the emergency room. There'd been no time for goodbyes. The realization twisted a tight knot in Cliff's stomach. "I know what thoughts must have been in your mind." He bowed his head at the grim realization of death. "I would have been filled with regrets, too."

A strange peace settled over Cliff, a peace beyond words. He relaxed, and a grin curved his mouth. "You'd be amazed at Joan and Katie. They're quite the young ladies now." Diana was letting both girls stand up with her today as maid of honor and bridesmaid. She'd sewn them each a beautiful long pink dress with lace overlays. Joan had claimed she looked at least fourteen. Heels, panty hose, the whole nine yards. Katie was excited about getting her hair done in a beauty shop. Cliff laughed out loud at the memory of the eight-year-old insisting they serve Kentucky Fried Chicken at the wedding reception. Joan had been thrilled with the prospect of having an extra set of grandparents at Christmastime. Within minutes both girls had had his parents eating out of their hands. They'd been enthralled with Diana's two daughters from the minute they'd been introduced.

"You'd have reason to be proud of your girls," he said thoughtfully. "They're fantastic kids."

The humor drained from his eyes as his gaze fell once more to the engraved words on the headstone. The word *father* seemed to leap out at him. "I guess what I want to say is that I don't plan on trying to steal you away from Joan and Katie." Stan would always be their father; he had loved his children more than Cliff would ever know until he and Diana had their own. Now Cliff would be the one to raise Joan and Katie and love and nurture them into adulthood, guiding them with a gentle hand. "I know what you're thinking," he said aloud. "I can't say I blame you. I'm new to this fatherhood business. I can't do anything more than promise I'll do my best."

Now that he'd gotten past the girls, Cliff was faced with the real reason he had come. "I love Diana," he said plainly. "I didn't expect to, and I imagine you'd be more than willing to punch me out for some of the things I've tried with her. I apologize for that." His hands knotted into tight fists inside his pants pockets. "I honestly love her," he repeated, and sucked in a huge breath. "And I know you did, too."

The sun had risen above the hills now, bathing the morning mist with its warm, golden light so that the grass glistened. After a long reverent moment, Cliff turned and traced his steps back to the parking lot.

He took a leisurely drive back to his condominium and found his brother parked outside waiting for him.

"Where have you been?" Rich demanded. "I've been all over looking for you. In case you've forgotten, this is your wedding day."

Undisturbed, Cliff climbed out of his car and dropped the keys into his pants pocket.

Still Rich wasn't appeased. "I didn't know what to think when I couldn't find you." He checked his watch. "We were supposed to meet Mom and Dad ten minutes ago."

"Did you think I'd run away?" Cliff joked.

"Yes. No. I didn't know what to think. Where the blazes did you go that was so all-fired important?"

Cliff smiled into the sun. "To talk to a friend."

"Mom, I've got a run in my panty hose," Joan cried, her young voice filled with distress. "What am I supposed to do now?"

"I don't like the feel of hair spray," Katie commented for the tenth time, bouncing her hand off the top of her head several times just to see what would happen to the carefully styled but stiff curls.

"I've got an extra pair of nylons in the drawer," Diana answered Joan first. "Katie, keep your hands out of your hair!" Her mother was due any minute, and Diana didn't know when she'd been more glad to see either parent. Surprisingly, she wasn't nervous. She was more confident about marrying Cliff than any decision she'd made in the past three years. He loved her, and together they would build a good life together.

"You're not wearing your pearl earrings," Joan said with astonishment, and loudly slapped her sides. "Good grief, is any date more important than this one?"

Diana wrinkled her brow. "What do you mean?"

"Don't you remember? Honestly, Mom! I wanted you to wear the pearls the first night you went to dinner with Cliff, and you told me you wanted to wait for something festive to impress him."

Diana smiled at the memory. "I think you're right," she said, and traded the small gold pair for the pearls. "Nothing's more important than today." Her knees felt weak, not with doubts, but with excitement, and she sat on the corner of the mattress. "How do you girls feel?" she asked, watching her two daughters carefully.

"We're doing the right thing," Joan said with all the confidence of a five-star general. "Cliff's about the best we're going to do."

"What?" Diana asked with a small, hysterical laugh.

"Really, Mom," Katie came back. "For a while, I thought we'd get stuck with that Danny fellow from Wichita."

"Or Owen," Joan added. Both girls looked at each other and made silly faces and cried, "Oou!"

"Who's Owen?" Diana's mother asked as she stepped into the bedroom.

"He's the major geek I was telling you about who brought the references," Joan explained before Diana had the chance. He really was a dear man and someday he'd find the right woman. Fortunately, according to Joan and Katie, it wasn't her.

"Ah, yes," Joyce said, sharing a secret smile with her daughter. "You look lovely, sweetheart."

"Thanks," Joan answered automatically, then looked and gave her grandmother a chagrined smile. "Oh, you mean my mom."

"All three of you look beautiful."

Joan and Katie beamed at the praise.

"Watch, Grandma," Katie said. Tucking her arms close to her side, Katie whirled around a couple of times so the hemline of her dress flared out.

"Stop behaving like an eight-year-old," Joan cried. "You're supposed to be mature today."

"But I am eight!"

Joan opened her mouth to object, then realized she'd already lost one of her press-on fingernails. For a wild minute, there was a desperate search for the thumbnail. Peace ruled once they located it.

"Mother, would you check Katie's hair?" Diana asked. "She can't seem to keep her fingers out of it."

"Sure. Katie," Joyce called to her granddaughter, "let's go into the ladies' room."

Three hours later, Diana stood in front of the pastor who had seen her through life and death in the church where she sat each Sunday morning. Her parents, Cliff's family and a small assortment of close friends were gathered behind them. Joan and Katie stood proudly at her side.

The man of God warmed them all with a rare, tranquil smile. Diana turned, and her gaze happened to catch Cliff's. He did love her, more than she'd ever dared to dream, more than she'd ever thought possible. He stood tall and proud and eagerly held her eyes, his love shining through for her to read without doubt, without question. He was prepared to pledge his life to her and Joan and Katie. The commitment she sought he was about to willingly vow.

Witnessing all the love in Cliff's eyes had a chastising effect upon Diana. The man she'd once considered an unscrupulous womanizer had chosen her to share his life. He was prepared to love her no matter what the future held for them, prepared to raise her daughters and guide their young lives. Out of all the beautiful women he'd known, Cliff had chosen her. Diana didn't know what she'd done to deserve such a good man, but she would always be grateful. Always.

The minister opened his Bible, and Diana focused her attention on the man of the cloth. Her heart was full. Happiness had come to her a second time when she'd least expected it.

When the moment came, Cliff repeated his vows in a firm, assured voice, then silently slipped the solitary diamond on her finger. Diana prepared to do the same.

Her pastor's words echoed through the church. When he asked her if she would take Cliff as her lawfully wedded husband, she opened her mouth to say in an even, controlled voice that she would. However, she wasn't given the chance.

Joan spoke first. "She does."

Katie chimed in. "We all do."

Fourteen

So much for the small, intimate wedding party, Cliff thought good-naturedly several hours later. Everywhere he looked, there were family and friends pressed around him and Diana, shaking his hand, kissing Diana's cheek and offering words of congratulations. Each wished to share in their day and their happiness, and Cliff was pleased to let them. If it wasn't their guests pressing in around them, then it was Joan and Katie. The two popped up all over the hall, jostling gaily around the room like court jesters. Every now and again Cliff captured Diana's gaze, and the aching gentleness he saw in her eyes tore at his soul. Beyond a doubt, he knew that she was just as eager to escape as he was.

Other than their meeting in the church, Diana hadn't had more than a moment to talk to this man who was now her husband. They stood beside each other in the long reception line and were so busy greeting those they loved that there wasn't an opportunity to speak to each other.

When there was a small break in the line of relations and friends, Cliff leaned close and whispered in her ear, but she scarcely recognized his voice. His aching whisper was filled with raw emotion. "I adore you, Mrs. Howard."

Her eyes flew to his as the shattering tenderness of his words enveloped her. So many things were stored in her heart, so much love she longed to share. Because she couldn't say everything she wanted to, Diana moved closer to Cliff's side. Very lightly she pressed her hip against his. Cliff slipped his hand around her waist, drawing her nearer and tighter to him. For the moment at least, they were both content.

Hours later they arrived at the hotel room, exhausted but excited. A bottle of the finest French champagne, a gift from Cliff's brother, awaited them, resting in a bed of crushed ice.

Cliff gave the champagne no more than a fleeting glance. He wasn't interested in drinking—the only thing he wanted was his wife. He wrapped his arms around Diana and kissed her hungrily, the way he'd been fantasizing about doing all afternoon. He was starving for her, famished, ravished by his need.

Diana eagerly met his warm lips, twining her arms around his neck and tangling her fingers in the thick softness of his dark hair. She luxuriated in the secure feel of his arms, holding her so close she could barely breathe. She smiled up at him dreamily and sighed.

"I didn't think we were ever going to be alone," she whispered, her voice shaky with desire. Pausing, she pressed her face against the side of his strong neck.

"Me, either." His voice wasn't any more controlled than hers. His gaze fell on the bed, and the desire to make love with Diana wrapped itself around him like a fisherman's net, trapping him. He didn't want to rush Diana—he'd hoped their lovemaking would happen naturally. It was only late afternoon. They should have a drink and a leisurely dinner first, but Cliff doubted that he could make it through the first course. "Shall we have a drink?" he asked, easing her from his arms. Over and over again, he silently told himself to be patient, to go slow. There was no reason to rush into this when they had all the time in the world.

"I don't want any champagne," Diana answered in a husky whisper.

"You don't?"

Smiling, she shook her head. "I want *you*. Now. Don't make me wait any longer."

Cliff's knees went weak with relief, and he turned to face her. His heart pounded like a giant jackhammer in his chest.

"Oh, Cliff," she murmured, holding out her arms in silent invitation. "I don't think I can wait a minute more. I love you so much."

His eyes glowed with the fire of his passion as he reached for her. He kissed her once, twice, hardly giving her a chance to breathe. Their bodies strained against each other, needing and giving more.

Wildly Diana returned his kisses, on fire for her husband, desiring him in a way that went beyond physical passion.

In response to Diana, Cliff wrapped his arms around her, bringing her close to him so she would know beyond a doubt how much he longed to make her his. Somehow, while still kissing, they started to undress each other. Deftly Diana loosened his necktie, rid him of his suit jacket and unfastened the buttons of his shirt. When she splayed her hands over his bare chest, she sighed and reveled in the firm, hard feel of him.

With some difficulty, Cliff located the zipper in the back of Diana's dress and fumbled with it. Diana sighed into his mouth and reluctantly tore her lips from his. She whirled around, sweeping up the hair at the base of her neck to assist him and resisted the urge to stamp her foot and demand that he please hurry.

Their clothes were carelessly tossed around the room one piece at a time. By the time they'd finished, Diana was breathless and weak with anticipation. She'd thought to hide her imperfect body from Cliff, eager to climb between the sheets and hide, but he wouldn't allow it.

Cliff broke away long enough to study Diana. His sharp features, hardened now with excitement, softened with indescribable tenderness. Just looking at her made the breath catch in his throat and the blood surge through his veins in a violent rush. His senses were filled with the sight of her as his eyes swept her body in one long, passionate caress. His breath was labored when he spoke. "You're so beautiful."

"Oh, Cliff." Tears pooled in her eyes. Her body carried the marks of childbirth, but her husband saw none of her flaws. He viewed her with such a gentle love that he was blinded to her imperfections. Her heart constricted with emotion, and Diana was certain she couldn't have loved Cliff Howard more than she did at that precise moment.

His self-control was cracking, Cliff realized as he pulled back the sheets from the king-size bed and tossed the pillows aside. He wanted Diana so much his breath came quickly, no matter how hard he tried to slow it, and his heart beat high in his throat. He kissed Diana again and pressed her back against the mattress. After the lovemaking their arms and legs remained tangled as they lay on their sides facing one another. Cliff was trapped in the web of overpowering sensation. He saw her tears and felt his chest tighten with such a tender love that he could have died at the moment and not suffered a regret. Everything in his life until this one moment seemed shallow and worthless. The love he shared with Diana was the only important thing there would ever be for him. He'd found more than a wife; he'd found his life's purpose, his home.

Murmuring her love, Diana slipped her arms around his neck and pulled his head to hers. Her kiss was full, holding back nothing. Again and again Cliff kissed her. They were soft, nibbling kisses; the urgency of their lovemaking had been removed. They both slept and woke late in the evening. While Diana soaked in a hot bathtub, Cliff ordered their dinner from room service. Her stomach growled as the smell of their meal wafted into the large pink bathroom. She was preparing to climb out of the water, when Cliff came to her, holding a fat, succulent shrimp.

"Hungry?" he asked,

Diana nodded eagerly. It'd been hours since she'd last eaten—morning, to be exact—and at the time she'd been too excited to down anything more than a glass of orange juice.

"Good." He plopped the shrimp in his mouth and greedily licked the sauce from the ends of his fingers. Darting a glance in her direction, he laughed aloud at her look of righteous indignation.

He left the room and returned a couple of moments later with an extra shrimp, taking delight in feeding it to her. Diana hurriedly dried off and dressed in a whispery soft peignoir of sheer blue. The lacy gown had been a gift from Shirley Holiday, with instructions for her to wear it on her wedding night.

When she reappeared, Cliff had poured them each a glass of champagne. He turned to hand her hers and stopped abruptly when he viewed her in the sheer nightgown, his eyes rounding with undisguised appreciation.

"Do you like it?" she asked, and did one slow, sultry turn for effect.

Cliff only nodded; to speak was nearly impossible.

Diana took a sip of the champagne and pulled out a chair. One by one, she started lifting domed lids to discover what he'd ordered. "Oh, Cliff, I'm starved."

He dragged his gaze from the dark shadow of her nipples back to their meal. His gaze fell to the table. Food. Their dinner.

"Filet mignon," Diana said, and sighed her appreciation. "I can't believe how famished I am." She looked up to discover her husband's eyes burning a trail over her.

Cliff moistened his lips. Diana's gown teased him with a soft cloud of thin material that fell open to reveal her thigh and the top of her hip. He found he couldn't tear his eyes off her. Wistfully he cast a glance at the bed. He dared not suggest it—not so soon after the last time. Diana would think he was some kind of animal.

"Cliff?" Diana whispered.

He squared his shoulders and forced a smile.

"Cliff Howard." Although he made a gallant effort to disguise what he wanted Diana knew. This man was a marvel. "Now?"

He looked almost boyish. "Do you mind?"

She glanced longingly at her dinner, grabbed a second shrimp and smiled. Standing, she reached for his hand and led him toward the bed.

"Married life seems to agree with you," Shirley Holiday commented three weeks later, after Cliff and Diana had returned from their honeymoon.

There'd been some adjustments, Diana mused. They'd recently moved into their two-story house, situated between Des Moines, and Salt Water State Park and were still unpacking. The girls had settled into their new school and were learning to adjust to sharing their mother, which was something they hadn't realized would happen once she and Cliff had married.

"It has its moments," Diana agreed. Like the first night they were in their new house! Cliff had just started to make love to her, when Katie burst into the bedroom, crying because of a bad dream. Cliff murmured something about having a nightmare of his own, while Diana scrambled for some clothes. The first thing the following morning, Cliff had put a lock on the bedroom door. Then, later in the same week, Diana and Shirley had planned on hitting a sale at Nordstrom's, when Cliff had shown up at the house unexpectedly. She'd thought, at first, that he'd come to take her to lunch, but he'd had other plans. Giggling, Diana had phoned her friend and said she'd be a few minutes late.

"I can't remember the last time I saw you this happy," Shirley said with an expressive sigh. "You know, I feel responsible for all this."

"For what?" Diana asked, joining her friend at the kitchen table.

"For the two of you getting together."

It took a supreme effort on Diana's part not to remind her former neighbor that she had done everything within her power to discourage Diana's relationship with the known playboy and womanizer, Cliff Howard.

"So when do you start your college classes?" Shirley asked while Diana poured them each a second cup of coffee.

The bride glanced in the direction of the kitchen calendar that hung beside the phone. "In a couple of weeks." After the wedding, Cliff had insisted Diana give up her job with the school district. As far as her future was concerned, Cliff had other plans.

"I think it's wonderful the way Cliff's encouraging you

to go back to school. How long will it take you to get your nursing degree?"

Grinning, Diana propped her elbows on top of the oak table. "About ten years, the way we plan it."

Shirley's eyes widened with surprise. "That long—but whatever for?"

"I plan to take a couple of long breaks in between semesters."

"But, Diana, that doesn't make sense. This is a golden opportunity for you. I'd think…"

"Shirley!" Diana stopped her. "We're planning on me having a baby as soon as possible." And another the following year, if everything went according to their schedule. From the way Cliff had been working at the project, Diana believed she was bound to be pregnant by the end of the month. Not that she was complaining. The lovemaking between them was exquisite, just as she'd always known it would be. Each time her husband reached for her, she marveled at how virile he was. And how gentle.

The conversation between the two women was interrupted by Cliff, George and the girls, who came through the front door, returning from a golfing match.

"We're back," Cliff said, leaning over the chair and kissing Diana's cheek.

"Cliff let me drive his golf cart," Joan announced proudly as she entered the kitchen. "It's only a few more years, you realize, till I'll be old enough for my driver's permit."

"All Cliff let me do was steer," Katie complained, plopping herself down in the seat beside her mother.

"Next year you can drive the cart," Cliff told her.

Katie responded by folding her arms and pinching her

lips together in a pretty pout. "It's not fair. Joan gets to do everything."

"The older one always does," Joan answered with a superior air.

"Are you going to let her talk to me that way?" Katie demanded. "Just what kind of a mother are you?"

"Girls, girls," Cliff said, without raising his voice. Joan and Katie stopped arguing, but when they didn't think he could see, Katie stuck her tongue out at Joan, and Joan eagerly reciprocated.

Cliff did his best to disguise a smile. He was smiling a lot lately. Marrying Diana and taking on the responsibility for Joan and Katie had changed him. There'd been so many wasted years when he'd drifted from one meaningless relationship to another, seeking an elusive happiness, finding himself chasing after the pot of gold at the end of the rainbow. But now he'd found real love, experienced it firsthand, and it had altered the course of his life.

That night, Diana fell asleep in her husband's arms. A loud clap of thunder woke her around midnight. She rolled onto her back and rubbed the sleep from her face.

"I wondered if the storm would wake you," Cliff whispered, raising himself up on one elbow in order to kiss her.

Diana kissed him back and looped an arm around his neck. "Have you been awake long?"

"About five minutes." Once more, his mouth tenderly grazed hers. "Have I told you lately how much I love you?"

"You *showed* me a couple of hours ago!"

He nuzzled her neck and the familiar hot sensation raced through Diana, and she sighed her pleasure.

Cliff kissed her in earnest then, wrapping her in his

arms. "What have you done to me?" He growled the question in her ear. "I can't seem to get enough of you."

"Do you hear me complaining?" Completely at ease now with his body, she touched and kissed him in places she knew would evoke a strong reaction.

"You little devil," Cliff whispered raggedly.

"Want me to stop?"

"No," he answered on a low growl. "I'm crazy about you, woman."

Diana stiffened and turned her head toward the bedroom door.

Cliff was instantly aware of the change in her mood. "What is it?"

"Katie."

"I didn't hear her."

"She's frightened of storms." Already Diana was freeing herself from his arms.

Mumbling under his breath, Cliff rolled onto his back and swallowed down the momentary frustration. "I'm beginning to relive a nightmare of my own. When are you going to be back?"

"In a minute." Diana climbed out of the bed and reached for her robe.

"Give me a kiss before you go," Cliff insisted, then yawned loudly. "Wake me if I go back to sleep."

Diana willingly obliged. "I shouldn't be long."

"Hurry," he coaxed, and yawned a second time.

Diana was gone only a matter of minutes, but by the time she returned and slipped between the sheets, Cliff was snoozing.

"Sweetheart," she whispered, gently shaking him awake.

He rolled over and automatically reached for her.

"Honey," Diana murmured.

"Just a minute," he whispered sleepily. "I need to wake up." He nibbled softly on her earlobe.

"It's Katie," Diana told him.

"What about her?"

"She's frightened by the storm."

"I'm frightened, too, but I understand—go ahead and go back to comfort Katie."

Diana pushed the hair from his face and gently kissed the side of his jaw. "She doesn't want me—she requested you."

"Me?"

"You."

A slow, easy smile broke out across Cliff's handsome features. Comforting his daughter in a storm. It was exactly the kind of thing a father would do.

* * * * *

ALMOST AN ANGEL

One

Bethany Stone's nimble fingers flew over the computer keys. Tears blurred her soft blue eyes as she typed the few short sentences that would terminate her employment with Norris Pharmaceutical Company and J. D. Norris. This was it. The end. She'd had it up to her ears and beyond!

Any woman who would waste her life for a man who treated her like a robot deserved to be unemployed. She had played the part of a fool for three long years, perfecting the role. But no more! It was long past time for her to hold her head high, walk away and never look back.

The words from a militant protest song played loudly in her mind as she signed her name with a flourish at the bottom of the letter. She straightened. From the way Joshua David Norris treated her, she might as well have been a machine. Oh, he might miss her efficiency the first few days, but he would soon find a replacement, and then she would quickly fade from his memory. A year from now, if someone were to casually mention her name, she was convinced he would have trouble remembering who she was.

The intercom beeped unexpectedly. "Miss Stone, could I see you a moment?"

With a determination born of frustration and regret, she

jerked the letter of resignation from her printer and stood. As an afterthought, she reached for her dictation pad, which he still insisted she use. Her shoulders were stiff and her back ramrod-straight as she opened the door that connected the outer office with the executive suite. She exhaled once, hard, and filled her steps with purpose as she marched into the executive office.

Joshua was scribbling notes across a yellow legal tablet with his thin scrawl. He didn't bother to glance up when she entered the room, and for a few brief moments she was given the opportunity to study the man she loved—fool that she was. He was sitting, the muscles in his broad shoulders relaxed. Not for the first time, she sensed the complexity of this man's character. He was strong and mature yet headstrong and obstinately blind. Often she'd been a witness to the way he concealed his emotions in the tight fabric of control that he wrapped around himself. In some ways she knew Joshua Norris better than he knew himself, but in others he was a complete stranger.

His hair was dark brown with faint highlights of auburn, the result of hours spent in the sun, sailing his boat on Lake Pontchartrain. His brows were thick and drawn together now in concentration as he jotted down his thoughts. The smooth contours of his handsome face were broken by a square angular jaw that revealed an overabundance of male arrogance.

His eyes were a deep rich shade of brown that reminded her of bitter chicory. She knew from experience that they could reveal such anger that she was sure one look was capable of blistering paint off a wall. And then there were those rare times when she'd seen his gaze flitter over the photo of his daughter, Angie, that rested on his desk. Bethany had seldom witnessed a gentler look. All she knew was that Angie lived somewhere in New York and was being raised by his wife's family. In all the years that Bethany had been employed by Joshua, he'd rarely mentioned his daughter. From everything she knew of the man—which was considerable, since they spent so much time together—J. D. Norris didn't seem interested in long-term relationships and created a thick outer shell that often seemed impenetrable.

Joshua dropped the pen on top of the tablet, leaned back in his chair, and pinched his thumb and index finger over the bridge of his nose.

"Miss Stone, do we have any aspirin?"

"Yes, of course." His request caught her by surprise. Quickly she crossed the room to the wet bar, amazed that he didn't even know where the aspirin were. She returned momentarily with a water glass and two tablets.

He gave her a fleeting smile of appreciation. "Thanks."

Now that she thought about it, Joshua *did* look slightly pale. "You aren't feeling well, Mr. Norris?"

He shook his head, then widened his eyes as though he regretted the action. "I've got a beast of a headache."

"If you'd like, I'll cancel your afternoon appointments."

"That won't be necessary," he informed her crisply. He tore the top sheet off the tablet and handed it to her. "Could you have these notes typed up before you leave tonight?"

"Of course." The letter of resignation remained tightly clenched in her hand. She hesitated, wondering if she should give it to him now, then quickly decided against it. The last thing he needed was another problem. Which shouldn't have been *her* problem, of course, but old habits died hard.

His glance revealed his annoyance. "Was there something more, Miss Stone?"

"N-no." She did an abrupt about-face and left the office, closing the door behind her. Maybe she'd been too hasty. She should give him that letter, headache or not.

Ten minutes later her best friend and roommate, Sally Livingston, stuck her head inside the door. "Well, did you do it? Did you give your notice? What did he say?"

Bethany pretended to be busy, but she should have known Sally wouldn't be easily thwarted. Her friend advanced toward her desk, folded her arms and tapped her foot, waiting impatiently until Bethany looked up.

"Well?" Sally demanded a second time.

"He didn't say anything." Okay that was a lie of omission. He hadn't commented because she hadn't given him the letter.

Her roommate's brow crimped into a tight frown. "Nothing? You handed J. D. Norris your two-week notice and he didn't so much as respond?"

There was nothing left to do but confess, but still Bethany avoided looking in Sally's direction. "If you must know, I didn't give it to him."

"Bethany," Sally whispered angrily. "You promised."

"I—I wrote the letter."

"That's a start, at least."

"I was going to give it to him—honest—but he has a headache, and he looks absolutely terrible. The timing just wasn't right, and you know how important that is in these situations."

"Beth, this is crazy! The time will *never* be right—you've got to do it today, otherwise you'll end up putting it off for heaven knows how long."

"I know." Defeat weighted Bethany's voice. She'd promised Sally and herself that she wasn't going to delay this unpleasant task another day, and here she was looking for an excuse to put off the inevitable. "I'll do it Friday."

"What do you think today is?" Sally asked, sending her dark gaze straight through her.

"Oh," Bethany mumbled, and lowered her eyes. "Monday morning, then—first thing—you have my word on it."

Sally unfolded her arms and rolled her eyes. "I've heard that line before."

"All right!" Bethany cried. "You're right. I'm weak. I've got all the backbone of a...a worm."

"Less!"

Bethany paused and surveyed her friend through narrowed eyes. "What could have less backbone than a worm?"

"You!"

"But, Sally," Beth said, wishing her friend understood, "Mr. Norris isn't feeling well. I don't want to add to his troubles now. I'm sure he'll be better on Monday."

"Maybe he knows what you're planning and this is his way of generating sympathy."

Bethany knew Joshua would never do anything like that. "No, he's pale, and his head hurts. I think he might be coming down with some virus."

"It serves him right."

"Sally!" It wasn't Joshua's fault that Bethany had been silly enough to give him her heart. The man didn't so much as guess that she cared one iota about him.

It was her own fault for allowing herself to become attached to a man who chose to live his life without emotional commitments. It wasn't that he ignored her in particular. He seemed to be uninterested in women generally, at least based on what she'd observed. The divorce from, and later the death of, his ex-wife had left him hard and bitter toward the opposite sex. In the long run, if she stayed on she would only get hurt even more than she already had been. She had to leave—it was best for everyone involved.

If only she knew how to crack the thick facade he had erected over the years. If she'd had a little more experience or been a bit more sophisticated, then perhaps she could have come up with a surefire plan to win his heart. But as it was, she'd simply stayed on, hoping one day Joshua Norris would look up at her and some mysterious magic would change everything. Twinkling lights would go off in the distance and little hearts would pop up around her head, and he would recognize the love she'd stored up just waiting for him to discover it.

"All right," Bethany returned forcefully, her hands knotting into tight fists of steely determination. "I'll do it."

"Today?" Sally looked skeptical.

"I'll place the letter on his desk when I leave." It was a coward's way out, but when it came to standing up to Joshua Norris, no one was going to award her a medal for valor.

"Good for you." Sally patted her across the back much as a general would before sending a raw recruit into battle. "Meet me at Charley's when you're through here."

Bethany nodded. Charley's was a popular New Orleans hangout. The two had taken to stopping there and relaxing with a glass of wine on Friday nights. A reward of sorts for making it through another difficult work week.

"I'll see you there," Bethany said. Once Joshua left the office she would simply walk inside, place her resignation on his desk and be done with it. Then there wouldn't be any time for second thoughts and looming regrets. She had to get on with her life, because clearly this was a dead end for her.

It was after six by the time Bethany made her way into the crowded lounge. Sally had already found a table, and she stood up and gave a short wave. Bethany forced a smile and joined her friend. When the waitress strolled by, she pointed at Sally's wine glass and said, "Give me whatever she's having."

The woman nodded and turned away.

"So? Did you actually do it?" Sally asked, her voice low. "Did you finally hand in your notice?"

The glass of pinot noir arrived, and Bethany reached into her purse to pay for it. "Not yet."

"Not yet?" Sally echoed.

"Because *just couldn't.* I'm a weak—"

Abruptly Sally raised her hand, stopping her. "We've already determined that."

"Listen," Bethany said thoughtfully. "I've been giving some thought to my problem, and I think I may be doing Joshua Norris a disservice."

"How do you mean?"

The hum of conversation and a Dixieland band playing in the distance forced Bethany to raise her voice slightly and lean her head closer to her roommate's. "Joshua doesn't have a clue how I feel about him." At Sally's perplexed look, she hurried to add, "I should have the courtesy to at least let him know."

"Oh, Beth," Sally muttered, and shook her head. "The man has to be blind not to know how you feel. The entire company knows you love him."

Bethany paled. She actually felt all the blood rush from her face and pool at her ankles. When she spoke, her voice came out scratchy, high-pitched and weak. "Everyone knows?"

"Maybe not maintenance."

"Oh, no." Bethany took a long sip of her wine to hide her distress. This was worse than she'd ever imagined.

"Calm down, I was just joking. Not everyone knows—but enough people do."

Bethany's shoulders sagged with relief.

"What do you plan to do?" Sally asked in a husky whisper. "Saunter into his office, bat your eyelashes a couple of times and offer to bear his children?"

"No... I... I don't know yet." Bethany pushed the short dark curls from her temple.

"You've had three years to get the message across. What makes you think you can do it now?"

"I... I've never actually *told* him."

"Not outright, true, but honestly, Beth, give the matter some thought here. You're much too gentle-natured and sweet to come right out and tell J. D. Norris you have feelings for him. He's bound to give you one of those famous dark looks of his and fire you on the spot."

"I've been thinking..."

"The first time is always hardest," Sally joked. She reached for a handful of salted peanuts, munching on them one at a time.

Bethany reached for the salted nuts, too, hoping to buy herself time. "Maybe that's for the best," she finally said.

"I disagree." Sally popped another peanut into her mouth. "If you were going to fall in love, why did it have to be with him?" Her elbows rested on the tabletop, and her eyes narrowed with a thoughtful frown. "Beth, face it, the man's soured on women, soured on marriage, soured on life. He's the big bad wolf, and you're an innocent lamb. As your best friend, I refuse to stand by and let you do this to yourself."

"But...he can be wonderful." Bethany knew Joshua in ways the other employees of Norris Pharmaceutical didn't. She'd been a silent witness to his generous contributions to charity. She admired his unwavering dedication to medicine. She was sure there were times when others viewed him as harsh, but she'd never known him to be unfair or intentionally unkind. In the three years she'd worked for him, she had gotten enough glimpses of the real man inside to convince her that the exterior of indifference he wore was only a shell.

Sally chewed on a peanut as though it were rawhide, then paused, surprise widening her gaze and giving her away. "Don't look now, but..."

Instantly Bethany jerked her head around.

"I told you not to look," Sally berated her friend. "He's here."

"Who?"

Immediately Sally's dark eyes narrowed into thin slits, a sure sign she was irritated. "I thought you said your precious Mr. Norris was coming down with some dreadful virus."

Bethany's brow tightened into a frown. "He looked dreadful earlier. I got him aspirin." Sally wouldn't realize how unusual that was.

"Well," Sally said, looking properly disgusted, "he seems to have made a miraculous recovery."

"He's here?" Bethany rose halfway out of her chair before Sally jerked her back down. She felt the muscles in her throat tighten. "He's with someone, isn't he? That's the reason you don't want me to look." Already her mind was conjuring up a tall luscious blonde—someone she could never hope to compete against.

"Nope." Sally's eyes followed him. "He just sat down at the bar." Another nut was positioned in front of her mouth. "You know, now that I have a chance to get a good look at him, you're right."

"About what?"

"He is... I don't know, compelling-looking. He's got a lean hardness to him that naturally attracts women. An inborn arrogance, if you will."

Sally wasn't telling Bethany anything she hadn't already known—for years. "You're sure he's alone?"

"I just told you that."

Bethany clenched her hands together in her lap. "What's he doing now?"

"Ordering a drink. You're right about something else,

too. He doesn't look the least bit like himself. Not exactly sick, though."

Bethany couldn't stand it any longer. She twisted her chair around so she could get a decent look at her employer herself. She braced herself, not sure what to expect. But when her gaze skimmed over Joshua, she stiffened and experienced a rush of concern. "Something's wrong," she whispered, surprised she'd spoken aloud.

"How can you tell?" Sally asked, her voice barely above a whisper as though the two of them were on a top secret reconnaissance mission.

"I just can. Something's troubling him. Look at the way he's leaning over his drink...how his shoulders are slouched. I wonder what happened. Something's got him worried—I can't remember the last time I saw him look so...so distressed."

Sally shook her head. "I don't know where you get that. The only reason he's slouching like that is because he wants to be left alone. Didn't you ever read a book on body language? He's letting others know he isn't in the mood for company."

"Maybe." Thoughtfully Bethany gnawed at the corner of her lower lip. "But I doubt it." Without any real plan in mind, she pushed back her chair, reached for her bag and wine glass, and stood.

"What are you doing?" Sally demanded in a tight whisper.

"I'm going to talk to him."

Sally briefly touched her arm. "Be careful, sweetie, wolves have sharp teeth."

Bethany's heart was pounding like a jackhammer as she advanced toward Joshua Norris. Luckily the stool beside his was vacant. She perched her five-foot-five frame atop it and set her glass of pinot noir on the bar, folded her hands and leaned forward. She gave him a minute to notice her and comment.

He didn't.

"Hello," she said softly.

It seemed like an eternity before he turned his head to look at her. When he did, surprise briefly widened his intense dark eyes. "Miss Stone."

She took another sip of her wine. Now that she was here, for the life of her, she couldn't think of anything to say. She tossed a glance over her shoulder, and Sally's eyes rounded as she nodded encouragingly.

"I didn't know you frequented Charley's," Bethany managed at last, amazed at how strange her own voice sounded.

"I don't." His words were clipped, and he turned his attention back to his drink, discouraging any further discussion.

"Are you feeling better?"

He turned back to her then. "Not particularly."

The bartender strolled in their direction, and Joshua motioned to the tall thin man that he wanted a refill. The man poured another shot glass of Scotch, then cast Bethany a questioning glance.

She shook her head. She had a one-glass limit, especially on an empty stomach. As it was, the alcohol was already rushing to her brain.

"I have aspirin in my purse if you need some."

"I don't." He answered without looking in her direction, as though he wished she would get up and walk away. He hadn't sought her company, and the stiff way in which he sat told her as much.

Not knowing what else to do, she took several more sips of her wine. Feeling more than a little reckless, she lightly placed her hand on his forearm. "We've worked together all this time, so I hope you feel you can trust me."

"I beg your pardon." His hard gaze cut into her.

"Won't you tell me what's wrong?"

"What makes you think anything is troubling me?"

"I've worked for you for three years. I know when something's wrong. I've seen that look in the past, and I..."

"I am well aware of the length of your employment, Miss Stone—"

"Bethany," she interrupted, her unflinching gaze meeting his. "I've worked for you all these years, and I think you should know my first name is Bethany."

His eyes formed glacial slits. "And what makes you think that I care to know your first name? Because, rest assured, I don't."

Her breath felt trapped in her lungs, and scalding color erupted in her cheeks. She'd seen Joshua be cold and insensitive before, but never intentionally like this. The look he gave her was more than embarrassing...it was humiliating. The corner of his mouth turned up in a sneer, as though he were looking at something distasteful. His eyes cut her to the quick before he dropped his attention to her fingers, which were lightly pressing against the sleeve of his jacket.

As though in slow motion, she withdrew her hand from his arm. Her whole body went numb. The uselessness of it all hit her then, more poignantly than all the lectures Sally had given her, more cutting than her own soul-searching efforts. The message in Joshua's taut gaze was sharp, hitting its mark far more effectively than he would ever guess. He didn't know who she was, not really, and he didn't care to know. The world he'd created was his own, and he wasn't ever going to invite her or anyone else inside.

Her gaze didn't waver from his as she slid off the bar stool and took one small step in retreat. "I won't bother you again." The words managed to wrestle past the stranglehold that gripped her throat muscles. What an arrogant jerk.

She didn't know where she was going. All she knew was that she had to escape. She walked past Sally's table without looking at her friend, and maneuvered her way through the crowded room and outside into the chill of the January night.

For a moment she thought she heard someone call her name, but she wasn't up to explaining what had happened to Sally or anyone else. Increasing her pace, she hurried down the crowded pavement of Decatur Street, which bordered the popular French Quarter. The road was crowded, the sidewalks busy, but she kept her head up, walking as fast as her feet would carry her. Not knowing where—not caring.

"Miss Stone. Wait."

She sucked in her breath at the sound of Joshua's impatient demand, swung her bag strap over her shoulder and pushed herself to walk faster.

"Bethany, please."

Surprisingly, once Joshua caught up with her he didn't say a word. She must have continued walking half a block with him, their steps in unison, before he spoke again.

"I owe you an apology."

"Yes, you do," she said, "You were arrogant and rude. I was only trying to help. Would it have hurt you to simply say you weren't in the mood for company?" She should have listened to Sally. His body language had said as much, but oh, no, her tender heart had wanted to reach out to him. Well, lesson learned.

Neither of them spoke for a minute, and when she looked up she noticed that they were walking past Jackson Square. Several park benches were spread across the lush green lawn in front of the statue of Andrew Jackson on horseback.

He motioned toward an empty bench. "Would you care to sit for a minute?"

She calmly took a seat, although her heart continued to beat erratically.

He sat down beside her. After what seemed like a hundred years, he spoke. "I apologize. It's Angie."

At the mention of his young daughter, alarm worked its way through Bethany, and adrenalin shot into her bloodstream. She turned so she was facing him, her hands gripping his sleeve. "Is she ill? Has she had an accident?"

"No, no." Abruptly he shook his head. "As far as I know, she's in perfect health."

She relaxed, dropped her hands and slumped against the back of the bench.

Joshua sighed, his look bleak, distressed. "What do you know about children, Miss Stone?"

"Very little, actually." She was an aunt several times over, but although she dearly loved her nieces and nephews, they lived in Texas, so she only saw them on summer vacations.

"I was afraid of that." Roughly he splayed his fingers through his hair. "Frankly, I don't know what I'm going to do."

Questions were popping up like fizz from a soda can in Bethany's mind, but after her earlier attempt to draw him out, she decided against a second try.

"Angie's mother and I were divorced shortly after she was born."

He paused as though he expected her to make some conventionally comforting statement. She had nothing to offer, though, so kept her half-formed thoughts to herself.

"Over the years I've visited Angie when I could," he went on, his brooding gaze seeking hers. "Heaven knows, I've tried to do everything I could moneywise."

"She's a beautiful little girl," she murmured, not knowing what else to say. Angie's photo was updated regularly, and each time Bethany looked at it she saw the promise of rare beauty in the ten-year-old.

He nodded sharply, his brow furrowed. "The thing is, I don't know anything about being a father."

"But you've been one for the past ten years," she couldn't help reminding him.

"Not really," he murmured, his facial features remaining tight. "Not a real father." He stood then, and rubbed his hand along the back of his neck. "I've never felt more inept in my life."

She was sure that the sensation was foreign to him. In all the time she'd worked for him, she'd never seen him this upset or unsure about anything.

As though forgetting his own problems for the moment, he hesitated and stared down at her. His hard gaze softened perceptibly, and a half smile teased at the edges of his mouth. "You didn't deserve my sarcasm earlier. I truly *am* sorry."

An earthquake wouldn't have been powerful enough to tear Bethany's gaze from his. In three years, this was the most personal comment he'd ever made to her. Forgetting her earlier reluctance, she asked him softly, "Won't you tell me what's happening with Angie?"

He nodded and slumped down into the seat beside her. "I talked with my mother-in-law yesterday afternoon. It seems both my in-laws have been in poor health recently."

Bethany nodded, encouraging him to continue.

"They feel it's time for Angie to come live with me. I'm supposed to pick her up at the airport in a couple of hours." He paused and inhaled sharply. His gaze sought hers. "Miss Stone… Bethany, would you consider coming with me?"

Two

The Louis Armstrong International Airport was a beehive of activity, just as Bethany had expected it would be. The first thing Joshua did once they'd entered the terminal was double-check the flight schedule on the television monitor positioned beside the airline reservation desk.

"The plane's on time." He sounded as though he'd been hoping for a short reprieve. After obtaining the necessary paperwork to pass security to meet his daughter, he hurriedly guided Bethany through the wide corridor to the assigned concourse. In all the time she had known him, she'd never seen him more unsettled. When it came to his business, he generally revealed so little emotion that it had become his trademark. She watched him now, amazed and also pleased at this evidence that he did indeed possess emotions.

Once they found the gate, he paced the area, his hands buried deep in his trouser pockets. After several tense minutes he parked himself beside Bethany at the huge floor-to-ceiling window and stared bleakly into the darkness.

"I appreciate your coming with me," he said. "I haven't seen Angie in almost a year." He jammed his fingers through his hair and released a harsh breath. "Do you think she'll recognize me?"

"I'm sure she will." Bethany searched for something more to say that would reassure him, but she wasn't sure he would appreciate her efforts. Joshua Norris was a difficult man to interpret. She didn't know how far she dared tread onto this carpet of unexpected trust he'd laid before her.

A series of flashing lights glowed in the distance, and she felt him tense. She checked her wrist and noted the time. "It's too early for that to be Angie's plane."

Her employer nodded and seemed to relax.

"Joshua," she whispered, unable to keep herself from speaking, "everything's going to work out fine."

At the sound of his name, his troubled gaze shot in her direction, and he frowned. His eyes revealed surprise mingled with bewilderment. "No one's called me that since I was a boy."

Color exploded in Bethany's cheeks, working its way to her ears until she was certain they glowed with the heat. She'd always thought of him as Joshua. The world knew him as J. D. Norris, but she'd found the initials too abrupt for the complex man she knew him to be. "I...apologize. I..."

"It wasn't a reprimand... Bethany, but a statement of fact." He said her name as though it felt awkward on his tongue, yet as if he had recognized she had a name other than Miss Stone. When he continued to stare at her for a long moment, she had the impression he was seeing her for the first time. She knew her clear delicate features were unlikely to attract attention. Her eyes were a pale shade of blue not unlike a thousand others. Her cheekbones were slightly high, her nose firm and straight. But she didn't possess any one feature that would distinguish her as a great beauty.

Friends had called her cute, but that was about the extent of it. She was neither short nor tall, just average height—a description that sounded so terribly boring. She was contemplating that fact when she realized that if Joshua were to take her in his arms the top of her head would just brush against his jawline. All he would need to do was bend his head to kiss her and her lips would meet his without...

With an effort she tore her gaze from his, her composure badly shaken by the brief encounter. "Are Angie's grandparents traveling with her?" she asked, purposely diverting her thoughts.

"No." Joshua abruptly shook his head and turned back to stare out the window. "It couldn't be helped. She's flying alone."

"Oh." Poor Angie. With the time difference between New York and New Orleans, the little girl would probably be exhausted—or as keyed up and full of energy as a fresh battery.

"Has her room been fixed up?"

"Room?" Joshua echoed the word as though it were something totally foreign. "I thought I'd put her in the guest bedroom for tonight.... I hadn't stopped to think beyond that. I suppose she'll need something more, won't she?" His gaze clouded.

"I'm sure the guest room will be fine for now."

"Good."

A fresh set of wing lights blinked in the distant night. "I think that's her flight now," Bethany said.

Joshua stiffened, seeming to brace himself, and nodded. "She should be one of the first ones to disembark—I arranged for a first-class ticket."

"The flight attendant will escort her off."

He exhaled sharply. "I can't tell you how glad I am that you're with me."

She couldn't have been more pleased herself. She'd been granted a glimpse of a whole new facet of Joshua Norris's personality. When it came to his daughter, he was as uncertain as any new father, which to all intents and purposes he was. It seemed completely contradictory that this same man could bring a room full of board members to silence with one shattering look. She'd witnessed glares from Joshua that were colder than a tombstone in midwinter. No one would ever guess that the man who was nervously waiting for his young daughter was the driving force behind a thriving business. She had trouble believing it herself.

A few minutes later an airline official opened the door to the Jetway, and two businessmen were the first to step into the terminal, carrying briefcases and garment bags. They were followed by a female flight attendant escorting a little girl with straight dark hair that fell to the top of her shoulders. Two pink ribbons held it away from her face, which seemed to be made up solely of round eager eyes.

"Daddy!" The girl broke away from the attendant and ran toward Joshua.

He looked startled, then fell to one knee as his daughter hurled herself into his waiting arms.

Angie tossed her arms around her father's neck and squeezed for all she was worth. Slowly, almost as if it were against his will, he closed his eyes and returned the bear hug.

Bethany felt moisture brim in her eyes at the tender scene and bit into her bottom lip, determined not to say or do anything to disturb their reunion.

Finally Joshua released his daughter and stood, claiming her hand. "Angie," he murmured, looking down on the ten-year-old, "this is Miss Stone. She works for me. She's my assistant."

"Hello." Angie's wide dark eyes stared up at Bethany.

"Hello, Angie. Welcome to New Orleans."

"Thanks." The little girl grinned and let loose with an adult-size sigh. "I can't tell you how boring that flight was. I was beginning to think I'd never get here."

"I believe your father was feeling much the same way."

Angie's smile grew wider. "I don't suppose there's a McDonald's around here? Grandma told me not to trust anything the airlines served, and I'm absolutely starved."

"Miss Stone—a McDonald's?" Joshua was looking at her as though he expected her to wave a magic wand and make one instantly appear.

"Any hamburger will do," Angie offered, her gaze growing desperate.

"There's a McDonald's a few miles away," Bethany said, checking her Blackberry.

"Thank goodness." The little girl sighed, shrugging her small shoulders. "I swear I could eat one of everything on the menu."

Come to think of it, Bethany hadn't had dinner yet, either. Her stomach growled eagerly at the mere thought of a burger.

Angie prattled on about New York and her grandparents as they moved down the concourse to the baggage claim area. In addition to her backpack, she had three gigantic suitcases.

As soon as they were seated inside Joshua's car, Angie leaned forward so her head was positioned between Bethany and Joshua.

"You're a winter, aren't you, Miss Stone?"

"A winter?" She hadn't a clue what the ten-year-old was talking about.

"Your coloring—haven't you ever been analyzed?" Angie smothered a yawn with her palm. "It was a big deal a few years ago. My grandmother says every woman should know her season."

"I guess I actually hadn't given it much thought. I need to look into that." Bethany shared a smile with Joshua.

"Oh, no need to do that. I have a gift for these things, and you're definitely a winter," Angie returned confidently. "You should wear more reds, blues, whites, those kinds of colors."

"Oh." Bethany wasn't sure how to respond. As it was, her wardrobe consisted of several bold colors, but she wore more subdued ones for the office—tans and soft blues mostly, pencil skirts, business attire.

"There's a wonderful TV series about it. You should watch that for a few fashion hints."

"Yes," Bethany said, hiding a grin. "I suppose I should."

Sitting back and buckling her seat belt, Angie turned her attention to her father. "How's the sailing going, Dad?"

"Good," he said distractedly. He seemed more concerned with getting out of the heavy airport traffic than with talking.

"I saw an interview with some guys on TV last night. You might think about studying tacking techniques if you want to be a really great sailor. Personally, I think the New Zealanders are the ones we have to watch out for in the next America's Cup."

"It wouldn't be their first win." Joshua's smiling gaze bounced off Bethany's as he briefly rolled his eyes.

Angie leaned forward again, crossing her arms over the seat and resting her chin on top of her folded hands. She hesitated for a quick moment, then said, "We're going to get along just fine, don't you think?"

"Just fine," Joshua echoed. "What I'd like right now, though, is for you to sit back and stay in your seat the way you're supposed to."

Bethany sucked in her breath. His words were clipped and far more harsh than necessary. He was right, but there were gentler ways of telling his daughter so.

"Oh, sure." Angie immediately obeyed, flopping back and tightening her seat belt. "You should have done this years ago."

"Done what?" Joshua's tone was absent-minded as he pulled to a stop to pay the parking attendant.

"Sent for me," Angie said on the tail end of a yawn.

He didn't answer for what seemed like an eternity. "You may be right," he murmured at last.

Bethany noted how his face eased into a relaxed smile. It struck her then how rare it was for him to show pleasure at something. He ran a tight ship, as the saying went. He lived his life according to a rigid schedule, driving himself and everyone who worked closely with him to the brink of exhaustion. The control with which he molded his existence was bound to change now that his daughter had arrived. For the better, Bethany suspected.

She curved her fingers around the purse that rested on her lap. The letter of resignation neatly folded inside would stay there. Exciting things were about to happen at Norris Pharmaceutical *and* with Joshua Norris, and she planned to stick around and witness each and every one.

The living room curtain was pushed aside and Sally's eager face was reflected in the glass when the taxi deposited Bethany in front of her apartment two hours later.

"It's about time you got home!" Sally cried the minute Bethany walked inside the door. "What happened? I've been dying to talk to you. You should have phoned." She inhaled a huge breath and sank onto the deeply cushioned sofa. "But don't worry about apologizing now. Talk."

Bethany hung her jacket in the hall closet. She wasn't exactly sure where to start. "Mr. Norris followed me out of Charley's...."

"I know that much. I just hope he had the good grace to apologize. I don't know when I've seen you look more... I don't know...stricken, I guess."

"He did apologize," Bethany assured her.

"And it took him two hours?"

"No."

"The two of you had a romantic dinner together?"

"No."

Sally's shoulders sagged with disappointment. "What *did* happen?"

"Nothing, really. He told me his daughter is coming to live with him."

Sally folded her pajama-clad legs under her and leaned back, her look thoughtful. Her brows arched speculatively as she bounced her finger over her closed lips several times. "Well, that's news."

"Angie arrived tonight, and Mr. Norris asked me to go to the airport with him."

"So that's where you've been?"

"Part of the time." Bethany slipped off her low-heeled shoes and claimed the overstuffed recliner across from her roommate. "After that we went to McDonald's."

Sally grinned at that, her smile slightly off center. "How romantic."

Actually, in a weird way it had been, but she wasn't

about to explain that to her friend. She was convinced it was the first time Joshua had ever been to a fast-food restaurant, and he'd looked as uncomfortable as a pond fish during a summer drought. "We went to the drive-through window, because it was obvious Angie was going to conk out any minute."

"And did she?"

"The poor kid was fast asleep by the time we arrived at his house."

"You saw Mr. Norris's house?" Sally uncrossed her legs and leaned forward. Rumor had it Joshua Norris lived in a mansion.

Bethany answered with a short nod, remembering her first impression of the breathtaking two-story antebellum home. It was constructed of used brick in muted shades of white and red. Four stately white gables peeked out from the roof above the second floor. The front of the house was decorated with six huge brick columns that were lushly covered with climbing ivy. The house was a tasteful blend of the old South and her warm traditions with the new South and her willingness to adapt to change.

"What happened once you got there?" Sally pressed, clearly unable to hide her curiosity.

Bethany answered with a soft shrug. "I helped Angie get ready for bed, Mr. Norris brought in her luggage."

"And?"

"And then he phoned for a taxi so I'd have a way home."

He'd also thanked her and apologized again for his behavior earlier that evening. And as he did, she'd realized that he was closing himself off from her again. She could see it as clearly as if she were standing before a huge gate that was swinging shut. She'd tried to read his features, but it was impossible. She suspected that once the crisis had passed, he'd regretted having confided in her.

She didn't mention any of this to Sally, nor did she tell her roommate how Joshua had walked her to the cab once it arrived and paid her fare. He'd lingered outside for a few moments, hands buried deep in his pants pockets, his face lined with a frown that left her brooding all the way home.

"That's it?" Sally asked, looking sadly disappointed. "You were gone for hours, and that's the extent of what happened?"

"That's all there was." On the surface it didn't sound like much, and really it wasn't, but so much more had been accomplished. So much more than Bethany wished to share with her friend.

For the first time since she'd been hired as Joshua Norris's executive assistant, her employer had seen her as something more than an automaton. She chose to think he'd been pleasantly surprised by what he'd found.

Bethany was at her desk by the time Joshua arrived on Monday morning. She glanced up expectantly and was disappointed when he did nothing more than offer her a crisp good-morning, the way he'd done every day of the past three years, as he marched past her desk and into his office.

Reaching for the mail, she followed him inside. She'd taken his daughter's advice and chosen a dark blue business suit with a white silk blouse and a ribbon tie. Briefly she wondered if he would notice anything as mundane as the way she dressed. Probably not.

Following ritual, she poured him a mug of hot coffee and delivered it to his desk. He reached for the cup and took a sip before quickly leafing through the mail. He gave brisk instructions on each piece, handed back the ones she could deal with directly and kept the rest. Once he'd finished, she hesitated, standing beside his desk, uncertain.

"Yes?" he asked. "Was there something else?" He didn't so much as look up at her.

"I…wanted to ask you about Angie. How's she adjusting?"

His facade was back, and from the hard look about him, it had been heavily reinforced.

"Miss Stone, in case you've forgotten, I have a business to run. My daughter is none of your concern. Now, may I be so bold as to suggest that you do the job for which I pay you a very generous salary?"

It took Bethany a moment to quell her anger and not tell him to stuff his precious job. He wasn't paying her nearly enough to put up with his rudeness. After a moment she managed to say, "Yes, of course." Her voice was hardly more than a whisper. She found that her hands were trembling with outrage by the time she'd returned to her desk. Her legs weren't in much better shape. In fact, she had to walk around her desk two or three times before she was calm enough to sit down. She knew she should march right back into his office and hand him her resignation. But she wouldn't. She couldn't make herself do it, despite her fury.

By rote she managed to finish the morning's tasks, but by the time Sally arrived at noon, Bethany had worked herself into an uncharacteristically angry state. She shook from the force of her feelings, furious with herself for allowing Joshua to speak to her in that demeaning tone.

"He's impossible," she hissed when her friend stuck her head in the door.

"Mr. Norris?" Sally's gaze travelled from her roommate to the closed door to his office.

"Who else?" Bethany pushed back her chair so hard, she ended up six feet from the desk.

Frowning heavily, Sally stepped into the office. "Good grief, what happened?"

"I've had it!" Bethany declared, and cringed when Sally rolled her eyes toward the ceiling. Okay, so she'd been saying the same thing for weeks, but today was different. She would show Joshua Norris that she deserved respect. She refused to allow any man to talk to her the way he had. Never again. The worm had developed a backbone at last.

She reached for her purse and headed toward the door.

Open-mouthed, Sally lingered behind. "Aren't you going to let the great white shark know you're leaving?"

"No. He'll figure it out for himself."

Sally closed her mouth, then promptly opened it again. "Okay."

Bethany was halfway out the door when she glanced over her shoulder at Joshua's office. A great sadness settled over her, and she exhaled a soft sigh of regret. Her relationship with him seemed to be a case of one step forward followed almost immediately by two giant leaps back. She'd been given a rare glimpse of the man she knew him to be. It might well take another lifetime to be granted a second peek.

Unusually quiet, Sally led the way to the company cafeteria on the third floor. They ordered their lunch, then carried the bright orange trays to a round table by a window that overlooked the rambling Mississippi River.

"You're right, you know." Bethany spoke first. "I should have quit long before now." Like a romantic schoolgirl, she'd believed their relationship had shifted and he'd begun to view her as someone other than his executive assistant.

Instead, their time together with Angie was an embarrassment to him, something he obviously regretted.

"I'm right about what? J. D. Norris?" Sally asked, watching her friend carefully. When Bethany didn't respond right away, she peeled open her turkey-on-wheat sandwich to remove the lettuce. She reached for the salt shaker in the middle of the table, then changed her mind and replaced it.

A long minute passed before Bethany nodded.

"Well?" Sally demanded. "Are you going to spill your guts or not?"

"Not," Bethany answered in a small voice that was filled with regret. She couldn't explain facts she herself had only recently faced. She had been pining away for three good years of her life, and just when she'd been given a glimmer of hope, she'd been forced to recognize how futile the whole situation was.

Eventually Sally would wear her down, Bethany knew. Her friend usually came up with some new way of drilling the information out of her. But she wasn't ready to talk yet. She lifted her sandwich and realized she might as well have been contemplating eating Mississippi mud for all the appeal her lunch held. She returned the sandwich to the plate untouched and pushed it aside.

"You know I've heard all this a thousand times before."

"Of course I do. But this time is different."

"Right," Sally said with a soft snicker.

"No, I really mean it," Bethany returned. "I recently read that the best time to find a job is when you're currently employed. I'm going to start applying for new positions first thing tomorrow morning."

Sally's narrowed gaze said that she wasn't sure if she could believe her friend or not. Bethany met that look with a determination that had been sadly absent in the past. This time she was serious—she honestly meant it. She was leaving Joshua Norris for good.

When Bethany returned to the office, the morning paper tucked under her arm, Joshua's door was open. He must have heard her, because he stepped out and stood at her desk as if to wait for her. Although she refused to meet his gaze, she could feel him assessing her. He left without a word a couple of minutes later.

The instant he was gone she opened the newspaper to the jobs section, carefully read the help-wanted columns and made two calls, setting up appointments.

An hour later Joshua returned, but he didn't speak to her then, either, which was just as well.

The afternoon passed quickly after that. He requested two files and dictated a letter, which she typed and returned within the half hour. No other communication passed between them, verbal or otherwise.

Finally he left for a meeting with accounting, and fifteen minutes later Bethany walked out to meet Sally for their afternoon coffee break. Apparently Sally had decided to keep her opinions to herself, because the subject of J. D. Norris didn't come up.

When Bethany returned to the office, she decided she would ask Joshua for Thursday morning off. She would tell him she had an appointment, which was true; it just wasn't the kind of appointment he would no doubt assume. The appointment was to fill out a job application. And next time she accepted a position, she was going to be certain that her employer was happily married and over fifty.

"Miss Stone. Hi."

Bethany's gaze flew to her desk, where Angie sat waiting.

The girl jumped up and smiled, looking pleased to see Bethany again. "I didn't think you'd ever get back."

"Hello, Angie." The little girl's welcoming smile would rival a Louisiana sunset. "How was your first day of school?"

The ten-year-old wrinkled up her nose. "There are a bunch of weird kids living in this town."

"Oh?"

"Not a single girl in my class has ever heard of Bobby Short or Frank Sinatra."

"What a shame," Bethany answered sympathetically.

"Anyone who knows anything about music must have heard about Bobby. Why...he's world famous. Grandma and Grandpa knew him. A long time ago they would go to the Carlisle Hotel in New York City to hear him." She crossed her arms and gave a short little pout. "I never got to go, but Grandma has his CDs."

"Do you enjoy his music?"

"Oh yes, and Frank Sinatra, too. I'm not going to tell Dad this," Angie continued, her voice dropping to a soft whisper, "because it would upset him, but the kids here have no class."

Making no comment, Bethany deposited her bag in the bottom desk drawer and took her chair.

Angie came around the other side of the computer to face her. "Do you like Britney Spears?"

Containing a smile was impossible. "Quite a bit, as a matter of fact."

The youngster seemed surprised that Bethany would openly admit as much. "I do, too, but Grandma says she's a hussy."

"And what does that mean?" A laugh worked its way

up Bethany's throat but she quickly shut it down when her gaze met a pair of dark, serious brown eyes.

Angie shook her head. "I'm not sure, but I think it has something to do with getting her body pierced."

Bethany sincerely hoped the ten-year-old hadn't noticed her ears. Heaven only knew what she would think of someone who had each lobe pierced *twice*. To divert the child's attention, she turned toward her computer.

Angie dragged a chair over to the side of the desk. "Dad said I'm not supposed to bother you when you're working. The new housekeeper can't come until tomorrow, so I'm here for the afternoon."

"You won't be a bother, sweetheart."

Angie looked relieved at that. "What are you doing now?"

"I'm about to type a letter for your dad."

"Can I watch?"

"If you want." Bethany's fingers flew over the keys. She finished in a few minutes.

"You're good."

"It takes practice."

"Can I look up something on your computer? Mine is at the house."

Bethany moved aside. "Of course. If you need any help just say the word."

For the next hour Angie became Bethany's shadow. The little girl was a joy, and more than once Bethany was unable to hold back a laugh. Angela Norris was unlike any ten-year-old Bethany had ever known. Despite the fact that she'd been raised by her grandparents and had attended a small private school, she appeared utterly unspoiled. Bethany found that fact remarkable.

It was nearly five o'clock by the time Joshua returned from his meeting.

"Hi, Dad," Angie said happily. "Bethany let me use her fingernail polish. See?" She held up both hands, revealing pink-tipped fingers.

The phone rang before Joshua could respond.

"I'll get that." Bethany sucked in her breath as Angie reached for the receiver. "Mr. Norris's office, how may I help you?"

"Miss Stone?" Joshua arched his brows in a disapproving slant. "Is this your doing?"

Bethany's response was to offer him a guilty smile.

Angie pressed the receiver to her shoulder and looked at Bethany. "It's someone named Sally asking for you."

Joshua's gaze sliced into Bethany, dark with disapproval. "As soon as you're finished, Miss Stone, I'd like to see you in my office."

Three

"You asked to see me, Mr. Norris?" Bethany asked in a brisk businesslike tone, devoid of emotion. She trained her gaze on a point on the wall behind him so she wouldn't have to subject herself to his cool assessing eyes. No doubt she'd done something more to displease him. Again. It wasn't as though she hadn't been trying. All day she'd been thinking of petty ways of getting back at him for his cold treatment of her earlier.

She didn't like to think of herself as a mean person, but working with Joshua had reduced her to this level. That on its own was reason enough to find other employment.

"I wanted to apologize for Angie being here," he said.

Bethany relaxed. "She hasn't been a problem."

"Good. The housekeeper I hired starts tomorrow, so this will be the last time Angie will need to come to the office."

"I understand." Although it required willpower, Bethany kept her gaze centered on the landscape drawing behind Joshua. "Will that be all?"

"Yes." He sounded hesitant.

She turned and marched with military precision toward the door, then paused when she remembered her plan to look for another job and turned to face him again. "Mr. Norris?"

"Yes?"

"I'll need Thursday off."

"This Thursday?"

"I've got an appointment."

"All day?"

She straightened her shoulders. "That's correct."

He didn't sound pleased, but that wasn't her problem.

"All right, Miss Stone, arrange for Human Resources to send me a substitute, then."

"I'll do that, sir."

"Miss Stone," he called out impatiently. "Kindly drop the 'sir,' will you? You haven't used it in the past, and it's unnecessary to call me that now. Is that understood?"

"Perfectly, Mr. Norris."

He expelled his breath in what sounded like a frustrated sigh. "Miss Stone, is there a problem?"

She kept her face as devoid of emotion as possible. "What could possibly be wrong?" she asked in as much of a singsong sarcastic voice as she dared without invoking his full ire.

"That's my question!" he shouted.

"Then that's my answer."

His eyes rounded with surprise, and he looked as though he wanted to say something more. But when he didn't speak immediately, she quickly left the room. She'd never spoken to him in that tone before or revealed any of what she was thinking. But she wouldn't be in Joshua Norris's employment much longer, and the sense of freedom she felt amazed her.

"Miss Stone?" Angie asked, her wide eyes studying Bethany. "Is my dad upset with you?"

"No, honey, of course not."

"Good." The little girl released a long sigh that seemed to deflate her until her small shoulders sagged with relief.

"He's always saying things in this deep dark voice that scares people. It used to make me want to cry, but then I realized he talks that way most of the time, and he isn't really mad."

"I know, Angie. If you'd like, you can call me Bethany."

"I can?"

"But only if we can be friends."

The ten-year-old released another one of those balloon-whooshing sighs. "After the day I've had, believe me, I could use one."

Bethany laughed at the adult turn of phrase, although she could see that the little girl was dead serious.

"It's true," Angie murmured, her dark eyes round and sad. "I don't think anyone in my new class likes me. I don't know what I did wrong, either. But I think Grandma would say I was trying too hard."

"Give it time, sweetheart."

Angie nodded and grinned. "That's something else Grandma would say."

"By the end of the week you'll have all kinds of new friends."

"Do you honestly think so?"

Bethany opened a word processing program and brought up a fresh page. "How would you like to type a letter for me?"

"I can do that?"

"Sure. I've got some filing to do, and since you're here, you can be *my* executive assistant." She laid a form letter on the tabletop for the little girl to copy.

"I'll do my best, Miss Stone. I mean… Bethany." Angie slid the chair toward the computer, looking as efficient and businesslike as it was possible for a ten-year-old to look.

Within a couple of minutes Angie's brow was furrowed with concentration as her fingers went on a seek-and-find mission for each key on the keyboard. It took her an hour to finish the few short sentences of the letter, but when it was done, she looked as proud as if she'd climbed Stone Mountain unaided.

"You did a fine job, Angie," Bethany told her, glancing over the finished product.

"Oh, hi, Dad," Angie said, flew off her chair and went running toward her father. "Guess what? Bethany said I can be her executive assistant. I can come back tomorrow, can't I? You aren't really going to make me stay with that stuffy old housekeeper, are you? Bethany needs me here."

Bethany opened her mouth, then closed it. She'd only been trying to entertain Joshua's daughter, and now it looked as though she'd created a problem instead of solving one.

"There may be an occasional afternoon when Miss Stone could use your help," Joshua admitted thoughtfully, his gaze resting on Bethany. "But Miss Stone is quite efficient, so you shouldn't count on coming every day."

"But, Dad…"

"Miss Stone is usually able to handle all the work herself," Joshua said in a voice that brooked no argument.

"I *want* to help her, though. As often as I can, and I should be able to come every afternoon, don't you think, Bethany?"

"I said you may come occasionally," Joshua reiterated, "and that's all the argument I'm willing to listen to, Angela."

"Yes, Daddy." She didn't look pleased, but she wasn't completely deflated, either.

Considering everything, Bethany felt Joshua had offered a decent compromise. In fact, thinking it over as she left the office later, she was actually pleased with the way he had handled the situation with his daughter. He might not have had a lot of opportunity to do much parenting, but he seemed to be adapting nicely. No doubt once she found another job, Angie and Joshua would get along fine without her.

Late Thursday afternoon Bethany was sitting in front of the television, her feet propped up on the coffee table and a hot drink cupped in her hand, when her roommate let herself into the apartment.

"You look like you had a rough day," Sally commented.

"It's a jungle out there," Bethany said forcefully. Her feet ached, her spirits sagged, and she wondered if there would ever be a job that would free her heart from Joshua Norris. She'd gone on two interviews earlier and applied for several other openings on-line.

"I take it you didn't get a job offer?"

"The woman's a mind reader."

"What'd you find out?"

"Nothing, unfortunately," Bethany admitted with a soft moan of discouragement. "I got the old 'don't call us, we'll call you' routine."

"What are you going to do?" Sally asked, the concern in her voice evident.

"What else *can* I do?" Bethany answered. "I'll stick it out with Joshua Norris until I find something suitable."

Her friend plunked herself on the sofa beside Bethany and rested her own feet on the coffee table. "Well, I've got news for *you,* too."

"What?" Bethany was in the mood for something up-lifting.

"Apparently Mr. Norris didn't have a good day without you."

"Oh?"

"He went through two substitutes before noon."

"Good grief, who did H. R. send him?"

"I don't know, but the word was, Mr. Norris was in a foul mood all day."

Bethany tugged at the corner of her lower lip with her teeth. "I wonder why?"

"So does everyone else. I'll tell you one thing, though. There isn't an executive assistant in the entire company who isn't glad you're coming back tomorrow morning. Every one of them spent an anxious afternoon fearing they were going to be sent to work for him next. It's like ordering a vestal virgin to walk into the dragon's den."

"He's not that bad!" Joshua might have faults, but he certainly wasn't a tyrant. She wouldn't have fallen in love with a slave driver.

"Mr. Norris isn't bad? Wanna bet?" Sally returned forcefully. "Rumor has it that he told the first substitute she was completely useless."

Bethany gritted her teeth to keep from defending Joshua. It was apparent to her, if not to her roommate, that if her employer had called her replacement useless it was highly probable the woman had done something stupid. Bethany didn't know who H. R. had sent up to replace her, but it seemed the problem lay with them and not Mr. Norris.

"You *are* planning to go back tomorrow, aren't you?" Sally asked expectantly.

Bethany nodded; she didn't have any choice but to return. She'd envisioned walking into his office and slapping down her two-week notice, all the while smiling smugly, but that wasn't going to happen. She knew it had been foolish to expect to receive an offer on the spot, but still, she had dared to hope.

"That will save me a good deal of telephoning."

"Telephoning?"

"Yeah," her roommate said, looking pleased. "I promised I'd call the other exec assistants and let them know if you weren't going to work, because in that case, every one of them was planning to call in sick."

"But that's ridiculous."

"You weren't at the office today, Beth. You couldn't possibly know what rumors have been circulating. I swear, there isn't a woman in all of Norris Pharmaceutical who doesn't think you should be nominated for sainthood."

Bethany grinned at that. It did her ego a world of good to have others think of her as irreplaceable. Unfortunately, Joshua was the only one who mattered, and he didn't seem to care one way or the other.

The following morning proved her wrong.

Bethany was at her desk when Joshua strolled into the office. He paused just inside the door and looked relieved when he saw her. It might have been the lighting, but she actually thought she saw his gaze soften. A brief smile touched his mouth; of that, she was sure.

"Good morning, Bethany."

"Mr. Norris." She stood and was halfway into his office when she realized he'd called her by her first name. Her heart ping-ponged against her breast. For the first time in years she was a real person to him and not some kind of motor-driven robot.

By the time she delivered a cup of freshly brewed coffee to his desk and handed him the mail, she'd managed to compose herself and wipe the last traces of triumph from her face.

He leafed through the correspondence and gave his instructions the way he did each weekday morning. When he was finished, however, he paused.

"Miss Stone?"

She'd already stood, but he gestured for her to sit down again. "Yes?"

"How long have you been working for me now? Three years?"

She nodded.

"When was the last time I gave you a raise?"

"Four months ago." Her generous salary was part of the problem in finding another suitable position. Once she listed her current wages, most places were unwilling to meet or match her price. At least that was what she surmised from her experiences the day before.

"You've done an excellent job for me, Miss Stone."

"Thank you."

"I tend not to tell you that often enough."

As she recalled, he'd never said it, certainly not directly.

"We seem to work well together. Until you were gone yesterday I didn't realize how much you do to keep this office running smoothly."

"Thank you." She knew she sounded as if her vocabulary was limited to two words, but he'd taken her by surprise, and she couldn't find anything else to say that made any sense. There must have been some truth to what Sally had told her about her replacements, but she had been absent from work before. Not often, but a day or two now and again, or an annual vacation.

"You anticipate my needs," he went on, looking slightly embarrassed. "You seem to know what I'm thinking and act on it without my having to comment. I don't think I appreciated that before. It's a rare quality in an employee."

"Thank you." She hardly knew what to say.

"I feel it would only be fair to compensate you for a job well done." He paused and looked pleased with himself.

"I beg your pardon?" She wasn't sure what he meant.

"I'm giving you another raise."

He mentioned a sum that made her gasp. The amount was nearly twenty-five percent of her already more than adequate salary. "But I told you, I just received a raise last October."

Joshua arched his brows speculatively. "Does that mean you don't want this one?"

"Of course I want it."

"Good," he said briskly, turning his attention to the papers on his desk, dismissing her. "That will be all, then."

"Thank…you, Mr.…Norris," she said, getting awkwardly to her feet. A couple of the envelopes she was holding nearly slipped from her fingers, but she managed to grab them before they fell to the floor.

He grinned, and his look was almost boyish. "I believe you've thanked me quite adequately, Miss Stone."

She couldn't return to her desk fast enough. The first thing she did was call Sally, who worked in the accounting department.

"Sally," she said under her breath. "Meet me in the cafeteria."

"Now? In case you haven't noticed, it's barely after nine."

"Okay, at ten." It would kill her to wait that long, but she didn't have a choice.

"Bethany?" her friend said, sounding vaguely concerned. "We've been meeting for coffee every day at ten for three years. Why would today be any different?"

"I got a raise!" Bethany cried, unable to hold the information inside any longer.

"Another one?"

To her way of thinking, Sally didn't sound nearly as pleased as she should have been. "What you said about yesterday must have been true, because Mr. Norris seemed more than pleased to see me this morning."

"Beth, does this mean you won't be looking for another job?"

"Are you nuts? Where else would I ever make this kind of money?"

"Where else would you risk breaking your heart?" Sally asked.

The question echoed through Bethany's mind like shouts bouncing off canyon walls. The reply was equally clear: nowhere else but with Joshua Norris.

Two weeks passed, and although nothing had actually changed, everything was different. There didn't seem to be any one reason that Bethany could pin down, but she felt more at ease with Joshua. Their routine remained exactly as it had been for the last three years, but he seemed more content. He was less formal, less austere. She guessed that the changes were a result of having Angie come to live with him. The ten-year-old was such a great kid that Bethany knew her employer couldn't be around his daughter and not be affected.

Bethany was hungry for news of the little girl, but she dared not topple this fragile peace between them after that first morning when Joshua had made it clear that he didn't wish to discuss his daughter.

"Miss Stone?" He called for her when she returned from her lunch break Friday afternoon.

She reached for a pad and pencil, and stepped into his office.

Joshua was leaning back in his chair, his hands forming a steeple under his chin; his look was thoughtful. "How much do you know about fashion for ten-year-olds?"

"Fashion?" she repeated, not certain she'd heard him correctly.

"Yes. Angela recently informed me she's 'out of it' and seemed quite concerned. Apparently not wearing the latest fad is a fate worse than death."

Bethany smiled and nodded, remembering her own teen years. Ten seemed a bit young, but she could understand Angie's wanting to fit in with the other girls her age.

"Short of dying her hair orange and piercing her nose, I have very few objections to the way my daughter dresses."

Bethany nodded. She didn't particularly agree with that statement, but it wasn't her place to share her opinions on the matter with Joshua.

He straightened and looked uncomfortable. "I was wondering if it would be possible for you to take Angie shopping. She specifically asked for you, and I don't mind admitting I know next to nothing about how girls her age dress these days. Naturally I'd pay you for your time. It would mean a good deal to Angie."

"I'd enjoy it immensely."

He sighed, and then actually grinned. "You don't know how relieved I am to hear that. I had visions of Angela dragging me through the women's lingerie department."

The following morning, Bethany met Angie and Joshua in a local shopping mall. The minute Angie saw Bethany approach, she let go of her father's hand and came running toward her as though they hadn't seen each other in years.

"Bethany, hi. I didn't think you'd ever get here."

Surprised, Bethany glanced at her wrist. "Am I late?" According to her watch, she was five minutes early.

"It seemed to take you forever," the ten-year-old said.

"We've been here ten minutes," Joshua admitted with an off-center grin that took away five years.

He looked so good that Bethany had to force her gaze back to Angie. "I take it you're excited?"

"Do the Saints play football?" Joshua asked, referring to the New Orleans football team, which had just finished an exceptionally good season.

"Dad said the sky's the limit. Are you ready?" Angie asked, her face a study in eagerness. "'Cuz I am."

"Good luck," Joshua said, and paused to look at his watch. "I'll meet you for lunch. Where would you suggest?"

Before Bethany could answer, Angie called out, "McDonald's! There's one in the food court."

"You game?" Joshua asked Bethany, looking more amused by the minute. She had trouble seeing him as the same man she worked with five days a week. For the first time in memory, he wasn't wearing a suit but was dressed casually in slacks and a light sweater that accentuated his eyes.

"McDonald's? Sure!" The last time she'd been to one had been the night they'd picked up Angie from the airport. If Joshua was game, then so was she.

By one o'clock Bethany was exhausted and Angie was just hitting her second wind. The child seemed tireless— a born shopper. It amazed Bethany how selective the ten-year-old was about her clothes. Although they'd been in at least fifteen different stores, Angie had chosen less than a dozen items. Mostly T-shirts and acid-washed jeans, and a couple of pairs of sandals and tennis shoes. Bethany did manage to talk her into one dress and a pair of dress shoes, but according to Angie she had a closet full of frilly dresses already. She needed casual clothes like the ones the other girls in her new school wore.

Joshua was sitting in a booth in McDonald's munching on a French fry when Angie and Bethany joined him.

"How's it going?" he asked.

"Bethany really knows her stuff," Angie announced, already reaching for the burger he'd ordered for her. "I knew the minute you told me she was going to take me shopping that today would be special, and it has been."

Bethany felt her heart constrict at the little girl's praise. If anyone was special, it was Joshua's precocious daughter.

Angie dabbed a French fry in the ketchup and lowered her gaze to the tabletop. "I just wish I could see Bethany more often."

Neither adult spoke. Bethany gave her attention to her own hamburger.

"Miss Stone is busy, Angie. She has other friends."

"Why do you call her Miss Stone, Dad?"

"I don't have that many other friends," Bethany said quickly. "I'd enjoy seeing Angie more often."

Joshua's eyes drifted from one female to the next, his gaze bewildered, as though he weren't certain who he should answer first. It was clear from his expression that he felt outnumbered.

"I call her Bethany, and I bet you could, too." Angie added, "Grandma told me it was all right to call an adult by their first name if *they* said it was okay. I bet Bethany wouldn't mind if you called her that instead of Miss Stone all the time. You see her every day."

"Yes, well, I suppose I could—if Miss Stone doesn't object."

"Of course I don't mind."

"And you should call Dad J.D. like everyone else," Angie continued, speaking to Bethany.

"She prefers Joshua," he explained, his eyes holding Bethany's briefly. He grinned.

"Joshua." Angie rolled the name over her tongue as if the sound of it were something rich and rare. "I like that, too. When I was born, if I'd been a boy, what would you and Mom have named me?"

"David. It's my middle name."

"Not Joshua?" Angie sounded disappointed.

"Too confusing," her father explained.

"What made you decide on Angela?" the little girl asked, closely studying her father. She was so intent that she stopped eating, a French fry hanging limply in her hand, halfway to her mouth.

"You looked like a tiny angel when the doctor first showed you to me," Joshua explained, and his gaze softened as it rested on his daughter. "I suggested the name Angela Catherine to your mother."

Angie nodded, not looking overly pleased. "I wish you'd thought I looked like a Millicent."

"Millicent?"

"Perhaps a Guinevere."

"Guinevere?" It was Bethany's turn to become an echo.

"Or even better, a Charmaine." Dramatically, the ten-year-old placed her hand over her heart, gazed into the distance and heaved an expressive sigh.

"Charmaine?" Bethany and Joshua repeated, and glanced at each other.

"Oh, yes. Those names sound pretty and smart. Angie sounds… I don't know…ordinary."

"Trust me, sweetheart, the last thing you are is conventional."

From the way Angie's eyes darted down to the table, it was apparent she didn't understand Joshua's meaning.

"That's another way of saying ordinary," Bethany explained.

"I knew that!"

Once more Bethany and Joshua shared a brief smile.

"Bethany is such a pretty name. I wouldn't have minded that name, either."

"Thank you. My father named me, too."

"He did?"

"Yes, and when I was ten I wanted to be called Dominique because it sounded sophisticated and mysterious. I used to make up stories where I was the heroine who saved all my friends from certain death."

"You did?" Angie's eyes were growing rounder by the minute. "What about you, Dad? Did you ever want to be called something else when you were ten?"

"No."

Bethany resisted the urge to kick him under the table. Even if it was true, there wasn't any need to squelch the game.

"I believe I was eleven at the time," he answered thoughtfully. "I wanted everyone to call me Mordecai. I felt it was a name that revealed great character. When I said it, I felt stronger."

"Mordecai," Angie repeated slowly. "I like that almost as much as Joshua. Oh, Dad, this is the most fun I've had since moving to New Orleans."

Joshua grinned, and the smile Bethany had felt was so rare only hours before looked almost natural.

"Dad, can Bethany come home with us? Please? I want to show her my bedroom, and my new television and computer and everything. You don't mind, do you?"

Four

"Come see my bedroom next," Angie insisted, dragging Bethany by the hand down the long hallway. "Dad had a lady come in and decide on my colors and everything... only, I wish..." She paused and glanced over her shoulder before adding, "I like lavender much better than the yellow she picked."

Bethany paused in the doorway of the little girl's room and swallowed a soft gasp. The bedroom was elaborately decorated with ornate French-provincial-style furniture. A huge canopy bed dominated the space, with a matching desk and armoire close by. Thick canary-yellow carpeting covered the floor and was used to accent a lighter shade of sheer priscilla curtains. The bedspread had the same flowery pattern as the curtains.

"Don't you think it's simply divine?" Angie asked in a falsetto voice that Bethany was sure was an imitation of something she'd seen on TV. Angie's wide-eyed gaze made it clear she was waiting for a response.

It was all Bethany could do to nod. Yes, the room was lovely, but it didn't personify Joshua's daughter. The little girl who now preferred acid-washed jeans and sweatshirts hadn't once been consulted regarding what she wanted in her bedroom. Bethany would stake her career on that. This room belonged to a soft, feminine, demure child, and Angie was direct, tomboyish, and full of vitality and life.

"Look at this," Angie said, stepping around her to the armoire. She opened the top doors and revealed a thirty-two-inch screen. "I can sit on my bed and watch television or play computer games as late as I want."

"What about bedtime?" Bethany immediately wished she hadn't asked. She might be curious, but it was better that she not know, because she already knew that she was going to disapprove. And she was powerless to say or do anything about it.

"Dad says I'll go to sleep when I'm tired, and I do." She flopped down across the mattress on her stomach, legs raised and crossed at the ankles. She reached for the remote control, held it out like a laser gun and pressed a button, turning on the TV. "Sometimes I fall asleep with it on, and then Dad turns it off for me before he goes to bed."

Bethany managed a weak nod.

"He's always real busy after dinner," Angie explained, her eyes a little sad. "He has a lot of homework to do... reading papers and stuff like that. You know."

Bethany did. "What do you do while your father's busy working?"

"Oh, nothing much. I come to my room and play on my computer or watch TV. Sometimes I read."

"What about homework?"

"Oh, Mrs. Larson, the housekeeper, has me do that as soon as I get home from school," she said, and sighed expressively. "Mrs. Larson's all right, but I wish she'd let me play with the other kids, and after class is the only time I can do that."

"Have you made new friends?"

"Sure, lots—just like you said I would."

Pleased, Bethany patted the top of the little girl's head. At least that adjustment had seemed to come easily enough.

"As soon as I admitted I like Lady Gaga all the girls knew I wasn't a geek." She paused, pressed a button on the remote control and turned off the television. "The afternoon you let me paint my fingernails helped, too, I think." Her gaze dropped suggestively to her clear nails, and she let loose with a hopeful sigh and raised pleading eyes to Bethany.

"I think I just may have a bottle of that same polish in my purse. If it's all right with your father, we'll do your nails again before I leave."

"Oh, Dad won't care," Angie said, flying off the bed and throwing her arms around Bethany's waist in a bear hug.

"What won't I care about?" Joshua asked, leaning against the doorjamb, looking relaxed and amused.

His eyes sought out his daughter, then drifted, almost reluctantly, to Bethany. The warmth of his gaze did funny things to her equilibrium, and she reached out to steady herself against the bedpost.

"You won't care, will you, Dad?"

"About what, sweetheart?"

"If Bethany paints my fingernails again."

"No," he murmured, his gaze continuing to hold Bethany's. "I think that would be just fine."

"Do you want to come outside and look at the patio next?" Angie asked, her voice raised and eager. "Dad wanted to buy me a swing set, but I told him I was too old for that kind of kid stuff." She rolled her eyes for effect, and it took all Bethany's self-control not to laugh outright.

Joshua led them to the patio off the family room and

gestured toward the white wicker furniture for Bethany to take a seat.

"Would you care for something to drink, Miss Stone?"

Angie slapped her hands against her thighs in a small display of disgust. "Honestly, Dad, I thought you were going to call her Bethany."

"Old habits die hard," he said, clearly trying to appease his daughter.

"I'll take a soda," Angie said, sitting beside Bethany, swinging her stubby legs.

"Bethany?"

"Iced tea, if you have it. Thanks."

He cocked one brow and grinned broadly, his eyes alight with mischief. "What, no white wine?"

Bethany quickly averted her gaze to Lake Pontchartrain, whose waters lapped lazily against the shore only a few yards away. Joshua was teasing her about the Friday night she'd approached him at Charley's, and she didn't know how to respond.

"I'll be back in a minute."

"Do you want to walk down to the water?" Angie offered, jumping to her feet and holding out her hand to Bethany.

Bethany nodded eagerly. She'd always loved the lake and was more than willing to escape Joshua for a few moments. Questions were pounding against the edges of her mind like children beating against a locked door. She'd hungered for so long to know him better. She'd been just as anxious for him to like her. Now it was finally happening, and suddenly she was afraid. Terrified.

Sally would be furious with her for not having a witty comeback when he'd suggested the wine. He was accustomed to sophisticated women who knew how to spar verbally. Bethany could be witty, too, but it generally took a glass of wine or some time. She wasn't as quick witted as some, much to her regret. Feeling the way she did about him didn't help, either. Every time he looked at her with those warm lazy eyes, she felt light-headed and dizzy.

Angie slipped off her sneakers and socks, and tested the water with her big toe. "It's really warm."

The day was almost balmy, even though it was only the beginning of February.

"Do you think it would be all right if we waded a little bit? I think it would," Angie answered her own question and stepped out into the water until she was up to her calves.

Bethany slipped out of her sandals and followed, letting the lake lap at her toes. It was probably a silly thing to do, but she didn't care. The impulse to enjoy the water was too strong to resist.

"I love this lake," Angie said wistfully. "Dad says we'll be able to swim in a couple of months if the weather is nice, and it should be. I only wish he would let me swim alone, but he says I can't go in the water unless he's with me."

"He's right," Bethany said forcefully, frightened by the thought of Angie in the lake without an adult close by. "Don't ever go in the water alone. It's much too dangerous."

"Oh, I won't. I don't think Dad will ever go with me, though," she said regretfully. "He has too much work to do. All he does is work, work, work. I tried to talk him into reading his papers on the patio so I could play by the water, but he said no to that, too."

Bethany silently agreed with that decision. It would be much too easy for him to become involved in whatever he was working on and forget about Angie.

"Your dad's right, honey."

"I knew you'd say that," she answered with a soft pout.

Bethany laughed, enjoying the warm breeze that mussed her hair about her face. As she moved deeper the water felt cool and refreshing, and before she knew it, she had lifted the skirt of her soft pink dress and was almost knee-deep.

"Hey, look!" Angie called excitedly, waving frantically toward the house. "Dad's watching us."

Bethany twisted around and answered Joshua's wave with one of her own. In her dreams she'd often pictured a scene where they stood together by the lake with the wind whispering gently around them. She wished he would come down by the waterside and make her dream a reality. If she hadn't known better, she would have thought he was thinking the same thing, because the smile left his face and his gaze captured hers, holding it, refusing to let it go. The tender look was enough to cause her pulse rate to soar.

She wasn't sure what happened next, or how she lost her footing, but suddenly, unexpectedly, she was slipping. Her arms flew out in a desperate effort to maintain her balance. She should have known that if she was going to make a complete fool of herself it would be in front of Joshua Norris. By the time she hit the water, she'd accepted her fate.

"Bethany, Bethany, are you all right?"

Mortified, Bethany sat in the chest-deep water and buried her red-hot face in her hands, unable to answer the little girl.

"Daddy, Daddy, I think Bethany's hurt!"

Bethany heard Angie shouting as she ran toward the house. Knowing there was nothing to do but face Joshua, she stood awkwardly and walked out of the water. Her once pretty dress was plastered over her torso and thighs, and the ends of her hair dripped water. Bethany didn't understand how her hair could be wet and her shoulders dry, but they were.

Joshua stood on the shore, his hands braced against his hips, doing an admirable job, she thought, of not laughing.

"Well, Miss Stone, how's the water?"

"Fine, thanks," she said, and her voice came out an octave higher than normal.

"I've sent Angela for a towel."

Bethany nodded her thanks, and rubbed her hands up and down her chilled arms. Water pooled at her feet.

"Here, Dad," Angie said breathlessly, rushing onto the scene, her arms loaded with a drawerful of soft thick towels.

Joshua draped one across Bethany's shoulders and held it there momentarily. "Whatever possessed you to wade in the lake?" he asked in a low growl. "For heaven's sake, it's February."

"The water was warm." The excuse sounded weak even to her own ears.

"Bethany, honestly." He pressed his forehead against hers. "Come in the house before you catch your death."

"I... I think it would be best if I just went home," she whispered, utterly miserable.

"Like this? Wet? You could catch a cold, and you must be uncomfortable, besides."

She didn't care. She was willing to suffer any discomfort in order to extract herself from this awkward situation.

"Stay," he urged, "and dry off here."

His gaze sought hers, and she found she couldn't refuse him.

With his arm cupping her shoulder, he led her toward the house. At loose ends and wanting to help in some way, Angie ran circles around them like a frolicking puppy. "Are you all right, Bethany?" she asked.

"She's fine, sweetheart," Joshua said, answering for her.

"It's all my fault."

"Bethany doesn't blame you. It was an accident, and sometimes those happen." Again he was answered for her.

Not knowing what to say or do to calm the distraught child, Bethany held out her hand. It was immediately clasped by a much smaller one.

Joshua led her through a set of sliding glass doors at the other end of the house into what was obviously the master bedroom. Bethany hesitated, not wanting to drip water all over his pearl-gray carpet, but he urged her forward and into the large master bathroom.

"Take a warm shower," he ordered, but not unkindly, much less in the coldly unemotional voice she was accustomed to hearing from him. "Give Angie your wet things, and I'll have Mrs. Larson put them in the drier."

Bethany nodded.

"When you've finished, slip into my robe." He pointed to the thick navy blue robe that hung on the back of the door. "I'll have a hot drink waiting for you."

Again she answered him with a short nod. He left and closed the door.

"I feel terrible," Angie wailed, close to tears. "You'd never have gone into the water if it hadn't been for me."

"Sweetheart, don't worry about it. I stumbled over my own two feet." She didn't mention that she'd been looking at Joshua at the time and daydreaming.

Angie slumped down on the edge of the bathtub, looking mournful. "I will always blame myself for this," she said, sounding like a true drama queen.

"I refuse to let you," Bethany said, her teeth starting to chatter. "If you do, then I'll be forced to keep my nail polish in my purse."

"Well, actually, now that you mention it," the ten-year-old said as she nonchalantly stood and walked to the door, "it really *was* all your own fault. Are you normally this clumsy?"

"Always," Bethany muttered, and turned on the shower.

When she was finished, both Angie and Joshua were sitting in the living room waiting for her. She tightened the belt of the thick robe, which was so long on her that the hem dragged across the carpet. Her hair hung in limp strands about her face, and she felt as if she should stand on a street corner and beg for quarters.

Joshua stood when he saw her coming and made an admirable effort not to smile.

"Don't you dare laugh," Bethany warned him under her breath, at the same time reassuring Angie with a grin. She didn't know what she would do to Joshua if he did, but she would find a way to make him regret it.

"I wouldn't *dream* of laughing."

"Ha!"

"I'll pour you a cup of coffee."

She sat in a velvet wingback chair, and accepted the mug from Joshua when he brought it to her. "Thank you."

"You're quite welcome."

She had the distinct feeling he was showing his appreciation for giving him the single biggest laugh of his life.

The first sip of coffee seared its way down her throat and made her eyes widen at its potency. It was apparent the moment the liquid passed her lips that it had been liberally laced with whiskey.

"This is… Irish…coffee?" she stammered in a breathless whisper, having trouble finding her voice.

"I didn't want you to catch a chill."

"Dad was real worried about you," Angie piped in. "He said you were lucky you didn't swallow a fish."

Bethany's narrowed gaze sliced through her employer. How she wished she could say exactly what she was thinking!

"I've instructed Mrs. Larson to set the table for three this evening," he said.

Bethany had no idea it was so close to dinnertime. "I can't stay," she said hurriedly. "Really, I have to get home."

"You can't just leave," Angie said, her voice tight with disappointment. "We're having pork roast and homemade applesauce and fresh peas. But you don't have to eat the peas if you don't want. Dad makes me, but he won't make you…at least, I don't think he will."

Joshua stiffened and strolled to his daughter's side, resting his hand on her small shoulder. When he looked at Bethany, his gaze was guarded. "Miss Stone might have a date this evening, Angie. We shouldn't assume she's free."

"I… I'm not meeting anyone," Bethany said quickly. She shouldn't have been so eager to let him know that, but the truth was, she rarely dated anymore. There was no reason to, when she was already in love.

"Then you'll stay for dinner?" Angie asked eagerly.

Bethany's gaze fell to the steaming coffee. "All right," she said. She couldn't find an excuse not to, except that she'd hoped to salvage what remained of her pride. Not that there was much left—most of it had drowned in Lake Pontchartrain.

"Oh, good," Angie said gleefully. "Mrs. Larson's a terrific cook."

By the time the meal was served, Bethany's clothes were out of the drier, and she'd had time to deal with her hair. She felt infinitely better.

"I'm starved," Angie announced, claiming the chair

beside Bethany and carefully unfolding the linen napkin across her lap.

"Swimming does that to me, too," Bethany added.

The corners of Joshua's mouth quivered before he burst into a full rich laugh. Soon they were all laughing.

"Rare is the woman who can find humor in her own misadventures," he announced, his face transformed by his careless smile.

Flustered, Bethany looked away, unable to hold his gaze any longer.

Before the meal was served Joshua poured her a glass of wine. She wasn't sure she should drink it on top of the laced coffee, but she decided it wouldn't hurt. A second glass followed toward the end of the meal.

Angie fell asleep on the sofa while Bethany and Joshua lingered over their second glass of wine in the living room. Candles cast flickering shadows across the wall, and the light in the room was muted, creating an intimate feeling.

"I enjoyed today," he said.

"I did, too."

"I'm grateful you were willing to take Angie shopping. It meant a good deal to us both. I want you to know I was serious about paying you for your time."

"Oh, don't, please. Being with Angie is a delight." She didn't add that spending her day with him had been equally wonderful. Thrilling, even. He was a completely different person away from the office. Having his daughter move in with him had sanded away the rough edges of his brusque personality. Her gaze shifted affectionately to the sleeping child. Knowing Angie had opened a door for Bethany that she had thought would be forever closed to her. She would be eternally grateful to the little girl.

"Angie really seems taken with you."

He said it as though he couldn't understand why, "That surprises you, doesn't it?" she asked and hated how defensive she sounded. She couldn't help it, though.

"What?" He frowned and looked confused.

"That...that anyone could be taken with me."

He looked completely shocked. "Not in the least."

She decided it was the wine that had given her the courage to speak frankly, to question him. Heaven knew she never had before...wouldn't have dared.

"You certainly can be a prickly thing," he added, frowning.

"Me?" That just went to prove how much attention he'd paid her over the years.

"I meant to compliment you when I said how much Angie liked you."

"I apologize, then."

"Fine."

A throbbing silence followed, during which she was convinced they were both searching for ways to bring the conversation back to an amicable level.

"I suppose I should think about getting home," she murmured, discouraged. The day had held such promise, but the evening had been a disaster. She should never drink wine. It went straight to her head and disassociated her tongue from her brain.

"Before you do, I'd like to ask another favor of you, if I may," he said.

Once more she could feel his reluctance, as though he didn't like to be in her debt. "I'd be happy to do anything for you...for Angie," she hurried to add.

"It's about Mardi Gras next week. Angie is looking forward to attending the festivities, and, well, you know my schedule better than anyone. Would you be willing to take her to the parade? I could meet you afterward, and we could have dinner, the three of us. That is, of course, unless you've got other plans. I certainly wouldn't want you to cancel a date with someone special."

"I'd love to take Angie to the parade."

Joshua nodded and grinned. "Bethany?"

"Yes?"

"*Is* there someone special?"

To tell him that he was the only one who mattered in her life would have been ludicrous, and even after the wine, she had the good sense to resist.

"No...not lately." She didn't know why she tagged that comment on, but she did, for better or worse.

"I see."

Bethany wasn't sure what he read into her answer—or what there was to read. "You don't have to meet us for dinner if you'd prefer to make other plans," she blurted out, then snapped her mouth closed, hardly able to believe she'd made the offer. "I mean...well, if you'd rather meet 'someone special' yourself, I'll understand."

He rotated the stem of his wineglass between his open palms. "There hasn't been anyone for me, either," he said in a low, well-modulated voice. "Not lately, anyway." He raised his eyes to hers and grinned.

She relaxed against the back of the chair and smiled, more relaxed with Joshua than she could ever remember being. She'd often imagined quiet romantic moments such as these with him. But she'd always felt it was impossible.

"More wine?"

"No," she answered, and shook her head. "I'd better not, since I still have to drive home."

"I'll take you."

Although the thought was tempting, it would only be

an inconvenience for him, and then she would need to ask Sally to drive her over to pick up her car tomorrow. Knowing Sally, and what her friend would read into her leaving her car at Joshua's...no, that just wouldn't work.

"Thank you, but no, I'll drive myself."

"What do you think of Angela's room?" he asked, and glanced proudly toward the hallway that led to the bedrooms.

She wasn't sure what to say. "It's very...yellow, isn't it?"

"You don't like yellow?"

"Oh, yes, it's a favorite color of mine."

"Then why do I hear that bit of derision in your voice?"

"No reason." It wasn't her place to tell him Angela would have preferred lavender.

"You know, Miss Stone, you don't lie the least bit convincingly."

"No, I suppose I don't."

"Now, tell me what you don't like about the very expensive bedroom I had prepared for my daughter."

"You've certainly made it appealing with all that technology." She hoped that would appease him, but one look at his frowning gaze told her differently.

"Yes. I realize she may be a bit young to appreciate some of that equipment."

"I just think—" She stopped herself in time, silently cursing the wine for loosening her tongue.

"You think what?"

"Never mind." She shook her head so hard her hair whipped across her face. She brushed her index finger across her cheek to free a maverick strand.

"Bethany, I wouldn't ask your opinion unless I wanted it." His eyes were unusually dark and solemn.

"I worry about her, that's all," she said, scooting forward a little in her chair. "You've created her own self-contained world, and I don't know if that's the best thing for a ten-year-old who's recently left the only home she's ever known."

"You think because I can afford to give her a television and a game system—"

"That's not my objection," she interrupted heatedly. Now that she'd started, the floodgate of opinion couldn't be held back. "Angie needs to be introduced to *your* world. She's got to spend time with you—not by herself in front of her own television while you watch yours. When you come home at night, she has to feel that she's more important to you than some report."

Joshua looked shocked. "I see."

"I don't mean to criticize you, Joshua, really I don't. It's just that I care so much about...about Angie." If she didn't shut up soon, she would give him more than one reason to fire her.

"Well, you've certainly given me something to think about."

She stood. It would be better if she left, before she said anything more.

"I'll walk you to your car," he murmured when she reached for her purse.

He escorted her outside and opened the driver's door. Scant inches separated them, and she moistened her dry lips, feeling the night air fill with tension. The silence seemed to vibrate between them, thick with awareness, with unspoken words. She felt it and wondered if he did too.

"There's more to you than I ever realized," he admitted. He reached out and touched her cheek, gently gliding his finger down the side of her jaw as though he were touching the most valuable thing in the world.

Bethany closed her eyes to the delicious sensation that overtook her like an unexpected weakness. Her pulse began to beat wildly. He was so close, so wonderfully close, she could feel the heat radiate from his body. She knew her lips had parted with expectation. She wanted him to kiss her. Needed him to kiss her. With her eyes still closed, she raised herself on tiptoe.

With a soft groan, Joshua settled his mouth hungrily over hers. He kissed her until she was flushed and trembling, sliding his mouth back and forth lazily across hers, soaking in her softness, savoring her gentleness. And yet he gripped her shoulders as though he wanted to push her away and couldn't find the will to do so. If it were up to her, he would go on holding and kissing her forever. It was as she'd always imagined it would be in his arms. Her whole body felt as though all the strength was draining out of her, leaving her weak and wanting, and oh, so needy.

With an indrawn breath and a shudder, Joshua dragged his lips from hers and took a step back. "Bethany," he whispered in a voice she barely recognized. "You'd better go."

She wanted to argue with him, lock her arms around his neck and tell him she didn't ever want to leave him, but that would be impossible.

"Thank you," he whispered, his voice still husky.

For one wild second she didn't know why he should thank her for anything. Then her mind cleared, and she realized he was talking about helping with Angie. If anyone should be grateful, it was her.

By taking her in his arms, Joshua had just proven that dreams actually *do* come true.

Five

Monday morning Bethany sat at her desk, her stomach a mass of nerves. The wine, she told herself. It had been the wine that had done all the talking Saturday night. In retrospect it astonished her that she could actually have told her employer how to raise his daughter. Who in heaven's name did she think she was?

She was an executive assistant. The closest she'd ever come to mothering anyone was burping her three-month-old niece. Sure, she liked kids, got along well with them, but that didn't make her an expert when it came to Joshua's relationship with his daughter.

And if the wine had been talking for her, then it might well have been responsible for Joshua's kissing her, too. She knew her employer well enough to believe that when he walked into the office this morning, he would pretend Saturday night had never happened. He'd crossed the line, no doubt regretted it, and would immediately step back, hoping she hadn't noticed—or had the good sense to forget.

But she would never forget being in Joshua's arms. It had felt so wonderfully right and good. But instead of fulfilling a need, it had created an even greater one. The innocent emotion she'd held against her breast and nurtured had blossomed, leaving her craving so much more.

The door opened, and she held her breath as Joshua stepped into the office. He didn't glance in her direction, which was exactly what she'd expected. She'd been right. He regretted everything.

"Good morning, Miss Stone," he said tersely on his way past her.

She closed her eyes and firmly gritted her teeth. It was even worse than she'd thought. He'd barely been able to look in her direction.

Picking up the mail, she reluctantly followed him into the executive suite, pausing long enough to place the sorted correspondence on his desk. As was her habit, she delivered a cup of freshly brewed coffee and set it on the corner of his desk.

He leafed through the stack of letters, then paused and glanced in her direction. "How are you feeling, Miss Stone?"

"Fine." From the hoarse way the one word slipped past the tight constriction in her throat, it was a wonder he didn't call for a paramedic.

"Good. Then there were no lingering effects from your... swim the other day?"

"No...none—" she dropped her gaze so fast she nearly dislocated a disc in her neck "—except for a loose tongue." She felt the necessity to apologize. "Mr. Norris, I feel terrible that I took the liberty of criticizing. How you raise your daughter is none of my concern, and I sincerely hope that—"

"Miss Stone, kindly sit down."

She nearly missed the chair in her eagerness to get off her feet. Her hold on the pencil was so tense it was a credit to American craftsmanship that the wood didn't snap in two.

He reached for the coffee mug and leaned back in his

chair, his look contemplative. "Ah, yes, your advice regarding Angela had slipped my mind."

Oh, no. He'd forgotten, and she'd gone out of her way to remind him! "It was the wine, you see," she said hurriedly. "I should never drink more than one glass, and I'd had two when we spoke, not to mention the Irish coffee earlier…and I can honestly say I wasn't quite myself Saturday evening."

"I see," he said with a frown. "So you have regrets?"

"Mr. Norris, please understand that under some circumstances…like those on Saturday…sometimes my tongue says things I have no intention of speaking aloud."

His frown grew darker, his brows crowding together until they formed a straight narrow line. He stiffened, seeming to shut her out completely.

She hated it when he did that, but she was powerless to do anything more than react. "I truly am sorry," she finished weakly.

"I believe you've apologized sufficiently. Shall we deal with the mail now, or is there anything else you care to confess before we get down to business?"

"The mail…of course."

Fifteen minutes later she stood, her head buzzing. She didn't exactly know where matters had gone wrong, but nothing seemed right. Joshua had been terse and impatient, issuing orders faster than she could write down his instructions. When he did look at her, his handsome face was devoid of expression.

She stood in front of the door that connected their two offices. Gathering her courage, she hesitated and turned around. She held the dictation pad to her breast like a shield of armor, her eyes infinitely sad. "Mr. Norris…one last thing."

"Yes. What is it now, Miss Stone?" he asked impatiently.

"I don't regret *everything* about Saturday night," she

admitted in a raspy whisper, wanting to clear away one misconception, even at the cost of her own pride. "I can understand why *you* would prefer to forget what happened, but I don't. However, I... I promise not to embarrass either of us by ever mentioning it again."

She hurried to escape then, not waiting for a response, but several minutes later she was stunned to hear her employer whistling from behind the door.

At lunchtime she pressed the button of her intercom. "Mr. Norris, I'm leaving now."

"Miss Stone," he said hurriedly, "last year...did I do anything special for you for Assistants' Day?"

She had to think about it. "You had flowers delivered, I believe."

A soft laugh followed. "As I recall, you ordered those flowers on your own. I had nothing to do with it."

"We...we did discuss it. Briefly."

"It seems to me most employers take their assistants to lunch. Is that right?"

"I'm not sure."

"Lunch appears to be the proper protocol. If that's the case, it seems I owe you a meal. Are you free this afternoon?"

Her mouth opened and closed several times, a bit like a trout, she was embarrassed to realize.

"Miss Stone?"

"Yes, I'm free."

"Good, I'll be finished here in about ten minutes."

She released the intercom and sat there with her mouth gaping open for a full minute before reality settled in. Joshua Norris had requested her company for lunch!

Sally stuck her head in the door. "Hey, are you coming or not? I'm hungry!"

Words square-danced on the tip of Bethany's tongue, but

when she couldn't get them to cooperate with her brain, she jerked around and pointed her thumb towards Joshua's door.

"You mean the beast won't even let you leave to eat lunch?"

Bethany shook her head wildly.

"What, then? Good grief, you look like you're about to keel over. What did that monster do to you this time?" Sally walked into the room and planted her hands on Bethany's desk, her eyes afire with outrage.

"I'm taking Miss Stone to lunch," Joshua announced, standing in the suddenly open doorway. "Is that a problem, Ms. Livingston?"

Sally leaped back from Bethany's desk as though she'd been struck by lightning. "No problem. Not for me. Well, I guess I should be getting along now. Enjoy your lunch, Bethany. It was good to see you again, Mr. Norris."

"Good day, Ms. Livingston."

Bethany's friend couldn't get out of the office fast enough. "See you later," she said weakly, and waved, all but jogging in an effort to escape quickly.

Joshua leaned against the doorjamb, indolently crossed his arms and legs, his face amused. "So I'm a monster. I wonder who could have given Ms. Livingston that impression?"

Bethany stood and tightly clutched her purse to her side. "There have been times in the past, Mr. Norris, when the description was more than apt."

"Is that a fact?" He seemed to find the information more humorous than offensive. "Then I'd best repent my obnoxious ways. I made reservations at Brennan's."

"Brennan's," Bethany repeated in an excited whisper. She'd lived in New Orleans most of her life and had never eaten at the world-famous restaurant.

"You approve?"

"Oh, Joshua... Mr. Norris, I'm... I'm very pleased. Thank you."

Their table was waiting for them when they arrived. If Joshua thought she was going to order a dainty shrimp salad and a glass of iced tea, then he was in for a surprise. She informed him that her appetite had always been healthy, and started off by ordering an appetizer plate and turtle soup, and then, for the main course, Buster Crabs Béarnaise, a Brennan's specialty.

"You don't mind, do you?" she thought to ask, after the waiter had left their table.

"Of course I don't. I can see you plan to make up for all the years I didn't take you to lunch."

He was teasing her, but she didn't mind. "That's not it."

"Just where do you plan to put all that food?"

"Oh, don't worry. None of it will go to waste. I've never had a problem with my weight. None of the women in my family do until after they get pregnant, or so my mother and sisters tell me. From then on, keeping their figures is a constant battle. So I plan to enjoy all the goodies while I can." Bethany knew she was chattering, but she couldn't make herself stop. Already she felt light-headed, and the wine hadn't even been poured yet.

"So you want children?" he asked, watching her with smiling eyes.

She spread a thick layer of butter over the top of a crisp French roll. "Of course."

"You're not afraid it'll ruin your figure?"

She shrugged, pleased he hadn't noticed how thin she was. "Actually, I'm pretty much a toothpick. I'm looking forward to adding a few curves. I'm just hoping they'll show up in the right places. With my luck, my bust is likely to sink to my waistline." She paused in shock, amazed at what she'd just said and hoping that Joshua wasn't shocked.

He chuckled, and then his eyes grew warm and serious. "I don't think you need to worry, Bethany."

"I hope not," she said, and paid close attention to her roll in an attempt to calm her heart rate. She knew she shouldn't try to read anything into their conversation, but she couldn't help it. Her guess was that Angie's mother hadn't wanted children, and consequently Joshua thought all women felt the same way. It took everything in her not to announce that she would gladly bear his children. At her errant thoughts she decided to forgo the wine.

"I told Angie you'd be escorting her to the Mardi Gras parade, and she's excited, to say the least," he went on, changing the subject as if aware of her discomfort.

"I'm looking forward to it myself."

"You honestly enjoy my daughter's company, don't you?"

Bethany found that a strange question. "Yes. She's delightful."

He added a teaspoon of sugar in his coffee and stirred it vigorously. "I gave some consideration to what you said Saturday night. You may be right about me shutting Angie out of my life. It isn't easy, after living all these years alone. But I wanted to tell you that I appreciate your insight."

"You do?" She fingered the tassel on the wine list. Maybe alcohol wasn't such a detriment to her thought processes, after all. Maybe it was just the thing to burst this romance wide open.

"I'm making an effort to spend more time with Angie, and I think we're both enjoying it. I have you to thank for that."

She smiled, more pleased than she could remember being about anything in a long while.

"Unfortunately, time is at something of a premium in my life," he added in a thoughtful tone. "These next six months are crucial to the future of Norris Pharmaceutical. There's a great deal at stake."

She watched him carefully. She knew another firm had made a takeover attempt several months back, and that it had taken everything Joshua had to hold off the other company. His business was still small, but the potential for growth was huge if the firm were managed properly.

"What I'm trying to say is that for the next little while I'm not going to be able to be the kind of father I'd like to be. I'm literally not going to have the time."

She opened her mouth to tell him that time had little to do with being a good father. All Angie required was to know he loved her and that she was important to him. She needed him to listen to her problems and occasionally to laugh with her.

"Angie hasn't stopped asking about you since that first afternoon she spent at the office before Mrs. Larson, the housekeeper, arrived. She seems to like you better than anyone."

Bethany's smile grew more forced by the minute. So this lunch hadn't been an excuse to get to know each other better, as she'd imagined...as she'd hoped. It was a bribe—pure and simple. Joshua wanted her to babysit his daughter. No doubt he was willing to pay her handsomely to become a lonely ten-year-old's surrogate parent.

"I'm going to be busy for the next several weekends," he continued. "And I was wondering if you'd be willing to entertain Angela for me. Naturally I'd be more than happy to pay you for your time."

"Naturally," she repeated dully.

The waiter delivered the appetizer tray, but she knew she wasn't going to be able to swallow a single bite.

* * *

"I'm such a romantic fool," Bethany said to Sally. She should have known—she should have at least suspected—that something was up when he'd asked her to lunch. But the instant he'd mentioned children she had made assumptions. Optimism had poured into her heart as she'd wondered where the conversation was going. Well, now she knew. He was looking for a weekend babysitter.

"I can't believe I was so gullible," she continued. She hadn't told her friend the details of what Joshua had asked of her over lunch, much less her fantasies, which were simply too embarrassing to repeat.

"Honestly, Beth, no amount of money is worth this," Sally said, shaking her head.

Actually, Bethany agreed with her, but it wasn't that easy. "I can't quit now."

"Why not?"

"Angie needs me."

"J. D. Norris is using his daughter to blackmail you into staying on as his executive assistant? No wonder you're so upset."

"It isn't exactly blackmail," she said miserably. But the one who would suffer if she were to refuse to look after Angie would be Angie herself. The little girl had endured enough turmoil in the past few weeks. If Joshua was planning on using her to keep his daughter occupied and out of his hair, Bethany would do it—for Angie's sake. But she had learned her lesson when it came to her employer. She was going to guard her heart well. She was not going to be made a fool of for a second time.

"At least tell me what he pulled this time," Sally said, clearly frustrated that Bethany hadn't let her know anything beyond the basics. "If you tell me what he said, then I can hate him, too."

Bethany shook her head forcefully. She didn't know why she'd held anything back. Sally knew everything...or almost everything, anyway.

"The raise..."

"Yes?"

"The lunch..."

"Yes," Sally said, and took a step forward. "Go on."

"They weren't because Joshua is interested in me. He wants a weekend babysitter."

"What?" Sally exploded.

"He was buttering me up so I'll be willing to watch Angie over the weekend."

Sally's eyes narrowed, and she plopped herself down on the couch and crossed her long legs, looking more furious by the moment.

"I should have known he'd never be interested in me as a woman. For one thing, that would be against company policy, and nothing's more important to him than his company."

A loyal friend, Sally gave her a gentle hug, but when she finished the fire was back in her eyes. "You're not standing still for that, are you?" she asked with grim determination. "I won't let you."

"So just what do 'I' plan to do?"

Sally tapped her finger over her closed lips as she mulled things over. "*You're* going to find yourself a man, a real man, someone who will give J. D. Norris an inferiority complex."

"And just where am I supposed to meet this paragon?"

Sally's gaze narrowed. "I think you already have. In fact, we've both met him."

"Oh, sure," Bethany muttered. If Sally had met someone so fabulous, why wouldn't she would want him for herself? "What makes you think Joshua Norris would care if I dated a hundred men?"

"He'll care," Sally said, nodding. "Trust me, by the time you're through with him, he'll care."

"Bethany, look!" Angie cried, pointing at the flambeaux carriers lining both sides of the wide cobblestone street. A golden arch of flame shot from one torch to the other. In the background a blast of music from a jazz saxophone pierced the night, followed by the unmistakable sounds of a Dixieland band.

"This is the most exciting night of my life," Angie said, and dramatically placed her hand over her heart.

Even the blue funk that Bethany had been in since her lunch with Joshua evaporated under the excitement of New Orleans during Mardi Gras.

"I've never seen so many people in my life…not even in New York." Angie shouted to be heard above the heavy noise of the milling crowd. "How's Dad ever going to find us?"

"Don't worry," Bethany answered, her voice equally loud.

"Do you think he'll like my costume?"

Bethany nodded. "He'll love it." She paused and adjusted the halo on top of the little girl's head. After hearing the story of how she'd gotten her name, Angela Catherine had insisted on dressing up like an angel, with elaborate feather wings and a golden halo. Bethany's own outfit was far less elaborate. She'd rented an antebellum-style gown, intent on doing her best imitation of Scarlett O'Hara. Sally had advised her to flirt and flitter, and play the part of a vamp and a tease. Not in front of Angie, of course, but much later, for Joshua's benefit. Bethany remained convinced such a ploy was useless, but she didn't have any better ideas.

Just thinking about Sally's plan to make Joshua jealous was enough to cause Bethany to peel open her fancy lace fan and cool her flushed face.

"Oh, look," Angie said next, pointing toward the street once more. "There's a man on stilts."

"I certainly hope those are stilts," Bethany answered with a soft laugh. "He must be all of eight feet tall." She checked the pendant watch pinned to the bodice of her gown and reached for Angie's hand. It was time to leave their position on the pavement if they were going to meet Joshua on time. "We'd better start working our way toward the restaurant."

"But the parade isn't over."

"It won't be for hours yet, but I don't want to keep your father waiting."

"OK," Angie agreed, although reluctantly.

"We'll still be able to see most of it." Bethany wasn't eager to leave, either. There was so much to see and do. Excitement arced like static electricity through the air. People were singing and dancing in the streets. Strangers were hugging and kissing one another. Laughter echoed all the way from the French Quarter to the exclusive Garden District.

Tightly gripping Angie's hand so as not to lose the little girl, Bethany wove her way through the milling mass of humanity.

"Bethany, Bethany, stop!" Angie shouted, her voice filled with panic. "I lost my halo."

By the time Bethany turned around to investigate, the headpiece was gone. "Oh, dear." There was nothing she could do. The halo had apparently come loose and been quickly carted off by a masquerader who considered the golden circle fair game.

"Now I can't be an angel," Angie said, looking as if she was ready to burst into tears if something wasn't done quickly.

"I'm sure this happens all the time," Bethany said, thinking on her feet. "Real angels must have a difficult time holding on to their halos, too, don't you think? I know I would."

"What happens then?"

"Then they're considered almost-angels, and they have to work hard to regain their status as full angels," she suggested, improvising.

"Oh, I don't mind that, because it must be difficult to be perfect all the time."

"Then we'll consider Angie Norris to be almost an angel."

"Right," Angie answered, apparently appeased.

Bethany couldn't remember ever being in a larger crowd in her life. Making progress down the people-filled streets was difficult, and the restaurant wasn't even within sight.

"Look, Bethany, there's Prince Charming."

Bethany looked up in time to see a tall handsome man astride a huge white stallion trotting down Bourbon Street. A mask covered his face.

"He's stopping!" Angie cried, her voice shrill with excitement.

Just as Angie had said, the handsome prince pulled back on the reins of the powerful stallion and came to a halt opposite them. Bethany watched in amazed wonder as he gave the horse over to a stranger, jumped down into the crowd and worked his way through the throng of partygoers until he stood in front of Bethany and Angie.

"Madam," he said softly to Bethany, "your loveliness has captured my heart."

He wore a mask, so Bethany couldn't see his face, but she would have recognized that mouth anywhere. Joshua. It had to be him. It looked like him. It even sounded like him. But he was tied up in a meeting and wouldn't be joining them for another half hour. It couldn't possibly be him. In addition, he would never do anything this wildly romantic.

"Oh, Bethany, he's so handsome. Don't you think so?"

The prince held out his palm, silently requesting her hand. By this time several people had formed a circle around them, watching the unfolding scene.

"Are you going to stand there all night, or are you going to kiss her?" a gruff male voice shouted.

"If he wants a kiss, I'm willing," a boisterous female voice added, and the crowd laughed.

Clearly trying to appease the rowdy group of merrymakers, the handsome prince took Bethany in his arms, swung her around with a flair that drew a round of applause and draped her over his forearm. Her eyes went as round as satellite dishes when he lowered his mouth to claim hers. She had half a mind to object. After all, she wasn't in the habit of kissing strange men. But this was Mardi Gras, a special once-a-year time to let down one's hair and participate in the unconventional.

The prince's mouth took hers in a warm moist kiss that was as soul-stirring as a religious revival and as deep as a bottomless sea. The kiss gentled as the fierce hunger was satisfied, and his lips moved over hers like the gentle brush of a spring sun on the hungry earth.

The crowd approved heartily.

When the prince released Bethany it was a wonder she didn't melt onto the pavement. Breathless and weak, she placed her hand over her heart, heedless to anything but the man who had held her in his arms. She blinked and took a step back.

"Wow," Angie said, her eyes round and wide. "I thought he was going to suck your lips off."

Had Bethany been any less affected she might have laughed, but even breathing was difficult…laughing would have been impossible.

Three or four women formed an impromptu line. "I've got dibs next," the first one called out, waving her fingers.

The prince, clearly being a true gentleman, kissed the hand of each woman in turn, and then, before they could object, gracefully remounted his white stallion and rode off.

"Bethany, why did he kiss you?" Angie wanted to know.

"I… I don't know." She continued to stare long after he rode out of sight. "Angie—" she paused and looked down at the little girl "—did that man…the one who kissed me… did he remind you of anyone?"

"Oh, yes," Angie admitted. "He looked like the prince in *Cinderella*. The one who kept trying the glass slipper on all the women's feet. I always thought that was silly, you know. What woman wears glass shoes?"

"Oh." Bethany couldn't help being disappointed. It was nonsensical to think it could have been Joshua when it simply wasn't possible. The logistics were all wrong.

And yet…

Six

The noise level decreased by several decibels when Bethany and Angie left the street and entered the restaurant where they were supposed to meet Joshua. Antoine's was probably the most famous restaurant in New Orleans, having been in operation close to 150 years. Bethany secretly hoped her employer wouldn't be there. If the prince who'd kissed her *had* been Joshua, then it would have been close to impossible for him to have changed outfits so quickly and arrived at Antoine's ahead of them.

Her gaze searched the plush interior, and to her bitter disappointment she found Joshua casually sitting at a table awaiting their arrival.

"Dad, Dad, guess what I saw!" Angie went running past the maître d', weaving her way between tables to her father, then hurling her arms around his neck and squeezing for all she was worth.

The maître d' offered Bethany a strained smile and formally escorted her to Joshua's table. He paused and elegantly held out a shield-back chair for her to take a seat.

"There was a man eight feet tall," Angie was telling him, the words running together, she was speaking so fast.

"And other men who tossed fire at each other, and then... *then* we met a handsome prince on a big white horse who kissed Bethany. It was soooo romantic."

Joshua's eyes widened, and when he glanced toward Bethany the edges of his mouth were quivering with the effort to hold back a smile. "It sounds like you've had quite an evening."

"Oh, yes, and, Dad, there are so many people, and everyone dresses like it's Halloween." Angie paused, and her hand flew to her hair. "I lost my halo. I was going to surprise you by being an angel because you said I looked like one when I was born, and then I lost the most important part, but Bethany said that's okay, because angels are supposed to be perfect, and well, you know me."

"I do indeed know you." He looked up and grinned in Bethany's direction. "I'm pleased to see you made it safely."

She managed a nod, still watching him closely, hoping to prove, if only to herself, that the prince who'd kissed her had been Joshua. She so desperately wanted it to be him and would always choose to believe that it had been.

"Do you usually kiss strange men on the street, Miss Stone?" he asked, seeming to read her thoughts.

"I... I..." she stammered. She couldn't very well announce that she thought the man had been him, and that was the only reason she'd allowed the prince to take her in his arms.

"It wasn't like she had much choice, Dad," Angie inserted, climbing off her father's lap and taking her own seat.

"So he forced you?"

Bethany managed a weak smile. "Not exactly."

He leaned forward, rested his elbows on the table and clasped his fingers together. "I'm curious why you would allow a complete stranger to sweep you into his arms and kiss you in front of a crowd of onlookers."

Hope fired through Bethany's blood like running water shooting off the edge of a cliff. It *had* been Joshua! It must have been, because no one had told him about the prince taking her in his arms, or that a crowd had gathered around to watch.

Boldly she raised her gaze to his. "He didn't seem the least bit dangerous," she said softly. "I... I felt that I knew him."

He cocked his thick eyebrows. "I see."

She certainly hoped he did, because her heart was pounding like a crazed pogo stick.

"Dad, is Bethany coming over Friday night?" Angie asked, sticking her head around the side of the huge menu. "You said she was."

"Bethany?" Joshua directed the question to her. From the way he turned away and started studying the menu it appeared her answer was of little consequence to him.

Despite her desire to see more of him out of the office, Bethany was aggravated. Joshua hadn't said anything to her about needing her Friday night. He'd taken it for granted that she didn't have any other plans, which fortunately she didn't, but his blatant assumption irked her.

"I suppose I could be there Friday night," she mumbled somewhat ungraciously.

"Mrs. Larson would be more than willing to stay," Joshua announced in a flat emotionless voice. "There's no need to feel obligated, especially if you have other plans."

"I'm not doing anything special." The admission took some of the bite out of her irritation.

"Oh, good," Angie said with an elaborate sigh. "Weekends are a bore, and being with you is always fun."

"Have you thought about inviting a school friend to spend the night?" Bethany asked. "We could order pizza and rent movies."

Angie slammed the menu down on top of the table, her eyes round and excited. "We could do all that?"

"Mr. Norris... Joshua?" It gave Bethany a small amount of pleasure to toss the question back into his court.

"Pizza and movies and a friend for the night?" He didn't sound overly enthused. "I suppose that won't be any problem."

"I think I'll ask Melissa over," Angie murmured thoughtfully, nibbling on her lower lip. "No, I like Wendy Miller better. She wants to be a writer, like me, and when we get tired of watching movies we could make up our own stories."

"That sounds like an excellent plan," Bethany said, pleased. "Don't you think so, Joshua?"

He mumbled something under his breath about pizza and little girls running around the house at six in the morning, and left it at that.

The remainder of the week passed quickly. What Joshua had said about the next few months being especially busy for him and the company was true. Rarely could Bethany remember a time when he had more meetings and appointments scheduled. He was working too hard, and it showed. She wished there were some way she could lessen his load.

"Do you have the Harrison report ready?" he asked on Thursday at quitting time.

"Not yet," she admitted reluctantly, feeling guilty. The report was nearly two hundred pages in length and highly complicated. "I can stay late tonight if necessary."

"No." He shook his head. "But give it top priority first thing in the morning."

"Of course. I apologize, but there were a thousand interruptions the past couple of days." She felt obliged to explain why it was taking so long, although he didn't appear to be upset with her.

"Don't worry about it, Bethany, I understand."

Friday, Bethany skipped her lunch hour to work on the report so Joshua would have it for his meeting that evening. It was on his desk when he returned late that afternoon.

He called her into his office soon afterward and motioned for her to sit down.

"You did an excellent job with this," he told her, granting her a rare smile.

"Thank you." She was rather proud of it herself.

He hesitated and leaned back in his chair, looking anxious. "The dinner meeting this evening is with a group of financiers. I don't know what time I'll be getting back to the house. I'm afraid it could be quite late."

"Don't worry. I can stay with Angie and her friend until you get home."

"I really appreciate your help, Bethany."

She nodded, unable to voice the emotion that ran like a river deep within her heart. Helping Joshua, sharing his joys and easing his worries, was something she yearned to do every day. Since Angie's arrival their relationship had changed drastically, and yet she wanted so much more.

It was after eleven by the time Bethany heard Joshua let himself into the house. She'd been sitting in the family room reading. Both Angie and Wendy had fallen asleep at ten, exhausted from a busy week at school. They were sleeping in Angie's bedroom, and the house had been blissfully quiet since they'd gone to bed.

She set her book aside and stood, eager to talk to Joshua about what she knew had been an important meeting. She knew that the future of Norris Pharmaceutical rested on the decision of the financiers, although Joshua had never directly told her as much. Still, she would have had to be blind not to know the problems his company was currently facing.

She met him in the living room and greeted him with a warm smile. "Welcome home," she said softly, not wanting to wake the girls.

"It's good to be here." He set his briefcase down, peeled off his suit jacket and folded it over the top of the sofa. "How did everything go with the girls?"

"Great, what about you?"

Joshua shrugged. "I won't know their decision until next week sometime."

So Joshua and Norris Pharmaceutical were going to be forced to play a waiting game.

"Are you hungry?" she asked.

He nodded, looking slightly chagrined. "Starved, as a matter of fact. I didn't have much of an appetite earlier."

Knowing the importance of his meeting, she could well believe that. She'd eaten sparingly herself. "There's plenty of pizza left."

"You'll join me?" he asked. When she nodded, he looked pleased and led the way into the kitchen. "I think I've got a couple of cold beers. Do you want one?"

"Please."

While he was searching through the refrigerator for the beer, she placed several slices of cold pizza on a plate and warmed them in the microwave. By the time they were heated he had brought out paper napkins, and set those and the two bottles of beer on the small kitchen table.

The pepperoni pizza was excellent—better than the first time around, she decided. They didn't talk much at first. He asked her a couple of questions about how her evening had gone, and she told him how the two girls had been far too keen to make up their own stories to be interested in watching a DVD.

"I've set up the television and DVD player so all Angie has to do is turn them on first thing in the morning, and they can watch then. Hopefully that'll give you an extra hour or two of peace so you can sleep in a little." She worried that he wasn't getting enough rest. Heaven knew he worked long enough hours, especially lately.

"That was thoughtful of you."

A short silence followed before he spoke again. It was clear that the meeting with the financiers continued to weigh on his mind. He told her his general feelings about how his proposal had been received, the vibes he'd felt, the mood that had persisted throughout the long dinner meeting.

She leaned back and listened attentively while he rummaged through and sorted out his thoughts. He finished, sat quietly for a moment, then downed the last of his beer.

"I suppose I should be getting home," she said, standing.

His gaze flew to his gold watch. He looked surprised when he noted the time. "I didn't mean to keep you so long, Beth."

She stopped in front of the dishwasher, turned back to him and smiled.

"Does something amuse you?"

She set their dirty plates inside. "Here you are using a

nickname, when there was a time not so long ago when you didn't even know my first name."

"I knew," he whispered. He was so close behind her now that she could feel his warm breath against the side of her neck. "I've always known."

A shiver of awareness scooted down her spine, and she braced her hands against the counter as he gently cupped her shoulders, his touch so light that she thought at first she might have imagined it. His fingers gently stroked her skin as he ran his hands down the length of her arms. At the same time he tenderly drew her back so her body fitted against his full height. His movements were slow, deliberate, as though he expected her to object and was granting her ample opportunity to pull away if she so desired.

She went completely immobile. She couldn't have moved if her life had depended on it.

He rested his chin on top of her head for a short moment before he lowered his mouth to the slender curve of her neck. The instant his lips touched her sensitized skin and located the pulsing vein there, heat erupted like a fiery volcano throughout Bethany's trembling body.

She didn't know who moved first. She might have turned and slipped her arms around his waist, or his hands could have directed her. She didn't know which. It didn't matter, though, nothing did except that she was in Joshua's arms and his mouth was hungrily locked over hers. He was kissing her as if he'd thought of doing nothing else for endless hours. Again and again he dragged his lips over hers, as though the thought of releasing her so soon was too much to bear.

A helpless moan escaped her. To have him kiss her was almost like drowning, then bursting through the water's clear surface and feeling more alive than at any other time in her life.

Still holding her, he buried his face in the curve of her neck and exhaled a deep unsteady breath.

"The most important meeting of my life," he whispered, his voice husky and moist against her flushed skin. "And all I could think about was you."

"Oh, Joshua." She tucked her hands under his arms and leaned against him for support, bracing her forehead against his hard chest.

"This shouldn't be happening," he said, but there was no regret in his voice.

"I wanted it, too," she admitted, hiding her face in his chest and closing her eyes to the warm happy feeling that enveloped her.

"You've been so good for Angie," he whispered.

Some of her good feelings left, and she stiffened, fearing he was going to use her love for him to keep her as a willing babysitter. She tried to break away, but he wouldn't let her.

"What's wrong?" he asked anxiously. "Bethany, you've gone all cold on me. What did I say?"

She shook her head rather than explain.

"You're upset because I appreciate what a good friend you are to my daughter?"

He lovingly caressed the side of her jaw and lifted her chin so that she couldn't avoid meeting his gaze. "No, of course not. I love Angie."

"And she loves you." He bent forward and brushed his mouth over hers, his lips settling naturally onto hers for another swift taste.

She kept her eyes closed, still trapped in the lingering sensation, and yet her heart felt as if it were weighted down with bricks. It wasn't right that she should be in his arms and feel so terribly insecure. He should know her feelings. "I sometimes think Angie's the only reason you…you want to be around me."

The room went suspiciously quiet. The smallest noise would have sounded like a sonic boom in the silence that stretched between them. Her eyes fluttered open, but she dared not look at him, dared not meet the fiery anger she could feel radiating from him.

"You don't honestly believe that, do you?"

"What else am I to think?"

He freed her arms and took a step back from her. His eyes were dark and solemn. Sad. "If you don't know the answer to that by now, then I've failed us both."

"Failed us both?" She tossed his own words back at him. "The only time you ever want me around is to…to baby-sit for Angie."

The muscles in his jaw leaped as though it was an effort to control his anger. "I can't see how you could think that."

She felt miserable. Only a minute ago he'd been holding and kissing her, and now he looked as though he couldn't wait for her to get out of his house.

Rather than continue the argument, she turned toward the kitchen table and removed their crumpled napkins.

"Leave those," he said.

"I… I was just going to put them in the garbage."

"I don't want to be accused of using you as my personal maid sometime later. Believe me, I'd prefer to do the task myself."

"Okay." Swallowing hard, she dropped the napkins back on the tabletop. The only thing left for her to do was walk away. Holding her shoulders stiff and straight, she collected her purse and her book. She was almost to the front door when Joshua reached out and stopped her.

She didn't turn to look back at him.

"Beth," he said starkly. "I'm sorry."

Her head whirled around, and she saw the regret written boldly across his face.

"I'm sorry, too, Joshua." Sorry to have doubted him, sorry to have been so willing to believe the worst of him, but she couldn't help it. She might have done him a grave injustice...but she couldn't help feeling the way she did.

He kissed her again, but this one lacked the urgency or the hunger of the others. With his arm wrapped around her waist, he walked her out to her car. As she drove off, she could see his image in her rearview mirror, standing alone in the night, watching her as she pulled away.

"Okay, everything's all set," Sally announced, standing in front of Bethany's desk. She wore that off-center silly smile that indicated she was up to something.

Bethany paused with her fingers poised over the keyboard. She would play along with Sally's game for a while, until she figured out what card Sally was hiding up her sleeve, but that wouldn't take too long. "What's all set?" she asked.

"Your hot date."

"What?" Bethany exploded, and jerked her gaze toward the connecting door, grateful it was closed so Joshua wouldn't overhear their conversation. "A hot date with who?"

"Whom," her roommate corrected with a mischievous grin.

"Whom, then!"

"You honestly don't remember, do you?" Sally looked surprised, then disbelieving, then impatient. As each emotion cross her face in turn, Bethany thought it was like watching the flickering movements of an old-time silent film. "You really don't!"

"Obviously not," Bethany answered. "What are you talking about?"

With a look of disgust, Sally crossed her arms and aimed her chin toward the ceiling. "Does the name Jerry Johnson ring a bell?"

Bethany mulled it over in her mind. She knew Sally had been up to something the past couple of days, but she hadn't a clue what. "The name sounds vaguely familiar."

"Well, you *should,* since you've agreed to a date with him."

"I've what?" This nightmare was growing more vivid by the minute. "When?" Bethany demanded.

"I've arranged everything for Thursday night."

"Not *that* when," Bethany said. "When did I ever say I'd have anything to do with the man?"

Sally cast a suspicious glance towards Joshua's door. "The afternoon you sat in our living room after your lunch with Mr. Big Shot. Remember? We made plans, you and I."

The words jarred Bethany's memory. She could remember her friend telling her what a fool she was being and that she would be an ever bigger one if she continued to let Joshua Norris take advantage of her. Sally had rambled on about finding a man to make Joshua jealous, but Bethany had been too miserable to listen carefully. Now she realized her mistake. "I seem to remember you making a suggestion or two," she admitted reluctantly.

"I did more than suggest," Sally said righteously, and lowered her voice to a whisper. "I *acted,* which is more than I can say for you."

"But things are progressing between me and Joshua,"

Bethany answered, keeping her voice as low as possible. "I don't want to do anything to topple the cart."

"Sure, it's going just great between the two of you... now," Sally scoffed. "You're taking care of his little girl every free moment. You don't have time for anything else."

"But..."

"Just answer me one thing, Bethany. Has your precious Mr. J. D. Norris ever taken *you* out without dragging Angie along? Has it ever been just the two of you alone? Well, other than that lunch when he asked you to fill in on weekends for him?"

Her roommate had knocked away Bethany's argument as easily as if she'd toppled a stack of children's building blocks. Bethany lowered her gaze. Sally was right.

"See what I mean?" Sally muttered. "Mr. Norris is using you. He has been from the first, and as your best friend I refuse to stand by and let it happen any longer. You've got to start circulating again. I'm going to introduce you to the *right* kind of men, and I won't let you stop me."

"But, Sally..."

"I refuse to hear any more arguments. Thursday night, got it?"

"All right," Bethany agreed, but she couldn't have cared less about Jerry Johnson or Jerry anyone. She was in love with Joshua, and nothing would change the way she felt about him.

When Joshua called for her to take some dictation an hour later, Bethany briskly stepped into his office.

He smiled when he saw her, but her return smile was strained. He handed her a stack of papers. "Collate and get me fifteen copies of each of these at your convenience. There isn't any big rush."

"Is tomorrow morning soon enough?"

"That'll be fine."

She would have returned to the reception area, but he stopped her. "One minute, Miss Stone." He paused to write something across the top of a yellow legal tablet, and when he glanced up, he looked pleased about something, relaxed in a way she hadn't ever seen him. "Would you happen to be free tomorrow night, Beth?"

She felt as if a loaded logging truck had parked on top of her chest. "Thursday night?"

"That's tomorrow, yes. I realize it's short notice. Is there a problem?"

Her palms felt unexpectedly moist, and she shifted the papers she was holding to get a better grip on them. The small stack felt as though it weighed thirty pounds. "I'm sorry, Joshua… Mr. Norris, but I've already got plans."

"There's no problem. I should have asked you earlier." He frowned and went back to his task, scratching notes across the top of the pad.

"If… I hope Mrs. Larson will be able to stay with Angie, but if she can't—"

"Mrs. Larson can, so don't worry about it."

Bethany could feel her heart's thundering beat all the way to her toes.

As soon as she was back at her desk, Sally stuck her head around the door. "Have you got a moment?"

"Sally…" Bethany groaned. "What is it now?"

Her friend strolled into the office. "I've got his picture."

"Whose?"

"Jerry Johnson's." She looked as pleased as if she'd managed to smuggle secret papers out of the Kremlin. "It was in the bottom of my purse. I forgot I had it."

"Sally, honestly, I don't even want to go out with this guy."

"Don't say that until you've seen his picture." She waved the photograph under Bethany's nose, as though the blurred image would be enough to convince her how lucky she was to be dating such a hunk.

Bethany grabbed the small glossy picture from her friend's hands and studied the handsome smiling face. Jerry Johnson was attractive—okay, he was downright show stopping.

Sally leaned her hip against the side of Bethany's desk, crossed her arms and looked exceedingly proud of herself. "He knows you, too."

"Why don't I remember him?" She frowned, because he *did* look vaguely familiar.

"You only met him once," Sally said, and studied the fingernails on her right hand. "Christmas, last year, at the Dawsons' party."

Bethany could hardly remember who the Dawsons were but finally recalled they were family friends of Sally's.

"Trust me, Beth. Thursday night with Jerry Johnson is a date you won't soon forget."

"Ms. Livingston," Joshua said in a cold voice from the open doorway. "Seeing that you have nothing to do but traipse in and out of my office at all times of the day, I'm wondering just how much your work performance contributes to my company."

Sally bounced away from the desk as though she'd been sitting on a hot plate. Her eyes filled with shock as she glanced at Bethany, silently pleading for help.

"Sally was making a delivery," Bethany said, stretching the truth as far as she dared.

"Yes, I heard. The photo of your hot date."

Bethany's face flushed with brilliant color.

"I trust you two have more important business to see to on company time?"

"Yes, sir," Sally mumbled, and was gone.

"Are those papers collated yet?" Joshua demanded.

"I...no. I thought we agreed... I'll take care of that first thing in the morning."

"I need them now."

"But you said—"

"Don't argue with me, Miss Stone. I want those papers collated before you leave tonight. Is that clear?"

"Perfectly, Mr. Norris."

"Good. And the next time I see Ms. Livingston in my office talking to you on company time instead of being where she should be, she'll be looking for another job."

"If Sally leaves, then I'm going, as well."

"That decision is your own, Miss Stone." With that he spun around and returned to his office, soundly closing the door.

Seven

"Have aliens captured your brain?" Bethany demanded of her roommate. "Of all the crazy things you've pulled over the years... Couldn't you have waited until after work to bring me Jerry's photo or, better yet, have emailed it to me?"

"I know, I know," Sally said, still shaken from her earlier confrontation with J. D. Norris. "Honestly, I thought he was going to ask for my head."

"He nearly did." She didn't mention that hers would have rolled with her friend's. Joshua had been in such a bad temper that even hours after their confrontation, talking to him about the situation would have been impossible. Not that Bethany had tried. She knew her employer well enough to recognize his mood. And honor it.

"You're still going Thursday night, aren't you?" Sally asked, glancing surreptitiously toward her friend.

"Of course I'm going." But Bethany didn't feel nearly as confident as she sounded. This whole idea of dating a man she'd briefly met at a Christmas party months earlier didn't appeal to her, especially since she'd been drinking spiked eggnog at the time. Eggnog and wine were synonymous with trouble, as far as she was concerned.

* * *

Friday morning, Joshua was already at his desk when Bethany arrived. She paused between the doorway that connected their offices, surprised to see him and dismayed at the picture he presented. He looked terrible. Even from where she was standing, she could see and feel his fatigue. Dark smudges circled his eyes. His jacket had long since been discarded, his tie loosened and the top two buttons of his wrinkled shirt unfastened. One glance convinced her that he hadn't bothered to go home the night before.

"Joshua," she whispered concerned, "how long have you been here?"

Deliberately he set his pen aside, though he continued to hold on to it. "When we're at the office, Miss Stone, kindly refer to me as Mr. Norris."

"As you wish," she returned stiffly, and proceeded into the room. So that was the way it was going to be. All right, she would deal with it. Holding her back as straight as possible, she brewed a fresh pot of coffee and went back to her own desk to sort through the morning mail. When she'd finished, she returned, poured Joshua a cup of coffee and delivered it to him the way she had every morning for the past three years.

"So, Miss Stone," he said sardonically, "how did your 'hot date' go?"

His voice was so thick with sarcasm that she had to bite down on her bottom lip to keep from responding in like tones. Seeing the mood he was in, she decided against saying how her dates went was really none of his business.

"Fine, thank you." She handed him the sorted mail. "The letter you've been looking for from Charles Youngblood arrived."

"Good." He picked through the stack until he located it. "Are you planning on seeing him again?" he demanded.

"Charles Youngblood?"

"You're being deliberately obtuse. I was referring to your...date," he said impatiently.

Now he'd stepped over the line. "I hardly think that's any of your business," she snapped, her own patience a slender thread. "What happens outside this office isn't your concern."

"When your action directly affects the productivity of this company, I'd say it becomes my business."

Icy fingers wrapped themselves around Bethany's vocal cords. She couldn't have answered him had her job depended on it, and considering the horrible mood he was in, it very well could be.

"Miss Stone, I asked you a question. I expect an answer."

It was in her mind to shout that he was demanding and unreasonable, and that she refused to discuss the details of her personal life with any employer. Instead, she squarely met his gaze and said, "My personal life is my own." With that, she turned and walked out of the office.

An hour later her hands were still trembling. If she lost her job, then so be it. The door to Joshua's office opened, and just the sound was enough to cause her to stiffen her spine, readying herself for another confrontation.

He walked over to her desk and set down the mail. A list of handwritten instructions accompanied the large stack of letters.

"Cancel my appointments for the rest of the day, Miss Stone," he said in a raspy tone.

She refused to look at him, but with her peripheral vision she saw him lean momentarily against the edge of her desk and pinch the bridge of his nose. He paused and wiped his hand down his face.

"I'm going home," he announced.

She nodded once, a quick jerky movement.

Joshua hesitated once more. "I apologize for my earlier behavior. You're absolutely right—your personal life is your own. I had no business laying into you that way."

Again she remained silent.

"If there's anything that requires my attention, you can contact me at the house. Good day, Miss Stone."

"Mr. Norris."

"J. D. Norris said all that?" Sally murmured when they got together during their break, her eyes narrowed and thoughtful.

"I've never seen him so angry and unreasonable. I'm just glad he left, because I couldn't have stood another minute.... I think I would have quit on the spot if he'd said one more word."

Sally broke off a part of her sugar-coated doughnut and paused with it in front of her mouth. "I think he could be falling in love with you, Bethany."

The sip of coffee Bethany had just swallowed jammed halfway down her throat and refused to budge. She slapped her hand over her chest and gasped. Once she'd composed herself enough to speak, she murmured, "Hardly."

"I mean it," Sally countered with a contemplative look. "He's acting like a jealous little boy, which is exactly what I thought might happen. His behavior confirms my suspicions."

"A more likely scenario is that I was a convenient scapegoat for him to vent his troubles." Bethany wasn't blind to the company's current financial problems. Having recently held off one takeover effort, Joshua had been hit almost immediately by another. His resources had been depleted by the first attempt, and he was holding on to control of the company by the thinnest of threads. Naturally, most of the information was privileged, so she wasn't at liberty to discuss it with anyone, including her best friend. A good deal of what transpired without Bethany being present. But she'd garnered enough information from the numerous transcripts she'd typed. Unfortunately, she didn't have a clue how Joshua was surviving this latest takeover bid.

"I don't know," Sally muttered, the same piece of doughnut still level with her lips. "I've been doing a lot of thinking about the way Mr. Norris has been acting these past few weeks, and it's obvious he's really into you."

"Sure he is," Bethany muttered scornfully. "Angie thinks I'm loads of fun, and he thinks I'm a soft touch when it comes to his daughter."

"Well, aren't you?"

Bethany was reluctantly forced to agree. "I...won't be able to meet you at Charley's after work," she said, almost as an afterthought.

"How come?"

"I... I've got to take some papers over to Mr. Norris's house for him to sign."

"Ah." Sally's eyes brightened, then were quickly lowered as she pretended an interest in her paper napkin. "Listen..." She paused, placed the half-eaten doughnut back on her plate and brushed the sugar granules from her fingertips. "Since you weren't really all that interested in Jerry, I was wondering..."

"Go ahead," Bethany said, having trouble disguising a smile, almost enjoying her friend's discomfort.

"Go ahead and what?"

"Date Jerry yourself. Do you honestly think I didn't know you're attracted to him? Sally, you drool every time you mention his name."

"I do?"

"I can't believe you'd fix *me* up on a date with him when you're so obviously taken with him yourself." Actually, knowing Sally's twisted way of planning things, this scheme of hers was probably the only way she'd been able to come up with to talk to him again.

"When did you figure it out?" Sally demanded.

"Not right away," Bethany was slow to admit. She'd been so caught up with what was going on between her and Joshua that she hadn't been paying attention to her friend until the obvious practically hit her over the head. After all, how many women carried a picture of a man they'd only met once in their purse for an entire year? Not many, she would bet. Only someone as sentimental and romantic as Sally.

"So you don't mind if I—"

"Not in the least. Jerry Johnson is all yours, with my blessing."

Bethany finished the last of her duties at five and left the office to drive directly to Joshua's home on Lake Pontchartrain. Her excuse for stopping at the house was flimsy at best, but she felt terrible about what had happened that morning and longed to straighten things out—even if it meant admitting she wouldn't be seeing Jerry again.

Mrs. Larson opened the front door. "Miss Stone, how are you this evening?"

The portly widow had thick silver hair, and wore the traditional black uniform and white apron. She was kind and gentle-hearted, and on the few occasions that Bethany had met her, she'd been impressed with the older woman.

"I'm fine, thank you," Bethany answered. "How's Mr. Norris?"

Mrs. Larson's lips thinned with worry as she shook her head. "I swear, it's a miracle that man hasn't worked himself into an early grave."

"I know," Bethany said miserably. "Has he slept at all?" The more she thought about their argument that morning, the guiltier she felt for her part in it. Joshua was obviously exhausted beyond reason.

"He slept an hour or two when he came home this morning, and now he's at his desk in the den, working. Would you like me to take you to him?

"Please." Bethany followed Mrs. Larson to the large den, which was built off the living room and faced the lake.

The older woman knocked politely, then opened the door. "Miss Stone is here to see you," she announced, and stepped aside.

Joshua half rose. "Bethany." His eyes widened with surprise. "Is there a problem? You should have phoned."

"I'm sorry to interrupt you...."

"It's no problem. Sit down."

She lowered herself into a huge overstuffed leather chair and folded her hands on her lap, watching him expectantly. If she hadn't known better, she would have sworn he was pleased to see her, and that made her feel good about her unscheduled visit.

He returned her look, his gaze expectant, and she suddenly remembered the excuse she'd invented to explain her presence. "There are some letters for you to sign, but... I seem to have left them in the car." She rushed to her feet. "I'll get them and be right back."

She all but jumped out of the chair and hurried back outside. Instead of troubling Mrs. Larson a second time after she grabbed the letters, she let herself into the house and Joshua's den.

"Taking the time to bring these over was thoughtful," he said, scribbling his name across the bottom of the first letter without bothering to read it.

"Yes…well, I felt badly about this morning," she murmured. Her face was growing warm, and she knew she was blushing. "You'd obviously been up all night and, although it really wasn't any of your concern, it wouldn't have hurt me to let you know about Jerry and me."

"Yes?" he coaxed when she didn't immediately continue. "Have you decided to continue dating Ms. Livingston's friend?" Some of the pleasure drained from his eyes. "That's understandable."

"No, Joshua… I mean, Mr. Norris. I won't be seeing Jerry again."

"You won't?" Five years disappeared from his face as his expression lightened. "Well, that's certainly your business."

"Yes, I know," she countered softly. With no excuse to linger any longer, she stood, wishing she could find a plausible reason to stay. "How's Angie?" she asked with a flash of brilliance, and reclaimed her chair.

"She's doing just fine," he answered eagerly. "Really good. She's spending the night with her friend Wendy."

Silence followed.

She stood once more.

"She seems to have made the adjustment from New York to New Orleans rather well," he said.

She sat back down, almost gleeful with relief over the excuse to stay. "Yes, I thought so."

Another moment of silence fell between them.

"I know this is spur-of-the-moment, but would you care to have dinner with me?" he asked.

"Yes." She felt excited enough about the prospect to stand up and cheer, but she restrained herself. "I'd like that a lot."

The smile he tossed her was almost boyish. He paused and glanced her way, eyeing her clothes, and frowned slightly.

"I can go home and change if you want." She was wearing a dark blue business suit with a straight skirt and short double-breasted jacket.

"No, you're perfect just the way you are."

"You're sure?" She was curious to know where he was taking her. When he'd asked her to dinner, she'd assumed at first that he meant that they would be eating there at the house.

"I'm positive," he answered, although he was dressed far more casually than usual himself, in trousers and a thick Irish cable-knit sweater the color of winter wheat.

After pausing to let Mrs. Larson know he was leaving, he reached for Bethany's hand and led her out to the car. He drove into the heart of the city and parked on a side street a few blocks off the French Quarter.

"Do you like beans and rice?" he asked.

She nodded eagerly. The popular New Orleans dish had been elevated by the on-going interest in Cajun and Creole cooking. The recipe had originated in the slave quarters, and many a Southerner had grown up in a time when each day's menu revolved around rice and beans.

"A friend of mine runs a café that serves the best Louisiana cooking in the world." He hesitated, then smiled. "But be warned, the food is fantastic, but the place rates low on atmosphere."

"You needn't worry about that with me." She wondered what he would think if he were ever to join her large family for a Sunday dinner. How would he fit in with mismatched place settings and the ever-flowing stream of conversation?

He slipped his arm around her waist, holding her close to his side. "I wasn't worried that you'd disapprove, I just wanted to warn you."

"Okay, I consider myself properly warned," she told him, her eyes smiling. This was the man she was just beginning to know, the man she'd been granted rare glimpses of over the years. Excitement filled her at spending this time alone with him.

He directed her down a narrow alleyway. She had been up and down the streets of the French Quarter most of her life, but she didn't recognize this one.

"Are you sure there's a restaurant back here?" she asked.

"Positive."

The place was small and cramped, with only a handful of tables. The chairs were mismatched, and the Formica tabletops were chipped, but the smells wafting from the kitchen were enough to convince her that Joshua knew what he was talking about.

"What you doin' bringin' that skinny girl in my kitchen, J. D. Norris?" a huge black woman asked as she stepped out from behind an old-fashioned cash register.

"Bethany, meet Cleo."

The woman wiped her hands dry on the smudged apron that was tucked into the folds of her skirt. "You look like a strong wind would blow you away," Cleo announced, cocking her head to one side as she studied Bethany through narrowed dark eyes.

"Then I sincerely hope you intend to feed me."

Cleo chuckled, and her whole body shook with the action. "Honey chil', you have no idea how Cleo can feed a soul." She ambled across the room and pulled out two chairs. "Sit," she ordered. With that she started toward the kitchen, paused and looked over her shoulder. "You bring your horn?"

Joshua nodded. "It's in the car."

"It's been too long, Dizzy, much too long."

"Your horn? Dizzy?" Bethany asked once Cleo was out of sight.

"I play saxophone now and then, when the spirit moves me."

Shocked speechless, she studied him for a moment, astonished at this unknown side of the complex man she loved. There was nothing in her knowledge of Joshua that so much as hinted at any musical interest or talent. "I had no idea," she managed to say after a moment.

He grinned, as if to say there was a lot about him she didn't know, and she couldn't doubt it.

Cleo returned with plates piled high with rice and smothered with rich beans in a red sauce. "This is just for openers," she warned, setting down the food. She returned a minute later with a third plate stacked high with warm squares of corn bread oozing with melted butter.

"She doesn't honestly expect us to eat all this, does she?" Bethany asked between bites. She'd tasted beans and rice in any number of restaurants but never anything that could compare with this unusual blend of spices, vegetables and meat. No other version of the classic had ever tasted anywhere near this delicious.

"She'd be insulted if we left a crumb."

She didn't know how she managed it, but her plate was clean when Cleo returned.

The woman gave her a broad grin and nodded approvingly. "Maybe you be all right, after all," the massive woman said with a sparkle in her dark eyes.

"Maybe you be, too," Bethany returned, holding in a laugh.

Cleo let loose with a loud burst of laughter and slapped Joshua across the back. "I like her."

Joshua grinned, sharing a look with Bethany. "So do I."

"You got room for my special sweet-potato-pecan pie?" Cleo eyed them both speculatively, as if to say they were too skinny to know anything about good food.

Joshua leaned back, splayed his fingers over his stomach and sighed. "I think you better count me out. I'm stuffed to the gills. Bethany?"

"Bring me a piece."

Cleo nodded several times. "You done yourself proud, Dizzy. She don't look like much, but there's more to her than meets the eye."

The pie was thick, sweet and delicious.

Joshua watched, eyes wide, as Bethany finished off every last bite.

"You amaze me."

She licked the ends of her fingers. "I told you before, I've got a healthy appetite."

Cleo returned carrying two steaming mugs of coffee. "You takin' this pretty gal to St. Peter's?"

Joshua nodded, and Cleo looked pleased.

After he paid for their meal, he led Bethany out of the café and further down the narrow alley to another set of doors. "I hope you like jazz, because you're about to get an earful."

"I love any kind of music," she was quick to tell him, feeling closer to him than ever before. He opened the door off the alley, and a cloud of smoke as thick as a bayou fog enveloped them as they walked inside. It took a second for her eyes to adjust to the dim interior. She couldn't see much as he led her to a vacant table and pulled out a chair for her. The sounds of clicking ice, the tinny tones of an old piano and the hum of conversation surrounded her like the familiar greetings of old friends.

"What would you like to drink?" he asked, and had to lean close in order for her to hear him above the conversational roar. "A mint julep?"

She answered him with a shake of her head. "A beer, please."

He turned to leave her, but he must have forgotten something, because he hadn't gone more than a couple of steps when he turned back. She looked up expectantly, and he leaned down to press his mouth over hers in a kiss so fleeting that she hardly had time to register it.

In the front of the room was a small platform stage. A man was playing the piano, and another was setting up a drum set. Bethany watched Joshua weave a path between tables to get to the bar. He was waylaid several times as people—obviously friends—stopped to greet him. In a few minutes he returned with two frosty mugs of cold beer.

She had barely had time to taste hers when he stood and offered her his hand. She didn't understand at first, then realized he was asking her to dance. The small dance floor was crowded when they moved to the edge of it. He wrapped her in his arms, and they soon blended in with the others.

The minute he had pulled her into his embrace, a wave of warmth had coursed through her. She leaned her head back and looked up at him, realizing anew how much she loved this man.

He touched her cheek, and his fingers felt like velvet

against her cool skin. His lips were only a few inches away, and she longed with everything in her for him to kiss her again.

"Beth," he whispered urgently, "don't look at me like that."

Embarrassed, she lowered her gaze, all too aware of what he must be reading in her eyes.

"No, forget I said that," he went on, and moved ever so slightly to lift her chin and direct her mouth to his.

She felt as if her bones were melting. She tasted the malt flavor of his beer as she opened her mouth to his. If his first kiss had been an appetizer, this second one was a feast. He slid his hands down her spine, molding her body intimately to his as he kissed her again. He moved his lips over hers in eager exploration until she was convinced she would faint from the sheer pleasure of being his arms.

When he broke off the kiss, she sagged against him, too weak to do anything but cling to the only solid thing in a world that was spinning out of control. He nuzzled the side of her neck and then investigated the hollow of her throat with his tongue. She was gathered as close as humanly possible against him. When he kissed her again, his mouth was so hot it burned a trail all across her face.

"Let's get out of here," he whispered in a voice so thick and raspy she could hardly understand him.

She answered with a nod.

He kept her close to his side as he led them back to their table. They were about to leave when a tall dark man with a huge potbelly and a thick dark beard stopped him.

"C'mon, Dizzy. You can't leave this place without playing the blues."

"He's right… Dizzy," she murmured, looking up at Joshua.

"Good to see you again, Fats." Joshua shook hands with the other man.

"You got your horn, brother?"

Joshua nodded reluctantly. "It's in the car."

"Get it."

Joshua looked almost apologetic as he led Bethany back to their table. "I'm sorry, sweetheart," he whispered.

She pressed her hands onto his shoulders and was so bold as to reach up and brush her lips across his. "I'm not. I want to hear you play."

The man Joshua had called Fats jumped onto the stage when Joshua reappeared, carrying his saxophone with him. Fats had brought a bass trombone. The man who'd been playing the drums reappeared carrying a trumpet. The first couple of minutes were spent checking valves and tooting a few notes. No one seemed to mind that the dancing had come to an abrupt halt. The room seemed to vibrate with a charged sense of anticipation.

Bethany sat back, watching Joshua and loving him more each minute. He stepped to the front of the stage and his gaze sought hers. The look he sent cut straight through her, and then he smiled and brought the instrument to his lips.

The blast of music split the air and was followed by shouts of encouragement from the audience. Soon the sounds of the other instruments joined Joshua: the piano, the trumpet, the trombone, each in turn.

Bethany couldn't have named the tune, didn't even know if it had a title—the players weren't following any sheet music. The melody appeared improvisational as each player in his own time bent the notes his own way, twisting and turning, soaring and landing again. She flew with them, and she wasn't alone. Every patron in the club joined the flight, ascending with the music. The men played as if they were one, yet each still separate. Bethany soaked in every note of Joshua's music as if her heart had become a sponge meant only to take in this man and his music. She experienced the bright tension of the piece as though each bar of music were meant for her and her alone. When they were finished, her eyes burned with unshed tears.

She remained in an almost dreamlike state when Joshua rejoined her. His face was close to hers, and she could see the beads of perspiration that wetted his upper lip and brow. She raised her fingertip to his cheek, needing to touch him, needing to say what was inside her and unable to find the words to explain how his music had touched her heart.

He gripped her hand with his own and kissed her fingertips.

"You liked it?" he asked, his gaze holding hers.

She nodded, and a tear escaped and ran down the side of her face. "Very much," she whispered.

"Bethany, listen." His hand continued to squeeze hers. "I'm going out of town next week."

She already knew he had a trip planned to California.

"I haven't any right to ask this of you." He stopped and tangled his fingers in her hair. "I want you to come with me."

If he'd asked for her soul at that moment, she couldn't have refused him. "I'll come," she replied.

His eyes ate her up, seeming almost to ask her forgiveness. "Angie will be with me. She wants you there, and so do I."

Eight

"When we're in California," Angie said thoughtfully, sitting beside Bethany in the first-class section of the Boeing 767, "will you call me Millicent?"

"If you like."

The little girl nodded eagerly. "At least for the first day or two. I might want to change to Guinevere or Charmaine after that."

"I may slip up now and again," Bethany admitted, doing her utmost to remain serious. There were days she couldn't keep track of who *she* was, let alone a fun-loving ten-year-old.

"That's all right," Angie said, and went back to flipping through the pages of the flight magazine. She paused abruptly and looked back to Bethany. "Do you want me to call you Dominique? I could."

Bethany hesitated, as if to give the child's offer serious consideration, then shook her head. "No thanks, sweetheart."

Joshua was sitting across the aisle from the two of them. His briefcase was open, and he was busy reviewing documents. His brow was creased in concentration, his gaze intent. Bethany was convinced he'd long forgotten both her and his daughter, and her heart ached a little with the realization.

Inhaling a deep breath, she pulled her eyes away from her employer and tried to involve herself in the plot of the murder mystery she was reading. It didn't work, although the author was one of her favorites. Instead, Sally's dire warning played back in her mind like a stubborn voice mail that refused to shut off. It was happening again, her roommate had warned. Bethany was allowing Joshua to use her as a convenient babysitter. Bethany didn't want to believe that, but...

After Friday night, when Joshua had taken her to meet Cleo and she'd heard him play the saxophone at St. Peter's, she had been convinced he felt something deep and meaningful for her. She wasn't so naive as to believe he loved her—that would have been too much to hope for so soon. But she couldn't deny that Joshua had shared a deep personal part of himself with her, and that went a long way toward making her forget she would be left solely in charge of Angie while he tended to his business meetings.

"Daddy." Angie leaned across Bethany and called to her father. When he didn't immediately respond, his daughter took to waving her hand.

Joshua obviously didn't hear or see her, too wrapped up in the report he was reading to break his concentration.

"What is it, Angie?" Bethany asked.

The girl leaned back in her seat. "How much longer? Will we be able to go to Disneyland today? I can hardly wait to see Mickey Mouse and Snow White."

Bethany checked her watch. "It'll be another couple of hours yet before we land."

"Oh." The small shoulders sagged with disappointment. "That long?"

"I'm afraid so."

"What about Disneyland?"

"There just won't be enough time after we leave the airport and check into the hotel."

"But Dad said we—"

"We'll see Mickey and Minnie, Snow White and everyone else first thing in the morning. I promise."

It looked for a moment as though Angie was going to argue, but she apparently changed her mind and quietly settled back in her seat for a while. Then she squirmed once more.

"Is Dad going to be in meetings the whole time we're in California?"

Bethany nodded. She didn't like the idea of Joshua being constantly busy any better than Angie did. When she'd originally made the arrangements for this trip, he had requested that she schedule in a couple of days' free time so he could spend it with Angie, sight-seeing. However, once Bethany had agreed to accompany them, the days he'd set aside for vacation had quickly filled up with appointments and other business affairs. Now he would be occupied the entire five days of their visit.

Their flight landed at LAX at five that evening, but by the time their luggage had been collected and the limousine had driven them into Anaheim, it was much later. Because of the time difference, Angie was overly tired, hungry and more than a little cranky.

Bethany wasn't faring much better after the long trip. Keeping Angie occupied had drained her completely. When Joshua had first asked her to accompany him, she'd been thrilled. Now she felt abused and disappointed at the role she would be playing during the next few days. Her back was stiff, she was hungry, and she felt like Cinderella two nights after the ball, when her hair needed washing and there was a run in her tights.

Joshua had requested a hotel close to the amusement park, where Bethany and Angie planned to spend a good deal of their stay. He had reserved a large suite. By the time they were settled, Angie was close to tears. Cranky because she was hungry, grumpy because she was tired, and yet too excited to sleep.

It took Bethany the better part of an hour to convince the little girl to eat the hamburger Joshua ordered from room service. More time was spent persuading Angie that although it was still daylight, she really needed to rest. She was a little more cooperative once she took a bath, at which point she climbed into bed with hardly a complaint and was asleep within five minutes.

Bethany felt as if she'd worked straight through a double shift when she joined Joshua in the suite's living room. She plopped herself down beside him on the davenport, slipped off her shoes and sagged against the back of the sofa, more exhausted than she could remember being in a long while.

He set aside his papers and reached for her hand. His gaze revealed his appreciation—and no wonder, she thought. It had been obvious from the moment Angie started to whine that he wasn't going to be able to deal with his daughter patiently. He raised Bethany's hand to his mouth and brushed his lips over her knuckles. "I don't know what I'd do without you," he murmured.

A polite nod and a weak smile were all the response she could manage.

"I don't mean for you to work while we're here." He scooted closer and wrapped his arm around her, cupping her shoulder. "My intention had been to make this a vacation for you, as well.... I didn't realize Angie would be such a handful."

"She was just tired and cranky."

He kissed the top of her head. "I know it was completely selfish of me to ask you to make this trip."

She didn't answer. Couldn't. Sally had been telling her what a fool she was from the minute Bethany had told her she would be travelling to California with Joshua and his daughter.

"The thought of spending five days without seeing you was more than I could bear."

She desperately wanted to believe him. She tucked her head under his chin and snuggled closer, almost too exhausted to appreciate the comfort his arms offered.

"I'm being unfair to you."

Her eyes drifted shut when he raised her chin and kissed her, his mouth brushing over hers in a swift kiss. She sighed and smiled contentedly. Tenderly he smoothed wisps of hair away from her face and slowly glided his fingertips over her features.

"Such smooth skin," he whispered. "So warm and silky."

She felt as if she'd gone ten rounds with a prize fighter, but one kiss from Joshua wiped out everything but the cozy tranquil feeling of being held in his embrace. She slipped her left arm around his middle and tipped her head back, seeking more of his special brand of comfort.

When he didn't immediately kiss her again, her lashes fluttered open. What she saw in his eyes made her heart go still. He was staring at her with such naked longing that she felt she would break out in a fever just looking at him. The words to tell him that she loved him burned on her lips, but she held them inside for fear of what voicing them would do to their relationship.

"Oh, Bethany, you are so beautiful." He whispered the words with such an intensity of emotion that she felt her heart melt like butter left sitting too long in the hot sun.

She wanted to tell him that it wasn't necessary for him to say things like that to her. He owned her heart, and had for three years.

His gaze held her a willing prisoner for what seemed like an eternity as he slowly slid his hand from the curve of her shoulder upward to her warm nape. He wove his fingers into her thick dark hair, and with his hand cupping the back of her head, he directed her mouth toward his. The kiss was full and lush. Rich. The man who was kissing her wasn't the arrogant man she worked with in the office. This was the same man who'd revealed a part of himself to her she was sure few others knew existed. The same man who had soared to unknown heights on the wings of a song he'd played just for her. The same man who gazed into her eyes and revealed such need, such longing, that she would spend a lifetime basking in the pure desire she viewed there.

She was shaking so fiercely inside that she raised her hand to grip Joshua's collar in a futile effort to maintain her equilibrium. Her flesh felt both hot and cold at the same time.

When he lifted his mouth from hers, he drew several ragged breaths. "Having you with me could end up being the biggest temptation of my life," he whispered in a raspy voice. He captured her hand and flattened her palm over his heart. "Feel what you do to me."

"I don't need to feel… I know, because you're doing the same thing to me."

"Bethany…listen, this isn't the right time for either of us and—"

She cut him off, not willing to listen to his arguments. All she longed to do was savor the sweet sensations he'd aroused in her with a single kiss. She slipped her hands around his neck and offered him a slow seductive smile as she gently directed his mouth back to hers.

His eyes momentarily widened with surprise.

She answered him with a smile, her lips parting, deepening the kiss.

"Bethany, oh, my sweet, sweet Bethany." He closed his eyes like a man enduring the worst kind of torture.

The distinctive ring of his cell didn't penetrate her consciousness at first. But he reacted almost immediately, jerking his head up and groaning aloud.

"Yes?"

It wasn't until he spoke that she realized he had left her and gone to find his phone. She blinked a couple of times, her eyes adjusting to the glaring light. Ill at ease, she sat upright and tried to catch her breath.

"The flight was on time. Yes…yes, first thing in the morning. I'm looking forward to it. I've got those figures you asked to see. I think you'll be impressed with what's been happening the past couple of months. Yes, of course, eight. I'll be there."

He spoke in crisp clear tones, and no one would have guessed that only a few moments earlier he'd been deeply kissing her. The transformation from lover to businessman was as slick as black ice on a country road.

It took her several minutes to gather her composure enough to stand. Her knees felt shaky, and she was sure desire lingered in her expression. She brushed the hair out of her face, her hands trembling. He was sitting with his back to her, intent on his conversation. As far as he was concerned, she could have been back in New Orleans. He had completely forgotten she existed.

She didn't wait until he was finished with his call. With her heart pounding like a battering ram against her rib cage, she walked across the floor, opened the door to the darkened bedroom she would be sharing with Angie and slipped inside. The little girl was sound asleep, and Bethany didn't bother to turn on any lights. She undressed silently, and found her way into the bathroom to brush her teeth and wash her face. Then she eagerly slipped between the clean sheets. Within minutes she felt herself sinking into a black void of slumber, but not before she heard Joshua's footsteps outside the bedroom door. He paused, then apparently thought better of waking her and walked away.

Angie was wearing Mickey Mouse ears and carrying a series of colorful balloons, two huge stuffed animals and other accumulated goodies when Bethany opened the door to their suite late the following afternoon.

"Hi, Dad." Angie flopped down in a chair and let out a giant whoosh of air. "Boy, am I tired."

Joshua grinned and sent a flashing query to Bethany. "How did you survive the day?"

"Great—I think. Only there isn't enough money in the world to get me back on some of those rides."

"Bethany screamed all the way through Big Thunder Mountain," Angie announced in a tattletale voice. "I thought she had more guts than that."

"At least I didn't hide my eyes when I rode through the Matterhorn."

"The abominable snowman frightened me," Angie announced, accepting the ribbing good-naturedly.

Joshua leaned back in his chair and grinned at them. "It looks to me like you both had a great time."

"Did we ever! We saw Donald Duck and Goofy and Snow White."

"Did Bethany happen upon another Prince Charming?"

Joshua asked. His gaze met hers, and it was filled with curiosity.

"Unfortunately, no."

"A shame," he muttered, looking appropriately disappointed.

"The only white stallion I encountered was connected to an old-fashioned fire truck," she told him, sharing his amusement. "I didn't have time to investigate further."

He chuckled.

"How did your meeting go?" She was all too aware that the future of Norris Pharmaceutical rested on the outcome of this trip. She was worried for Joshua and prayed everything would go his way.

"It went well." But he didn't elaborate.

"I'm starved."

Bethany nearly fell out of her chair at Angie's sudden announcement. "You just ate two hot dogs, cotton candy and a bag of peanuts."

"Can I help it?" the girl asked. "I'm a growing child—at least that's what Mrs. Larson keeps telling me."

"And I'm one pooped adult." The thought of leaving the comfort of the suite on a food-seeking expedition so soon after getting back didn't thrill Bethany.

"Is anybody interested in taking a swim?" Joshua asked, diverting his daughter's attention.

"Me!" Instantly Angie was on her feet, eager to participate in anything that involved her father.

Bethany shook her head, too exhausted to move for the moment. "Maybe later—give me a few minutes to recuperate first." Her feet were swollen, although she'd worn a comfortable pair of shoes. Her back ached, and her head continued to spin from all the rides Angie had insisted they go on.

"I'm ready anytime you are, Dad," Angie said, and ran into the bedroom to change.

Joshua walked over to Bethany's side and bent down to lightly kiss her lips. "You look exhausted."

She smiled and nodded. "I'm too old to keep up with a ten-year-old."

"Go ahead and rest. I'll keep Angie occupied for the next hour or so."

"Bless you." She wasn't teasing when she'd told Joshua how exhausted she was. The energy level of one small girl was astonishing. They'd arrived at Disneyland when the amusement park opened that morning and then had stayed for the full day. On the monorail ride back to the hotel, Angie had casually announced that she intended to return to the park the following morning and then had wondered what there was to do that evening. All Bethany could think about was soaking in a hot bath and taking a long uninterrupted nap.

"We're off," Joshua said, coming out of his bedroom. He was wearing swimming trunks and had a thick white towel draped around his neck. He made such an attractive virile sight that Bethany nearly changed her mind about accompanying the two of them.

"Bye, Bethany," Angie said, and waved, looking happy and excited. "Rest up, okay? Because there are still a whole lot of things to do."

Opportunities for the little girl to spend time alone with her father were rare. Bethany was pleased that Joshua was making the effort to fit Angie into his busy life.

The door closed, and, with some effort, Bethany struggled to climb out of the chair. With her hand pressing against the small of her back, she made her way into the bedroom, deciding to forgo a soak in the tub and instead rest her eyes a few minutes.

The next thing she knew an hour had slipped away, and she could hear whispered voices.

Angie stuck her head in the bedroom door and announced to her father, "Bethany's asleep," then withdrew.

Bethany's mouth formed a soft smile as she bunched up the feather pillow beneath her head and pulled the blanket more securely over her shoulders. She'd been having such a pleasant dream that she wanted to linger in the warm bed and relive it. In her mind, Joshua had been telling her how much he loved her. The scent of orange blossoms wafted through the air, and she was convinced she could hear the faint strains of the "Wedding March."

"Dad," Bethany heard Angie whisper. "Have you ever thought about getting married again?"

Bethany's eyes popped open.

"No," Joshua muttered, and the tone of his voice told her that he found the subject matter distasteful.

"I've been thinking a lot about what it would be like to have a mother," Angie continued, apparently undaunted by the lack of enthusiasm in her father's voice.

Bethany lifted herself up on one elbow, wondering what she should do. If she were to make some kind of noise, then Angie and Joshua would know she was awake and end their talk. However, if she lay there and listened, she was going to regret it and feel guilty about eavesdropping when their discussion clearly wasn't meant for her ears.

"Angie, listen to me. I—"

"You're supposed to call me Millicent," she interrupted, impatience ringing in her young voice.

"Millicent, Guinevere, whoever you choose to be at this moment, I don't think my remarrying is a subject you and I should be discussing."

"Why not?"

Joshua seemed to have some difficulty answering, because only silence filtered into the bedroom where Bethany lay listening. She knew she should let them know she was awake. Obeying her conscience, she made a soft little noise that apparently went undetected.

"I've been thinking about what it would be like if you married Bethany," Angie continued. "I like her a whole bunch. She's a lot of fun."

"Bethany's too young," Joshua answered shortly. "I'm nearly eleven years older than she is and—"

"Oh puh-lease," Angie said dramatically. "I saw you kiss her once, and you didn't seem to think she was too young for that!"

"When?" Joshua demanded.

"A long time ago. I forget exactly when, but you did, and I saw you with my own two eyes."

Too young! Bethany mouthed the words in astonished disbelief. It was obvious that Joshua was pulling excuses out of a hat in an effort to appease his daughter.

"You *did* kiss her, didn't you?"

"Yes," Joshua muttered.

"And you liked it?"

"Angie." He paused, and Bethany could hear his sigh of frustration. "All right… Millicent, yes I *did* like it." The admission was ungracious, but it filled Bethany with joy, anyway.

"Then I think you should marry her."

"A whole lot more than liking the way someone kisses has to happen before a man considers marriage," Joshua explained with gruff impatience.

"It does?" Angie questioned. "Like what?"

"Things that a man doesn't discuss with his ten-year-old daughter."

"Oh," Angie muttered.

"Now for heaven's sake, don't say anything to Bethany about this or it'll make her uncomfortable." He paused, and in her mind Bethany could see him pacing the floor. "You haven't talked to Bethany about this, have you?"

"No," Angie admitted reluctantly. "I wanted to discuss it with you first. You told me I could talk to you about anything, and I thought I should let you know that if you wanted to marry Bethany I'd approve. She'd make a great mother."

"Whatever you do, Angela, don't say anything to her!"

"I won't." Bethany heard Angie make a disparaging sound, but she wasn't sure what had prompted it. "Do you want more children, Dad?"

"What?" The word seemed to explode from him.

"You know, another kid, like me?"

"I... I hadn't given it much thought. What makes you ask that?" It was clear from his tone of voice that Angie's questions were exasperating him.

"I don't know," Angie admitted, "except that if you and Bethany were to get married, then you'd probably have more children, and I'd like that. I want a little sister and then a little brother."

"Did Bethany put you up to this?" Joshua's low voice was filled with suspicion.

Bethany was so outraged that she nearly flew out of bed to argue in her own defense. How dare Joshua Norris think she would use his daughter to achieve her own ends. The very thought was despicable! If he believed for one second that she would resort to such underhanded tactics, then he didn't know her at all, and that hurt more than anything else he'd said.

"Bethany doesn't know anything yet. I told you, I wanted to talk to you first."

"I see," Joshua muttered.

"You *will* think about marrying her, won't you, Dad?"

A year seemed to pass before Joshua answered. "Maybe."

Bethany's face was so hot she was sure she was running a fever. Her heart constricted, and she closed her eyes, wishing with everything in her that she'd been asleep and oblivious to this rather unpleasant conversation.

After lingering in the bedroom for another forty minutes, Bethany opened the door and stepped into the living area, only to discover that Angie and her father were engrossed in a television movie.

"I didn't think you were ever going to wake up," Angie announced. "I'm starved, but Dad said we had to let you sleep."

"I'm sorry to keep you waiting," she said, having trouble sounding normal. "You should have gone without me. I wouldn't have minded." The way she was feeling now, she didn't know that she could maintain her composure and not let Joshua know what she'd innocently overheard.

Angie didn't seem to notice a change in Bethany's attitude, but Joshua certainly did. He studied her, and his gaze narrowed. "Are you feeling all right?"

"I'm fine," she said, and to prove it she smiled brilliantly in his direction.

"Good. I hope your healthy appetite is in place, because I've picked out an excellent Italian restaurant for dinner tonight."

"That sounds great," Angie said, reaching out to claim Bethany's hand. "Come on, let's go, Dominique."

The remainder of their days ran together, they were so filled with activities. Angie and Bethany visited Knott's

Berry Farm, Universal Studios and every other tourist attraction they could find. In the evenings Joshua took charge of his daughter, finding ways of entertaining her and relieving Bethany of the task. There were plenty of opportunities for Bethany to spend time alone with Joshua, but she avoided them as much as she could without, she hoped, being obvious.

The final night of their stay, Angie fell asleep in front of the television. Joshua carried the little girl into the bedroom and gently laid her on top of the mattress.

Bethany pulled the covers over the small shoulders and bent down to plant a swift kiss on the smooth brow. Joshua followed suit.

"I think I'll turn in myself," Bethany murmured, avoiding his eyes.

He arched his brows in surprise. "It's only a little after nine."

"It's...it's been a long day."

"Come on, I'll order us some wine. We have a lot to celebrate."

"Then the meetings went well for you?"

He grinned and nodded.

She was relieved for his sake. Now perhaps his life could return to normal, and he could go back to keeping regular hours instead of working day and night.

He had a chilled bottle of Chablis sent to their room. The waiter opened it for them and poured.

"I have a one-glass limit," Bethany said, feeling awkward.

"You had more the other night, as I recall."

"Sure, but I'd just swan dived into Lake Pontchartrain, too, if you'll remember."

A smile broke out across his handsome features. "I'm not likely to forget."

They sat in the living room with the lights dimmed, looking out over the flickering lights of the city. Neither spoke for a long time.

"I want you to know how grateful I am that you accompanied me and Angie," Joshua started off by saying. "Since Angie's come to live with me, things have changed between us, haven't they?"

She stared into her wine and nodded.

"I always thought of you as an efficient executive assistant, but bit by bit I've come to learn you're a warm, caring, nurturing woman."

"Thank you."

"I know you're attracted to me, Beth, and I haven't made any secret of the way I feel about you."

Her brain filled with an agitated buzzing. He was going to ask her to marry him. She knew it as clearly as if he'd removed a diamond ring from his pocket and waved it under her nose. Angie had specifically requested her for a mother and Joshua was simply complying with his daughter's wishes.

She glanced up and tried to hold back the emotions that were clamoring for release.

His intense gaze held hers.

"I know this must seem rather sudden, Beth, but I'd very much like you to consider marrying me."

Nine

"Bethany?"

With deliberately calculated movements, she set aside her glass of Chablis. Her mind was spinning like a child's toy top, wobbling precariously now as the momentum was slowing. Her heart was shouting for her to accept Joshua's proposal, but her head knew it would be wrong, especially since she'd heard him declare he had no intention of marrying again. All she could think was that over the last few days Angie had pleaded, whined and convinced Joshua against his better judgment to propose.

"For a moment there I actually thought I could do it," she whispered, feeling both miserable and elated at the same time.

Joshua's face sobered. "I don't understand."

She raised her hand to his face and lovingly pressed her palm against the side of his jaw. "I don't expect you to. I'm honored, Joshua, that you would ask me to be your wife, but the answer is no."

"No?" He looked positively stunned. "You didn't even take time to think it over. You're turning me down? I thought... I'd hoped..."

She hung her head. "I want so much more out of marriage than to be a replacement mother for a lonely little girl."

Joshua's brow creased into a deep dark frown. "What gives you the impression I'm asking you to be my wife because of Angie?"

"Joshua, please..."

"I want to know why," he demanded, his words as stiff and cold as frozen sheets.

If he was looking for an argument, she wasn't going to provide one. She stood and offered him a sad but strong smile. "At least you didn't lie and tell me how much you love me. I've always admired that inherent streak of honesty in you. It's been ego shattering at times, but I've come to appreciate it." She swallowed tightly and then whispered, "Good night."

"Bethany." He ground out her name from between his teeth. "Sit down. It's obvious, if only to me, that we've got a great deal to discuss."

She shook her head. If they talked things over, she would be forced to tell him that she'd overheard his exchange with Angie. To admit as much would be humiliating to them both.

"Good night, Joshua."

He clenched his jaw, and a muscle leaped at the side of his face. She knew he was struggling to hold back his anger. She looked away, determined to leave the room with her pride, even if nothing else, intact.

The return to New Orleans was as much of an ordeal for Bethany as the flight to California had been five days earlier. At least this time Angie slept a good portion of the way. Once again Joshua sat across the aisle from her, but he might as well have been on a different airplane for all the attention he paid her. The silent treatment was exactly what she had expected, but it still hurt. His protective shield was securely fastened in place, and with no apparent regret or effort he'd shut her out of his heart and his life. Whatever possibility there had ever been for her to find happiness with Joshua Norris was now lost. He wouldn't ask her to marry him again and no doubt was sorry he'd done so the first time.

When they landed, Joshua saw to their luggage with only a few clipped instructions to Bethany to wait with Angie for his return.

"Did you and my dad have a fight?" Angie asked, tucking her small hand in Bethany's and studying her carefully.

"Not an argument." Bethany knew it would be wrong to try to mislead Joshua's daughter into believing everything was as it had been earlier in the week, but she had no idea what to say.

"How come ever since we left California you look like you want to cry?"

The best answer Bethany could come up with was a delicate shrug, which she knew wasn't going to appease a curious ten-year-old.

"Dad's been acting weird, too," Angie murmured thoughtfully, glancing toward her father, who was waiting for their suitcases to appear on the carousel. "He hardly talks to you anymore." She paused, as though waiting for Bethany to respond, and when she didn't, Angie added, "Dad and I had a long talk, and we decided that it would be a good idea if you two got married." She slapped her hand over her mouth. "I wasn't supposed to tell you that."

"I already know," Bethany said, feeling more miserable by the minute.

"You *are* going to marry Dad, aren't you?" Eyes as round as oranges studied her, waiting for her response.

"No." The lone word wavered and cracked on its way

out of Bethany's mouth. She loved Angie almost as much as she did Joshua, but she couldn't marry him to satisfy his little girl.

"You *aren't* going to marry my dad?" If Joshua had looked stunned when she'd refused his proposal, it was a minor reaction compared to the look of disbelief Angie gave her. "You really aren't?"

"No, sweetheart, I'm not."

"Why not?"

Bethany brushed the soft curls away from the distraught young face and squatted down to wrap her arms around Angie, who wanted to be called Millicent. "I love you both so much," she whispered brokenly.

"I know that." Ready tears welled in Angie's eyes. "Don't you want to be my new mom?"

"More than anything in the world."

"I don't understand…"

Bethany didn't know any way to explain it. "Your father will find someone else, and…"

"I don't want anyone else to be my mother. I only want you."

Fiercely Bethany hugged the little girl close, and Angie's tears soaked through her silk blouse. "I…have to go now," Bethany whispered unevenly, watching Joshua make his way toward them, carrying their suitcases. "Goodbye, Millicent."

"But, Bethany, what about…?"

Remaining there and listening to Angie's pleas was more than Bethany could bear. She lifted her suitcase out of Joshua's hand without looking at him and hurriedly walked away.

"Bethany, don't go!" the little girl cried. "Don't go… please, don't go."

The words ripped through Bethany's heart, but she didn't

turn around. Couldn't. Tears streaked her face as she rushed outside the terminal and miraculously flagged down a taxi.

"You honestly refused Joshua's proposal?" Sally demanded, pacing in front of Bethany like an angry drill sergeant. "You were delirious with fever at the time and didn't know what you were saying. Right?"

"No, I knew full well what turning him down would mean."

"Are you nuts, girl?" Sally asked, slapping her hands against the sides of her legs and stalking like a caged panther. "You've been in love with him for years."

"I know."

"How can you be so calm about this?" Sally slapped her thighs a second time.

Bethany shrugged, not exactly sure herself. "I wouldn't even mention it except I'm going to be looking for another job right away. And I knew as soon as you realized what I was doing, you'd hound me with questions until I ended up confessing everything, anyway."

"He fired you!"

"No," Bethany whispered. But she couldn't continue to work with Joshua. Not now. It would be impossible for them both.

"I thought you were crazy about the guy?"

"I am." Crazy enough to want the best for him. Crazy enough to want him to find his own happiness. Crazy enough to love him in spite of everything. For Joshua to marry her to provide a mother for his little girl wouldn't be right. "When he first asked me, I honestly thought I could do it. The words to tell him how much I wanted to share his life were right there on the tip of my tongue, but I had to force myself to swallow them." It had been the most difficult task of her life, but she didn't feel noble. Her emotions ran toward sad and miserable. Perhaps someday she would be able to look back and applaud her own gallantry. But not now, and probably not for a long time.

"But why would you refuse him?" Sally was looking at her as though it would be a good idea to call in a psychiatrist.

"He doesn't love me."

"Are you so sure of that?" Her roommate eyed her carefully, clearly unconvinced.

"I'm positive."

"Well, big deal! He'd learn to in a year or so. Some of the greatest marriages of all time were based on something far less than true love."

"I know that, but the risk is too high. He might come to love me later, but what if he doesn't? What if he woke up a year from now and realized he loved another woman? I know him. I know that he'd calmly accept his fate and let the woman he really loved walk out of his life."

"What about *your* life?"

Bethany ran her hand down her skirt, smoothing away an imaginary wrinkle. The deliberate movement gave her time to examine her thoughts. "I'm not being completely unselfish in all this. Yes, I love him, and yes, I love Angie, but I have a few expectations when it comes to marriage, too. When and if I ever marry, I want my husband to be as crazy in love with me as I am with him. When he looks at me, I want him to feel that his life would be incomplete without me there to share it with him."

"So you've decided to give J.D. your two week-notice first thing Monday morning?"

Bethany nodded. "You should be glad, Sal. You've been after me to do it for months."

"I don't feel good about this," Sally muttered, folding her arms over her chest, her brow furrowed with a frown. "Not the least bit."

Monday morning, Bethany had her letter of resignation typed before Joshua arrived at the office and had left it on his desk, waiting for him.

She gave him a minute to find it before entering his inner sanctum. He was sitting at his desk reading it when she delivered his coffee and handed him the morning mail.

"I hope two weeks is sufficient notice?" she asked politely, doing her utmost to remain outwardly calm and composed.

"It's plenty of time," he said without looking in her direction. "I'd like you to review the resumes yourself, decide on two or three of the most qualified applicants and I'll interview those you've chosen."

"I'll contact personnel right away."

"Good."

She turned to leave, but he stopped her. "Miss Stone."

"Yes?"

His gaze held hers for an agonizingly long moment. "You've been an excellent executive assistant. I'm sorry to lose you."

"Thank you, Mr. Norris." She hesitated before turning and walking out of his office. She longed to ask him about Angie but knew it would be impossible. She hadn't contacted the little girl, believing a clean break would be easier for them both. But she hadn't counted on it being this difficult, or on how much she would miss the little ray of sunshine who was Joshua's daughter.

A week passed, and Bethany was astonished that she and Joshua could continue to work together so well, even though they rarely spoke to each other, except for a few brief sentences that were required to accomplish the every-day business of running the office. She was miserable, but she knew she was right, and however painful it was now, the hurt would eventually go away.

Following Joshua's instructions, she reviewed all the applications personnel sent up. She chose three who she felt would nicely fill her role. Joshua interviewed all three and chose a matronly woman in her early fifties. For the next week Bethany worked closely with the woman so the transition would be as smooth as possible.

On her last day Joshua called her into his office, thanked her for three years of loyal service and handed her a bonus check. She gasped when she saw the amount, pressed her lips together and calmly said, "This is too much."

"You earned it, Miss Stone."

"But…"

"For once, Miss Stone, kindly accept something with-out arguing with me."

It wouldn't do much good, anyway, so she nodded and whispered brokenly, "Thank you, Mr. Norris."

"Have you found other employment?" he asked her un-expectedly, delaying her departure.

She shook her head. She hadn't taken the time to look. With everything else going on in her life, another job didn't seem all that important.

"I wish you the very best, Miss Stone."

"You, too, Mr. Norris." She couldn't say anything more, fearing her voice would crack. As it was, tears hovered just below the surface. "Thank you again."

"Goodbye, Bethany."

She lowered her gaze and worried the corner of her lower lip. "Goodbye, Joshua."

With that, she turned and walked out of his life.

* * *

"Well, did you get the job?" Sally asked one afternoon.

The whole day had been gorgeous and sunny, and Bethany knew she should be like everyone else in the city and enjoy this unusual display of summerlike weather. Instead, she was inside, reading a book.

Shaking her head, she said, "They offered the position to someone else." Amazingly, she couldn't have cared less.

"You don't look all that disappointed."

"Sally, I don't know what's wrong with me," she said on the tail end of a drawn-out sigh. "I don't care if I ever find another job. All that interests me is sleeping, and if I'm not doing that, I'm reading. I've read more books in the past month than I did all last year."

"You're escaping."

"Probably." All she knew was that it didn't hurt as much when her face was buried in a good book—as long as it wasn't a romance. True love wasn't exactly her favorite topic at the moment. Murder mysteries appealed to her far more. Bloody battered bodies—that sort of thing.

Sally looked at her watch and gasped. "I've got to change and get ready," she said, and hurried toward her bedroom.

"For what?" Bethany asked, following her friend.

Sally blushed. "Jerry and I are going on a picnic."

"You've been out with him every night for the past week."

"I know," Sally admitted, and sighed sheepishly. "I'm in love, and I'll tell you right now—if Jerry Johnson proposed to me, I'd accept." She grew serious. "Tell me, honestly, Bethany, are you okay?"

"I'll be fine," she said, feigning a smile. "I've got everything I need. I stopped off at the library on my way back to the apartment. I've got enough reading material to last most people a lifetime, though at the rate I've been going I'll be done in a week." Her small attempt at humor fell decidedly flat.

Ever the true friend, Sally rolled her eyes toward the ceiling and mumbled something under her breath about misguided love and Bethany not knowing what was good for her.

The apartment felt empty with Sally gone. Bethany figured she might as well get used to it. The way her roommate's romance was progressing, Sally could well end up marrying her attorney boyfriend before the end of the summer.

At about seven, the doorbell rang. Bethany climbed off the sofa to answer it, unsure who it could be.

She pulled open the door and then nearly sagged against it. "Joshua?" She had never been more shocked to see anyone in her life.

"Is this a bad time? I know I should have phoned, but I was detained and…" He let the rest of what he was saying dwindle off.

"No, I'm not doing anything important. Please come in." She stepped aside to let him enter the apartment.

She hurried to get ahead of him and picked up an empty soda can and a banana peel, feeling embarrassed and foolish. "Sit down." She gestured toward the couch. "Can I get you something to drink?"

"No, thank you."

She deposited the rubbish in the kitchen and rushed back into the living room, holding her hands behind her back in nervous agitation. "Is something wrong at the office? I mean… I'd be happy to help in any way I can."

"Everything's fine."

Alarm filled her when she realized there could only be

one reason why Joshua would come to her. "It's Angie, isn't it? She's had an accident—"

"No. Angie's doing very well. She misses you, but that's to be expected."

Relief flooded through her, and she sagged into the chair across from him.

He sat uncomfortably close to the end of the sofa. "The purpose of my visit is to see if you'd found another job."

"Not yet...." She couldn't very well announce that she'd taken to job hunting the way a cat does to a bath. If she spent the rest of her life reading and eating bananas, she would be content.

"I see." He braced his elbows against his knees and laced his fingers together. "I thought I might be able to help."

"Help?" It came to her then. The purpose behind his visit should have been as clear as Texas creek water. Anyone but a blind fool would have figured out that Joshua wanted to hire her as a babysitter for Angie. If he couldn't convince her to marry him, then he would no doubt be willing to pay her top dollar for her child-rearing services.

"Yes, help," Joshua said, ignoring her look of outrage. "I have certain connections, and I may be able to pull a few strings for you, if you'd like."

"Strings?" Bethany repeated. So he hadn't come because of Angie. She narrowed her gaze suspiciously, not knowing what to believe.

"Is something wrong?"

"No," she returned quickly.

"I understand Hal Lawrence of Holland Mills is looking for an executive assistant, and I'd be happy to put in a good word for you."

"That would be thoughtful."

"I'll call him first thing in the morning, then."

"Thank you." She continued to watch him closely, unsure what to make of his offer.

He stood, but she could tell he was reluctant. "I was wondering…" he said after an awkward moment.

"Yes?" she prompted, tilting her head back so far that she nearly toppled in her effort to look up at him.

He jammed his hands inside his pants pockets, then jerked them out again. "What makes you so certain I don't love you?"

Briefly she toyed with the idea of asking him outright what he *did* feel for her.

"Bethany," he said softly, "I asked you a question."

"I wasn't asleep," she answered weakly, her voice trapped and unstable.

"Asleep?" he demanded. "What are you talking about?"

"The first day in California," she continued, refusing to meet his impatient gaze. "I overheard Angie ask you if you'd ever thought of remarrying."

"Ah," he whispered, sounding almost relieved.

She didn't like his attitude. "Perhaps more important, Joshua Norris, I heard your answer."

"You're basing everything on that?"

"As I recall, you seemed to think I'd put her up to asking. That was the worst of it…that you assumed I would use Angie that way."

"I knew you wouldn't do that—you must have misunderstood me."

"Perhaps." She was willing to concede that much. "Even if I hadn't heard you talking to Angie…that night you ordered the wine…"

"Yes?" He was clearly growing impatient with her, shifting his weight from one foot to the other.

"You didn't tell me how you felt then, either. I may have

been too willing to jump to conclusions, but it seems to me that if you honestly love me then that would've been the time to tell me."

"Did it ever occur to you that a man wouldn't ask a woman to marry him without feeling something for her?"

"Oh, I'm sure you do...did," she corrected stiffly. "I haven't worked with you all these years without knowing how you operate. Unfortunately, I want more."

He paced back and forth a couple of times before sitting down again. He leaned forward, braced his elbows on his knees and exhaled sharply.

"The word *love* frightens me," he said after a moment, his gaze leveled on the worn carpeting. "I loved Angie's mother, but it wasn't enough. Within a year after we were married, Camille was discontented. I thought a baby would keep her occupied, but she didn't want children. I should have listened to her, should have realized then that nothing I would ever do would be enough. But I was young and stupid, and I loved her too much. Angie was unplanned, and Camille had a terrible pregnancy. When she was about five months along, she moved to New York to be with her family. She never cared for Angie, had never wanted to be a mother. Whatever instincts women are supposed to have regarding children were missing in her. Her mother was the one who took care of Angie from the very first.

"Camille insisted she needed a vacation to recover after Angie's birth and stayed with her parents, while I took what time off I could to fly between the two cities.

"Angie was only a few months old when Camille asked for the divorce. She was in love with another man." He paused and wiped a hand over his face, as if the action would clean the slate of that miserable portion of his life. "Apparently Camille had been involved with him for months after she moved to New York—even before Angie was born."

The pain in his eyes was almost more than Bethany could stand. She stood, walked over to the sofa and sat beside him. He clasped her hand in his.

"She died in a freak skiing accident a few months later."

"Oh, Joshua, I'm so sorry." She closed her eyes and pressed her forehead against his shoulder.

"Why?" he asked, almost brutally.

"Because...because she broke your heart."

"Yes, she did," he admitted reluctantly. "I'd assumed I was immune to love until Angie came to live with me. I felt safe from emotional attachments."

A tear rolled down the side of her pale face.

He paused and gently wiped the moisture from her cheek. He gripped her shoulders then, turned her in his arms and firmly planted his mouth over hers. His kiss was unlike any they'd shared in the past. His mouth moved urgently in a ruthless plundering, as if to punish both of them for the misery they'd caused each other. He slid his hands from her shoulders to her back, crushing her into his chest. This was a trial by fire, and she felt herself losing control, surrendering all she was, all she would ever be, to Joshua. Like a hothouse flower peeling open its petals, she blossomed under his expert lovemaking.

When he'd finished, her body was aflame and trembling. He straightened and sucked in deep gulps of air. His gaze was narrowed and clouded.

"Honestly, Bethany, if this isn't love, I don't know what is."

With that, he stood and walked out.

She was too weak to do anything more than lift her hand

to stop him. Her voice refused to go higher than a weak whisper when she called out to him.

The door shut, and she sat there for a full minute, too stunned to do anything except breathe. Gradually the beginnings of a smile formed. A shaky kind of hopeful happiness took control of her. Joshua had never been a man to express his emotions freely. Maybe, just maybe, she'd misjudged him. He'd swallowed his considerable pride and come to her, and although he hadn't admitted that he loved her in words, he'd come so close as to make no difference. In thinking back to his proposal, she felt she hadn't given him the opportunity to tell her how he felt.

An hour later the phone rang. She reached for it and was pleasantly surprised to hear Joshua answer her greeting.

"Oh, Joshua, I'm so pleased you called. I've been thinking ever since you left and—"

"Bethany, have you heard from Angie?"

"No," she admitted, a little hurt by the cutting tone of his voice.

"You're sure she hasn't called you?"

"Of course I'm sure." His implication that she would lie to him was strong, and she didn't like it.

"Joshua, what's going on?"

A long moment passed before he spoke. "Angie's missing. Mrs. Larson saw her after school, but she hasn't been seen by anyone since."

The memory of the little girl telling her how much she enjoyed swimming and how she wished her father would go with her more often rang in Bethany's mind like a funeral gong.

"Joshua," she whispered through her panic. The evening was gorgeous. Sally and Jerry were on a picnic. "Could Angie have gone to the lake?"

Ten

Bethany didn't bother to ring the doorbell to Joshua's Lake Pontchartrain home. She barreled through the front door, breathless and so frightened she could barely think clearly. Her mind continued to echo Angie's words about wanting to swim alone in the lake like ricocheting bullets, and the fear Bethany experienced with each beat of her heart was debilitating.

"Joshua?" she called, stepping into the living room.

He walked out of his den, and his eyes held a look of agony. "She hasn't been seen or heard from since right after school. At least there's no evidence she went down to the lake. At least none that Mrs. Larson or I could find...."

Tears blurred Bethany's vision as she rushed across the room and into his arms. She wasn't sure what had driven her there—whether it was to lend comfort or receive it. Perhaps both. His chest felt warm and solid as she pressed her face into it and breathed in deeply in an effort to regain her equilibrium.

He held on to her desperately, burying his face in the gentle slope of her throat, drinking in her strength, her courage, her love.

The thought passed through her mind that perhaps this was the first time Joshua had ever truly needed her.

"I think she may have run away," he confessed in a voice that was thick with emotion. "She told me once she'd thought about it. There's no other plausible explanation."

"But why?"

He dropped his arms and momentarily closed his eyes. "I'm rotten father material. From the first, I've done everything wrong. I love Angie, but I'm just not a good parent. Heaven knows I've—"

"Joshua, no!" Bethany reached for his hand, holding it between her own and pressing it to her cheek. "That's not true. You've been wonderful, and if you've made mistakes, that's understandable...really. No parent is perf—" She stopped speaking abruptly, cutting off the last word. Her eyes grew round as the horror of her actions struck her... the consequences of refusing Joshua's proposal. "It's me, isn't it? Angie's been upset because I haven't talked to her since...since the California trip, hasn't she? I bet she assumed I turned you down because of her, and, Joshua... oh, Joshua, that just isn't true." She took a step away from him and folded her hands over her middle as the reality burned through her. "That's...that's why you came to see me today, isn't it? You were worried then that something like this would happen, and you thought..." Everything was so amazingly clear now.

"No," he said gruffly, regretfully. "I'm not going to lie. Angie and I *did* discuss the matter before I proposed and... and after, but she accepted your decision...." He paused and looked away, his expression tight and proud. "In fact, she took it better than I did." He turned away and raked his hand impatiently through his hair. "Telling you this no doubt confirms the worst."

"Confirms the worst," she repeated. "I don't understand."

"You chose to believe I asked you to be my wife because I was looking for a mother for Angie."

She hadn't been able to help thinking exactly that, of course. But it wouldn't have mattered if Joshua truly loved her. She looked at him, her soul in her eyes. "It was true, though, wasn't it? About wanting me to be a mother to Angie?"

His shoulders sagged a little, and a sad smile briefly lifted the edges of his mouth but didn't catch. "I can't say the way Angie loves you didn't weigh into my decision, and I suppose that condemns me all the more. But my daughter loves Mrs. Larson, too, and the thought of marrying her never once entered my mind."

Bethany's heart began to do a slow drumroll.

"I know you probably don't believe this, but I *do* love you, Bethany. I have for weeks."

His words had the most curious effect on her. She stared at him, her blue eyes as wide as the Mississippi River. She was too stunned to react for a wild second, and then she calmly, casually, burst into tears.

It was clear from the way Joshua stepped forward and then quickly retreated that he didn't know what to do.

"Then why didn't you once so much as hint at the way you felt?" she asked, tears still streaming.

"I did," he countered. "Every way I knew how."

"But…"

"You weren't exactly a fountain of information yourself," he told her.

"You knew how I felt. You couldn't have missed it."

"Yes," he admitted reluctantly. "I caught on the evening we bumped into each other at Charley's...the night Angie arrived."

That soon. She gulped at the information. Her thoughts were interrupted when a glimpse of color flashed in her peripheral vision. She turned abruptly to see the tail of a flowered summer shirt disappear into Joshua's sloop.

Angie.

"Joshua..." She folded her fingers around his forearm and pointed toward the sailboat moored at the end of the long dock at the edge of the lake. "I just saw Angie."

"What?" He was instantly alert. "Where?"

"She's hiding in the sailboat."

"What on earth! Why would she do that?"

"I...don't know."

"Well, I intend to find out. Right now." He jerked open the French patio door hard enough to practically pull it off its hinges.

"Joshua..." She ran after him. "Calm down."

"I'll calm down once she's been properly disciplined."

Bethany was forced to run to keep up with his long strides.

He marched onto the dock like an avenging warlord. "Angela Catherine!" he shouted, and his voice was furious.

The top of a small brown head appeared, followed slowly by a pair of dark eyes.

"Angie! How could you have worried us this way?" Bethany cried, and covered her mouth with her hand, both relieved and upset.

"Hi, Dad." Hesitantly Angie stood and lifted her hand to greet him. "Hi, Bethany."

"Come out of that boat this minute, young lady," Joshua demanded.

"Okay." As though she'd recently returned from a world

tour, Angie retrieved a pillowcase stuffed full of her clothes and tossed it to her father. She handed Bethany another, this one crammed to the top with a week's supply of snack foods. Finally she made a show of climbing over the side of the boat and onto the dock.

Bethany had to give the child credit for sheer courage.

"I suppose I'm going to get the spanking of my life," Angie said, calmly accepting her punishment. "I don't mind. Really." She squared her shoulders and offered her father a brave smile.

"Go to your room and wait for me there," Joshua ordered.

"Okay." The girl glanced from her father to Bethany and back again. "Can I ask Bethany something first?"

Joshua expelled his breath in a burst of impatience and nodded.

"Are you going to marry my Dad and me?"

"Angela Catherine, go to your room." Joshua pointed in the direction of the house. "Now!"

The girl's head dropped. "All right."

The two adults followed Angie through the patio doors. Bethany deposited the pillowcase full of food in the kitchen, then followed Joshua into the family room. Standing there, she rubbed her palms back and forth as she gathered her thoughts.

"I was right," he said, looking pale and troubled. "Angie *did* run away."

"I don't think she was planning to go far."

He sat on the edge of the sofa and dragged his hands over his face. "But why?" He tossed the question to her and seemed to expect an answer.

"I... I don't know."

"Angie and I have been closer than ever the past few weeks," he said, and every feature of his handsome face revealed his bewilderment. "I can hardly believe she would do this."

Unable to understand it herself, Bethany sat beside him, her legs weak with relief that they'd found the little girl.

"I'm not cut out for this parenting business. I've done everything wrong from the minute that child was born," he muttered, his discouragement palpable.

"I sincerely hope you don't mean that," she whispered, and rested her head against the outside curve of his shoulder.

He turned to her then, his gaze narrow and curious.

"I'd like us to have a family someday," she whispered, gladly answering the question in his eyes.

"You would?" His voice was taut, strangled.

"Yes," she answered with a short nod. "Two, I think. Three, if you want."

"Bethany, oh, Bethany." His eyes went dark, the pupils dilating as he continued to stare at her. "You mean it, don't you?"

"Of course I mean it! I love you so much."

His eyes closed, as though he had paused to savor each syllable of each word. "Then you *do* plan to marry me?"

"I'd prefer to do it before the children are born," she answered with a soft teasing smile.

He pulled her into his arms and kissed her with hungry desperation, rubbing his mouth back and forth over hers, sampling her lips as a man would enjoy an expensive and rare delicacy.

She wound her arms around his neck and leaned into him, offering him everything. He broke off the kiss, but his lips continued a series of soft nibbles down the side of her face.

"That night at Charley's..." he whispered.

"Yes...?"

"Having you come up to me at the bar, your eyes so full of concern, your love so open...it shook me to the core. I'd worked with you all that time, and I'd never seen you as anything more than an excellent executive assistant."

"I know," she said with a tinge of remembered frustration. She ran her fingers through his hair and down the side of his face to his neck, reveling in the freedom to touch him. "I was ready to give you my notice then. Everything felt so hopeless."

"I think I realized that, too...and for a time I thought it would be for the best if you *did* find other employment. Then you were gone that one day, and the office seemed so empty and dark without you. I thought if you left, nothing would ever be the same in my life again, and I couldn't let you go."

"Oh, Joshua."

"My reasoning wasn't so selfless," he admitted. "I didn't intend to fall in love with you...that took me by surprise. The day you fell in the lake, I knew it was useless to pretend anymore. Oh, my beautiful, adorable Bethany, what a sight you made that afternoon, with water dripping at your feet."

She groaned at the memory.

"But you held your head high and walked out of that water as though drenching yourself had been your intention all along. I stood on the shore and knew right then and there it wasn't going to do the least bit of good to fight my love for you any longer. I was hooked for all the days of my life."

"The prince..." She lifted her face to watch him, needing to know if the man who'd swept her into his arms at the Mardi Gras parade had been Joshua.

"Yes?"

"It *was* you, wasn't it?"

He looked sheepish when he nodded. "I can't believe I did something so crazy…. It's not like me, but I wanted to kiss you again, needed to, because I didn't know if I'd ever get the chance given what was happening with the com—"

"But why?" she interrupted.

He took her hand and lifted it to his mouth. "You were aware of only a fraction of what was going on with the business at the time. I nearly lost it, Bethany, nearly lost everything. I was in the middle of the biggest financial struggle of my life. The timing for falling in love couldn't have been worse."

"Telling me you loved me would have gone a long way, Joshua Norris."

He grinned. "Now, perhaps…but not last month. Everything I had in the world was on the line. I had to deal with the financial issues before I could pursue our relationship."

"I could have helped." She wasn't sure how, but surely there would have been some way.

"You couldn't—there wasn't anything you could have done. I was sure if I lost Norris Pharmaceutical, I'd be losing you, too."

"How can you say that? I would never have left you…."

"I know that. Now." He held her face between his hands and kissed her again. "I died a thousand deaths when I heard Sally arrange that date for you."

"She…she was convinced you were using me."

Joshua leaned his forehead against hers. "As a babysitter? There wasn't a single moment I needed you to watch Angie—they were all excuses to have you close, to spend time with you. I thanked God for that excuse. I was so afraid I was going to lose you to someone else while I was forced to deal with the second takeover bid. I invented reasons to keep you close."

"But in California, when Angie suggested you marry me, you didn't sound pleased with the prospect."

"I wish you'd been asleep that day," he admitted with a frown. "Everything was still up in the air—I'd only met one day with Hillard and his group. I loved you then, Bethany, but a man can't come to a woman without something to offer her."

"But it really did sound as if you thought I'd put Angie up to that conversation."

He grinned. "If I *did* suggest that, then it was with a prayer and a smile, because I wanted you so much, and I was hoping you wanted me, too. I could hardly stand the wait myself. The day the negotiations were finalized, I asked you to marry me. Delaying it even a minute longer was intolerable."

"But you didn't tell me you loved me, and…"

"Bethany, I was a nervous wreck. Surely you noticed? I'd been as jumpy as a toad all evening, waiting to get you alone, and then, when I finally managed it, you didn't seem the least bit inclined to want my company. All day I'd been rehearsing what I wanted to say, and instead I blurted out the question like a complete idiot. You could have bowled me over with a Ping-Pong ball when you refused."

"I thought…"

He interrupted by sliding his mouth over hers. "I know exactly what twisted thoughts you'd been harboring…and I'll admit my pride took a beating that night and all the nights that followed. It wasn't easy to come to you this afternoon, but I've grown to accept that my life isn't going to be worth anything if I can't share it with you."

"Oh, Joshua." Tenderness filled her eyes, and a precious kind of sweetness pierced her heart. She found his mouth with hers and kissed him with all the love she'd been holding in for so long.

"And then I blew everything a second time and came home to discover Angie was missing."

At the mention of his daughter, Bethany straightened. "I think we should talk to her. Together."

"All right," he agreed, standing. His hand was linked with hers as he led her down the hallway to the bedrooms.

Joshua rapped at Angie's bedroom door and then let himself inside. Angie sat on the edge of the mattress, her head bowed and her hands clasped in her lap.

"All right, young lady, what do you have to say for yourself?"

"Nothing."

The word was so soft Bethany had to strain to hear it.

"Surely you know how worried Bethany and I would be?"

Angie nodded several times, still not looking at them.

"If you knew that, then what possible reason could you have had for doing something like that?"

Her small shoulders jerked up, then sagged.

"Are you unhappy, sweetheart?" Bethany asked.

The little girl shook her head. "I like living here better than anyplace in the world."

"Then why would you want to run away?" Joshua demanded.

A short pulsating silence followed. Finally Angie said, "So Bethany would come."

"I beg your pardon?" He advanced a step toward his daughter.

"So Bethany would come," Angie repeated a little louder.

"I heard you the first time, but I don't understand your reasoning."

"When you talked to me last week, you said we might have been hoping for too much with Bethany, because she didn't want to marry you, and I knew that was wrong. I knew she loved you and I know she loves me, so I figured if something bad happened, then she'd come and you two would talk, and then maybe she'd want to marry us."

Bethany gasped at the logic, because that was essentially what *had* happened.

"Your intentions may have been good, but what you did was very wrong."

"I know." For the first time Angie raised her eyes to meet her father's. "Can you let me know how many swats I'm going to get? If you tell me that, I can hold on and not cry."

Joshua seemed to be contemplating that when Angie went on.

"I saw Bethany from the sailboat, and she looked real worried, and then I saw you talking and I could hardly wait to hear what you said, so I snuck out of the boat and came to the patio to listen." A smile as wide as the Grand Canyon broke out across her face. "I wasn't sure, but it sounded like Bethany wants us."

"Oh, sweetheart, I've always wanted you." Bethany wasn't sure if Joshua would approve of her comforting Angie, but she wrapped her arms around the little girl and hugged her close.

"So are you going to marry us?"

Bethany nodded eagerly.

"Oh, good!" Angie beamed at her father and added, "You can give me as many swats as you want, and I bet I won't even feel them."

Bethany was just preparing to move into the role of stepmother, and she didn't want to cross Joshua, but she couldn't bear the thought of Angie being spanked. She tried to tell him as much with her eyes.

He answered her with a look of his own, cleared his throat and announced, "Seeing as everything's worked out for the best, I believe we can forgo the spanking."

"We can?" Angie all but flew off the bed. Her arms groped for Joshua's waist, and she hugged him with all her might.

"However, you caused Bethany, Mrs. Larson and several others a good deal of concern. You're grounded for the next two weeks, young lady."

Some of the delight drained out of Angie's eyes. She sank her teeth into her lower lip and nodded. "I won't ever do it again, I promise. I... I thought it would be fun, but it wasn't. I was bored to tears."

"Good. I sincerely hope you've learned your lesson."

"Oh, I did." She slipped one arm around Bethany's waist and the other around her father, and stood between the two adults. "We're going to have such a good life together."

"I think so, too," Bethany agreed.

"Especially after the other kids arrive," Angie said, looking vastly pleased with herself. "I want a sister first, okay? And then a brother."

Joshua's gaze reached out to Bethany and wrapped her in an abundance of warmth. "I'm more than willing to do my part to complete the picture."

Bethany couldn't have looked away to save the world from annihilation. Joy welled up inside her, and she nodded. "Me, too."

Angie released a long slow sigh. "Good. Now when can I tell my friends about the wedding? I was thinking Saturday the fifteenth would be a good choice, don't you? At the reception, we'll serve Big Macs and macadamia nuts."

"Sounds good to me," Joshua said with an indulgent chuckle.

"I couldn't think of anything I'd like more," Bethany added.

"Now, about the honeymoon..."

Joshua's gaze didn't leave Bethany as he spoke. "That's one thing I plan to take care of myself."

"Anything you say, Dad." Angie looked up at Bethany and winked. "We're going to be so happy."

And they were.

* * * * *

For preschool teacher Kayla Harris,
Tony DeNunzio's arrival in town with his young nephew
just before Christmas could be what fills her holiday
stocking with everything she's always dreamed of.

Don't miss First Kiss at Christmas, *the next book in*
Lee Tobin McClain's The Off Season series,
available November 2021 from HQN Books!

Read on for a sneak peek!

KAYLA HARRIS CARRIED a bag of snowflake decorations to the window of her preschool classroom. She started hanging them in a random pattern, humming along to the Christmas music she'd pulled up on her phone.

Yes, it was Sunday afternoon, and yes, she was a loser for spending it at work, but she loved her job and wanted the classroom to be ready when the kids returned from Thanksgiving break tomorrow. Nobody could get as excited as a four-year-old about Christmas decorations.

Outside, the November wind tossed the pine branches and jangled the swings on the Coastal Kids Early Learning Center's playground. A lonely seagull swooped across the sky, no doubt headed for the bay. The Chesapeake was home to all kinds of wildlife, year-round. That was one of the things she loved about living here.

Then another kind of movement from the playground caught her eye.

A man in a long, army-type coat, bareheaded, ran after a little boy. When Kayla pushed open the window to see better, she heard the child screaming.

Heart pounding, she rushed downstairs and out the door of the empty school.

The little boy now huddled at the top of the sliding board, mouth wide open as he cried, tears rolling down round, rosy cheeks. The man stood between the slide and a climbing structure, forking his fingers through disheveled hair, not speaking to the child or making any effort to comfort him. This couldn't be the little boy's father. Something was wrong.

She ran toward the sliding board. "Hi, honey," she said to the child, keeping her voice low and calm. "What's the matter?"

"Leave him alone," the man barked out. His ragged jeans and wildly flapping coat made him look disreputable, maybe homeless.

She ignored him, climbed halfway up the ladder, and touched the child's shaking shoulder. "Hi, sweetheart."

The little boy jerked away and, maybe on purpose, maybe not, slid down the slide. The man rushed to catch him at the bottom, and the boy struggled, crying, his little fists pounding, legs kicking.

Kayla pulled out her phone to report a possible child abduction, eyes on the pair, poised to interfere if the man tried to run with the child.

One of the boy's kicks landed in a particularly vulnerable spot, and the man winced and adjusted the child to cradle him as if he were a baby. "Okay, okay," he murmured in a deep, but gentle voice, nothing like the sharp tone in which he'd addressed Kayla. He sat down on the end of the slide and pulled the child close, rocking a little. "You're okay."

The little boy struggled for another few seconds and then stopped, laying his head against the man's broad chest.

Apparently, this guy had gained the child's trust, at least to some degree.

For the first time, Kayla wondered if she'd misread the situation. Was this just a scruffy dad? Was she maybe just being her usual awkward self with men?

He looked up at her then, curiosity in his eyes.

Her face heated, but she straightened her shoulders and lifted her chin. She was an education professional trying to help a child. "This is a private school, sir," she said. "What are you doing here?"

The little boy had startled at her voice and his crying intensified. The man ignored her question.

"Is he your son?"

Again, no answer as he stroked the child's hair and whispered something into his ear.

"All right, I guess it's time for the police to straighten this out." She searched for the number, her fingers numb with the cold. Maybe this situation didn't merit a 911 call, but there was definitely something unusual going on. Her small town's police force could straighten it out.

"Wait. Don't call the police." Tony DeNunzio struggled to his feet, the weight of his tense nephew making him awkward. "Everything's okay. I'm his guardian." He didn't owe this woman an explanation, and it irritated him to have to give one, but he didn't want Jax to get even more upset. The child hated cops, and with good reason.

"You're his guardian?" The blonde, petite as she was, made him feel small as her eyes skimmed him up and down.

He glanced down at his clothes and winced. Lifted a hand to his bristly chin and winced again.

He hadn't shaved since they'd arrived in town two days ago, and he'd grabbed these clothes from the heap of clean, but wrinkled laundry beside his bed. Not only because he was busy trying to get Jax settled, but because he couldn't bring himself to care about folding laundry and shaving and most of the other tasks under the general heading of personal hygiene. A shower a day, and a bath for Jax, was about all he could manage. His brother and sister—his *surviving* sister—had scolded him about it, back home.

He couldn't explain all of that, didn't need to. It wasn't this shivering stranger's business. "Jax is going to enroll here," he said.

"Really?" Another wave of shivers hit her, making her teeth chatter. Tony didn't know where she'd come from, but apparently her mission of mercy had compelled her to run outside without her coat.

He'd offer her his, but he had a feeling she'd turn up her nose.

"The school is closed on Sundays," she said.

Thank you, Miss Obvious. But given that they'd slid through a gap in the playground's loosely chained gate, he guessed their presence merited a little more explanation. "I'm trying to get him used to the place before he starts school tomorrow. He has trouble with..." Tony glanced down at Jax, who'd stopped crying and stuck his thumb in his mouth, and a surge of love and frustration rose in him. "He has trouble with basically everything."

The woman shook her head and put a finger to her lips, then pointed at the child.

What was that all about? And who was she, the parenting police? "Do *you* have a reason to be here?" he asked, hearing the truculence in his own voice and not caring.

She narrowed her eyes at him. "I work nearby," she said. "Saw you here and got concerned, because the little guy seemed to be upset. For that matter, he still seems to be."

No denying that. Jax had tensed up as soon as they'd approached the preschool playground, probably because it was similar to places where he'd had other bad experiences. Even though Jax had settled some, Tony could feel the tightness in his muscles, and he rubbed circles on his nephew's back. "He's been kicked out of preschool and day care before," he explained. "This is kind of my last resort."

She frowned. "You know he can hear you, right?"

"Of course he can hear, he's not..." Tony trailed off as he realized what she meant. He shouldn't say negative things about Jax in front of him.

She was right, but she'd also just met him and Jax. Was she really going to start telling him how to raise his nephew?

Of course, probably almost anyone in the world would be better at it than he was.

"Did you let the school know the particulars of his situation?" She leaned against the slide's ladder, her face concerned.

Tony sighed. She must be one of those women who had nothing else to do but criticize how others handled their lives. She *was* cute, though. And it wasn't as if *he* had much else to do, either. He'd completed all the Victory Cottage paperwork, and he couldn't start dealing with the program's other requirements until the business week started tomorrow.

Jax moved restlessly and looked up at him.

Tony set Jax on his feet and gestured toward the play structure. "Go ahead and climb. We'll go back to the cottage before long." He didn't know much about being a parent, but one thing he'd learned in the past three months was that tiring a kid out with active play was a good idea.

Jax nodded and ran over to the playset. His tongue sticking out of one corner of his mouth, forehead wrinkled, he started to climb.

Tony watched him, marveling at how quickly his moods changed. Jax's counselor said all kids were like that, but Jax seemed a little more extreme than most.

No surprise, given what he'd been through.

Tony looked back at the woman, who was watching him expectantly.

"What did you ask me?" Sometimes he worried about himself. It was hard to keep track of conversations, not that he had all that many of them lately. None, except with Jax, since they'd arrived in Pleasant Shores two days ago.

"I asked if you let the school know about his issues," she said. "It might help them help him, if they know what they're working with."

"I didn't tell them about the other schools," he said. "I didn't want to jinx this place, make them think he's a bad kid, right from the get-go. He's not."

"I'm sure he isn't," she said. "He's a real cutie. But still, you should be up front with his teachers and the principal."

Normally he would have told her to mind her own business, but he was just too tired for a fight. "You're probably right." It was another area where he was failing Jax, he guessed. But he was doing the best he could. It wasn't as if he'd had experience with any kids other than Jax. Even overseas, when the other soldiers had given out candy and made friends, he'd tended to terrify the little ones. Too big, too gruff, too used to giving orders.

"Telling the school the whole story will only help him," she said, still studying Jax, her forehead creased.

He frowned at her. "Why would you care?"

"The truth is," she said, "I'm going to be his teacher."

Great. He felt his shoulders slump. Had he just ruined his nephew's chances at this last-resort school?

MONDAY MORNING, KAYLA WELCOMED the last of her usual students and stood on tiptoes to look down the stairs of the Coastal Kids preschool. Where were Tony and Jax?

She'd informed two of her friendliest and most responsible students that a new student was coming today and that they should help him to feel at home. If he didn't get here in time for the opening circle, she'd tell all twelve of the kids about Jax.

But maybe his uncle had changed his mind about enrolling him.

Maybe Kayla's mother, who was the principal of the little early learning center, had decided Jax wasn't going to be a good fit and suggested another option for him. That would be rare, but it occasionally happened.

Mom said Kayla fretted too much. Probably true, but it was in the job description. Kayla felt a true calling to nurture and educate the kids in her care. Sometimes, that meant worrying about them.

The Coastal Kids Early Learning Center was located in an old house that adjoined a local private school. Kayla's classroom was one of three located upstairs, and from hers, she could see down the central staircase to the glassed-in offices. Her mother was welcoming a few stragglers, but there was still no sign of her new student.

She turned back to face her students. "Good job sharing," she said to redheaded Nicole, who was holding out a plastic truck to her friend. "Jacob, we don't run in the classroom. Why don't you look at the new books on our reading shelf?"

After making sure all the kids were occupied with their

morning playtime, she stepped out into the hall. If she could flag down her mother, she'd try to find out what was going on with Jax.

And then Tony came into the school, holding Jax's hand.

Kayla sucked in a breath. Wow. He cleaned up *really* well.

Not that he was entirely cleaned up; he still had the stubbly half beard that made him look a little dangerous, and his thick, dark hair was overlong. But he wore nice jeans and a green sweater with sleeves pushed up to reveal muscular forearms. He knelt so Jax could jump onto his back for a piggyback ride, then stood easily, and Kayla sucked in another breath. There was something about a guy who was physically strong.

He stopped and spoke to Kayla's mother—she'd been occupied with another parent right inside the office, apparently—and then, at her gesture, headed up the stairs toward Kayla's classroom.

Maybe it was the fact that the school was dominated by kids and women, but Tony seemed very, well, *large*. He took the stairs two at a time, still carrying Jax on his back. "Sorry we're late," he said as he came to the door. "Here you go, buddy. You met Miss Kayla before."

He bent to set Jax down, but the boy clung to him like a monkey.

That wasn't surprising, but Kayla had seen every reluctant-new-kid trick in the book. She was ready. "We have a special day for you, Jax. If you like trucks and cars, we have a whole tub of them, and friends who like to play with them too."

Jax turned his face away and clung tightly to his uncle.

Should I come in? Tony mouthed to her.

"Better if he comes in on his own," she said quietly, then

stepped to Tony's side to be closer to Jax, who still clung to Tony's back. "Jax, honey, after playtime, and circle time, would you like to have the job of feeding our hamster?"

The little boy peeked in her direction for a nanosecond, then buried his face against his uncle's shoulder.

"Come on, buddy," Tony said. "Get down, and we'll go see the hamster." He peeled the boy's hands apart, releasing their death grip on his neck, and swung him to the ground.

Immediately, Jax crouched and grabbed Tony's leg and clung to it. "You come too."

"Is that okay?" Tony asked her. He knelt and, by holding Jax's hand, managed to get the child to stand on his own two feet.

Having a parent or guardian come in with a new student wasn't ideal, but Jax seemed to have a *lot* of separation anxiety. Which made sense, if he'd had bad experiences at other schools. Kayla made one more try. "How about if we show Uncle Tony the hamster when he comes back to get you?" she suggested. "He'll come back. Moms and dads— and uncles—always come back."

At her words, Tony winced. Jax stared at her for a half second, then his face contorted and he flung himself to the floor, his legs kicking, grabbing desperately at Tony's ankle.

"His mom didn't come back," Tony explained to Kayla over the child's ear-splitting screams.

Kayla pressed a hand to her mouth. "I'm so sorry. That was just the wrong thing to say, then." Behind her, she heard the kids in her class murmuring and gathering around the door. Another kid's tantrum always drew an audience.

Tony knelt and patted his nephew's back. "It's okay, buddy," he said, his voice a low rumble. "You're okay."

"Not okay!" Jax wailed.

Kayla blew out a sigh and looked from Jax to the cluster of children in her care. A couple of them looked upset. Kids this age were starting to develop empathy, which was great, but it also meant that meltdowns could be contagious.

She glanced down the stairs. No help there. "I'm going to get the other kids busy," she said to Tony. "If he can settle down, maybe bring him in for a bit and stay with him?"

He nodded, and she went into the classroom, half closing the door in an attempt to give Tony and Jax some privacy.

She never failed with kids, but she'd failed with Jax this morning. She shouldn't have made an assumption about his family life. With a college degree in early childhood education and three years of full-time experience here at Coastal Kids, she knew better.

She would make it up to him. That was central to her identity as a teacher. It had nothing whatsoever to do with his uncle's concerned brown eyes.

Don't miss First Kiss at Christmas, *the next book in Lee Tobin McClain's The Off Season series!*